MOOSE WILLOW

Mystery

A *Yooper* ROMANCE

TERRI MARTIN

Modern History Press

Ann Arbor, MI

Moose Willow Mystery: A Yooper Romance
Copyright © 2022 by Terri Martin. All Rights Reserved

ISBN 978-1-61599-689-6 paperback
ISBN 978-1-61599-690-2 hardcover
ISBN 978-1-61599-691-9 eBook

Published by
Modern History Press   www.ModernHistoryPress.com
5145 Pontiac Trail   info@ModernHistoryPRess.com
Ann Arbor, MI 48105

Tollfree 888-761-6268 (USA/CAN)
FAX 734-663-6861

Distributed by Ingram Book Group (USA/CAN/AU)

Library of Congress Cataloging-in-Publication Data

Names: Martin, Terri, 1951- author.
Title: Moose Willow mystery : a Yooper romance / Terri Martin.
Description: Ann Arbor, MI : Modern History Press, [2022] | Summary: "A suspicious death in a game processing meat locker is just the beginning of bizarre events happening in the Upper Michigan village of Moose Willow. It all starts when a mysterious woman appears at the Methodist church during choir practice. Janese Trout and her best friend, State Trooper Bertie Vaara, team up to connect the woman to a growing number of disturbing occurrences around town including the disappearance of Janese's eccentric lover, George LeFleur, and an undeniable increase in Bigfoot sightings. Meanwhile, Janese faces a multitude of personal challenges as she grapples with a sagging career at the Copper County Community College, an elusive pregnancy test, and a controlling mother who inserts herself into every hiding place of Janese's life"-- Provided by publisher.
Identifiers: LCCN 2022037603 (print) | LCCN 2022037604 (ebook) | ISBN
    9781615996896 (paperback) | ISBN 9781615996902 (hardcover) | ISBN
    9781615996919 (epub)
Subjects: LCGFT: Detective and mystery fiction. | Romance fiction.
Classification: LCC PS3613.A786238 M66 2022   (print) | LCC
PS3613.A786238
    (ebook) | DDC 813/.6--dc23/eng/20220808
LC record available at https://lccn.loc.gov/2022037603
LC ebook record available at https://lccn.loc.gov/2022037604

Dedicated to all the good folks
who proudly call themselves Yoopers.

Prologue

He had hidden his truck off in some brush to wait, then when the coast was clear, he sneaked in on the weedy two-track that came up behind the Indian's place. The road was used by every kid and dick-hound in town looking for a spot to screw around, drink, and smoke weed—and things had been busy. The man was used to waiting, being dead quiet, sometimes barely breathing. And the bottle of liquor tucked in his coat made the wait a whole lot easier. He couldn't see much from where he was concealed in the brush but caught an occasional blink of light— probably when car doors opened and closed. Two cars in and two cars out. Time to go. The man had kept his headlights off as he drove around to the back of the building and shut off the engine.

If there had been a padlock on the door handle, it was gone now. No surprise there. The bonehead who owned the place was dimmer than a two-watt bulb and crooked as the winter was long. The man tripped over a wooden pallet next to the door and almost went down. "What the hell?" he muttered, giving the pallet a shove with his boot. He slipped inside the building, flicked on a light switch, and quietly shut the door behind him.

The front part of the place was a big walk-in cooler where animals, mostly deer, hung in a gruesome row, eyes blank, stiff tongues protruding. He tried not to look at them or think about their grisly end. It reminded him of things he wanted to forget.

The next room was even worse. It smelled of blood and decaying flesh. The only light came through a slat around the door from the "hanging" room. The man turned on the glaring overhead lights, instantly regretted it, and flicked them off. It was pretty clear that this was where the butchering took place and four-legged creatures were transformed into roasts, steaks, and burgers. An ugly assortment of saws, grinders, and knives lurked in the gloom. A propane stove held an enormous kettle. The man had heard of skull boiling. He had no idea how or for that matter why it was done. If the animal had a good rack, then the head would be mounted and become a trophy. Why the hell would anyone want a skull hanging in his den?

The man figured that the Indian probably stashed the illegal stuff in the next room. It only made sense to keep it frozen. He staggered a little as he pulled open the freezer door and lurched into the vault-like room, groping along the wall. The door slammed shut behind him, plunging him into darkness. After fumbling around, he found a light switch and flipped it on. Damn it was frickin' cold and his head felt like it was lost in a fogbank. Maybe he should have gone easy on the booze. He looked around and wished he could see better. Hadn't thought about it being so dark in the place. He tried to beat back the panic that sometimes came with darkness. The man took a deep breath, working to refocus on why he was there. The one crappy bulb in the whole room was making it a bitch to see anything. He reached for his cell phone, planning to use the flashlight. When he felt the pocket where he kept his phone he fingered instead a partial pint of Canadian whiskey. He remembered taking the phone out of his jacket to make room for the liquor. Left the damn thing sitting on the truck seat and he didn't want to go back for it.

Eventually his eyes adjusted to the dark and he started with the boxes, tearing them open one by one. Next he dumped the contents out of a dozen plastic tubs and riffled through columns of pull-out trays mounted on shelving units. But he came up empty. Just a bunch of venison steaks and bear gonads wrapped in butcher's paper. Indian thinks he's so slick. *Well, I'm slicker*, he thought.

The man shivered and swayed unsteadily as he pawed angrily through the mess he had created, knowing it was useless. He couldn't miss something so obvious. Then off in one corner, shoved behind some big plastic barrels, he spotted a dozen or so empty five-gallon pails along with a pile of oddly shaped plastic tubs. *Not started yet, eh?* Well, the cheater would have to get to it pretty soon. Time was running out. Bastard wasn't gonna get away with it, though. *Not again*, thought the man. He was cold and woozy and disappointed that he didn't find any real "evidence." But he knew how to bide his time. The man knew he'd be in deep shit when he got home. It was way past suppertime and she'd be wondering where he was, calling around, working herself up. He'd say he had a flat. She'd believe anything, except the truth. Truth be told, he *was* getting hungry. It had been a while since he had his grilled cheese and hot cocoa for lunch.

The man worked his way out of the freezer and through the butchering area to the hanging room. If he could just catch his breath, maybe open a window—except there weren't any windows. Only the door. Okay, he'd leave, but he'd be back. Yessir, he'd be back. Was chased off by the Indian last time. This time he got in. Next time he'd find what he was looking for.

The man braced against the wall, trying to steady himself. A deep growl filled the room, startling him. The noise continued, steady and methodical. The man felt stupid for being so jumpy. Damn refrigeration compressor had kicked on, that was all. He tried to slow his breathing. Maybe it was a panic attack or maybe just the lack of air in the damn place. Like being buried alive. That's what it reminded him of. A tomb, sealed up for all eternity. He labored to breath: In. Out. In. Out. A lot of work and it made him dizzy. He'd go outside, get some air. He pushed on the knob that was supposed to release the door latch. Goddamn: jammed. He tried again and again, fighting terror, lungs burning, heart hammering in his ears. His legs buckled and he went to his knees. The door was fuckin' stuck and so was he.

Suddenly, he found everything incredibly funny and started to laugh. *What the hell, he'd gone through worse in 'Nam,* he told himself.

Good thing he brought his hooch. Yessir. A man's best friend. Funny, he wasn't feeling cold anymore. He'd just cozy up under the swaying carcasses and wait for the sumbitch to find him. The man smiled. He couldn't wait to see the look on the Indian's face when the door opened in the morning.

⚬ 1 ⚬

She just showed up one night, and said, "Hi. I'm Derry. I'd like to sing in the choir."

It sounded a bit like an AA introduction. Nonetheless, we all smiled idiotically and mobbed her in order to extract as much information as possible, mainly if she sang soprano (God, please) or alto.

"Welcome," said our choir director, Hannu, who extended a limp hand toward her. She touched his fingertips delicately, as a Victorian lady might do.

Where had this woman come from? She had not been within the humble walls of the Moose Willow Methodist Church that past Sunday. Usually, people shopping around for a church sneak in after the service has started and sit discreetly in the back pew. However, anyone—especially anyone female—who wanders in does not get past the Moose Willow Methodist Women or MW-MW.

The Methodist Women are a tenacious group of church ladies who strive to fulfill their God-mandate of recruitment for "auxiliary activities." Any woman, lady, or slut, who dares enter the handicap-accessible doors of the Moose Willow Methodist Church will undergo an inquisition. Before her hand has cooled from multiple welcoming grips, she will be asked to join the MW-MW.

This new woman appeared to be in her thirties. Blonde hair cascaded around her head like a flaxen halo. I judged her jeans to be about a size six. She wore a stretchy top that displayed a tease of cleavage. She studied her surroundings with hooded light-blue eyes— bedroom eyes. In spite of blushed cheeks and bright lipstick, the woman exuded a pale, haunted presence.

"So, Dairy is it?" I asked. "Spelled like Humbolt's Dairy?" Maybe she was from Wisconsin where they take their dairy products very seriously. I was used to odd names. I lived in the Upper Peninsula of Michigan, or U.P. where people *proudly* called themselves "Yoopers."

Our small village got its name from an Ojibwe moniker, *Mooz Oziisigobiminzh*, which basically translates as Moose Willow. Perhaps at one time the area abounded with moose munching on their favorite willowy browse. However, today, sightings of Bigfoot were more frequent than those of a moose.

"Well, actually, it's spelled D-E-R-R-Y," she said. "Parks. The last name's Parks."

"Very glad to meet you," I said. "I'm Janese – rhymes with geese. JanESE," I repeated. "Last name's Trout, like the fish."

Needless to say I had gone through my whole life with my first name being mispronounced and my last name being ridiculed.

A warm presence prickled the back of my neck. It was James. Not Jim, mind you, James, like in the Bible. Although our James was no saint. Quite the contrary.

"James Rush," he said, extending a manicured hand toward Derry. "Baritone," he added, "and your friendly television news reporter. Perhaps you've seen me anchoring the TV13 news?"

"I'm afraid not. I haven't been in town long and don't watch much television."

James regaled Derry with a toothy, veneered smile and reached up to correct any hair that may have strayed. He did this with his left hand in order to display his bare wedding-ring finger. James had been married and divorced three times, much to the consternation of our pastor. Not that I had any room to judge, what with my supposed "jaded" living situation. I needed a roommate and George LeFleur came along, with benefits; so there you have it.

"Will your husband be joining us?" James asked. He could be so obvious.

"I'm a widow," Derry said.

That took us aback for a sec.

James arranged his face into a perfect display of condolence. "I'm so terribly sorry—and you are so young."

"Thank you," she muttered.

I was beginning to feel like a third wheel or fifth wheel or whatever.

"Let's get started," our choir director shouted. His name, Hannu, is Finnish, and trying to pronounce his last name is hopeless, so he's just Hannu. Like "Cher" or "Prince" or "Lassie." Well, maybe Lassie isn't a good example. Hannu was a saint and hardly ever yelled at us. I attribute his tolerance to his strong Christian spirit. I do not believe, for one minute, that the rumors are true about the misuse of communal wine or prescription drugs. Alcohol, though frowned upon by the Methodist Church, can serve a legitimate purpose when carefully monitored. I allow myself one glass of wine a day, except on days when two glasses seem more appropriate, such as after a long, meeting-plagued day at the Copper Country Community College where I work.

5

"All right people," Hannu bleated as he banged his baton on the music stand. "Take your places."

Our pianist, Azinnia Wattles, pounded out a few scales while we noisily clambered up onto the choir platform we shared with the pulpit and the stained-glass window of Jesus. The scene depicted in the window suggested good times. Jesus was surrounded by bunches of fruit, sunshine, and lush foliage. He wore a toga and sandals and held a lamb in the crook of his arm. No matter where you were in the sanctuary, you could not escape Jesus' gaze. His normally benevolent expression had taken on a more reproachful look that evening.

"Where do you want me?" Derry asked.

"Squeeze in there next to Janese," Hannu said.

This bit of shifting would cause the usurping of Eleanor Heimlich from her ordinary seat to a folding metal chair perched on the edge of the platform, and she was not a person to take such a maneuver lightly.

"Oh for heaven's sake, Eleanor, scoot over," Hannu snapped. "It won't kill you to sit on the folding chair."

Eleanor was apparently unaware of the logistical problem she created. While of average height, her towering "Marge Simpson" hairdo tended to block voices from the back row. I suspected this was a strategic move on Hannu's part who hoped to position Eleanor where she would block the fewest number of voices. If she capitulated to the folding chair, which she had not yet done, she would be sitting smack behind the pulpit. Anyone stuck there spent the entire church service staring at the assortment of mundane items on the hidden shelf within the unit. One can ponder a box of tissues and the "pennies for pastors" jar only so long before boredom sets in.

But it was a matter of status, not scenery that caused Eleanor to glower at the folding chair. She fancied herself a reverent rock star and likely viewed a folding chair as spiritually degrading. I couldn't help but stare at her coif. It truly defied all principles of physics. I thought of the toy—Weebles, I think they were called, with the marketing phrase "Weebles wobble, but they don't fall down!" I couldn't suppress a giggle thinking about Eleanor's wobbly hair, which earned me a deadly look from Eleanor. A chill passed over me. Rumor had it that Eleanor was once part of an obscure religion from down South (I did detect a drawl) where they spoke in tongues and performed satanic rituals. Of course, it was all rumor churned up by the Moose Willow Gossip Mill. Eleanor moved to Moose Willow, where she had "connections," and took a job as secretary at the elementary school. Eventually, she found her way to the Moose Willow Methodist Church where she quickly moved up in rank among the MW-MW—mostly because she terrified them—and became the queen/president of the organization.

Eleanor shifted her disdain for me to the substandard chair that was to be her new place.

"I can sit on the end," Derry said.

Azinnia was still hammering out scales. Most of the choir had started to warm up their voices—except the soprano section, which was in turmoil because of the seating debacle.

"I want you between Janese and Eleanor. Sit!" Hannu barked.

We all sat abruptly with a unified thud. The piano music trickled to a stop.

Hannu always gets testy during cantata time. Every year, in addition to our regular Sunday anthems, we pull a musical program together for the community. Predictably, it has a religious theme, and the plot is generally the same each year: People of the world are living in darkness, despair, and gloom. They have nothing to look forward to, since the afterlife has not yet been confirmed. Christ Child is born in a manger in a lowly stall because the inn is full. This is the innkeeper's "humanitarian" solution for a young woman in the throes of heavy labor. A special star shines—presumably a sign from God that a major event is occurring in Bethlehem. Shepherds, while tending their flocks at night, marvel at the heavenly phenomenon and summon up some angels from the realms of glory. Wise men come from afar, following the star. They bring some nice gifts of gold and frankincense, and also the myrrh, which is a funeral embalming material. This particular gift does not bode well for the youngster's future. The story plays out through the robust singing of the choir. The practices are brutal. Hannu's sparse hair takes on a maniacal Gene Wilder appearance and large rings of sweat stain his underarms.

This year's cantata may have a welcome shot of freshness, due to the timely entrance of Derry. She was not only a soprano, but we quickly learned during warm-up that she was also solo material. This would do nicely for the solo piece where Mary sings to Baby Jesus laying all the world's problems on the little tyke and telling Him, with a multitude of high notes, that He is the world's savior. Derry sat primly, staring down at her lap. She smiled, but it wasn't a joyous expression—more fixed, like a mannequin.

7

The whole thing put Hannu in a very good mood. Perhaps, if the rumors about his habits were true, which I am not saying they are, he would be able to sleep without help that night. However, Eleanor Heimlich, likely still stinging from the chair downgrade, had been singing the solo "just for practice purposes." Eleanor, nostrils flaring, glared at Derry who focused rigidly on the music folder she held in her lap.

Somehow, James had managed to position himself behind Derry, which was not his normal place. As choir practice got into full swing, Derry and I were assaulted with James' vigorous singing—obviously intended to impress. I felt, as I'm sure she did, his spittle land on the back of my neck with each word beginning, ending or in any way containing the "S" sound. I was plotting ways to decommission James when Hannu noticed that something was askew in the back row.

"What are you doing there?" Hannu snapped at James. "You move to where you are supposed to be. You won't project there. And watch the S's. You sound like a leaky radiator."

James slunk to his normal place where he would properly project for the baritone solo he was to sing. Now, when he sang of the lonely shepherd in the desert doing God-knows-what with all those sheep, the S-induced spit would find its way elsewhere, possibly hydrating the poinsettia plants, which looked a little droopy anyway.

Once practice ended, I managed to elbow my way through the crush of yakking choir members into the brisk night air. I flapped open my coat, trying to catch the brace of cold. Snow had begun to fall, lazy and innocuous. What seemed so lovely that night—so Christmassy and all—would lose its appeal as winter progressed. The sparkling fairy-tale world would all too soon evolve into a cold, white monster that would make the gloom and despair people endured B.C. seem like a walk in the park.

"Pretty, isn't it?" Derry said. "Oh, sorry, I didn't mean to startle you."

There she was again. The woman simply materialized.

"So, where are you from?" I asked, trying to sound as if she hadn't unsettled me.

"Oh, originally not too far from here."

"Back to see family?"

"You could say that."

"Well, welcome, um, we are happy to have you." Boy, was that lame.

"My pleasure," she said, equally as lame.

The unmistakable voice of our very own Channel 13 newscaster and baritone soloist wafted into the night air. I turned to look at the door as the choir straggled out, with James leading the way. He always talked in a booming voice, as if on stage for a Shakespearean play.

The Pastor's wife, Kaaron Saaranen, worked her way through the crowd and brushed up against me. "We have a funeral on Monday. Could I get you to bring something in on Sunday to contribute to the luncheon?" she said.

"Sure, I guess," I said. "Who passed away?"

"Paavo Luukinnen, poor dear. He was ninety-three."

I had no idea who Paavo Luukinnen was, but suspected he was another nursing home casualty. I had only rudimentary kitchen skills and always resorted to making a trip to either Tillie's Bakery or the IGA to buy bakery items. For purposes of a funeral luncheon, IGA peanut butter bars were my go-to contribution. Of course, I removed them from the plastic store container and put on a plate to pass off as homemade.

"Bring your peanut butter bars?" Kaaron said as if reading my mind. "They are always so much better than the ones from the IGA?"

The question at the end of her comment implied that she was on to my fraudulent bakery offerings.

"See you Sunday," she said.

"Peanut butter bars—Sunday. You can count on it," I said.

When I turned back to find Derry and suggest we carpool next time (a clever way to find out where someone lives), she was gone. No crunch of footsteps in the snow, no car door shutting, no engine turning over. Just gone.

2

I went straight home after practice to my little cabin in the woods. I liked where I lived, all snug in the forest with the nearest neighbor a half mile down my road—Silver Road—and they went South for the winter.

"Hello? Hey George, I'm home!" I hollered as I tromped into my miniscule entryway, stomping snow off my boots. There was no answer, so I slipped off my boots and went up the steps to the loft where I found George throwing a pot. The throwing did not involve a random act of violence, but rather the creation of something sloppy on a spinning potter's wheel. Wet clay hung from George's beard and his bib overalls were a mess.

"Damn. Too wet," he muttered.

I could have been standing there buck naked with my hair on fire and George wouldn't have noticed. When he was working on one of his pots, you might as well forget finding out if he wanted peas or corn for dinner or if he had paid the electric bill. All of those trivial things didn't matter one iota when George was in a creative mood.

That didn't stop me from trying. "Did you have any dinner?" I asked.

"Hmmm." He was furiously working a long funnel of clay that looked a teeny bit lopsided to me.

"Want a cheese sandwich?"

"Hmmm," he repeated as he moved his hands to the top of the piece where he tried to close it in a bit, presumably to form a neck. I figured he was making a vase. He actually made some nice ones, considering he had only been doing pottery for about a year. It was something his doctor recommended—as therapy. George's craft had moved very quickly from therapeutic to a job teaching at the Copper Country Community College where I worked. The Community Center—located on campus—couldn't get enough of G. LeFleur pottery, which never sat on display long before someone snapped it up. Some said each piece had a story hidden within it. I admit the blobby, drippy stuff that he glazed on did seem a bit peculiar. Sometimes a face would emerge. Sometimes a tree. It was a little creepy if you ask me. I'm not much of an art critic.

I turned and went back down the loft steps into the compact kitchen of my cabin and poured my first glass of white zinfandel.

"Well, I'm hungry and I'm making a grilled cheese. You can just be a starving artist," I yelled. I knew darn well that I'd make a sandwich for George, too. I thought about opening a can of tomato soup.

I heard a soft, tragic *splut* followed by a string of curses; the whir of the potter's wheel stopped.

Uh oh, I thought, taking a generous swig from my wineglass.

George thudded down the steps from the loft. It had originally been a guest loft for the occasional visitor that wanted to see how "Mrs. Henry David Thoreau" lived, as Mother called me. When George moved in, he converted it into his pottery studio. I broke out into a cold sweat every time I looked at it: clay hardened on the floor, walls, and windows—even the skylight. If Mother ever saw it...

"Fuck it," George said, and headed toward the bathroom, presumably to remove the clay from his person and deposit it on the walls and floor of the shower.

I buttered some bread, slapped it on the griddle, and added a few slices of shiny, yellow cheese. I decided not to bother with the tomato soup. I topped off my wineglass.

Eventually, George emerged from the shower. He slumped down into his seat at the table and absently picked up half of his sandwich. His dark blond hair, still wet from the shower and in desperate need of cutting, gave him a slightly wild look. The beard could have used a trim, too. However, his body—well, no complaints there—had kept good muscle tone from a few years of working for a logging company. While he made his way into the second half of his grilled cheese, he seemed to come out of his defective-pot funk.

"Hey, Trout, thanks for making this," he said. Calling me by my fishy last name was George's way of being affectionate. Of course, if we got married, my last name could be LeFleur. I would gladly abandon "Trout," which was the last name of Mother's original husband who had also been my father. I was their little surprise. My father, whom Mother described as a free spirit, died hang-gliding while stoned on cannabis. A double high, so to speak. His death, which occurred when I was still toddling, left Mother with nothing but me. I guess it was tough, bringing me up alone with no family to speak of. Mom managed a motel and restaurant in town and worked long and hard to make ends meet. I think that was when the church became so important to Mother and me. Just about the time I graduated from college, Mother met husband number two: Sherman C. Caldwell *the third* who took a vacation every year in the Copper Country where he could shoot animals and gamble at the casino. Shermie, as Mother called him while they were courting, conveniently died during the honeymoon (probably because he was 86) leaving Mother a sizeable fortune. Tragic yet fortunate that Shermie had no offspring. This enriching turn of events helped build my cabin in the woods. Mother sometimes shared her good fortune, but there were always strings.

Currently, Mother—known to most as Madeline and to her closest friends as Maddie—was on a cruise in the Gulf of Mexico, taking a break before the holiday rush at The Straights Inn. She owned the place, which was clear at the other end of the Upper Peninsula (praise God) in St. Ignace. Thanks to Shermie, Mother no longer worked at a motel: she owned one.

George let out a huge sigh. "I guess I tried to make the damn vase too tall," he said. "I still got the other two to go to work with you tomorrow for firing."

Since the average home doesn't include a kiln room, George used the one in the art center at the Copper Country Community College—we called it the 4Cs for short—to fire his masterpieces. That was where we met—not in the kiln—but at the art center in an enrichment class. My job at the 4Cs, among other things, included coordinating community enrichment classes, such as art, dancing, basket weaving, *kantele* lessons, and other life-altering opportunities. One night I had decided to stop in and try pottery. What the heck, it was free to 4Cs' employees. However, since I never will see a blob of clay for more than a potential mess (George says I'm anal), I gave up my wheel to a senior lady who wore a bright floral smock and, God love her, called me young lady. Though I failed miserably at pottery, George and I hit it off.

I thought about Mother and her occasional surprise visits. I had not yet told her about George, who was forbidden to answer the phone. Quite frankly, I was sure she would either try to run George off or trick him into marrying me. Even though my biological clock was ticking along at an alarming rate and the potential for grandparent-hood remote, Mother was intent on meddling in my life, giving me ridiculous advice about men. According to her, a woman should be married at least once, even if she were to get divorced. Like having lots of shoes, it was something women did. I looked at my wineglass, which was empty again. Had I already had my daily allotment?

"Earth to Janese," George said.

"Huh? Oh, sorry, I was thinking about Mother."

We sat in silence for a while, George probably thinking about clay and me thinking about *her*.

"Um, so how much for the pieces I'm taking?" I asked.

"Oh, seventy-five—the usual. Ah, how was choir practice?"

"Same ol'—except there is this woman, Derry, who just showed up. She sings beautifully and wanted to join. She's never been in on Sunday and I have no idea why she's in town." My glass was still empty and I got up to refill it. I didn't offer George any because he didn't touch the stuff.

"Yeah? Well, maybe they came here because of the hiring at the prison," George said.

"See, that's the thing," I said, sitting back down at the table. "There is no *they*. She says she's a widow. Don't you think it's strange that a single woman—a widow at that—would come here? I mean she might have family, but she was kind of vague about it. And she's drop-dead gorgeous, but a little—haunting," I added. Those pale blue eyes were still with me.

"Ah, then I bet Rushinski was sniffing around her."

Rushinski was James's real last name. He had shortened it to "Rush" for show-biz purposes. On those rare occasions when George attended church, he made a point of calling James *Jimmy* or *Jimbo*, just to annoy him. In retaliation, James responded by calling George *Georgie* or *Georgie Boy*. Somewhere over the Wisconsin border, George and James shared a history. I could never find out much about it, except it went back to their days of working for Plante Forestry Products. As one might guess, forestry products are trees. To Plante, trees are potential logs, but they don't call them logs, they call them forestry products, which is more politically correct.

"So this Derry woman just showed up, eh?"

"Yeah, and she can sing. I think she's going to do the solo for the cantata. I don't think Eleanor is happy, either."

"Oh yes, Heimlich. She's the old battle ax that screwed me outta getting that custodian job at the school," George said.

"Well, you have your teaching job at 4Cs now," I said.

"True. But I'll never get anywhere there," he said. "Don't have the degree."

It was true, George didn't have a higher ed degree, which interestingly wasn't mandatory to teach but essential for job security.

Mother had insisted that I go to college in spite of the economic hardship. I did okay and got my bachelor's degree from Upper Michigan University. I majored in business and minored in partying.

George looked a bit forlorn, so I offered: "There's always the prison. They're always hiring." I really didn't want George to apply at the prison. It was a sucky job, but they hired regularly and had benefits.

George smiled. "Don't think I'd check out with them."

"How come?"

"Oh, that's between me and my shrink," he said.

"Same as the logging accident."

"What do you want to know about the accident?"

"You never said what *really* happened, only that someone died, and that you could have prevented it."

"Yeah, well I don't exactly remember it; that's why I go to the head doctor, who says I'm suppressing things."

"And he—or she—is trying to *un*-suppress you?"

"I guess. Let's not talk about it, okay?"

George had been living with me for several months and refused to open up. He went to regular court-ordered appointments with a psychiatrist or psychologist—someone in the mental health field. I hadn't seen much progress.

I cleaned the congealed cheese off the griddle while George put the dishes in the dishwasher. I retired my wineglass for the evening and headed for the bedroom. Since the guest loft had become a potter's studio, George had the choice of sleeping up there on the futon or with me in my nice pillow-top bed. The man liked his comfort, and since I wasn't collecting rent in the conventional sense, I felt due some sort of compensation. Normally, George was quite accommodating. However, that night he instantly fell asleep. I thought about his vase that apparently self-destructed when it was stretched too thin. Sometimes I felt that way, stretched too thin and ready to ooze into an amoebic puddle. I envied George's quiet strength—his resolve to invert his soul and emerge with a new identity; to reshape like a lump of clay. It made him maddeningly unreachable, and alluring. George was different than the other men I had known who basically wanted sex, beer, food, fishing, and football, in varying order.

I dozed off, thinking about ropes of clay and the stacks of projects on my desk at work. I dreamed that I was ensconced in an igloo with no windows and no doors. I lay there, cocooned in the oppressive, hot confines of a mummy sleeping bag with no zipper. The heat was overwhelming. The igloo started to drip, melting away. I was in my office and angry people pounded on my door, calling me names.

And then George shouted something weird that sounded like "gaaa," which jolted me awake, *thank God* not in a mummy sleeping bag or an igloo, but instead in George's house of horrors.

George moaned like a distant foghorn, low and painful.

"George, wake up," I whispered, nudging him gently. "You're doing it again."

More deranged moaning.

"George! Wake up!" This time I jabbed him. That did it.

He sat up in the darkness. "Hey Trout, was I snoring? Take it easy. I'm gonna have a bruise," he said massaging his ribs.

He turned to me. "Was I having the dream?"

"Apparently."

"I guess we're both wide awake," he said.

"Yeah. I was having a doozie of a dream myself."

"What about?"

"Igloos."

We were quiet a moment.

"Igloos," George said.

"Uh huh. Probably because of the New Year's Eve thing," I said.

"Mmm?"

"You know, the igloo building competition that 4Cs sponsors. It started out as a spur-of- the-moment-fun-alternative-to-getting-drunk on New Year's Eve and now it's, well, it's just ugly. Do you know that people cheat?"

George gave a snort. "Really?"

"I mean they're supposed to wait until December 26th," I said. "They can't start until the day after Christmas, and I've heard that Bucky Tanner—you know Bucky's Game Processing and Taxidermy—supposedly stores items for his igloo contest entry that he makes ahead of time in the freezer of his meat locker. And all this trouble so he can beat Weasel Watkins."

"What people won't fight over," George said absently. "So, you have to run the thing?"

I gave George my most withering look. I had told him all about how coordinating the igloo contest had fallen on my desk. This was the second year, not counting the spontaneous teen/quinzhee competition that had started the whole thing. It had been my colleague, Brenda

Koski's idea, supposedly to turn it into something "way cool," as she described her alleged epiphany. Most likely the college president, Patrick Neil, had planted the idea with Brenda, hoping it would grow there. However, Brenda lacked the brainpower to "grow" anything, and the project had somehow gotten shoved off on me. Brenda was the resident floozy at the 4Cs. Her title varied, depending on who she was chummy with. I had been racking my brain to come up with a way to pay her back for shoving the igloo contest off on me, but so far had only been able to think of things that would get me fired or possibly arrested.

George and I lay in the semi-darkness, listening to the silence. George shivered.

"Want some hot cocoa?" I said.

"Nah," he said looking at me.

I had seen that look; I liked that look. It was my turn to shiver. I preferred to think it was desire causing my chill rather than the drying perspiration from my bad dream. Whatever the cause—and I was pretty sure it was George's finger tracing down my... Anyway, I didn't want any cocoa, either.

≋ **3** ≋

As I parked in Lot B at the Copper Country Community College, I noticed that I had beaten Brenda Koski in—or at least her big, pretentious SUV was not there. When I got to my office, the evil red eye on my phone message light blinked at me. I started some coffee, booted up my computer, and dialed into my voice mail. The first two messages were people asking about getting entry forms for the igloo contest and the third was from someone inquiring about folk dancing lessons. The fourth message took me a while to figure out.

"Yeah," it began. "Tell that prick—'scuse my French—tell that jerkwad Weasel Watkins to quit poking around my place, eh? If he's gotta beef, he needs to come face to face. Next time I call the cops—or worse."

The gravelly smoker's voice was unmistakable: Bucky of Bucky's Game Processing and Taxidermy. As I told George, last year when Bucky won the igloo contest, Weasel Watkins swore he had cheated. What had begun as a wholesome and fun activity had evolved into a monster.

It all began on a New Year's Eve when we had a big, wet snowfall—perfect for packing. Kids were out cruising the three blocks of Moose Willow when the girls challenged the boys to a quinzhee-building contest. While igloos are constructed of ice, quinzhees are basically hollowed-out piles of snow that provide emergency shelter in a winter wilderness setting. The kids who built the makeshift quinzhees selected one boy and one girl to be lodged in their respective shelters and see who could stay there the longest. Plans were made for food, soda pop, and sleeping materials. However, sanitary facilities were not part of the construction, which forced the girl—who had had an extra-large diet pop for dinner—to default. In the spirit of fairness, (the girl being at an anatomical disadvantage and less inclined to seek relief where she was to sleep and eat) a tie was declared and the couple was crowned King and Queen of the quinzhees. A brief coronation ceremony took place, which involved snowballs being crammed down the king and queen's backs and the brutal destruction of the quinzhees.

During the contest, the citizens of Moose Willow abandoned the neighborhood bars and holiday parties, and came outdoors to cheer the kids. Everyone sang Auld Lang Sang and went home sobered up from the cold. The next year, the Copper County Community College had agreed to sponsor an annual contest. The activities expanded to include the whole community and involved an "igloo" building contest, which concluded with an awards banquet wherein the winners were announced and prizes were given out. The term igloo was a loose term for "something constructed of snow and/or ice."

Somewhere along the line, it got ugly.

I deleted Bucky and cued the last message. I got up to get a cup of coffee while it played. I stopped mid-pour to listen. It wasn't anyone calling to kibitz about the igloo contest, that was for sure. The voice, which was being disguised but sounded female, gave me goosebumps.

Tell George I'm so glad I finally found him. The voice, unmistakably menacing, was definitely not like a long-lost friend tracking down an old pal. There was a pause, then: *If you wonder who this is, just ask George. Tell him I'll be in touch.* No name, no number, no reason for calling. The mystery of George continued to grow. I did not delete the message.

Speaking of George, I remembered that I had his pottery in my car, which needed to go over to the art center for firing in the kiln. I vaguely recalled him warning me that it shouldn't get too cold or too hot or something. I dashed out of my office—never did get my coffee—and hurried to the parking lot. Brenda Koski's big SUV was parked so close to my car that my driver's car door could only be opened about six inches. Perhaps someone anorexic could squeeze through, but not me. I also noticed that the wheel wells of her SUV had huge mounds of snow packed up in them. For some reason, I loved kicking snow out of wheel wells—felt compelled to do it. George said it was my obsessive compulsive disorder. There, on Koski's car, was a prime icy snow hump begging to be dislodged. I casually gave it a kick, which scuffed the toe of my boot and hurt my instep. The ice held steady. I opened the hatch of my car and got a hammer out of my tool kit. My blows with the hammer only produced a few chips of ice, one of which lodged in my right eyeball. I blame my blurred vision on the inaccuracy of my next hammer swing. Did you know that splash guards are really flimsy—brittle, actually, especially when encrusted with ice? There was a bad noise—a cracking sound, and an impressive slab of ice fell to the parking lot with a fractured piece of plastic splashguard embedded in it.

Uh oh.

I stood and looked around. I was the only one in the parking lot. The distant scrape of a snow shovel reverberated off the buildings. I was certain that Brenda had insurance—good insurance. Anyway, that's what happens when you park so close to another car. It gets the owner all upset and the adrenalin pumping. I would have just gotten into my Subaru and driven off to deliver George's vases to the kiln room. Besides, you see all kinds of things that are far more intentional than a little chip in the splash guard—well, okay, a fairly good-sized break. You see obscene things written in the salt residue, such as "wash me bitch" or scratches that you know were intentionally done with keys, or major dings in the doors. No, a little nick—well, okay, a fairly good snap—in the splashguard, which is really just ornamental anyway, is certainly no cause for concern. Just a victim of the harsh Michigan winters, as I saw it.

I quickly put my hammer away, took one more look around, and climbed into my car through the passenger door. I crawled over the console, careful to avoid a bodily violation by the shift lever, and maneuvered around until I managed to slide into the driver's seat. In the process, I tore my coat pocket, which hooked on the shift knob and one of my gloves (leather—a gift from Mother) fell into the muddy slush on the floor mat. I was feeling less guilty about the tiny bit of damage that had happened to Brenda Koski's car.

* * *

My brain was completely numb after enduring one of those long, boring meetings that makes you either contemplate suicide or vow to cast off civilization and become a subsistence-living recluse. Or, I could have a little wine and enjoy a quiet dinner with George. After all, it was Friday, with two glorious days of no bizarre phone messages, long-winded meetings, or moral dilemmas. I did a mental inventory of my wine and food supply. I was pretty sure the wine was low and certain that there was nothing much to eat in the fridge. Also, I (miraculously) remembered that I had promised to bring "bars" to church Sunday for what's-his-name's funeral on Monday afternoon. I would have to stop at the IGA. Of course, their wine prices were exorbitant. If I wanted a bargain, I knew I had to stop at the Bayview Bar and Grill for a box of my favorite white zin. I hated going in there, with all the old farts sitting at the bar, watching me as if I were a bikini model strutting the runway.

The IGA had the peanut butter bars and I picked up some ground beef and hamburger buns, a bag of chips, and some deli baked beans and slaw. As an afterthought, I selected an apple pie from the bakery. I had sworn off desserts until my clothes quit shrinking. George, of course, looked like an ad for a crop walk (also an event that I coordinate) and could eat all he wanted without gaining an ounce.

Inside the Bayview Bar and Grill, the air hung stale with decades unwashed humans and a spilled-beer-Friday-night-fish-fry smell. It was dark, which was probably for the best. At one time, there had been a large picture window with a view of the bay. Herb Heinki, who is the Bayview's proprietor and perpetual bartender, boarded it up after the health department nearly shut him down. His logic is that if they can't see the grime, nobody cares. I shudder when I think about the kitchen.

Country music thumped so loudly that I suspected the cockroaches were packing up to move. Eventually, my eyes adjusted to the gloom and I headed toward the wine cooler that stored the take-out beverages. Several men sitting at the bar rotated on their stools and watched my progress. I endured this inspection, as did every woman, each time I came in the place. I took a quick look around. It was pretty empty. Two guys were playing pool; one had a toothpick hanging on his lip, apparently a substitute for smoking, which was no longer allowed in bars or restaurants. A couple sat huddled at the far table, crouched over their drinks. I recognized the coiffed back of the man's head. It was none other than our church choir's finest baritone, James Rush. And, well, I'll be damned, I thought, if it isn't the lovely and mysterious Derry Parks sitting across from him. She appeared to be rummaging in her purse for something, so didn't notice me—I hoped. I admit that I was a little surprised to see that Derry had succumbed, at least to the degree of meeting in a north woods bar, to one of James' propositions. I sidled over to the cooler and selected a box of low-end white zinfandel and set it on the bar by Herb.

"Hey, Janese," Herb shouted to be heard over the blaring music. Then he said something about my cottage.

"What? My cottage? I yelled back.

"COLLEGE. HOW-ARE-THINGS-AT-THE-COLLEGE?

"GREAT, HERB, JUST GREAT," I shouted back, straining my vocal cords. They were out of whack anyway, since cantata practice had started. At least I didn't have to worry about James and Derry overhearing me.

I think Herb told me how much for the wine and I slid my debit card toward him. He looked at the card as if were toxic. Of course, he couldn't fudge the books if there was a record—like from a debit card. Mercifully, the song ended.

"Sorry. I forgot to hit the ATM—no cash." My voice rasped as if I'd been shouting at a football game. He sighed and scanned the card, then tossed it back. I signed the appropriate slip and scuttled past the men at the bar.

"Ya gonna have a little party, eh?" One of them said. Another snickered. I wondered if saving a few bucks on wine was worth the harassment. I risked a quick glance over my shoulder at Derry and James. She had her head tossed back and was laughing. I'd have bet anything he had his hand on her knee, but of course I couldn't see. Well, to each her own, I thought as I passed through the squealing door into the brace of fresh air and brightness. I remembered how aloof Derry had been toward James at choir practice, or was she being coquettish? In any event, he could be charming in his own, narcissistic way. When I got to the parking lot, I saw that someone had parked a truck so close to my driver's door that I couldn't possibly get in. Ditto on the passenger-side. I may have said a bad word or two as I hit the unlock button and flung open the back hatch. "Why me?" I muttered. Perhaps I should have reported the damage to Koski's car. After all, even though there were no witnesses, God was watching, and He sends signs. Monday, first thing, I'd fess up. Maybe.

* * *

It was nearly dark when I pulled onto my road. A couple of inches of snow had fallen and a single set of fresh tire tracks wound its way down the middle of my street. George may have taken the truck and run out somewhere. Sometimes he went to the Silver River Tavern to get a deep-fried donut. It was a strange thing, having fried donuts and beer on the same menu. I wondered if I should try to grill the burgers in the garage or fry them in a pan. I had pretty much decided on the frying pan when I pulled into the driveway and saw not only George's truck still parked there, but another car as well. It looked vaguely familiar but was so caked with road salt that I couldn't even tell what color it was. Whoever it belonged to had blocked the garage door, forcing me to lug the groceries in through the service door.

I clamored into the entryway of my cabin, as the peanut-butter bars slipped out the grocery bag and smashed onto the floor.

"Well, sh—MOTHER!—what're you doing...I thought...aren't you on a cruise?"

She was sitting in George's favorite chair and he was perched on the edge of the couch, as if ready to bolt.

"Hello to you too, Janese," Mother said, rising from her chair. She and I met in the middle of the living room and exchanged an airy kiss. "Cruises do come to an end—thank God. Are you growing out your hair, dear?" she asked, her eyes scrolling me like the cursor on a computer screen.

I absently touched my hair. Perhaps the roots were starting to show.

"Being a blond is so much trouble, isn't it? That's why I'm back to my natural color," she said.

I hadn't noticed, until then, that Mother's hair was an unlikely shade of red. Was that new? She sat back in her chair and smiled. "George, here, has been a wonderful host. Thank heavens for instant coffee!" She took a sip, winced, and set the mug on my oak coffee table. My eyes shifted to the mug, wondering if it would leave a ring.

"I am so sorry I couldn't reach you, Janese. I tried, but I kept getting your answering machine."

"Did you leave a message?" I asked.

"Of course not dear. I refuse to talk to machines." Her eyes shifted around the room. "I see you've done some, uh, rearranging of things." She gazed up at the vaulted ceiling of the living room and her eyes darted toward the loft/erstwhile guest room. She lowered her chin and looked at George who moved even closer to the edge of the couch.

"Well!" I chirped, "Isn't this just lovely? I'm going to fix some burgers for dinner. George, come help me."

George shot off the couch and retrieved the box of wine that I had dropped in the middle of the hallway. We stopped briefly in the kitchen to deposit the groceries and, without speaking, moved toward the bedroom door where we became entangled until George backed off and allowed me to enter. I gently shut the door behind us.

"What is she doing here?" I hissed. "Why didn't you answer the phone?"

"You told me not to. Remember? And I tried to call and text *you*," he snarled. "Don't you ever have your cell on?"

"I keep forgetting. Why did you let her in?"

"Like she gave me a choice." George shot back. "I was doing some sketching in the loft when someone knocks on the door. When I open it, she hardly gives me a look then sashays in and asks where are you and who am I."

"And you said...?"

"I told her you were at work and that I was George, a friend. And she says is that so? I still didn't know who the hell she was and when I asked, she said she was Madeline, your mother. I had just gotten her some coffee and sat down when, thank God, you came home. Why the hell do you pay for a stupid smartphone if you never turn it on? Christ, it feels like the inquisition has arrived."

"It *has* arrived, George," I said in a chilly, calm voice. "And if you choose to leave—and it is a choice that I would not make lightly—please know that I will put all your stuff out in the driveway and set fire to it. That includes your potter's wheel."

George looked as though he were considering his options.

Could he fit through the bedroom window? It was one of those crank-out jobs with a screen and a feisty mini-blind that always catches on the window crank. There really was no escape, except directly through the belly of the beast whose name was Madeline.

I slid into the kitchen and put the groceries away. Mother was no longer sitting in the chair and I spotted her fiery-red hair moving about in the loft. That hair would keep her safe in the woods during hunting season. I also noticed her overnight bag—a very large one—sitting at the base of the steps. She came to the loft railing and looked down at me.

"What, in God's name, is all this—this, stuff up here?"

I stuck my head in the fridge, trying to buy some time.

"Wine, Mother?" I asked.

"I asked you a question, Janese. What is this…mess? And yes, wine would be nice. I need to get that nasty taste of instant coffee out of my mouth."

Thumping came from the bedroom. Maybe George was trying the window. I was deadly serious about my threats of arson. All the men in my life had abandoned me: my father along with a couple of boyfriends. Of course my father died, but that was because he was acting like a fool rather than a responsible family man. The others, well, they—

I heard a crash. Had George broken a window? No, it was Mother.

"Oh dear," she said. "I wonder what that thingy is—was."

George poked his head out of the bedroom. He was only wearing his boxers. "What th' hell was that?"

"Nothing, George, just a thingy," I said, waving him off. "Why did you take your clothes off?"

23

"I need a shower. Keep her away from my pottery," he snapped, slamming the door.

"Right. Keep her away," I muttered. For some reason it all seemed very funny and I started to giggle. I had poured two glasses of wine: one for *her* and one for me. Mine wasn't completely full anymore. I silently thanked the nectar gods for the brand spanking new box of white zin in the fridge.

"Mother, please come down, and leave, ah, George's things alone. Here's your wine."

"George's things?" she said. "I thought maybe you had taken up—whatever it is that's up there."

"No, it's George's," I said, not offering any more information.

Mom clacked down the steps into the living room. How she could stand those high heels was beyond me.

"So," she said, "tell me *all* about George."

I busied myself making hamburger patties and setting the table. "Nothing to tell. He's a friend. I gave him a place to, um, live for a while."

"I see."

She seemed thoughtful, which was unsettling. I got a pan out and slapped the hamburger patties in it. I opened the fridge and put my wine glass under the little spigot that came with the box of wine. As I emerged, I had the ketchup and mustard, and an onion of questionable vintage—and a full glass.

"Ah, well, men..." she said absently.

I gave her a covert look.

"So, tell me about the cruise to—where was it?"

"Well, truthfully, Janese, I never went. A bunch of old, desperate people trying to pretend they are having a great time. Not for me," she said as she took a generous swallow of wine. She smiled. "I'd rather be with my darling daughter than with a bunch of old farts who want to get it on with me, or worse yet, they want a nurse or a purse." She waved her wine glass around, miraculously not spilling any.

"What about the resort. Don't you need to be there, ah, overseeing things?" I asked as I sat on the couch.

"Yes, well, I closed it down for a few weeks—until just before Christmas—you know, while I was on the cruise and then had the renovations all lined up."

"What kind of renovations?"

"Oh, the usual. A little paint and personnel change."

24

"Personnel change?"

"Yes, dear. You remember Stephen?"

"Sure," I said. "He's a wiz, according to you; runs the restaurant and the motel. You positively *love* him."

The bedroom door opened. George sidled into the kitchen and touched the frying pan.

"He's a queer," Mother said matter-of-factly. "I let him go."

The bedroom door slammed shut.

"Queer, as in a homosexual or gay? You can't fire him for that," I said, straining to see toward the bedroom.

"Well, he was putting the moves on Rick, the nice young man who works the night shift. I can't have that kind of behavior. It's sexual harassment. I could be sued." She sighed. "So hard to get good help these days. Used to be the people you worked with were family—family," she repeated, looking directly at me.

I leapt off the couch and hurried into the kitchen.

"Need any help, dear?" she asked.

Oh, I needed help alright. "No thanks. So, you don't want to oversee the renovations—the painting and such?"

"Oh Janese, you know I'm allergic to latex," she said. "Do you have any more wine?"

I got her wine glass and refilled it. Mother had many allergies of convenience: paint, animals, cleaning products. "So how long will the fumes be keeping you, um, here?"

"Oh, only a week or two."

This time a crash came from the bedroom.

Mother smiled at me. "Are you still singing in the church choir, dear?"

"Sure," I said.

"Is Azalea still abusing the keyboard? God, she must be in her eighties."

"Her name is Azinnia," I said. "And the answer is yes."

"And that hunk—what's his name? His voice is positively hypnotizing—Peter, Paul, Matthew?"

"James," I said. "He's still there."

"And is he still single?"

"Mother!"

"Well, now that I've fired Stephen, I'm available."

"What!" I said. "Stephen and you...?"

"Well, I guess he was—how do you say—AC/BC?"

25

"That's AC/DC, Mother." I felt my face flush. Way too much information. Stephen was approximately my age, for God's sake. He and my mother?

"Well, there's nothing wrong with a younger man. After all, I don't want another repeat of Shermie. I mean the honeymoon killed him! God rest his soul. I think he had taken some special medication, not the prescription stuff, but something that they advertise on TV and meant for much younger men. I will say that he was really lively, I mean REALLY lively, until—"

"We have someone new in the choir!" I blurted out.

Mother seemed wistful for a moment, no doubt reflecting on that fatal wedding night. I told her about Derry, including spotting her in the Bayview with James. George re-emerged from the bedroom, tentatively lurking around the stove. I left Mom with her memories and went into the kitchen to cook the burgers and refill my wine glass. I was a little tipsy and tripped over a rug and fell into George. I glanced over at Mother and saw that she had her suitcase open and was rummaging around inside. I took the opportunity to turn to George and give him a meaningful kiss, complete with a little tongue. The hamburgers sizzled. It was going to be an interesting night. I was glad that George hadn't escaped. I really didn't have the energy to drag all his crap out into the driveway to burn it.

≉ 4 ≉

George was lucky. He had a pottery show that Saturday morning, which allowed him to vanish. When I awoke, only the faint smell of his cologne wafted from the bathroom. Mother and I sat bleary-eyed over our coffee and our giant home-fried, gut-bomb donuts from the Silver River Tavern. My stomach gurgled a little, trying to deal with the artery-clogging grease that accompanied each donut. (I'd had two.) Mother sipped her coffee and studied me. This always made me uncomfortable.

"Um, so was the futon ok?" I asked. When George and I had converted the loft into his studio, we had put a futon bed up there, which we had to cover with a drop cloth to protect it from splatters from George's pottery wheel. When it was determined that Mother would be best off sleeping in the loft, George had begrudgingly collected his pottery equipment and put it away for safekeeping. The floor and bath were given a quick cleaning.

She gave me a sour look. "What's in the mattress of that—that thing?"

"The futon?" I asked.

"Yes, the very same. Is it stuffed with ball bearings?"

"Well, no, I think it's stuffed with, ah, stuffing. You know, cotton and polysomething."

"What happened to the nice guest bed that I gave you?" she said.

"It was in the way, so we—I guess we donated it to a needy family."

It wasn't entirely a lie. Since there wasn't room for the bed because of George's potter's wheel and other paraphernalia, we had actually sold it and used the money to buy the futon. I was pretty sure only someone who was needy would buy a used mattress.

Mother sucked in her breath. "That was an expensive bed—motel quality. They make them to last. You simply gave it away?"

Before I could stammer out an answer, the telephone blessedly rang. I hurried into the living room and snatched the handset.

"Hello?"

I could sense someone on the other end, but they didn't speak.

"Hello?" I repeated. "Who is this?" I was getting tired of annoying phone calls. Until that moment, the mysterious call at the office had slipped my mind and I had forgotten to ask George if he had a clue.

"I can't hear you," I bellowed into the phone. I heard something faint. Cellphones were responsible for a lot of misunderstandings. Maybe someone was calling me from their cell.

Mother had gotten up and clattered around in the kitchen, which didn't help.

I gestured at her to be quiet. She cast me a scathing look and threw a dishtowel onto the counter.

"You're breaking up," I bellowed.

Then a very soft but clear, genderless voice said: "Tell George he's next. His partner's in the cooler."

"What? Who is this?" I demanded. I looked at the caller ID, but it displayed "unavailable." The line went dead.

George was next for *what*? And *I* was his partner. Cooler, like for beer? Sometimes cooler was a euphemism for jail. I stood there frowning and pondering the little mystery when the phone rang again. I looked at it for a moment before I ripped it off the stand; nobody was going to intimidate me.

"What the hell is this all about," I snarled.

"Janese?" said a tiny voice on the other end.

"Yeah?"

"Oh, well maybe this isn't a good time, I—"

"Who is this?" I demanded.

"It's Aileen Watkins. We met at the ecumenical church bazaar last fall. I was in charge of the white elephant sale. Clarence's wife."

"Clarence?"

"Well, of course most people call my Clarence by that disgusting name."

"Weasel!" I shouted. "Right, sorry Elaine, it's been a little crazy here this morning."

"Oh, I understand. It's Aileen, not Elaine," she said. "Why, things are perfectly crazy for me, as well. Besides my normal volunteer efforts, I've been trying to line up stitchers for making the Quilt of Faith. Have I ever talked to you about our quilting club, Janese? Now most of us are Lutheran, but we welcome any sister of Christ into our circle."

"Yes, well, I'm not very domestic," I said hurriedly. Mother had resumed poking around in the kitchen. She gave a snort, apparently in agreement with my statement.

"Think about it, dear," she said. "Anyway, I've gotten myself side-tracked—my Clarence says that I jump around more than a flea in a dog kennel—anyway, I called because it's just not like him."

It seemed that she expected some kind of response.

"You mean *Him* him, as in Jesus, or God?" I asked. "Perhaps your pastor—"

"No, for heaven's sake, Clarence," she said tersely.

"What about him—Clarence?"

She gave a loud, exasperated sigh. "My goodness and people call me scatter-brained. Anyway, well, it's got to be all about this gosh darned igloo thing, you know. That's the only reason he wouldn't come home. He's been sober for years, *years*. I'm calling you, dear, because you are the one in charge of all the nonsense and I thought you might know what happened to my Clarence."

Perhaps suicide? I thought. No, he would have killed her first then turned the gun on himself. I found my thoughts turning ugly. Also, I distinctly remembered seeing Clarence—Weasel to most of us—sitting at the bar at the Bayview when I picked up my box of wine the night before. Had it only been the night before?

"And since you are in charge, I am holding you responsible," she continued.

"Responsible for what?"

"Well, if he got himself all worked up—you know that Bucky cheats, and my Clarence is a good Christian man, and that would just be intolerable to him—and went and did something rash, or worse yet, turned to drink again, or, well, he does have issues and I just worry about him having a relapse."

I figured she was talking about Clarence falling off the wagon, which as far as I could see he was never riding on to begin with. "Maybe Clarence got an early morning start to go fishing," I said.

"Fishing! Are you insane, *insane*?" she shrieked. "There's barely a skim of ice on the bay. Oh dear. You don't think? No, of course not. He hasn't done anything so foolish since the spring break-up three years ago when they had to rescue him from that ice floe. That taught him a lesson. That was when his life turned around, you know, because he saw Jesus, *saw Jesus*, who took him in his arms and they huddled on that ice floe until that nice Native American man—John or Joseph something—was driving by and managed to get help, and—"

"Hunting!" I said.

"And his guns are still here, so I know he didn't go hunting," she added, without missing a beat.

I was somewhat relieved to know his guns were all accounted for.

"Elaine, I really don't know—"

"Aileen," she corrected. "My, but you are forgetful, aren't you? How do you manage with your important job when you can't remember names? Well, anyway, Janice—"

"JanESE."

"It's not pleasant to have one's name screwed up, is it?" she said, her voice icy.

I was speechless.

"I'm holding you personally responsible, *responsible!*"

"I—"

"I know it has something to do with that Bucky! You must go find him."

"Bucky?"

"You have an annoying habit of repeating everything, dear. Yes, Bucky. I think that Clarence went over to Bucky's to make certain that no shenanigans were going on. As I have said, my Clarence is a good Christian, and *someone* needs to oversee these things," she said, implying that I had not been living up to that responsibility. "And he never came home! Well, everyone knows that Bucky and Clarence have an ongoing—ongoing—"

"Feud?" I offered.

"Well, you see Bucky and Clarence were both sweet on me when I was just a young woman," she said, sounding wistful. "Bucky had the looks, but my Clarence had the brains."

As far as I knew, Clarence didn't get the nickname "Weasel" for his brains, although the name does imply someone crafty, underhanded, and sneaky. As I understood the story, it was a nickname he was given while deployed overseas.

"My Clarence won some silly contest and Bucky never got over it. He—Clarence that is—asked me out and we were married, um, a few months later," she said.

I tried to recall the story about Bucky and Weasel, and their pursuit of—what *was* her name? Aileen. I remembered that Weasel had just gotten a medical discharge from the military—maybe the Marines. He was always challenging guys, trying to start something. I recalled hearing about a beer chugging contest to see who would get to put the moves on Aileen, and Weasel won—or lost, depending on how you heard the story.

As for the blessed union, in the olden days, they called it a shotgun wedding. There was a pause on the line while each of us contemplated our version of the story. Mother came into the living room and looked at her watch. She had earlier announced that we were going into Marquette to shop. She had some scary ideas about decorating and fashion. She never could accept the fact that I hated to shop and that I'd rather spend the day shoving slivers under my fingernails.

"So it is your responsibility to go over there and find out what happened to him!" Aileen blurted out.

"Over where?"

She gave an exasperated sigh. "To Bucky's! *To Bucky's!*"

"Did you call him, *call him*?" I asked. Now I *was* repeating everything.

"Well, I tried and nobody answered. I just know something is terribly wrong."

The thought of going to Bucky's was marginally more appealing that shoving slivers under my fingernails, and wildly better than going shopping with Mother.

"Oh, okay," I said. "Give me your number, Aileen (was that right?), and I'll call you."

"Thank you, dear," she said, giving me her number. "Please consider the Quilt of Faith. We do have such fun, *such fun*! God's peace," she said, and abruptly hung up.

I carefully placed the handset back into the cradle and went into the kitchen to see if there was any coffee left. As I contemplated the inky dredges in the pot, someone pounded on the door, causing me to jump back and bump into Mother who was lurking in my blind spot. I felt something hot spill down the back of my neck.

"Sorry dear," Mother said. "Did I burn you?"

"I'm fine," I said waving her off. I hurried to the door and yanked it open. Bucky's hulking figure filled the doorframe.

"I tried to call yous, but the line's been busy," he said, wiping his feet ineffectually on the entrance mat.

Very little of Bucky's face was visible beneath the greasy, matted, beard. He was holding his Stormy Kromer hat in his hands, twirling it nervously. His large shoulders were hunched, as if he were trying to disappear into himself.

31

"I got trouble back at the place," he said. "I called the cops. I told them yous could vouch for me."

I could feel Mother's presence behind me. She seemed intent on dabbing at the back of my neck with a napkin.

"Mornin', ma'am," he said to Mother who nodded her head in response.

"Trouble—what kind of trouble?" I said.

"See, I wasn't cheatin', and he had no right to come around," Bucky stammered.

"Who—Bucky, what's going on?"

Mother quit dabbing; she was all ears.

"Well, see that darn fool got himself shut in somehow. It wasn't me that done it. I seen him first thing this morning. He's dead, eh?"

"Dead—who?"

"Watkins—Weasel, he's in my meat locker, deader 'n a doornail," Bucky said.

Mother sucked in her breath.

"I had nuthin' to do with it. The cops want yous to come out because of the igloo contest—I told them that Watkins was probably snooping around and got himself shut in. Probably passed out drunk. Yous need to come and explain things. That girl cop is there. She said more cops'r coming."

My head was spinning. Weasel Watkins dead? In a meat locker? Wasn't that sometimes called a walk-in cooler?"

"You need a ride?" he asked.

I remembered that Bucky had lost his driver's license some time ago and either drove an all-terrain vehicle or a snowmobile, depending on the season.

"No thanks. I'll drive my car," I said.

Bucky left, leaving a muddy puddle in the entryway. Where was George when I needed him? The art show—no phone and I had the cell. Mother reached for her coat and I felt instant panic. I did not think her presence at Bucky's would make things go smoother.

"Mother! Don't let this interrupt your trip to Marquette. Please go—to Marquette, I mean. I really do want you to get those things for the house we talked about. Valises."

"Valances, dear. For the windows."

"Yes, please. Get them. A whole bunch—I always say, the more valances, the better. Keep the receipts; I'll pay you back."

Mother gave me a look, snorted, and flounced out of the room.

32

⸗ 5 ⸗

Folks were boiling with excitement at church that Sunday. It wasn't every day that a member of the Moose Willow community died under "unusual circumstances." Clarence "Weasel" Watkins, though not a Methodist nor the most respectable member of the community, was nonetheless a resident of Moose Willow and this abrupt departure from his mortal husk was unsettling. Nearly as disruptive was the presence of Mother, who drew clusters of people more pleased with her visit than I was. She patted her hair at regular intervals, smiling and making modest gestures as old friends lavished attention upon her. Mother's visits seemed to breathe life into everyone but me.

The excitement in the narthex was of no concern to our choir director, Hannu, who was having a meltdown because two key members of the choir had not shown up, namely James and Derry. They were supposed to do a duet segment during the choir anthem, "You Raise Me Up."

"Where are they?" he shrilled as we robed up.

I was wondering the same thing. With Derry—well, she was new; she had not yet established a record of reliability or sustainability. It was not unusual for someone to try choir practice once and never be seen again. James, however, was a surprise. He never missed an opportunity to showboat. He and Derry had looked healthy and frisky when I saw them Friday night at the bar. In fact, if anyone was out of sorts, it was me.

* * *

I had spent several hours Saturday morning hanging out in the cold at Bucky's Game Processing & Taxidermy while waiting for the State Police crime lab to arrive and deal with the *deader 'n a doornail* Weasel Watkins. I was asked to stick around for a while since I had seen him at the Bayview, and then there was the igloo contest aspect of the debacle. A preliminary investigation by our local state trooper, Roberta "Bertie" Vaara, suggested that the victim had died of exposure, perhaps exacerbated by a high blood alcohol level, when trapped for an undetermined period of time in the refrigerated section of Bucky's Game Processing & Taxidermy. I had told her about my strange phone call, saying that George's partner was in the cooler, which didn't seem to connect any dots, since George and Weasel had no strong alliances. I hadn't erased the message, so Bertie said she'd stop by the house later to listen. Could just be a prank, she had said. I worked at a college where pranks were commonplace. It was no secret that George had a small, but determined set of art groupies, most of them young women. Maybe a jealous boyfriend made the calls. I mentioned that the caller ID had said "unavailable" on the display. Bertie said that was common with telemarketing, but maybe an individual could have his or her number blocked as well.

Bertie and I had known each other since grade school. We had taken turns tormenting boys, who we thought were stupid. Teachers generally tried to separate Bertie and me in the classroom, on the playground, during gym, and anywhere else we were likely to conspire. It seemed when we managed to hang out together, there was a strong risk of trouble and sometimes mayhem, which often led to detention and threats about our "permanent record."

Clarence Watkins' beater truck was parked out of sight behind Bucky's meat locker building. The police were having it towed in as potential evidence in possible foul play. Bucky said he hadn't noticed Weasel's truck when he went to open up in the morning. As soon as he turned on the light in the cooler, he saw Weasel sitting on the floor. He yelled out at him then went over and gave him a poke. He knew a dead guy when he saw one, but he still tried to find a pulse, with no luck. Next he ran to the trailer and called 911 and stayed put until the authorities arrived. Unfortunately, there were a slew of tire tracks and footprints in the churned-up mess of the emergency responders. Nonetheless, the police were looking for possible other tracks. Because of a fresh snowfall overnight, likely any other "visitor's" prints were gone.

Bertie had let me watch as she worked the scene along with someone from the crime lab who proceeded to take photos and collect possible evidence. Clarence Watkins had met his demise in the refrigerated section of the place, called a walk-in cooler, where a ghastly row of deer carcasses hung from a cable/pully system. This was where the deceased sat, as if waiting for someone to help him up. He appeared to have succumbed peacefully, though the vacant stare of his eyes—still open—indicated in no uncertain terms that he wasn't simply taking a snooze.

Bertie bent over Weasel and sniffed. "I smell booze," she said.

The body was very stiff, either from the cold or rigor mortis, or both. Bertie stood and straightened the kinks out of her back. "Mr. Watkins has been dead for some time," she said. "Rigor Mortis sets in about four to six hours after death," she added casually, as one might announce that the pot roast was done and dinner was served.

I, on the other hand, was feeling a bit light-headed. The scene in Bucky's meat locker was surreal, with Weasel sitting there, frozen, eyes staring and vacant from a pale, bloodless face. Bertie had gently closed his eyelids. The grisly scene wasn't at all like on television where the image is diluted during its journey from the TV to the viewer who, even if repulsed, knows it's not real.

An SUV pulled up and a man got out and walked over to the scene. He nodded at Bertie.

"Hey, Charlie, thanks for coming," Bertie said. "Charlie Adams is our ME—medical examiner," she explained to me. "He'll give the official word."

Charlie took one look and said, "He's dead. And that's official. What's the story?"

Bertie gave the ME a synopsis of the bizarre situation while I tried to focus on anything but the unfortunate Clarence Watkins.

The ME squatted next to Clarence. "For sure we'll need to do a blood alcohol," he said. "Maybe check for drugs, too."

Just as I was considering asking to leave, another vehicle raced in and slid to a halt. We all turned to look. Someone had called Clarence's wife, Aileen. She flew out of the car along with a swarm of sisters-in-Christ from the Lutheran church. Her entourage of support attempted to keep her away from the meat locker, but Aileen broke free and plowed in before Bertie could stop her. Aileen got a gander at her beloved.

Instantly, her voice rose to an impossible decibel level. "Claaaarreeeence," she wailed as she thrust herself at me, grabbing my coat. "You! You and your stupid contest. This is all your fault," she said while jerking at my lapels, then pushing me toward the antlers of a hanging deer.

"Aileen, I—"

Bertie hurried toward Aileen and me, muttering, "Damn that Bucky, he must have called her. Guess that's a positive ID." She gently pulled Aileen off me. "Mrs. Watkins, my deepest condolences for your loss." Bertie guided the woman out of the walk-in cooler. "You need to go home and rest, and we'll be in touch. Will someone be able to stay with her until we can notify her family?" she asked the group of women who huddled together like a herd of frightened sheep.

One of the women stepped forward and took Aileen by the elbow. "Of course," she said. "Come on honey, you can stay with me and Don." Another woman took Aileen's other elbow and said: "She don't have anyone."

Slowly they led her off, hopefully for a hot toddy, or better yet a dose of Valium. I did recall that the Watkins had lost a child at birth many decades ago and never had any more.

Eventually, Weasel's remains were removed from the freezer by two EMTs. At the direction of the medical examiner, they ensconced him in a humungous black zipper bag and placed him on a gurney. His legs seemed stuck in a bent, crossed position, which made it difficult for the EMTs to zip the bag closed. None too gently, they flattened Clarence's bent knees and worked the zipper until the bag was sealed. I wondered if the legs were so stiff that they might snap off, like icicles. That would be an interesting thing to explain to Aileen. *Oh, well, you only need a four-foot casket, because, well...*

The crime lab guy had taken photos, dusted for prints, and bagged a bunch of hair, which probably belonged to the dead deer. Once Weasel was removed, I was disappointed for some reason that there was no chalk line representing his final resting place.

As the ambulance was leaving, another car pulled up and a man got out and swaggered toward the scene.

"Oh, crap," Bertie said. "It's Burns here to save the day."

Burns and Bertie had a discussion. Since he was too late to even see the body and the so-called evidence was all collected and neatly labeled, it became clear that the detective was a day late and a dollar short. He honed in on me and decided to earn his detective pay by subjecting me to an interview. He asked my connection and why I was intruding.

"Hey," Bertie said. "She's a witness, sort of."

"That so?" Detective Burns said.

I explained all about the igloo contest and the situation between Bucky and Weasel and so on.

"So you think Mr. Watkins was snooping around in the freezer and somehow decided to just stay the night?" Detective Burns asked.

"Well, he was looking for igloo parts, I guess," I said

"Right. Really hard to believe grown men...Well, anyway, I understand that there was some animosity between Mr. Tanner and Mr. Watkins."

"Mr. Tanner? Oh, right," I said. I rarely if ever thought of Bucky as Mr. Tanner. "I guess you could call it animosity. They always had this friction, but I don't think—"

"And you say you saw Mr. Watkins at the bar on Friday night?"

"Yes. The Bayview. The owner can tell you that," I said.

"Bayview." Burns wrote this down in the same notebook that contained my vital statistics. "Did he seem intoxicated?"

"I think there was a good chance, but I didn't talk to him."

"Ok, thanks Miss—" he looked at his notebook— "Trout. Interesting name. Do you fish?"

"Um, sometimes," I said.

"We'll get in touch for a formal statement."

The detective slapped his notebook shut and went over to his 4x4 SUV and opened the door. You could hear the squawk of his police radio. He settled into the front seat, leaving the door open, and began typing on a laptop.

I saw Bucky hurry from his mobile home toward us. "I called the missus a while back," he said. "I meant to tell yous."

"Been here and left," Bertie said.

"Hey! Mr. Tanner." Burns yelled from his vehicle. "I need to talk to you."

Bucky turned and looked at Burns.

"But give me fifteen," Burns said turning back to his computer.

Bucky shrugged and came over to us. "I want yous to take some pictures," he said to Bertie. "Watkins made a real mess of things in the freezer." I might have to throw some stuff out."

The door of the walk-in cooler was propped open and we all filed inside. It was slightly less disturbing with Weasel's remains gone. Bertie paused at one of the deer carcasses and muttered something about a ten-pointer. We followed Bucky into a horrible room that only Hannibal Lecter could appreciate.

"This here is where I do the meat processing and some of the taxidermy," Bucky said. "Got state of the art equipment to make an easy job," he added, waving his arm at assorted instruments designed for maiming and dismemberment.

"So, what about all the stuff that got damaged?" Bertie said.

"In da freezer, eh?" he said.

He opened a door and we went into the freezer part of the unit, where presumably processed/packaged meat was stored—and, according to Weasel Watkins, illegal igloo parts.

The place was, indeed, a mess, with boxes torn open, things dumped out, drawers hanging open. Some of the packages had come unwrapped, exposing the contents.

Bertie looked around. "Offhand, I don't see any illegal igloo parts," she said.

"You won't find nothin' illegal in my freezer," said Bucky. "That dang fool Watkins. Anyways, yous can see that all these had nuthin' but game in them. They was all labeled proper with names, dates and wrapped up according to health department code. I keep everything right in here. See, I got a list posted on the wall too and check the temperature regular. The health department comes and checks all that."

Bertie took some pictures with her phone, then we filed out of the freezer, through the torture chamber, and back into the carcass room. Someone had had turned out the light and shut the exit door. Bertie turned on her phone flashlight and directed it toward the door.

"Who in hell turned off the lights and why'd you shut the door?" Bertie asked. "It's darker than a tomb in here."

"Hey, lights ain't free and I took the prop out so's the door could shut automatically. Otherwise the compressor will just keep running." He flicked on switch and a dim light came on, making the room almost worse.

"So how does this thing work?" Bertie asked, shining her phone on the door.

"Don't worry, there's an emergency release that yous push, right here. I just push on this knob and it turns the latch on the udder side of the door. I made it myself. It works perfect. That fool was so drunk that he didn't have the sense to work it," he said, giving the knob a good push. "That's funny."

"What's funny," Bertie said.

"She usually works like a charm." Bucky grunted, pushing with all his might on the release knob.

"Usually?" I asked.

"Seems jammed," Bucky said as he continued wrenching. "I've been in here a million times this week. Second week of deer camp, eh? My busiest time. Something's jammin' it."

"We be jammin'," I said, giggling. In addition to being anal retentive, I was also a teeny bit claustrophobic. I got "uncomfortable" in elevators, restroom stalls, and I hated stained-glass windows that blocked the view. Why have windows if you can't see out? Clearly, I needed to add walk-in freezers with cheesy homemade latches to my list of places to avoid. Bertie pointed the beam of her phone flashlight on my face for a minute. "You OK?" She remembered my hang-ups from childhood. She had shut me in a closet once. Bad idea.

In spite of the brisk temperature, the cooler was getting very close. Bucky was emitting a musky smell: a combination of B.O., woodsmoke, and tobacco breath.

Bertie trained her light on the release.

"I'll be," Bucky said.

"You'll be what?" I said much too loudly.

"Damned—ah, pardon me ladies—darned. I'll be darned. Looky here."

Bertie and I leaned closer, squinting at where Bucky was pointing.

"Look at what?" Bertie said.

"This here's been tampered with. Someone's jammed a knife blade in here," he said. "'til I get it out, we're stuck."

Tell George his partner's in the cooler. I thought about that phone call again. Was I smelling Bucky, or myself, or death? I wasn't sure what death smelled like but was pretty sure it wouldn't be pleasant. I was feeling a little woozy. Nothing made sense; I couldn't imagine a partnership of any kind between George and Weasel.

"Maybe it was Weasel, trying to get out," Bertie offered. "He was drunk and couldn't operate the release, so tried to use his knife."

"Maybe," Bucky said. "I didn't see no broken knife when I first come in."

"Well, I think the crime lab would have found it anyway. All they got was some hair," Bertie said.

"Will you please get this fucking door open!" I said in what I thought was a perfectly calm voice.

My cooler companions again turned to look at me. What was that smell? "Who cut one?" I said, giggling.

"We better get her outta here," Bertie said, waving her hand in front of her face. "We need something to pull the knife blade out. You got anything, Bucky?"

"Nope. Left my Leatherman in the house. What about you—yous're the cop. Don't you got a tool set or something? We need some needle-nose pliers."

"Sure, I keep them in my bra. You idiot! My tool kit's in the patrol car," Bertie said.

"Someone will miss us—right?" I said.

"Right, said Bertie. When they realize the patrol car's not back, they'll come looking—in two or three days."

"Two or three days!" I said. I might have started pounding my fists on the door. I felt my knees buckle. Something shrill, like an air-raid siren, was ringing in my head.

"Hey, Janese, I was kidding," Bertie said.

"You OK?" Bucky asked, grabbing my arm, slowing my fall to the disgusting, clammy floor. "Don't worry Janese, we'll get yous outta here. Ain't that detective still out there? Hey! Someone!" he shouted at the door, which suddenly burst open. Detective Burns was framed in the halo of the open doorway.

"You guys gonna screw around all day?" Burns said. "Who said you could mess around in here; this might be a crime scene. We'll know more about what happened to the vic after the autopsy." He looked at the hangers of deer carcasses swaying behind him, then to Bertie. "Hey Vaara, your old man get his buck this year?"

* * *

"I'm wery angry!" Hannu's Finnish accent became more prevalent when he got emotional. "Janese, Eleanor, Joe, and Tom—you sing the parts. Let's go now, we gotta practice."

The choir always sang an introit and an anthem during each Sunday's church service. The music we practiced was in addition to the cantata pieces we labored through each week. Due to time constraints, the anthem often got less attention than needed. And, of course, it didn't help one bit when the Derry/James duet was still MIA.

The whole situation seemed to please Eleanor Heimlich, who looked at me and raised an eyebrow; a corner of her mouth twitched into a smirk.

"I hope you can do the F sharp," I said to her. "I think my voice is a bit raspy from being out in the cold."

We didn't make it very far into our quickie rehearsal before Hannu flapped his arms with annoyance, bringing us to a dribbling stop. He gave me a withering look.

"Sore throat," I said, pointing to my neck. "Sorry."

40

Hannu released an ever-suffering sigh. James Rush and Derry Parks were on my list of people to seriously injure or kill. They sure looked cozy at the Bayview. I suspected they were enjoying a duet of the non-musical kind while I was deeply questioning my reason for being in the church choir, punishing my vocal cords beyond their limit, and under-mining my self-esteem. Furthermore, the music committee wouldn't even buy me my own choir robe, and I had a hand-me-down that was too long and tripped me constantly. It was Mother who had signed me up decades ago. I was all grown up now. I could quit anytime.

Hannu motioned to the pianist, Azinnia, to begin the prelude. This time we stumbled all the way through.

"Good enough," Hannu declared. "Line up."

Because of Derry's absence, Eleanor reclaimed her regular non-folding chair on the choir platform. Her hair towered impossibly high, dwarfing me.

"Don't screw this up," she hissed. "I have ways of making people suffer."

I felt a rush of heat followed by a cold chill. I was trying to remember the rumor about her husband dying under mysterious cir-cumstances. Heimlich's hemlock in the teacup, perhaps?

Then she smiled sweetly and turned her attention to Pastor Sam who started the service by bellowing out his usual: "Good morning!" To which we parroted: "Good Morning!"

"Friends, as you know, we have lost a long-time member of our community, who loved the land, his family, his God…"

That got the pot stirred up, and a din rose then fell in the congrega-tion as the pastor asked for a moment of silence for the shocking death of Clarence Watkins. Life goes on, and so did the service. Somehow, we had moved from the Gospel lesson on to testimonials.

George rarely went to church with me, and this day was no excep-tion. However, Mother certainly didn't miss the chance to immerse herself into the embrace of the congregation. She stood and said: "Well, I just want to say what a *joy* it is to be here with my church family." The congregation muttered its agreement then everyone looked at me, expecting me to leap up and sing a few choruses of "Halleluiah." I conveniently dropped my hymnal.

The pastor pushed on to the silent prayer time. My armpits began to tingle; the choir anthem was next. I could hear Hannu fidgeting, getting the anthem out of his music folder, fingering the pages. He moved to the music stand and signaled for the choir to rise. Joe and

Tom would have the first verse. I tried to swallow but my throat was dry. I wondered if this was how a snake felt when it had underestimated the size of its prey—stuck in the gullet, wiggling a little. Eleanor was crowding me, making it awkward to hold my music. Azinnia started the prelude. Hannu cued; Joe and Tom sang the first verse without a hitch.

Next came the chorus with the whole choir. Hannu shifted his attention from the choir at large to Eleanor and me. Showtime. He gestured ardently, giving us our cue.

YOU RAISE ME...

And then I was down.

Hannu fanned me with a church bulletin while Eleanor glared, pure hatred oozing from her. Mother was there as well, kneeling beside me, bright-red hair blazing as if she were consumed by fire.

"You're not pregnant, are you?" she asked, loudly. I think I heard tittering.

≈ 6 ≈

I retreated, mortified, into the bedroom after returning home from church. Mother's blatant comment about the possibility of me being pregnant had gone beyond humiliation. How could she? I hid in the darkened bedroom. Mother came in to fuss. I ignored her, pretending to be asleep. George brought me a small glass of wine, even though it was my policy not to drink on Sunday. There were always exceptions.

I sat up to take the wine glass.

"It's okay to have that—right, I mean alcohol?" George asked. He fidgeted with the bedspread, which was totally out of character for him. I figured Mother had filled him in about the spectacle I'd created at church.

"Sure, why not?" I said. "Oh." I looked at the wine. Mother had obviously filled George in on her speculation as to the cause of my fainting spell, and of course pregnant women weren't supposed to drink. Me, pregnant? Absurd. George and I had always been very careful when we got down to business, so to speak. Well, at least most of the time. I set the wine down and decided to change the subject.

I told him about the two phone calls: the first one in my office and the second at home, referring to George's partner being in the cooler.

George sat on the edge of the bed. He pushed my hair out of my face and kissed me, then straightened up. "Haven't a clue about the crank calls. Maybe someone you work with—or a student. What about caller ID?"

"When it's recorded, it doesn't display the number when I play back the message. When I looked at the missed call log, it was no help. It just said 'unavailable'. So did the one here at home."

"So you think there's a connection somehow with Weasel's body in Bucky's freezer?"

I gave him a steady look. "Do you?"

George lifted his hands, palms up. "Hey, I only knew Weasel from reputation. We might say hi if we passed in the woods."

"Maybe it was the wrong body," I said. I reached for the wine. If there was a fetus, a sip of wine was the least of its worries.

"I don't get it," George said.

"I mean, maybe someone thought they were shutting someone else in 'the cooler'."

George got up and started pacing the room. "Like who?"

I let the question hang there a moment. I took another sip.

George and I silently mulled this over until Mother popped her head into the bedroom.

"I'm making dinner," she announced. "Remind me to pick you up some new pots and pans, Janese. I don't think even Goodwill would take these. Also, I'm cleaning out the fridge to make room for the turkey."

I gave her a puzzled look.

"Oh, for heaven's sake, Janese, Thanksgiving is in four days. I'll have to buy a fresh one as it is. It takes a week to thaw out a frozen turkey."

I had completely forgotten about Thanksgiving and the idea of a family dinner had not occurred to me. Usually Mother was gearing up at the resort, getting ready for holiday guests. We had not shared a Thanksgiving since my college days.

"And you don't even have a casserole dish," she said. "How can I make my green bean casserole without a casserole dish?"

I loathed green bean casserole—all casseroles, for that matter. When I was a child, Mother had made her "surprise casseroles," which I had to gag down or sit and stare at until bedtime: my choice. Because we were dirt poor, the casseroles ranged from odd to downright scary. I was sure she had been kidding about her "toad surprise" and "road-kill scramble." Then again, maybe not. Mother could be very resourceful.

"What's for dinner?" George asked, prompted by all the food talk. In spite of the obvious discomfort between George and Mother, he did enjoy the regular meals we'd been having since her arrival.

"Tuna casserole," Mother said. "In a cake pan," she added.

I groaned. I hated tuna casserole more than anything on earth. Even more than the green bean thing. I felt a sudden rush of nausea and shot out of the bed to the bathroom.

When I returned, Mother and George were nowhere to be found. Cowards. The queasiness never came to fruition, thank God. I felt good enough to polish off the glass of wine and dozed to the sounds of Mother banging my inferior pots and pans around in the kitchen. During the twilight that precedes real sleep, I fantasized about exploring the deep, cool depths of an igloo. At the end of a long, dim tunnel, a group of people—all women—sat in a semi-circle of chairs: a committee, awaiting the accused. I awakened with a start and an overwhelming sense of doom, like prey fleeing a predator, and losing ground.

* * *

When I checked my voicemail at work on Monday morning, there were no messages, cryptic or otherwise. The mysterious phone calls I had received earlier reminded me of the single socks that come out of a dryer. Something was missing, but you have no idea where to look. The reference in those calls to George and the cooler simply didn't make sense. Weasel, the corpse in the cooler, was not George's partner, working, drinking, scheming, or otherwise.

When I checked my snail mail, I was blessed with three new entries for the igloo contest. One was from Bucky who proposed to build a beaver lodge. The other two entries included a hornets' nest—the sketch looked like a deranged Christmas ornament—and a bear's den. There was no sketch, but a note asking if costumes were allowed. I suspected a *Goldilocks* reenactment.

The igloo contest had become highly competitive. Especially this year with the grand prize of a shiny new off-road vehicle, or ORV, partially donated by Trail & Lake Motor Sports. Other prizes were token in nature: caps, tee-shirts, tote bags, food, and gift certificates from the local businesses.

There was a trophy that was passed around, which had been donated by the Northern Pride Gift Shoppe. The name of the individual, group, or business winning the roving trophy had his/her/its name engraved on it and displayed in a dusty case sitting in the town hall entryway. If you won it three years in a row, you got to keep it. Bucky's Game Processing & Taxidermy had won it the previous year, which was the first official contest. Bucky and his family had created a wigwam. The structure was built with chunks of ice made from freezing water in buckets, plastic totes, milk jugs, and five-quart ice cream buckets. Snow was used to chink the ice blocks and a few gallons of warm water poured over the structure smoothed it out and bonded it. The Tanner clan had salvaged some animal hides from the taxidermy business and draped them over the thing as a finishing touch.

This prompted a demand for disqualification because clearly—or maybe not so clearly—the expectation was that the structure would be made strictly of snow and ice, not animal hides or other exotic items. Of course rules had been sketchy, so Bucky couldn't be disqualified.

The Igloo Committee had not anticipated such nit pickiness. Now Bucky proposed a beaver lodge, which bore the same basic shape as the wigwam, only instead of a regular door, the entryway would be from underneath—somehow. "We ain't figured it out yet" was written on the entry form.

This year, the assumption that "anything goes" was to be squelched. Entries, complete with sketch, required committee approval. A hefty set of rules had been concocted for "the safety and enjoyment of all." A nice, *wholesome* theme was suggested in a memo from the 4Cs president, Patrick Neil, to the committee. The reason for this was because of the scandal surrounding one of the "igloos" from the past year. The inappropriate creation, submitted by The Quik Cash & Gun Pawn Shop had been a gigantic gun, barrel pointing phallic-like into the heavens in front of their business. The QC&G was an eyesore that was located on Main Street in Moose Willow and was passed by all who came into or went out of town. Many citizens would have liked the QC&G to disappear as the "retro" Colt 38 revolver did when it melted into a puddle with the spring thaw. However, it was owned and operated by the Ojibwe Tribe, and there was no getting rid of it. Besides, it was a dandy tourist attraction.

Unquestionably, the Quik Cash & Gun's Colt 38 revolver had been the most impressive entry: you could walk into the chamber where the bullets would go! The barrel reached about fifteen feet into the air and was made of ice formed in five-gallon buckets and "welded" by partially melting and refreezing the pieces together in a long, solid, semi-transparent cylinder. No other entries had shown such innovation. Yet Bucky and family had won with their unimaginative hump of ice and snow. Weasel Watkins occasionally worked at the QC&G as a fill-in and had been part of the "team" that build the gun. He had been furious about losing. *Poor taste! Wrong message? This here's the U.P. where guns is a way of life.* Weasel's tirade had gone on. The manager of the QC&G didn't really care, since the attraction had significantly boosted business. In addition to moving a lot of pawn shop inventory, they also sold T-shirts and other souvenirs to tourists during the boon. They even gave away coupons for a free beverage at the casino to anyone who guessed what kind of gun it was. It said Colt 38 right on it, so any fool could figure it out.

In its quest to ensure wholesomeness, the committee decided to have a limerick contest to establish a theme. Unfortunately, nobody, except the high school English teacher really knew what a limerick was, so the contest was dumbed-down to a "ditty" that rhymes. A fifth-grade girl submitted the only viable entry:

> *Walk on all fours*
> *Or fly or creep,*
> *A house of ice*
> *Is where they sleep.*

Perfect: Habitat for critters. What could be more wholesome and north-woodsy?

The girl not only got her name and poem published in the *Northern Sentry*, but also received a $100 savings bond from the local credit union. The photo in the *Sentry* showed her being handed the giant cardboard savings bond—one of those fake presentations staged for the camera. She looked completely bored. The branch manager, who presented the oversized replica, grinned idiotically at the camera.

President Neil sent a word-salad memo to the Igloo Committee congratulating them on its pursuit to unify the campus and larger community and the creative resourcefulness exhibited in establishing reasonable and satisfactory boundaries. What it meant, exactly, was not certain but the committee was fairly sure that they could breathe a unified sigh of relief.

At the Copper Country Community College, everything was done by committee. People were hired by committee, buildings were built by committee, academic programs came and went by committee, and the menu for the holiday party was selected by committee. Probably the toilet paper and pothole patch also required committee approval. There was actually a committee to establish and staff committees. Committees were safe. If a bad decision was made by a committee, then no individual need be held accountable. "I don't know why *the committee* decided on a kazoo band for the Christmas party!" If something went well, then the chair of the committee, all aglow, could step up to the microphone and say: "On behalf of the Campus Enrichment Committee, we would like to thank all who supported and attended the recent Nuts, Bolts, and Gears art exhibit!"

The Igloo Committee would meet that afternoon to approve the contest submissions we had received thus far and decide what type of non-snow/ice materials would be allowed. Important stuff. Competitors would likely try to push the envelope and attempt to incorporate colorful or eye-catching things such as deer antlers, plastic flowers, even blinking lights. Or in the case of Bucky, animal hides.

I had some ideas on how to handle these petty issues. My suggestion would be to allow "natural" enhancements. Then we could spell out what was natural. Of course someone would throw up a roadblock, such as Brenda Koski who, when she managed to actually show up for a meeting, would patronizingly reject all my ideas. I smiled and wondered if she had discovered her broken splashguard. My mind drifting from one paradox to another—parenthood, marriage, Mother—when someone knocked on the frame of my open door.

Speak of the devil.

"Hi Jan. Busy?"

I hated to be called Jan. There was no use feigning busyness, since, clearly, I had been daydreaming. "Hi Brenda, come on in."

"How are you feeling? Are you okay?" she asked in a syrupy tone.

"Sure, why?"

"Oh—well, just, you know, asking." Her words were full of innuendo. I knew she had heard of my fainting spell in church. The Moose Willow's Gossip Mill had been working overtime.

I decided to not give her the satisfaction of continuing that line of conversation. "So, Brenda, what can I do for you?"

"Well, I simply can't make the meeting today. You see, I have to meet with the president. It's very urgent." She was wearing stiletto heels, and shifted from one foot to the other, as if seeking relief.

The last time I had met with the college president, he called me Janice instead of Janese. But then, I didn't have legs that went on forever into itsy bitsy skirts, or breasts that spilled opulently from spandex tops.

"I don't think we should reschedule," I said.

"Oh, mercy, no," she said. "You go ahead and make all your fun little plans for the Eskimo contest," she said, inspecting a fingernail.

"Igloo."

"Excuse me?" she said, peering at me while nibbling on her fingernail.

"It's not Eskimo, it's igloo." I neatened some papers on my desk, squaring them up. "Actually officially the Habitat for Critters Igloo Contest."

"Whatever. Anyway, I'm afraid I must meet with Patrick about some very important stuff."

We were all encouraged to be chummy and call the president by his first name, Patrick. Most of us played it safe and called him President Neil.

"We may have to do some travelling—he thinks I could help him a lot in funraising."

"You mean fundraising," I said.

"That's what I said. I may get a promotion to VP of, um, oh what did he say. Oh yes, external affairs."

"Congratulations," I said flatly. I wondered what Mrs. Neil would think of this new partnership. She had gotten more than one person fired from the 4Cs.

"Thanks! And congrats to you, too!" Brenda said.

"For what?"

"Ooopsie. Gotta go," she said, pivoting on a heel and clacking off down the hall.

Bitch. Slut.

Would it really be so bad? I thought, if I were—pregnant? Would George stay or split like a cockroach caught in the kitchen light? Mother would stick around: a chilling thought. I absently looked in the mirror on my file cabinet. I had heard that pregnant women had a glow. I was not glowing. I looked like a zombie from *The Night of the Living Dead*. My hair was haphazardly pulled into a ponytail, with wayward tufts springing freely about my face and a significant amount of dark roots showing. I usually allotted at least two minutes every morning for applying makeup. I had cut the time in half that morning. My lack of grooming was a reflection of how a morning goes when there are at least one too many people in the house. As Mother established herself as a viable and obtrusive entity, George became scarce. Since she had taken over the loft as her guest quarters, George had no place to create pottery except at work. Therefore, he decided to go into the pottery studio at the art center every morning until further notice.

I stood at my office window; the snow was falling heavily. They predicted a lot of snow this year—something to do with global warming or climate change or the fact that we lived by a snow machine called Lake Superior. I was glad I had hired a local guy to plow my driveway. During my first winter in the cabin, I had believed that I could do it all: work, clean, mow, plow, varnish the logs, split my firewood, make my own soap—you name it. When I realized that I could barely maintain myself, let alone a homestead, I had come to my senses and hired Toivo Keskimaki to do odd jobs. I paid him in cash with an occasional bonus of his favorite twelve-pack. Toivo's wife, Iola, ran a little pasty shop in town and she regularly had Toivo deliver a fresh pasty, wafting the aromas of rutabaga, onion, and mystery meat all neatly sealed in a flaky, lard-based crust. Toivo drove an ancient Ford/Chevy 4x4 pickup, which owned very little of its original body. As pieces rusted and fell off, Toivo scrounged junkyards, dumps, and front yards for replacement parts. He did this only for essential items, so the exhaust system had not received much attention. You could hear him coming from at least a half mile away. An alarm clock was not necessary on snowy mornings.

As I pulled into my driveway after work, it looked like someone was building inventory for a used car lot. Mother's BMW was there as well as George's truck. An additional, vaguely familiar vehicle, parked snug to Mother's bumper, had joined the collection. Hail! Hail! The gang's all here! I wondered who was visiting *now*. It wasn't a police car, ambulance, fire truck, or other ominous vehicle. Was it a Mercedes? Hard to tell what was beneath the mantle of snow and caked-on mud. Perhaps Mother had plucked someone from the cast of Moose Willow citizenry and brought them home to enrich our lives. Maybe they could join us for Thanksgiving dinner and bring a sweet potato and turnip casserole. I took a closer look at the car; it was a Mercedes. That would be Mother's style.

When I entered my living room, I didn't recognize the visitor at first. He resembled a person who had been living off the grid. He bore several days' growth of beard, his hair was disheveled, and his clothing was soiled and torn. He stood, leaving a dark blotch on my couch.

"I'll get you some clean clothes," George said.

"Here, drink this nice herbal tea," Mother said, offering the man a cup.

"Thank you, Madeline," he said to my mother. The voice was unmistakable.

"James?" I said. The man who stood unsteadily before me barely resembled the normally immaculate TV Channel 13 anchor, choir baritone and ladies' man: James Rush.

"Hello, Janese," he said, taking the cup from Mother with a trembling hand. "Pardon the intrusion. But, you see, someone tried to kill me."

7

James looked over the rim of his teacup at me. "I didn't know where to go but then I thought of Georgie." He lifted his cup toward George who was coming back with a pair of jeans and a flannel shirt draped over his arm.

"Here are some dry clothes," George said. "Do you wear boxers or briefs?"

Mother's eyebrows twitched.

"Thanks, Buddy," James said, putting down his cup—not on a coaster—and taking the clothes. He started to leave the room, presumably to change in our bedroom. Had I made the bed? I was usually fanatic about making it, but lately things had been chaotic in the morning.

"And the boxer/brief question?" James said, "I'll never tell." He gave Mother a surreptitious glance and a wink.

"Hey, where are you going?" I said. "What's this all about someone trying to kill you?"

"I'll explain later," he said, turning and heading toward the bedroom. "Right now, I need a shower."

Weasel Watkins' demise had shaken our community and dispelled the notion that murder only happens in big cities. Not that they were calling it a homicide—at least not yet—but they weren't ruling out foul play. James Rush's atypical grubby presence in my living room, with claims of someone trying to kill him, certainly diminished my sense of well-being.

Moose Willow had enjoyed only natural-cause or accidental deaths in recent history, with one exception. The last so-called homicide in Moose Willow had occurred on St. Patrick's Day during my senior year at T.J. Harju High School. Folks called it a case of the "shack nasties," or cabin fever. People get a little crazy after being cooped up all winter.

Accurately predicting weather has always been sketchy in our neck of the woods, supposedly due to the influence of Lake Superior and air masses hitting areas of high country. The Channel 13 meteorologist said a bit of "weather" was approaching and would produce one to three inches or snow along with some wind gusts. Seemingly nothing to worry about. By two in the afternoon, an ominous front crept across

Lake Superior, accompanied by a biting north wind. The first flurries began to fall about the time I got out of school. By four o'clock, the day had turned to night and the snow fell so heavily that the plows couldn't keep up. By seven at night, the wind gusted up to 50 miles per hour, and people were advised to go home and stay there. Around 9:00, the plows were called in because of poor visibility. The bars closed—they were nearly empty anyway—and all signs of life in the village ceased to exist. By midnight, fallen trees and limbs had snapped power lines, which had blown out numerous fuses and transformers. This blacked out the entire county and it was too dangerous for repair crews to go out.

Any self-respecting U.P. resident was smart enough to have a couple days' worth of split firewood on hand in the event of just such a power outage. This was not the case at Lester and Eina Jokela's cabin, which was located in a remote, outlying area of the township. Lester and Eina were not the most loving couple, and the police had been called out frequently to mediate the prickly couple's disputes. Alcohol was always a factor.

On that particular St. Patrick's Day, Lester, being his usual lazy self, did not bring enough firewood onto the cabin porch to last through the blustery night and this apparently infuriated his wife. According to Eina, Lester refused to go to the shed for more wood (she would have herself but had a bad back) and remained planted in his recliner, drinking a thermos of green St. Paddy's Day beer that he had gotten from the tavern before it closed. Police speculated that the situation deteriorated when it was discovered that the green beer was the only alcohol in the cabin, and it was running low. A scuffle ensued, and the remaining beer was lost in the fray. Lester threw the empty thermos at Eina, who took the hit in her face. She picked up the last stick of firewood and threw it at Lester—strictly because she "feared for her life"—and made a direct hit to his head. The medical examiner said that the blow resulted in a massive brain hemorrhage and he was likely a doomed before he hit the ground. The thermos had badly damaged Eina's face, resulting in two black eyes, a broken nose, and purple forehead, which provided Eina's defense as a battered wife. Though she had beaten the manslaughter charge, everyone still called it the St. Paddy's Day murder.

"Do you want me to throw this stuff in the garbage?" James asked when he returned from showering and changing. He was clean-shaven and smelled of George's manly cologne. "Maybe we should burn them," he said, holding a sodden mass of clothing at arm's length.

Mother scurried over and snatched the clothing away from him. "You'll do no such thing," she said. "You just drink your tea and I'll go put these in the pre-wash. Of course your secret will be out!"

"Boxers, briefs, or commando?" James said, gazing at Mother.

Was I the only one who was horrified? Did George wink at James? Mother was much older, wasn't she? How old was she now? Almost sixty? And James, maybe thirty-five or forty? I was never good at figuring these things out because nobody was ever honest about their age.

James settled himself on the couch and looked at his teacup. "Got anything stronger, *Georgie?*" he said.

"You know I don't touch the stuff, *Jimmy*," George said.

Here we go with the insults, I thought.

Mother came bustling in, carrying a tumbler full of amber liquid. "Some nice scotch," she said, "to steady your nerves."

We all watched James sip the scotch Mother had magically produced.

"So, *Jimbo*, spill the beans," George said.

"All in good time," James said. "Madeline, you clearly have impeccable taste. Is this Glen Fiddich?" he said, holding up his tumbler.

"Well, yes it is," she said. "Shermie—God rest his soul—got me hooked on it."

"Very nice and clean tasting," he said.

"Enough chit chat!" I said. "Who tried to kill you?"

"Janese!" Mother said. "Don't hurry the man. He's been through an ordeal."

"It's okay, Madeline. I've barged in and I owe an explanation. Truth is, I have no idea," he said, taking another sip from the tumbler. "But I think it has to do with that new woman in town."

"Derry—whatshername—Parks, the mystery woman?" I said. "I noticed that you two were pretty chummy at the Bayview on Friday evening."

James feigned puzzlement for a moment. "Chummy?"

Mother looked at James.

George looked at me. "Bayview?"

"The wine's cheaper," I muttered.

"Yes," James said. "Derry and I did meet in the late afternoon on Friday to discuss a musical collaboration," James said. "I thought I was being a good ambassador, since she was new in town. Turns out she was supposedly interested in show business—wanted to be a news reporter for the station, and said she had a really *hot* story. Though in retrospect, she was obviously playing me like a well-worn fiddle. A bit of a user, I had thought, plying her charms to try to manipulate me. I have been around, you know, and she's not the first woman to be, well, enamored with me because of my position."

I stifled a cough. If his ego were any bigger, it wouldn't fit in my living room. I went to the kitchen and got myself a glass of wine. If he was having a cocktail, so was I; a small glass of wine wouldn't hurt anything.

"Janese, dear, why don't you freshen James' drink," Mother suggested.

"He found the shower, he can find the booze," I snapped.

Mother sounded as if she were choking on a marshmallow. I think George snorted. Impeccable hostess skills were not among my virtues.

"I'm fine," James said. "Boy, I can barely keep my eyes open. Of course, if I were to go back to my place, I wouldn't sleep a wink. Perhaps a motel..."

The implication that I would put a roof over yet another head was obvious.

"First off," I said, "as you can see, there is no more room in this inn. Second, you still haven't told us anything about this Parks woman and what she's got to do with someone trying to kill you. You will get no more Glen Fish scotch—"

"Fiddich," Mother corrected.

"—or so much as a cot in the garage without telling me what the hell is going on."

James sighed and set his glass on the coffee table, ignoring the coaster I had provided.

"Very well. Let's see. Derry contacted me at the TV station and asked if I'd like to go out for a drink. We met, as Janese pointed out, at the Bayview. It's a dreadful place, but it was convenient. The scotch is hideous. Nothing like this," he said holding up his empty tumbler.

"If I give you more, will you quit interrupting yourself and get on with it?" I asked.

"If you insist," he said, offering me the tumbler, which I ignored.

I went to the kitchen and got the bottle of scotch off the counter where Mother had left it. I returned to the living room and slammed it down next to his empty glass.

"Janese!" Mother said.

"Talk!" I said to James.

He sloshed some liquor into his glass. After an annoying, languid sip, James told us that when he and Derry met at the Bayview, she had told him that she was from somewhere in Wisconsin—he couldn't remember where. Her fiancé was tragically killed in an accident—she was vague about the details. She went to Ohio to be with family, which didn't work out so she came back to the north woods to seek "inner peace." Apparently, she had always loved our sleepy little village on the bay, with the sparkling view of Lake Superior and wintry Currier and Ives scenes.

"She wants to be part of the community—to fit in somewhere," James said. "That's why she came to choir practice—"

"Once," I said.

"Yes, well, I don't think we made her feel particularly welcome."

He had a point. I thought about Eleanor Heimlich's toxicity and Hannu's quirks—hell, everyone's quirks.

"Okay, you had a nice little chat session," I said. "I assume you didn't get past first base with her, and when you got forceful, she tried to kill you."

"Janese!" Mother said.

"Just kidding," I said. I looked at James, waiting.

James sighed, took a sip of scotch. "I'm just saying that it started the whole sequence of events that led to the attempt on my life."

"And how was this attempt made?" I asked.

"In that dreadful meat locker."

We all sat in stunned silence for a moment. What had happened to good old-fashioned weaponry, such as guns and knives—even fists? Why the sudden surge in murder, attempted or otherwise, by meat locker?

"You need to fill in some blanks, James," I said, rising and going for another touch of wine. "Keep talking."

Mother followed me into the kitchen and fussed over arranging some cheese and crackers on a plate. She also got herself a glass with ice, presumably to join in the cocktail hour.

"Is she always this impatient?" James asked Mother as he poured scotch into her glass. He topped off his own as well. "Anyway, as I said, Derry made a proposition. She said she would provide me with a really *big* story. In return, I would pull some strings at the television station and get her some airtime in the newsroom."

Mother clucked her tongue and muttered, "Tramp."

"I admit I was intrigued," James said, "so I agreed to *consider* her offer. I guess she took that as a yes. She was very anxious and said time was wasting. We would need to get on it that night before the 'evidence' disappeared."

George reached for the cheese and crackers. "What was this big story?"

"Bogus," James said. "She was nothing but a tease. I agreed to go to that God-forsaken place."

"*What* place?" I said.

"I already told you, the meat locker. You know, that Indian taxidermy place. Who knows what kind of germs I've been exposed to."

"You mean Bucky's?" George asked.

"That's the place, way the hell out in the middle of nowhere. Anyway, she said that she had some information on this Bucky fellow having something illegal stashed in his meat locker."

"Like illegal game or something?" George said.

"Or igloo parts for the contest," I said. "Hardly a major news story."

"She implied it would be a ground-breaking story. She wanted me to 'see it to believe it.' We were to go separately; she had to go home and change into different clothes, presumably something suitable for sleuthing around. She told me to head out and she'd meet me there. It was all so dramatic. I felt like I was participating in some B mystery movie. Foolishly, I fell for her scheme."

"So, you went to Bucky's?" I said. "Was she there?"

"I went to that meat locker building where she said to meet me, but she wasn't there. I damn near froze my bal—well, you get the picture, and it started to snow pretty hard, just to make it all the more miserable. I got up the nerve to go in—place wasn't locked—and suddenly the door slammed shut. I do not believe for one minute that it closed on its own. Clearly, someone intended to shut me in there to die either by exposure or asphyxiation. Perhaps it was the Parks woman, or perhaps it was that Bucky fellow, or maybe someone else entirely. I haven't a clue, but I was damn lucky to get out, because I believe that

that release latch had been disabled. More scotch, Madeline?" he asked as he sloshed more of the stuff into his tumbler.

James told us the rest of the story. His sense of the dramatic may have inflated a simple prank into attempted murder. It was even possible that a gust of wind had blown the door shut or that it just shut automatically, like Bucky said it was supposed to do. It was very possible that Derry had no intention of meeting him out at Bucky's for any big news exposé. Perhaps she was toying with him. But in God's name, why? According to James, after he found the light switch—though he did not spend a lot of time in the meat locker—he did not see a body, other than those of the antlered kind. This obviously meant that Weasel Watkins had not yet met his chilling demise. I made a mental note to let my State Trooper friend, Bertie Vaara, know. This might be significant.

James said that the escape latch was defective, but he managed to fiddle with it and finally got out. He did not use a knife—doesn't own one, he said. He couldn't see very well and had no idea if a knife blade was broken off in the latch. Also, something was wedged against the door, a board or pallet or something. He managed to force things and squeeze out. When he went home, James saw car tracks in his driveway and footprints leading to the service door to his garage. The door was standing open.

"Maybe it was just a UPS delivery, but I wasn't going to chance it. I was pretty spooked so I decided to head out to my hunting camp."

"Hunting camp?" I said. I could not envision the impeccable James Rush roughing it with a bunch of beer-guzzling, poker-playing, vulgar unwashed hunters.

"It's been in the family for generations. I've added electricity, running water, and even tore out the sauna and put in a hot tub. But, of course, I had the place winterized and the electricity shut off, so none of the amenities were functioning. In spite of the hardship, I stayed there for the weekend, freezing, living on canned beans, and terrified that I would be discovered. The snow was getting serious, too, and I was afraid I'd be snowed in for good, so I made a break for it. It was touch and go and then I got the Mercedes stuck. It is not made for this climate. I had to walk through the wet, heavy snow back to the cabin and get a shovel then walk back to my car and dig it out. The rear wheels were buried in mud. I made it though. Once out, I was still leery of going home, so I came here; it was the only place I could think of."

"Well, I'm certainly glad you did," Mother said. "I'm making us something to eat."

George perked up. Mother gave him a pitying look. I knew the implication: I was not properly caring for my man.

"Hungarian goulash," she said.

"Sounds great," George said.

I hated Hungarian goulash. Mother's visit was like reliving the gastric nightmares of my childhood. I wondered if she would make me sit in the hallway until I finished my veggie—maybe pickled beets or Brussels sprouts. Sometimes she would deny me dessert until I cleaned my plate. I had learned that cuffed pants provided a handy, temporary vessel in which to store unwanted food items.

"And I think I'll steam some nice green beans and whip up my five-minute pineapple dessert," she added. "Of course you'll stay for dinner, James."

"I graciously accept," he said, nodding his head dramatically at her.

Apparently, I was no longer queen of my castle and had been usurped by my own mother. Discussion took place about sleeping arrangements and, in spite of my lack of enthusiasm, it was decided that James would lodge with us and sleep on the sofa. He also pulled his car into the garage, so that nobody would spot it, and I left my Subaru out in the cold and snow, which always caused the hatchback to freeze up. James phoned somebody at the TV station and called in sick. He hadn't really missed any shifts thus far because he didn't usually go in on the weekend or Mondays. The crappy airtime was for the underlings. James suggested they get a sub to anchor the news for a few days, as he was most likely contagious. He coughed for dramatic emphasis. James lied smoothly and convincingly. No wonder women were so easily pulled into the vortex of his charisma. The way Mother was fawning over him, I suspected she might be the next. I smiled to myself. All of James' women had been amateurs, until now. With Mother, he was entering the professional league.

* * *

After dinner, I contemplated how to transfer the green beans discretely from the cuff of my pants into the garbage. I also contemplated the sequence and significance of events at Bucky's meat locker. What was the big story that Derry Parks was going to reveal to James? Was it a ruse, or did it have to do with Weasel Watkin's death? If James had indeed found the body based on this tip, he would have been glowing in the limelight for some time. Derry was the one with the answers, and she hadn't been seen since Friday afternoon at the Bayview. For all we knew, she was in the next state, laughing her pretty little head off. This was definitely something for Bertie and that Detective Burns to sort out. They would have to find the Parks woman.

George clicked on the TV and we all settled in to watch the late news before dispersing to our respective sleeping quarters.

"I wonder if they got Ted Weiner to sub," James said.

"Weener? An unfortunate name," Mother said.

"It's supposedly pronounced Vee-ner, but we call him Wee-ner."

The news came on after a local commercial featuring essential deer hunting attire sold at Bob's Bullseye & Bait. The camera panned the news desk. A doughy middle-aged man beamed at the camera. "Good evening out there in TV land!" he blurted.

James snorted. "TV land? What is this, the 50s?"

"I'm Ted *Vee-ner* sitting in for Jim Rush, who is in-dispensed. He chuckled. Maybe he is at deer camp?"

"James, not Jim you idiot," James sputtered. "And there's no such word as in-dispensed. You're illiterate, and you buy your clothes at the thrift store."

It was true about the clothes. Ted Weiner wore a cheesy bright blue polyester suit. His shirt was a dazzling white and topped off with a slightly crooked red tie. Very patriotic. It appeared that Dracula was his makeup assistant who relied on white chalk for face powder and Crisco to slick down Weiner's helmet of hair, which gleamed in the bright newsroom lighting.

"Speaking of deer camp," Weiner said, "we're going to break to pay some bills, but when we're back: the Yooper Bigfoot strikes again! Fact or fiction? You decide!"

"Hey, Jimbo, I don't think your job's in jeopardy," George said. "This guy is painful to watch."

"I can't take any more," James said picking up the remote.

"Hey, hold on partner, I want to see about the Yooper Bigfoot," George said.

"There is no Yooper Bigfoot—unless you've been tipping a few—or a lot," James said.

"I want to see the Wee-ner guy some more. He's starting to grow on me," I said.

James sighed and put down the remote.

A commercial for a local restaurant featuring the U.P.'s finest pasties ended and Ted Weiner reappeared, a smile frozen on his face.

"And now, as promised, we go out to the deer camp of (he glanced down at his papers) er, Buddy Lakkala and (another glance down, squinting) um Wilt? Wilt Cunningham, rather (this time he picks up the paper and holds it in front of his face) Wilt Kunninen. (The paper falls from his hand slips out of sight.) Yes, a remote deer camp near the mouth of the Huron River where there has been a reported sighting of an exceptionally tall, hairy primate spotted lumbering not twenty feet from Buddy and, er, Wilt's camp."

The scene changed from the newsroom to an outdoor scene. Weiner was holding a mic and wore a red buffalo plaid coat and matching Stormy Cromer hat. The camera operator panned the compound: a typical deer camp replete with disreputable cabin made from used lumber, chunks of old tin, logs, and other scavenged items. The camera zoomed in on a pair of deer antlers nailed over the door, swept across the cluttered "yard," and settled back on Weiner, who was standing with presumably Buddy and Wilt next to an H-shaped contraption constructed out of good-sized logs, designed for hanging deer carcasses. While it was possible a whole deer hung there at one time, all that remained was the head and part of the upper torso. The rest of the animal seemed to be missing.

"I'm standing here by this—(he turns to look)—at this rack thing with this mangled deer carcass where the alleged Bigfoot activity took place. Buddy—"

"I'm Wilt."

"Sorry, Wilt, tell the viewers about what transformed," Weiner said.

"Huh?"

"Tells us about your experience."

"Oh, you mean the Bigfoot? Well, he was bigger'n anything I ever seen, eh Buddy?"

Buddy said something, but Weiner still had the microphone poised under Wilt. He quickly moved it to Buddy.

"Could you repeat that?" Weiner said.

"Well, we was just having supper when we heard something, eh? And me and Wilt come out, thinking we got us some coyotes or maybe a bear sniffing around our deer, though bears should be denning up by now." He turned to look at the remains. "Well, I tell you I seen something going off into the woods, dragging a good chunk of our deer here, like it didn't weigh nothin'. Ain't that so, Wilt?"

Weiner feigned a look of awe and switched the mic over to Wilt.

"Fer sure," said Wilt. "That thing smelled worse than anything. Makes the outhouse smell like a bunch of posies." He tilted his head toward a crude outbuilding, presumably the camp privy.

"Some say it was probably a bear," Weiner said. "Do you have any proof that you spotted the Yooper Bigfoot? Maybe you took a photo with your phone?"

"Naw," Buddy said. "We don't have no cell service out here, so we don't bother with phones. But I'm telling you, the hair on the back of my neck just stood up, eh? That thing was huge. He just tore that deer carcass up like it was cotton candy."

"Maybe a bear come later," Wilt said, "But I know what a bear looks like, and that wasn't no bear. I caught a glimpse. It was upright, it was the Yooper Bigfoot, sure as shootin'."

"Well, there you have it folks. And exclusive story from me, Ted *Vee-ner*, your investigative reporter on the scene at a deer camp in the woods where these gentlemen spotted something, er, extraordinary! Ted Vee-ner, signing off."

The show went back to the newsroom where Weiner promised an update on the suspicious death of Clarence Watkins, right after a break for commercials. When Weiner was back on the air, he appeared to be blotting something off his gaudy red tie then his head snapped up and he stared for a moment like a deer caught in headlights.

"Oh, we're back so soon? Hi everyone. Well, as promised we have a news flash update about the hideous death of Clarence Watkins, whose corpse was found dead in a meat locker at a local taxidermy business."

"Aren't corpses usually dead?" Mother asked. "Isn't that an oxymoron?"

"No, actually it's redundant," I said. "Living dead would be an oxymoron."

"Well, Wee-ner *is* the living dead," James said.

Weiner continued the slaughter: "While the demise of Mr. Watkins could have been accidental, our gal cop, Bernice Vaara along with a Detective Barns seem to be poking around an awful lot. Is something sinister afoot? This reporter has heard from an undisclosed source that there may be a person of mistrust—I mean interest— that is yet unknown, I mean unnamed. We sure want to send our congratulations to the deceased person's wife, Aileen."

"Could he fuck anything up more?" said James. He looked at Mother. "Pardon my language, Maddie."

"Of course. You are entitled to be upset," she said.

"She's not a gal cop," I said. "She's a police officer—a state trooper!"

"Gal cop seems sexist," Mother said.

"And her name is Roberta, not Bernice, I said. "And I think the detective's name was Burns, not Barnes. Hey, he got Aileen's name right, I think, though I'm not sure why he's congratulating her."

"I think he meant to send condolences," Mother said.

Weiner turned away from the camera, giving us a close-up of his ear. "The police and the deceased widow have declined an interview with this reporter until more can be looked into."

"Deceased widow? Did Aileen die too?" Mother said.

"Makes an interview very difficult," I said.

James picked up the remote and switched off the set then buried his face in his hands.

⚡ 8 ⚡

Mother had prepared a big breakfast, which George and James were enjoying when I whisked through the kitchen. She had been taking good care of the menfolk ever since James arrived on Monday night. I didn't approve. It was Wednesday morning and James showed no signs of leaving or going back to work. He would never leave if Mother kept shoving home-cooked meals at him, not to mention the flirting and doting. Furthermore, Mother's domestic prowess gave George unrealistic expectations of me.

"Would you like some nice bacon and eggs?" Mother asked.

"No thanks," I muttered as I grabbed a cup of coffee.

Truthfully, the breakfast smells did not agree with me. I managed some juice and toast with the coffee while standing at the kitchen counter.

"Do you have choir practice tonight?" she asked.

"Nope, cancelled because of Thanksgiving tomorrow."

"Good, then you can pick up the pies I ordered from Tillie's Bakery."

"What kind?" I said.

"Pumpkin and mincemeat."

Mincemeat—yuck.

"You need to eat more than toast for breakfast," Mother said. "I could fix you some hot oatmeal—or Cream of Wheat with brown sugar. I could always get you to eat that, even when your tummy was upset."

"Not hungry," I said.

Mother gave me a reproachful look.

"But thanks," I added quickly.

I threw most of my toast in the garbage and poured my tepid coffee down the drain. After collecting my coat and purse, I approached George, hoping for a goodbye kiss. He quit eating barely long enough to give me a chaste peck on the cheek. The old adage that a way to a man's heart was through his stomach apparently had some substance. Sex, of course, usually trumped food, but in our neck of the woods, a Green Bay Packers' game took precedence over everything, including nuclear holocaust, pestilence, or a striptease act.

63

My calendar for the day included meeting with Trooper Vaara—Bertie—about the enigmatic Derry Parks and her possible connection to Weasel Watkins' death. Bertie said she'd stop by the college and meet me in my office some time that morning.

I arrived at work to an empty parking lot. Since classes were out for Thanksgiving break, there would be few students or faculty around. Maintenance had plowed the lot but hadn't shoveled the steps leading to the door, forcing me to tromp through the unbroken snow. When I checked my mail, I found half a dozen entries for the igloo contest. The December 10th deadline loomed.

One of the new entries requested the construction of a "Habitrail," whatever that was. The sketch was quite elaborate, with a labyrinth of passages and some sort of a wheel in the main chamber. The entry form said that rodents occupied the thing. It seemed overly ambitious. Another entry proposed a rocket ship, manned by a monkey. As far as I knew, neither monkeys nor spaceships were indigenous to the U.P. A wolf lair was another entry. No sketch. I loved the next one: a porcupine in an outhouse. Porcupines chewed wooden structures such as outhouses, apparently to fulfill some sort of sodium deficiency. The remaining two entries were anonymous and likely bogus: *The Old Woman in the Shoe* and *Peter, Peter Pumpkin Eater*. How droll. Maybe next year we would have a fairytale igloo contest. This year's theme of "Habitat for Critters" apparently failed to inspire.

I sat down at my computer and typed an e-mail to the committee about the latest entries. When I faced my computer, my back was to the door. Usually this wasn't a problem; I could often identify who was approaching by the familiar cadence of their footsteps. I heard the parking lot door open and close, then the rapid heel clicks of someone coming down the hall. Bertie. She was early.

"Down here, Bertie," I shouted. "I'm just finishing a—"

Something—a wastebasket—jammed over my head, releasing an avalanche of debris.

"What th—!" I inhaled something powdery, choked then gagged. The wastebasket, wedged around my elbows, pinned my biceps against me.

Someone wrenched me out of my chair and hurled me to the floor. I fell hard, squirming to free myself.

"*Boo ash a ga ga ak ala mak a roo!*" a woman said, gasping for air, her words unrecognizable.

She kicked—mostly glancing blows apparently aimed at my shins. I twisted away and struggled to sit up, clawing at the rim of the wastebasket. The woman shouted something else unrecognizable then kicked me again. I grabbed her foot, pulling hard. I heard her fall, hit the chair. Scuffling noises, chair coasters spinning. She squeaked like a mouse then shrieked something I couldn't understand.

I managed to get to my feet, working to shed the wastebasket. I heard running; she was getting away. I staggered out of my office, bouncing off the doorframe. I felt like a skunk that had gotten curious about a discarded drink cup: trapped and blinded. I crashed down the hall, deflecting off the walls, stumbling. I nearly had the trashcan off my head when someone grabbed me, trying to get a hold of my sweatshirt.

"Lemme go!" I said, kicking wildly and flapping the bottom half of my arms.

"Janese? Hey, it's me, Bertie. What the hell is going on?

By the time Bertie extracted me from the wastebasket, the woman had a lead on us. She must have gone the opposite direction from Bertie, otherwise they would have run into each other. Bertie and I rushed to the end of the hall opposite the parking lot and looked out a window over campus. There was no sign of the woman. We went back to the parking lot and inspected the footprints on the steps and found that the woman's tracks led around the building and up to the door. According to Bertie, when she arrived, my Subaru was the only vehicle in the parking lot. The woman must have parked in an inconspicuous place, then skulked over to my building, found my hallway, and launched her attack. There were many exit options if she went down to the ground-level floor, which housed some offices, the mailroom, and the several mechanical rooms.

"I think these footprints look like hers," Bertie said, motioning toward crisp impressions in the snow outside the boiler room service door. "Looks like a fairly aggressive sole on a boot. Hmmm. There's a kind of imperfection in the tread of the left foot, like a chunk is missing."

We checked with a couple of maintenance personnel who claimed they'd just got back from coffee, so they didn't see anyone leave or notice an unfamiliar car, though they weren't likely to notice, since there still was some traffic on campus. We gave up the chase and returned to my floor.

"You better go, um, wash up," Bertie said.

When I went into the restroom to tidy up, I gasped at my reflection in the mirror. I wondered why people had been giving me strange looks. It seems that the powdery substance I was choking on was black toner residue that had been thoughtlessly dumped in the hallway trashcan. I looked like Al Jolson getting ready to sing *Mammy*. I scrubbed most of the black off my face, but my hair, which now featured macabre blazes of the powder, would need a good shampooing. Maybe multiple shampooings. My clothing hadn't fared well, either.

When I returned to my office, Bertie—bless her heart—had straightened things a bit. She had also collected and bagged some hair, which she found wrapped around one of the caster wheels of my office chair and may have belonged to the assailant. She was attempting to sweep up the black ink powder but wasn't having much luck.

"Worse than fingerprint power," she muttered, as she smeared the toner around with a broom.

Turns out that Bertie had worked the midnight shift and just gotten off duty. She had come on her own time, probably to humor me, since she still believed that Weasel Watkins got drunk and died of hypothermia. I wasn't so sure, and Bertie had accused me of overreacting. Now, after what had just happened, she certainly would take me more seriously.

"You'll need to file a complaint," she said "and I need to make a statement, since I'm a witness. We can stop by the station. I'm assuming you want to go home and, well, clean up."

I nodded. Then, without warning, I burst into tears.

"I-I ca-can't st-stop," I blubbered.

Bertie, reached for me and held me while I sobbed uncontrollably into her shoulder.

"Hey, now," she said. "It's okay, we'll find out who's behind all this crap. You're safe now."

I continued to bawl, depositing black-laced snot onto Bertie's sweater. Then I got the hic-ups and nearly wet myself. As if a switch had been activated, my sobbing converted into giggling, occasionally interrupted by my hic-ups. Bertie started to laugh, too. We both sunk down into chairs, doubled over.

"Do you th-think (hic) that G-George w-will mmm mmm (hic) marry me, now?" I said.

"Of course," Bertie said. "Beauty is only skin deep."

We erupted into fresh laughter.

"Even—(hic) even if I—I'm pregnant?"

I was laughing alone; Bertie had abruptly stopped.

"Hey, girl, are you kidding?" she said.

I shrugged my shoulders and looked down at the floor. Large, polluted tears plopped onto my lap.

"Whoa. You need to get him to the little white church," she said.

"That's the Lutheran Church. I'm Methodist," I said.

"It was figurative or rhetorical—whatever. Are you sure? Did you do an EPT?"

"A what?"

"You know, an early pregnancy test. You pee on a stick. If it turns a color you are or aren't. You need to get a kit from the drug store. Except don't get it in town because everyone will know."

"An ET?"

"E-P-T. I'll get it for you. I'll get it in town. I love to get the old biddies going. They already think it's unconscionable that a wife and mother would wear a badge and uniform and go out to fight crime while her husband stays home and runs the household. *Unnatural* and against what God intended. But if they think I'm pregnant again—well, it'll be a hoot. Come on, we'll stop at the store then go into the station."

After we completed the paperwork, I gave Bertie the information on Derry Parks—how she had apparently lured James out to Bucky's Game Processing & Taxidermy along with James' entrapment then escape. I told her how James said she promised a big news story. Of course, there was no proof that she ever showed up and maybe it was all just a nasty little joke she played on James. The motive was elusive. Perhaps she really wanted to get into show biz but rinky-dink channel 13 wasn't exactly the big time. Whatever other motive she might have would remain a mystery for the time being. Besides, it was very possible that the door to the meat locker had swung shut automatically or maybe blew shut. The lock could have been defective all along, since it was "fashioned" by Bucky. And now the woman had vanished.

"I've checked out Parks' apartment where she is supposedly living, and nobody has been there for a while," Bertie said. "The super let me in. I wonder if she has some other place to go and lie low. Do you think she's the one who attacked you?"

"Could be," I said. "Though I sensed it was someone older—I don't know why, except I think I was gaining the upper hand, even with that damn wastebasket over me. And then there was all of that jibber jabber that I couldn't make out. It didn't sound like real words. But of course I couldn't hear much with that that trashcan over my head, like I was wearing earplugs—you know, you can hear a little, but I couldn't understand a word she was screaming at me."

"I wonder if it was glossolalia," Bertie said.

"What?" I said.

"You know, speaking in tongues—a religious verbal outburst of some sort," she said.

"More like from Satan! Well that just adds to the mystery as far as I'm concerned," I said.

Bertie and I mulled this over along with the other pieces of the mystery, including the weird phone calls I had received and Weasel Watkins' death. As usual, nothing added up.

"It could be a bunch of unrelated random things," Bertie said. "Who knows, maybe the woman who attacked you thought you were someone else—like a teacher who flunked her kid out of biology."

"That's possible, I suppose. I don't think she saw my face before she crammed that wastebasket over my head, so it could have been a case of mistaken identity. My nameplate fell off the door a while back and I haven't gotten around to sticking it back up. What the hell? It's all so bizarre—scary."

Bertie nodded. "I want you to watch your butt for a while. Don't go in anywhere without other people around. Get a big dog—whatever."

A dog would be nice. Mother was allergic to dogs, or so she said when I was growing up and wanted one. I wondered if a big, hairy pooch would send her packing back to her resort in St. Ignace. If she left, James would leave. As far as I knew, George liked dogs. Of course there would be the hair to vacuum and added expense. Still...

"First things first, though," Bertie said. "I have to ask, weren't you and George using—precautions? Aren't you on the pill?"

"I was having some side effects, so I went off and we used, um, other methods."

Bertie nodded. "Yeah, those 'other methods' are why we have our two boys. Anyway, you need to get the kit, take the test, and find out if you're going to be a mommy. Hey, this is exciting. I've got tons of baby stuff to lend you."

Baby stuff. I felt a large lump settle in my throat.

I arrived home earlier than usual, clutching my bag containing the EPT kit. Of course Mother's car was there and, presumably, James was still there. George's truck was gone. He tended to spend most of the day at the art studio, working on his next masterpiece. Finding a few moments of privacy was going to be tricky. Mother would be barking at the bathroom door, talking about casseroles and Thanksgiving, and—

Damn, I had forgotten to pick up the pies. Damn, damn, damn. It was nearly a twenty-mile round trip back into town. I decided to wait—maybe Mother would need something last minute from the grocery store. I went inside quietly, hoping to sneak into the bathroom. To my relief, the living room was unoccupied, as was the kitchen, though it bore evidence of serious activity. A bowl of cranberries sat in the sink next to a pile of potatoes. Another, bigger bowl on the counter contained cubes of bread. For stuffing? Is that how it started? The cutting board—the one that I had made in eighth-grade shop class— had been used to chop onions, some of which had spilled over onto the counter and floor. A newly purchased casserole dish awaited the dreaded green-bean casserole. Every spoon I owned had been used and cast into the sink or left to decay on the counter. I opened the fridge and was confronted by a wall of food, the most significant object being an enormous turkey. I slammed the door before things started to tumble out. Lights blazed everywhere, and music played seductively from Alexa. I had no idea where everyone was; perhaps Mother had taken James with her on her "daily constitutional." She was a big advocate of exercise. In any event, I decided to take advantage of the solitude and sneak into the bathroom.

I heard strange, muffled noises coming from the loft that made my scalp prickle. Someone giggled, someone grunted, then a simultaneous groan.

"Oh, God!" A male voice.

"Sweet Jesus!" A female voice.

My mouth dropped. Mother and James! Rhythmic sounds came from the loft, building... I didn't stick around for the ending.

Pies—I would get the pies and maybe something for the bile churning in my stomach. As I raced toward town, the Subaru struggling to keep traction on the corners, I tried to erase the sounds of their lovemaking. It was something a child should never hear. Once you are a parent, you should become celibate, should never...

I eased off the accelerator as I came into town. I didn't need the local constabulary stopping me, again. I snorted and started to laugh. My family was a freak show. Who was I to judge? I was still mottled with powdery ink and had an EPT—I panicked a moment—where was the EPT? Had I dropped it? I breathed a sigh of relief when I saw the crumpled bag jammed inside my purse on the seat next to me. Perhaps I would have to go to the Shell station to conduct my test. "Oh, look," the gas station clerk would say when emptying the trash. "Another positive pee stick. Why is it that women have to do this here?"

I wondered how long it had been going on—Mother and James. Right from the get-go, or was today the first? There she was, her frilly little apron tied around her petite waist as she fussed in the kitchen. A few strands of her striking red hair break loose from her chignon, dangling sexily down her forehead and neck. Music playing; Mother likes soft jazz. The rich tones of a saxophone, seductive and mellow, lure James into her kitchen/lair, where he falls victim to the enticing smell of her perfume and yeasty aroma of fresh-baked bread. They "accidentally" bump into one another. Perhaps he inadvertently touches her in an erogenous zone, feigning gentlemanly mortification over the transgression, but keeping the hand there. I shook my head, trying to obliterate the image. What the hell was the matter with me?

Well, it had been quite a day, hadn't it? Someone had assaulted me, then I walked in on Mother and James. What next? Maybe I'd hit a moose or get a flat on the way home. I realized that I was sitting in my car at the curb in front of Tillie's Bakery. Tillie was standing at the window glaring at me. Most of the shop lights were off and the sign of the front door said "closed."

I hurried inside. "I thought you closed at 5:30," I said.

"Well, I was hoping to get out earlier, Janese, since I still got to get my bird ready and my stuffing fixed and all don't I?" Tillie snapped.

"Sorry."

"What 'n hell happened to your hair? That some new kind of look?" she asked as she snapped up my money and shoved the cardboard boxes of pies toward me.

"Yes, I said patting my hair. Do you like it?"

"Well, it's different. Say hi to Maddie and have a good turkey day," she said as she hustled me out of the shop, slamming the door behind me. Tillie did not stay in business because of friendly customer service. She stayed in business because she used real butter, heavy cream, sugar, and rich imported chocolate. She was the dope pusher in The Village of Moose Willow, and we were all her junkies.

I had been in the bakery for less than five minutes, but during that time, the Bayview had opened for happy hour and the street was lined with trucks, two of which were parked on either side of me, effectively blocking all four doors. To say this was not "my day" would have been a monumental understatement. I sighed and shifted the pies into the crook of my arm and rooted my keys out of my pocket. I moved to the hatchback of my Subaru and hit the unlock button. Nothing happened. I shifted the pies again and tried the latch. Frozen. I hit the button several times but did not hear the familiar click of the latch releasing. I stared at my car for a moment. I could have "accidentally" keyed the trucks in retaliation, but they were a couple of rust buckets, and the doors were already marred with decades of dents and scratches too numerous to count.

I moved to the driver's door and punched the unlock button twice, and heard it click open. I set the pies on the roof of the car to free up arm so that I could squeeze it into the crack of the door and find the window button. Once the window was down, I was able to squirm into the car, headfirst, snagging my ear on the console shifter. Eventually, I maneuvered into a sitting position, started the car, and backed out. I assumed it was safe to go home.

Women need to understand the facts and limitations of home pregnancy testing in order to get accurate results. I sighed. This wasn't going to be as quick as I had hoped. After checking the turkey and starting the potatoes to boil, Mother and James had gone for a power walk. I was given stern instructions to keep an eye on everything—as if I were competent for such responsibility. George had run to the IGA to see if there were any pies left: bakery, not frozen. The store opened for a few hours on Thanksgiving to accommodate idiots like me who liked to see how far pies would ride on the roof of a speeding car before being flung into a snowbank, such as the ones that I had on the roof of the Subaru when I drove off from Tillie's Bakery the previous day.

In any event, I had a few minutes—a very few—of privacy. I had dug the EPT out of my sweater drawer and locked myself in the bathroom. The kit contained a mini pamphlet. *Caution: read before using.* I squinted at the tiny print. *Tests taken before the first day of an expected period, when the levels of human chorionic gonadotropin (hCG) hormone may be too low to be detected, can result in a false negative response for nearly one-third of pregnant women.*

This left me with several questions. First off, what was this hormone hCG? I had heard of estrogen and progesterone and, of course, testosterone. Were there other reproductive hormones I was supposed to know about? I also wondered how would one know exactly when to expect the first day of her period, when they always came unexpectedly? Every year I trudged into the OB GYN office for the dreaded annual physical and the nurse would always ask, rather brusquely, when the first day of my last period had taken place. Sometimes I just made it up. Other times I consulted a calendar, brow furrowed, as if working out Einstein's Theory of Relatively. Usually, I gave an honest answer and said I didn't have a clue. This never pleased the nurse.

Accurate results: EPT® Pregnancy Test is more than 99 percent accurate in laboratory tests at detecting typical hCG hormone levels (which vary by person). Now we were back to the hormones again. Women would go into labor before getting through all the disclaimers and hormonal mumbo jumbo. I skipped ahead.

1) Remove the EPT® test stick from its foil packet just prior to use.

Check.

2) Remove the purple cap to expose the absorbent tip.

Check.

3) Hold the test stick by its thumb grip. Keep the absorbent tip pointing downwards.

Downwards?

4) Place the absorbent tip in the urine flow for just five seconds, or dip the absorbent tip into a clean container of urine for just 20 seconds. Keep the absorbent tip pointing downwards.

I wasn't sure what would entail a five-second urine flow and furthermore, wasn't *a clean container of urine* an oxymoron? So, I could do the deed by free-flow or by cup: my choice. I decided on the cup. That way, if I screwed it up, I could drink a diet Dr. Pepper and have a second shot at it. I rummaged around in the bathroom for a drink cup. I finally found the package of plastic cups where Mother had moved them to an inconvenient place behind the toilet paper. I was no stranger to the specimen collection procedure. Along with the ineffective paper gown, stirrup maneuver, and rude probing, the annual exam also always required a urine sample. Sometimes there were elaborate instructions involving a sani-wipe, starting and stopping the flow, then starting again. In any event, one had to be a contortionist to successfully void into the tiny, clear cup with the hash marks running up the side. Inevitably, you felt the warmth trickle along your knuckles.

Just as I positioned the cup for the collection process, I heard the door slam. This startled me enough to drop the cup into the toilet bowl. My bladder, eager to be shed of my morning coffee, was beyond the point of no return.

"Shit. Damn," I muttered.

"Janeeeese!"

Mother. I quickly tidied things up, retrieving and disposing of the cup. I stuffed the test kit items back in the box and looked around in panic before deciding to stash it in the laundry hamper where I hoped it would be safe until wash day.

"Janese?" Mother repeated, her voice closer.

"In the bathroom," I yelled.

"Did you baste the bird, as I asked?"

"I was just going to do it again," I lied.

A few minutes later, I emerged from the bathroom into the bedroom where George was putting his wallet and keys in a tray on our dresser. He looked at me and arched an eyebrow.

"What?" I said.

"You're all flushed—you ok?"

"Sure. Did you get the pies?"

"Yeah. Good news: no mincemeat. I got pumpkin and apple. Bakery, too, not the frozen ones. Just as Her Highness commanded."

"Thank God," I said.

George pulled me to him and slipped his hand under my sweater up my back, making me tingle.

"Hmmm," I said. "What's this all about?"

"Well, it has been a while, you know."

"Yeah, I know."

"Janeeeese!" Mother trilled from the kitchen

George and I sighed in unison.

"Time to mash, dear," Mother shouted.

"Mash?" George said.

"The potatoes. It must be getting close."

George and I reluctantly broke our embrace and headed into the kitchen where, admittedly, wonderful smells wafted from every direction. Mother drained the potatoes and handed me the masher. James hoisted the turkey out of its roaster and onto a cutting board. George was given the simple task of putting the rolls and side dishes on the table. For a moment or two, we enjoyed the domesticity of it all.

"Get all the lumps out, Janese," Mother barked. "You always try to hurry and don't get the lumps out. George, put a hot pad under that dish. Honestly! A little common sense."

So much for domestic bliss.

I beat the potatoes furiously, my arm a blur of activity. Beads of sweat popped out on my forehead. The woman would not find a lump in her spuds.

"Oh, James," Mother purred, "you carve beautifully."

"I bet he does," I muttered.

"My father taught me a few tricks," he said.

I snorted.

"Janese, go blow your nose," Mother said.

I ignored her.

Mother insisted that we all hold hands around the table and she asked James, our special guest, to say grace. When he was finished extolling "Maddie's" Christian virtues and thanking God for all the food, we were all on saccharine overload. Mother wiped a tear from her eye and gazed at James. George stared steadily down at his plate, a smile twitching at his lips. I broke the circle-of-love-hand-holding-chain and grabbed the turkey platter.

"Who wants some breast?" I asked cheerfully.

George burst out laughing, while Mother glared at me.

"Oh, excuse me, *white* meat," I said. As a child, I was told that we called it white or dark meat, not breasts and thighs and legs and such.

After a flurry of dysfunctional passing, we all focused for a few minutes on our heaping plates of artery-clogging bliss.

Mother cleared her throat. "James and I have an announcement to make," she said.

My stuffing-laden fork dropped to my plate with a clank.

"Announcement?" I said.

"Yes, well, I was the bold one to ask, and James was kind enough to accept," she said with just a hint of discomfort.

My gaze shifted from Mother to James to George who was still eating—though his eyes had shifted up—and back to Mother. I waited for the bomb to drop.

"I'm needed back at the resort to make some decisions—don't worry Janese, I won't abandon you."

"Resort?" I said stupidly.

"Well, yes, dear, The Straights. I need to go make some personnel decisions and I've invited James to accompany me. I could *so* use his help."

"I'll take a short leave from the TV station," James said "and help Maddie search for a new manager. At first Bobby decided that he was gay and has moved to a more *tolerant* environment. Then the new manager—what's his name—only lasted two weeks."

"Christopher," Mother said. "*Less* than two weeks."

"I don't think you decide you're gay," I said. "I think you might discover it, but I don't think you can decide it."

Silence settled over us like a toxic fog. I took a vicious bite out of my drumstick and chewed the meat nosily. It was rude and childish, but I wanted to annoy Mother. She didn't seem to notice. She took a delicate bite of food.

"I do believe the cranberries are a bit tart," she said. "Anyway, I'm not sure why I attract these homos."

"I like tart things," James said.

"Everything's great," George said.

George was a clueless pig. He was more interested in food that the little drama that unfolded before us.

"Thank you, George," Mother said. She set down her fork. "We'll be leaving tomorrow first thing. We'll take my car and continue to leave James' Mercedes in the garage. He's still very concerned about his well-being, and I am too. I think getting away will be good for him—for both of us." She sighed. "In any event, I must tend to business. But don't worry, Janese, we'll be back in a few days."

Then it began to sink in. Mother gone—at least for a few days. This was great news!

"No rush, Mother. You've done plenty here already." I looked at George who had resumed vigorous eating. How did he stay so thin? "And I'm sure we'll have ample leftovers to sustain us." The sarcasm eluded George.

"It's settled, then," Mother said. "Eat your green beans," she added, looking at me. "Or no pie for you!"

"Me! You've hardly touched your food," I volleyed back. "Eat your potatoes, Mother. I worked hard to de-lump them, just to please you."

She looked perplexed. This rarely happened. I had her dead to rights, and she knew it. I felt a rise of adrenaline, preparing for battle. The ball was in her court.

"Who wants pumpkin and who wants apple, and who wants a little of both?" Mother blurted out, rising from the table.

* * *

George and I had celebratory sex that night, in anticipation of having the place all to ourselves for a few days. James still made a pretense of bunking on the couch, though I suspected he crept up to the loft when he thought the coast was clear. I had a moment of panic, wondering if he had listened at the bedroom door, waiting for the sounds to stop before making his move to Mother's boudoir. Too late now. George was snoring softly when I crept to the bathroom and locked the door. It clicked loudly, the sound seeming to bounce off the universe and into every corner of the bathroom. I turned on the light in the shower, which glared less than the vanity lights. I fished the test kit out of the hamper and fumbled around getting things ready. Then it occurred to me that I hadn't read all of the precautionary stuff. What if doing the test right after sex messed up the results? I squinted at the pamphlet, trying to skim through to find out what it had to say about it. It did talk a lot about hormones and there was no question that a boatload of hormones had been stirred up. Better wait. I took the kit into the bedroom and stuck it back in my sweater drawer.

* * *

Mother called me at work Monday morning and told me that she and James would be delaying their return for a few days. "The paint is wrong, all wrong," she said. Her erstwhile manager, Bobby, knew how to decorate, but of course she had to fire him. The morons who mixed the paint, according to Mother, screwed up royally and the lobby, which was supposed to be "Dijon" looked like baby poo. I agreed with Mother that it should be redone, and that she should supervise it. She should take as long as she needed. She informed me that she was leaning toward "pumpkin spice." I felt a wave of pity for the work crew. On the other hand, Mother's fickleness secured their jobs for a while.

"Hello, hello!" someone chirped at my doorway.

"Oh, hi Brenda," I said.

She stared at me; I could practically hear the gears grinding away in her pretty little head.

"Are those lo-lights in your hair?"

In spite of multiple shampooings, the black toner ink had been reluctant to wash out. I made a mental note to call Val, my stylist, and see what she could do. When I had gone home after the trash attack, Mother had been distracted by my loss of the pies and never got around to commenting on my hair. I never told her about being nearly smothered by a plastic wastebasket. I will give George credit, he noticed right away and held me for a few moments after I recounted the afternoon's drama. I had assured him that other than a few bruises, I was okay. My ribs and shin—which had turned an ugly purple—still hurt from the kicking attack. Otherwise, my main injury had been to my hair. "I kind of like it," George had said, lifting a limp strand of hair. "It's the latest rage amongst artists—to have these streaks. Some of the girls have purple, red, green—you name it."

I didn't answer Brenda, but gave her my brightest, boldest smile. "What's up?" I said.

77

She took a seat in my guest chair and crossed her legs. I wondered if all that exposed skin got cold. Giving the devil her due, she did have on some fairly serious winter boots, with fake fur bursting out of the top and what Bertie had called an aggressive sole. My eyes paused on the boots, especially the soles.

"Do you like them?" she asked, stretching out a foot for me to inspect.

Of course, there were a lot of winter boots around.

"I just got them. Can you believe they were half price? I think they're stylish, yet they really grip the ice. I mean, do the guys here ever think to throw down some salt? Anyway, you have to go to Marquette to get decent stuff," she advised. "Where do you go?

"Mostly Goodwill," I said. I needed to see if there was some damage to the tread, like Bertie mentioned from the tracks found outside my office after the assault. But the angle was wrong, and Brenda had a nervous foot bounce going that was making me dizzy. I needed to get ahold of those boots. I tried to remember—I thought Bertie had the crime lab take some kind of impressions or photos of the boot prints tracked in the snow. Everyone knew that Brenda and I weren't exactly chums. I didn't think she was the violent type, but I didn't know much about her outside of the 4Cs. I had heard that she was bulimic.

"What is Goodwill?" she asked. "Do they have designer lines?"

"They've got everything. I can't believe you haven't ever been there," I said.

"Well, I'll check it out, I'm sure," she said. "What I'm here for, anyway, is to get out of the meeting for, you know, the contest?"

"Igloo," I said.

"Yeah. I don't know why I can't remember that. Anyways, I have to miss the next meeting. Patrick has recommended I attend a training thing to, I guess, help me in the fundraising stuff."

She seemed a little less enthusiastic about her new VP position, perhaps because there was an effort to encourage productivity rather than promiscuity.

"Well, duty calls!" I chirped. "Hey, I'll cover for you if you'd let me try out those awesome boots." I was so smooth. "What size do you wear?"

"Huh? My boots? Oh, they're a size seven. I have small feet."

"Hey, that's my size, I lied. "I'd sure like to try them out before driving all the way to Marquette to try to find a pair. Maybe I could, you know, borrow them and just walk around some, just inside at home."

"Well, I guess that would be okay," she said.

Talk about gullible. We decided that she would wear something different the next day and bring them in for me to test drive. Janese Trout: super sleuth.

⸗ 10 ⸗

"The Pumpkin Spice looks like a jack-o-lantern on steroids," Mother said when she called me early Thursday morning. George and I had enjoyed nearly a week without Mother and James. We hadn't exactly been able to settle back into our old routine, because the loft was still marked territory for Mother, who presumably would be back like the poltergeist in the movie. Meanwhile, George still had to go to the studio to work on his pottery.

"I'm switching my strategy," Mother continued.

She was talking about the color of the lobby at The Straights Inn. Earlier she had rejected the baby-poo-Dijon-Mustard hue. Now the alluring Pumpkin Spice was another faux pas. I was barely listening, looking in the mirror inspecting the disastrous state of my hair. I had color issues of my own. In addition to the dark roots emerging from my scalp, the blond highlights that had been infused with toner ink seemed to be having a chemical reaction. Though not exactly iridescent, some weird color thing was going on. The ends of my hair were dry and split. Clearly, I needed a cut in addition to a color makeover.

"I'm going from warm to cool."

"Umm huh," I responded. "Good idea. "

"After all, we are on the Straits of Mackinac—*water*. Water is cool, not warm. I'm thinking either the Arctic Ice or Sea Foam. James is helping me."

"Good," I muttered. I lifted a limp strand of hair and let it flop back down. Hair is already basically dead. Interestingly, it continues to grow, along with the fingernails, even after we die. So, essentially, it's dead—the hair, that is—when we're alive, yet it lives on after we're dead. In spite of the hopelessness of it all, we fuss endlessly, trying to bring life where it cannot exist.

Mother said: "I'm leaning toward—" She giggled, "James, quit that. I'm talking to Janese."

God, spare me. He was probably feeling her up.

"*Anyway* I think the Arctic Ice would be nice, but the Willow—a lovely, whimsical green—would align so nicely with the woodland flora and fauna of the area."

"Go green," I intoned. "It matches your eyes."

"It would, wouldn't it?"

Actually, her eyes were hazel, but she claimed they were green, just as I claimed that I still weighed 120 pounds. (Perhaps after a severe bout of the flu.) Otherwise, no matter how much I shoved the scale around on the bathroom floor, the digital readout reminded me that things were not as they used to be.

"Thank you, darling," Mother said. "I'll let you know how it goes."

I absently hung up the phone. I had decided to take the day off from work so I could attend to certain personal matters, namely, the EPT, my hair, and cleaning my house—not necessarily in that order. I would have preferred to do the test first, but it seems that I needed to purchase a new kit, since the pee stick was now mysteriously missing from the original one. The only thing I could think of was that it got flushed in my haste to hide everything. At least that was what I hoped. The idea that it had been found on the floor or elsewhere by either Mother or George was unsettling. It was also unsettling that neither George nor Mother had brought up the subject of my possible pregnancy. Distracted by their self-interests, perhaps, or maybe waiting for me to broach the subject. Clearly, the ball was in my court. I needed to make an announcement, and we would all decide where to go from there. No matter what the outcome, my wish was that Mother would go away and George would stay.

I made an appointment with Val for an emergency hair session. She gave an ever-suffering sigh and agreed to squeeze me in between a perm and a waxing. After my hair was resurrected, I would try to discretely slip into the pharmacy for the pregnancy test kit. I would wear some sunglasses and a big puffy coat and pull a hat over my forehead. That way the salesclerk would not even be sure of my gender, let alone my name. Thereafter, I would conduct my test in the privacy of my own bathroom, uninterrupted. George had left early for the studio and Mother was several hundred miles away. I planned on whipping up something special for dinner for George and me. I'd stop at the store and get stuff for lasagna. It was my one specialty. Mother said we hadn't a drop of Italian blood in us and questioned its validity. I reminded her that we weren't Hungarian, either, yet she made Hungarian goulash. She also made chop suey, and we weren't Chinese. She often bragged about her enchiladas, curry rice, Swedish meatballs and Indian frybread, none of which reflected our ethnic origins.

Our ancestry was basically English and Scottish, and yet never has she made Yorkshire pudding or haggis. Anything goes in America, and the Italians would probably eschew my lasagna anyway. Truth be told, Mother was loath in admitting that I had a tiny skill not handed down by her. Lasagna and garlic toast would be filling the house with delectable aromas when George arrived home. I would prepare the scene for whatever announcement I needed to make: PG or not PG. We would have a nice quiet evening with a crackling fire in the fireplace, soft, sexy music—

Music. Damn, I had choir practice that night, which I couldn't skip. Things would be in turmoil with James and Derry gone. Hannu would be in a lather. I had to go. Damn.

* * *

"We need to do an all-over color and see what happens with the damaged parts. If they cover okay, then we can try a few foils—just a few. Your hair is in terrible shape. How long since you've been here?" my stylist, Val, said in a fussy, accusatory tone.

"It's been a while," I answered noncommittally.

"I'll do the best I can," she said. "No guarantees. Maybe a good cut. How attached are you to your ponytail?"

I was pretty attached to it since it allowed me to pull my hair into a scrunchie. Shorter hair required daily styling.

"I think a chin-length bob," she continued. "That would get rid of most of this damage."

There was no use arguing with her. She would have her way.

"We'll do that. No guarantees, though."

I perused the latest *Sentry* while my hair "processed." The article reiterated what the Weiner guy on Channel 13 reported. The headlines read "Yooper Bigfoot Raids Deer Camp?" It went on to mention that witnesses Buddy Lakkala and Wilt Kunninen, who were at their remote deer camp near the mouth of the Huron River, reported sighting an exceptionally tall, hairy primate lumbering not twenty feet from their cabin. Buddy claimed that he (Buddy) was just heading to the outhouse, and there was the creature, big and hairy and smelly. The reporter inserted some quotes and included a photo of the mangled deer carcass hanging from the rack. Also included was a photo of a cast taken from an alleged footprint left by the creature. There was even a yardstick laid out next to the photo, indicating that the foot for the thing was enormous. I didn't recall Weiner mentioning a foot casting.

The article went on to tell about an officer from the Michigan Department of Natural Resources—DNR—coming to inspect the scene and finding what he considered to be bear paw prints and scat all over the place. The article indicated that Buddy insisted that it wasn't a bear that he saw—maybe one did come later, but he knows what a bear looks like and he was sorry he didn't think to put the trail cam on the dressed-out deer.

There had been rumors of a Yooper Bigfoot for years, all basically unsubstantiated and always reported by unreliable people. Some said it was the color of a black bear, others said it was white like a polar bear. One report had him or her orange like an Orangutan. Some speculate that there is a whole colony of Bigfoots, with an assortment of shapes, colors, and temperaments. There have been endless reports of bird feeder damage, garbage can raids, hunting camps being pillaged, and even a pen of exotic birds—peacocks and an emu—being savaged. One would assume a black bear could be responsible, yet the alleged "creature" walked upright like a man, had that hideous odor, and when it encountered a person, would look at them with "intelligent curiosity." I was skeptical, to say the least.

Val finished waxing a woman's unibrow and came to inspect my progress. "Have you been to the rummage sale at the Lutheran Church?" she asked as she prodded my scalp with the rat-tail end of a comb.

"Nope," I said. I was not one to frequent rummage sales or yard sales or garage sales. Mother swore by them. I could never find anything useful amongst the tables of dusty vases, chipped cups, piles of used clothing, and boxes of tattered paperbacks. Mother, on the other hand, had purchased a Tiffany vase for a quarter and some antique furniture for practically nothing. It all looked like musty old junk to me.

"They have a craft sale, too, and a bake sale. That stuff goes fast. You need to get over there when we're done."

The bake sale was of some interest. Perhaps I could find something for dessert; maybe even pass it off to George as my own.

"So, what's new?" Val asked as she peeked inside a piece of foil that held a swatch of my hair.

"New? Oh, not much. Working hard, you know. Mother is gone for a while, she—"

"Uh huh. You're done, hon. Let's get to the wash sink."

Snow was falling earnestly as I went up the steps to the Lutheran Church fellowship hall. "Rummage Sale Today!" proclaimed a neon-orange poster board. "Man Stuff" was scribbled along the bottom of the sign. Man stuff meant tools, along with hunting and fishing gear. Normally, only the most henpecked man could be dragged to a rummage sale where he would be pressed into service to hold the various treasures that his wife had picked out. Most likely he had agreed to accompany her because he was doing penance for some marital transgression. However, *Man Stuff* was not your ordinary rummage/garage/yard sale. Now he had entered the testosterone zone where he hoped to find some worthwhile items likely disposed of by a wife on a mission to clean out the attic or garage.

I hurried to the bake sale table. Church women of all denominations hold the steady belief that things should be homemade and contain only the finest of ingredients—no high fructose corn syrup, palm oil, or xanthan gum in their offerings. I was instantly drawn to something that looked chocolate and gooey. It had a label calling it "double decadent" with a price of $10.00. I snapped it up and had it paid for and bagged within thirty seconds. The woman who took my money complimented me on my hair. I thanked her. It did look much better.

As I worked my way toward the door, I passed a table piled with shoes, boots, and purses. I gave a jumbo leather purse the once over. It was only $15.00 and looked expensive. I was pretty sure Mother would like it. Or not. A pair of black leather boots caught my eye. They had a lining but looked like they could be worn in or outdoors. Other than a bit of scuffing, they appeared to be practically new and were actually my size. I paid for my selections and headed out to my car. The snow had intensified with big, wet flakes coming down in earnest on my drive home. Even though it was daylight, visibility was terrible, and I clutched the steering wheel. I had to get my winter driving skills back up to snuff. I was annoyed that I had to park outside again, since James' car was still taking up the garage.

The phone was ringing urgently when I stumbled into the house.

"Hello?" I said breathlessly.

"Hey, Babe." It was George.

"Hey yourself," I said. He sounded pretty upbeat. Not his usual maudlin self. He had started calling me Babe ever since the pregnancy issue had come up, which, ironically, we never talked about.

"Guess what?"

"You cut your hair."

"Huh?"

"I cut mine," I said.

"Hey, great. Anyway, listen, Babe, there's a reporter from *The Potter's Wheel* coming to interview me."

"What's The Potter's Wheel?"

"It's a pretty well-known quarterly that features established and new potters. This woman—her name is Desiree Pruce—is coming to look at my stuff and write up an article. This could be my big break!"

I thought about the lasagna, double decadent—damn. I had forgotten all about the EPT How could I have forgotten the most important thing? And choir practice. I just remembered that again. My evening was falling apart.

"What time's she coming?" I said, my mood growing dismal.

"Well, the weather is pretty bad and she's coming from Marquette where she had an interview of someone else earlier. But she assures me she'll be here."

"Ok. Well, I have choir practice. Why don't we have dinner when I get back from that around 7:00?"

"Great, Babe. I'm so jazzed. This could mean a lot. I mean, *The Potter's Wheel!*"

He was positively giddy. Maybe it would all work out after all. I would make the lasagna ahead of time and put it in the oven on time bake so it would be done around 7:30. That would be the safest way to handle it. I could still get the test kit before choir practice and maybe have a chance to conduct the test before George got home.

"Gotta go. I need to tidy up," he chirped. "Love ya."

"Love you, too," I said.

The love ya stuff was something else that was new. George did periodically proclaim his love for me, but never in a casual format. I was pretty sure it meant that our relationship had moved to another stage; it was a good thing.

Just as I was putting the finishing touches on dinner, the phone rang again. I figured it would be a crestfallen George saying his interview had been cancelled.

"Hey, Janese—or should I say *Mommy?*"

"Hi Bertie," I said. "So far, it's just Janese."

"So the test was negative?"

I explained to her how the process had been temporarily derailed.

"Well, I do have some baby things set aside—just in case. Anyway, I'm calling to let you know you can give the Koski woman back her boots."

"Not a match?"

"Nope. Not even close. The ones you gave me were a size seven, and we figure your assailant was more like an eight, and the tread is wrong plus there's no damage or defect like the perp's. Nice, try, though. You have some sleuthing in your blood."

"It was worth a shot," I said.

"Yup. They're looking a little closer at Bucky. New evidence, I guess."

"Bucky? They think Bucky did in Weasel?"

"Well, they're looking at it. I caught hell for letting him into the crime scene. 'course I don't think he did it, but the dicks are calling him a 'person of interest'."

"Wouldn't it be pretty stupid to kill someone and store him in your own place like that?"

"Well, we are talking about Bucky," she said. "Still, it doesn't feel right to me. But I'm just a lowly patrol officer. What do I know?"

"You know a lot. I didn't like that detective—what was his name?"

"Burns. He's a pain," she said, matter-of-factly. "Hey, one more thing. Big favor. How would you like to doggie sit?"

"Doggie sit?"

"Yeah. I think Paul and I can wrangle a vacation to Hawaii. Beaches, tropical breezes, drinks with little umbrellas in them, snorkeling, sex! My mother will take the boys, but she won't take Woofie."

"Woofie?" I didn't remember Bertie having a dog last time I had been to her place.

"Yeah, he's a great pooch, a shelter dog we got a little while ago. The boys are crazy about him—Woofie, he's such a love muffin. I would kennel him, but he doesn't do well. We had to put him in the kennel a while back when we were gone for the weekend and apparently Woofie had 'separation anxiety,' probably a holdover from being abandoned in a shelter. Wouldn't eat, moped around, banged his tin dog dish on the chain link fence for hours and howled. He actually broke out and they had to chase him down the highway and capture him. Truth be told, the kennel asked that I not bring him back. He caused kind of a prison riot."

"Won't he have this separation anxiety when you leave him here?" I asked.

"Don't think so. We took him to Paul's brother's place once and left him there while we went to Appleton and shopped for school clothes.

He was fine. Didn't even care about us when we picked him up. It's the chain link that sets him off."

I owed Bertie a lot. She had been my steadfast friend through many life dramas. I thought taking charge of the dog was far more desirable than being asked to take custody of her two boys Robby and Jeffie, ages six and eight. I had watched them once, for about an hour, and barely came out alive. During that hour that lasted an eternity, the little dickens had managed to break George's recliner, permanently lose the TV remote, collapse the bed (an ad hoc trampoline), start a small fire in the woods, cause a flat tire on the Subaru (I backed over the roofing nails they had discovered), and dialed 911 without my knowledge, resulting in the police, rescue, and fire to respond. (The fine was waived when they found out it was Bertie's kids.) A dog was a piece of cake.

"Well, I guess I could. I'm at work all day, though," I said.

"Perfect. Woofie sleeps a lot."

I looked at my watch. I needed to leave.

Bertie told me they hadn't firmed up their reservations yet. She suggested that she bring Woofie over for the weekend for a trial run. If it didn't work out, then she would explore other avenues. When I asked what kind of dog Woofie was, Bertie said "mixed."

* * *

Choir practice was long and brutal. The lack of James and Derry did nothing to improve Hannu's prickly temperament and he seemed to hold me personally responsible for James' absence. Hannu had pretty much figured out that Derry was a one-practice wonder and, therefore, Eleanor was once again assigned the soprano solo for the cantata. She gloated lavishly and smirked at me. Clearly my downfall had been my fainting spell when assigned the semi-solo part with her in the anthem I had proven unreliable and lacking the moxie needed to handle the pressure. I simply wasn't worthy.

I was never certain what made Eleanor hate me. I had no desire to compete with her for vocal recognition. I was only in the choir because Mother put me there many decades earlier, and it became like a scab that you can't leave alone: I just kept at it. Perhaps it was a mission of God of sorts; a way to express my spiritual inner workings that were not apt to otherwise come out. The congregation always enjoyed the choir anthems—found them uplifting. So there you have it: my tiny donation.

But to those who come for personal glory, competition will rear its ugly head and jealousy will not be far behind. When a choir member falters, those who *compete* will silently rejoice, like the athlete wishing for his opponent to stumble and fall. True sportsmanship wants fair victory and feels reverence toward the victory of others. Choir practice is no place for competition. Eleanor exuded such ugliness in that all-knowing smirk. I was pleased with myself for taking the high road. I gave her a warm, generous smile and patted her on the shoulder. I muttered something about her being the best choice all along. I hoped it completely confused her.

In any event, I had other things on my mind. A new test kit sat on the front seat of my car. The time-bake on the oven would activate soon, starting the lasagna. I had already made a lovely salad, the bread was sliced, buttered, and wrapped in foil, and the bake-sale Double Decadent was displayed on the counter. I had laid a fire in the fireplace and a music playlist had been selected. Everything would be perfect when George got home from his interview with *The Potter's Wheel*. I hoped that the interview would go well. George needed a break. The frequent visits to his psychologist didn't seem to be getting him anywhere with his personal issues—issues that still eluded me.

Things began to unravel before I even got home. My route home via Big Lake Road took me through some high country in the Huron Mountains—really just hills, but famous for having their own weather system. I was instantly ensconced in a heavy snowstorm. I found myself completely over the centerline twice, nearly taking out mailboxes on the wrong side of the road. The wind whipped savagely, swirling blankets of snow all around the Subaru, creating a dreamlike feeling. There was no road, no houses, no mailboxes, no ditch, only white, blinding white, everywhere. It came at my windshield like a hoard of albino locusts, swirling viciously around in the useless beams of my headlights.

I slumped over the steering wheel when I finally arrived safely in my driveway, completely wrung out from the tension. I was certain that I had left the outside lights on, but the cabin sat engulfed in darkness. The reason became apparent when I went inside, flipped with light switch, and nothing happened. Damn. Another power outage. No baking lasagna smells, no music, nothing except cold and darkness. I found my emergency flashlight and stumbled around lighting some candles. One good thing: I could just strike a match to the fire that was ready to go in the fireplace. The flames dispelled the darkness somewhat, and soon a bit of warmth entered the rapidly-cooling cabin. I actually did have a generator for just such emergencies, but it was a pain to get started and I usually left it to George.

I took the lasagna out of the oven and put it in the fridge. Even though it wasn't running, it was still cold. The EPT would also be once again delayed as I couldn't possibly deal with its idiosyncrasies in the near darkness. I shoved the new kit into my sweater drawer. I changed into my warm-up suit then added another couple of logs to the fire. The cabin creaked under the impact of the buffeting wind. I sat in the shadowy darkness and stewed. George should not be driving in the storm. I needed to call him, but the landline didn't work without electricity. I fished my cell phone out of my purse and turned it on. The battery was nearly dead and reception was weak, but I was able to put through a call to the art studio where George was having his interview. The answering machine picked up the call to announce that the place was closed and would reopen at 9:00 a.m. Nothing to do but wait. Wait for the power to come on. Wait for the storm to subside. Wait for George.

⚡ 11 ⚡

Thumping awoke me. The fire had died and the cabin was cold. An eerie light broke the darkness and moved across the sliding doors, giving a distorted view of the living room. More thumping, scraping, the light reversed its path back across the patio doors. Closer. I strained to look at my watch. What time was it? A more troubling thought: where was George? The thumping transformed into a rumbling and seemed stalled somewhere toward the driveway side of the house. Someone pounded on the door. I jumped off the couch and immediately bashed my shin on the coffee table. I found the flashlight I had dug out the night before and fumbled my way to the door. More urgent pounding.

"Who is it?" My voice thin. Stupid question, as if someone or something evil would answer: "Hi, it's me the bogyman. I'm here to rip out your spleen!"

A muffled voice came from the other side of the door leading to the garage. Had I locked the door? "Who is it?" I repeated.

"Keskimaki—you okay in there?"

I jerked open the door. "Oh, Toivo, thank God you're here."

"Got you plowed out," he said. "Did a narrow strip here on your road, since the plows probably won't be down for a while. Why's your car outside? I tried not to bury it, but yous'll need to dig it out a little."

"It's out because I have someone else's damn car in the garage," I said. "I'll shovel it out later. I could use a little exercise."

"Hell of a storm. You got no 'lectric?"

"Went out sometime early last night," I said.

"I'll git the generator going for yous. Got any gas?"

We went into the garage with my dim, ineffective flashlight and found the gas can. Keskimaki rolled the generator around, filled it, and plugged it into a wall receptacle. After six or seven pulls, it reluctantly came to life, surging and choking.

"Shine that light over here by the choke," he said.

I didn't know a choke from a chicken wing but trained the wavering light in the general direction he was working. The generator smoothed out, chugging loudly. Next, we went into the basement and he flipped a switch on the wall. Instantly the furnace came on, the basement freezer began to hum, and a light filtered through from upstairs.

"Thank you so much. I want to give you something extra," I said as we trundled up the stairs.

"Ain't necessary. Can't leave a gal out here with no power. Where's your fella?"

That was a good question.

"I think he got stuck at the studio because of the storm."

"No lights in a lot of places, and they say more snow's comin' and the wind's shifting. Plows are out though. Yous aren't going to work are ya? I heard the campus was all closed along with the public schools, and even the supermarket is shut down because they got no 'lectric. Hospital's on emergency generator."

"How do you know all of this?" I said, amazed.

"Radio."

A radio, with batteries. Brilliant.

"Don't let her run too long. Yous need gas pretty soon and ya gotta shut 'er down to fill it. She'll run the water pump so's you can flush, but nothin' like a stove."

"Right." I had no idea what he was talking about. I hated being a helpless female.

"Guess the winds were worse'n when the Edmund Fitzgerald went down. Like a hurricane, they say, and it ain't even winter yet."

"Going to be a doozie of a winter," I said. What would we talk about if we didn't have the weather?

"Yep, a doozie for sure. You take care, eh?" he said as he hopped into his shuddering Ford/Chevy hybrid and rumbled off.

I started a pot of coffee, dialed the art studio and while it rang and rang, the answering machine didn't pick up the call, likely because the electricity was out. Still, George would have found a way to let me know he was all right, wouldn't he? Panic crept in, pushing out reason. Where could he be? The coffee pot apparently took a lot of juice and made the lights dim. I flicked off the light switch. I needed my coffee. I tried to call Bertie at the State Police post and got a very tired sounding dispatcher who told me that I had just missed her. As I debated whether to call Bertie at home and risk waking her, the phone rang.

"Darling! Are you all right?"

Words I would have loved to hear from George but, alas, it was Mother.

"Fine, why?" I said. I pulled the carafe out while the pot still brewed. Liquid hissed on the warmer. I poured a half cup and replaced the carafe.

"I tried to call all last night but got no answer. James and I have been worried sick."

I took a swig of coffee. Bitter, but reviving. "The storm. Lost power. In fact it's still out, but the generator is going, so everything is hunky dory."

"Oh, thank God. Of course you have George there. I shouldn't have worried."

I thought it prudent not to tell mother of George's disappearance and that Keskimaki actually came to my rescue. She would be certain that the old reprobate would be back to rape me and steal the family jewels, if we had any.

I added some more coffee to my cup and looked out the window. I couldn't tell how much snow had actually fallen. It had to be close to a record for this time of year, though.

"How's the weather there?" I asked.

"We only got a couple of inches. Windy, though, and the lights flickered. But the sun is out now."

I saw a vehicle pull into the driveway. It looked like Bertie, and something odd perched in the passenger seat.

"Did I tell you that the green is positively bilious? It reminds me of something you would put on the walls of a mental institution," Mother said. "We'll be delayed for a few more days, I'm afraid. I have reservations coming in soon. I hope the place doesn't smell like a paint store."

"Stay as long as you need. Gotta go," I said. "Someone's here."

I smirked a little thinking about Mother's so-called latex allergy, which apparently came and went according to the circumstances. I worked my way around the deafening roar of the generator and poked my head out the garage door. Bertie had gone to the passenger seat and opened the door. A large, hairy creature bounded out, ran to the snowbank where he lifted his leg and peed.

"What the hell is that?" I said, taking another swallow of coffee.

"Meet Woofie," Bertie said.

Woofie, after sniffing his work, lumbered over to me and jammed his nose in my crotch, causing me to spill a little coffee on his head. This didn't seem to faze him. His head, body and legs all blended into a large, indistinguishable mop of hair. He shook and I caught a quick glimpse of one eye, before it disappeared under a fringe of overgrown bangs.

"I brought him over to see how you all get along. George likes dogs, right?" Bertie said.

"Oh Bertie, I tried to call you at the post. George is missing, I guess." My voice quavered a little.

"Missing?" she said.

"Yeah, come on in. I'll get you some coffee."

"No coffee. I need to sleep in a while. I could use some decaf tea, though."

While the tea brewed and Woofie explored my living room, I told Bertie about George waiting for the reporter from *The Potter's Wheel* and how he didn't answer the phone at the studio.

"Well, the phone could be out. Service is spotty," she said. "I'm sure he's okay and just having trouble getting home. Some of the parking lots have six-foot drifts in them. Woofie, *no!*"

The dog had pulled a decorative pillow off my couch and had one corner chewed off.

"Don't worry, I hate that pillow. Mother bought it," I said. "Chew away, Woofie."

Bertie sighed. "He's really still just a pup. He just looks full grown."

"You mean he will get bigger?"

"Heavier, but probably not taller. He's a good boy, aren't you Woofie? Are you mommy's good boy?"

Woofie came over to Bertie, wiggling in delight, alligator tail thumping in his wake. She scratched him behind the ears and he rested his chin on her knee.

"I think George would have gotten through to me. I think something's happened. He's stranded somewhere. I'm worried, Bertie. And who was that woman from *The Potter's Wheel* coming during a snowstorm to do an interview? Under the circumstances, wouldn't she just do the interview over the phone?"

"Good point. What was her name?" Bertie said pulling a cell phone out of her pocket.

"Desiree something—Proof, Poof. I don't remember."

"I'll have dispatch check it out," Bertie said as she punched her cell phone. "Hey Brian, they got you on the radio? Do me a favor and get me a number for a magazine called *The Potter's Wheel*. Huh?" Bertie turned to me. "Any idea what city?"

"I think George said the woman was coming from Minneapolis, then to Marquette and then here. Maybe Minneapolis?"

"Try Minneapolis. Yeah. It's a magazine. The reporter's name is Desiree something—Poof, Proof, or something like that. Use your super detective skills. Sure, call me back."

Bertie laid her phone down and stretched out in her chair. "He'll get right on it. Brian's a good guy. He's on light duty because he got hurt on the job chasing some bad guys."

"Really?" I said. "What happened?" Woofie had left Bertie's lap and moved over to me. He flopped his head on my leg and shoved his nose against my hand.

"He likes to be scratched," Bertie said. "Woofie, that is, not Brian. Anyway, Brian was cruising Market Alley because there had been a string of B&Es. He saw some kids crawling out of the window at Pete's Hardware. They spotted Brian and took off down the alley and he went after them on foot because the alley was too narrow for the cruiser. They jumped a fence at the end of the alley. Brian, well, he's had a few too many cheeseburgers and didn't quite make it over the fence, fell and dislocated his shoulder. He still got the little thieves though."

Bertie's cell rang out the theme song to *Hawaii 5-0*. "Always my favorite cop show," she said, tapping the screen. "Hi Brian. Uh huh. Really, you sure? Okay, thanks. I'm gonna get some sleep soon."

She tapped the phone again and slid it into her pocket. "Well, there is a magazine called *The Potter's Wheel* published in Minneapolis. However, they have no reporter or editor or any employee named Desiree Proof, Poof, Puff, or otherwise. It's a shoestring operation and they only got like four employees. The one woman that works there is named Ruth Johnson and she currently is in the hospital recovering from surgery."

Bertie and I looked at each other. I knew what she was thinking. George had someone else on the side and he had fed me the well-worn "away on business" excuse.

"Did you tell him you might be PG?" Bertie said. The implication was clear. She thought George had fled. "Or did you finally take the test?"

"Things keep interrupting me," I said. "He knows I could be, but he, well doesn't seem too—anyway, he'd never leave his wheel."

Bertie sipped her tea and studied me. "What are you waiting for? You need to find out if you're pregnant."

"I will, today," I said.

"Something's fishy," Bertie said. "Too much going on. I'm calling in a BOLO—a be-on-the-lookout—we'll check the hospital, too. I gotta go get my kids from Ma's. I'll call Brian back and have him check things out. Don't worry. George is a big boy. I'm sure he's fine."

Woofie rushed to the door.

"You stay with Aunt Janese," Bertie said. "His toys, food, leash, and dishes are in the duffle bag. I wrote down how much food. He has to poop right after he eats. Keep him on the leash. You be a good boy Woofie. Mommy will be back in a couple of days."

Woofie continued to stand at the door.

"Here Woofie, come here," I said.

He ignored me.

"Aunt Janese has your squeaky—get his squeaky toy out of the duffle."

I did as told and gave the rubber bone a few squeaks. Woofie perked up. I tossed it and he lumbered after it, retrieved it, and came to me, squeaking loudly all the way.

"Well, that did it. Dogs are fickle. Don't forget the test, and I'll let you know about George. Maybe a cruiser can break free and go check out the studio."

I tossed the bone a couple of more times for Woofie, refilled my coffee cup, and unpacked Woofie's paraphernalia. I filled his water dish and stuck it in a corner of the kitchen. Woofie went to the dish and had a long, noisy drink.

"Thirsty, huh?"

Woofie's tail thumped loudly against the wall. He made his way back into the living room and jumped up into George's chair, made a few awkward circles, grunted then lay down. I had no idea if his eyes were open or shut, since they were hidden beneath a panel of hair.

"Make yourself at home." I sighed. "Guess this is as good a time as any, huh Woofie?"

Once again, I headed to the bathroom with my EPT test. I went through all the steps, dipped the stick and took it over to view under the one dim light I had on in the bathroom. Just as I was trying to decipher the thing, the distant drone of the generator cut off and I was plunged into darkness.

"Damn and hell!"

I fumbled my way out and made my way to the garage. I remembered a couple of things Keskimaki showed me. I found my very weak flashlight, went downstairs and switched the main circuit from "generator" to "REA." This meant when the REA—Rural Electrification Association—got the lines fixed, I would have my power back. Meanwhile, I would have to learn how to fill and restart the generator. Switch the circuit back—too much trouble. Besides, I thought Keskimaki had said he used up all the gas in the can and I needed to get some. Until I did, there would be no hot coffee, running water, phone, or heat. I took my flashlight back to the bathroom and found the EPT stick lying in a small puddle of water in the sink. I couldn't make out any markings, so I set it on the edge of the sink to dry out.

I wasn't sure if anything would be open in town but decided to drive in and see if I could find gas—I thought the Ojibwe station had a generator—and maybe the local mom and pop diner, The Copper Café, would be open. They had the world's best western omelets. My stomach rumbled as I slid into my down parka. Woofie raised his head and leapt out of the chair.

"Ok, you can ride in the back," I said, heading out the door.

My heart sank as I saw the mounds of snow piled around the Subaru from Keskimaki's plowing. Woofie wandered around, sniffing the driveway, and relieving himself while I shoveled. Sweat trickled down my spine by the time I could get the driver's door open. Woofie bounded into the car and sat on the front passenger seat. I debated if I should belt him in. I slid into the driver's seat and turned the key. An ominous, low moan came from the battery, then nothing. Dead. I wondered if I had left the interior light on again, or maybe it just couldn't deal with the cold. James had not left the keys to his car, which was a moot point anyway, since the electric garage door opener wouldn't work.

"Ok, Woofie, we're screwed. I guess we rough it until REA gets around to fixing things. Then I'll call for a wrecker."

Back inside, I rekindled the embers in the fireplace and made myself a peanut butter and jelly sandwich. Woofie sat at my feet, strings of drool slipping from beneath the hair. I offered him pieces of crust, which disappeared into the vicinity of his mouth.

"Just you and me, Woofie. How about a game of Gin Rummy?"

Once the sandwich was gone, Woofie returned to George's chair. A small tingle of panic crept over me. I was alone in my secluded cabin. I had no phone and my car wouldn't start. This might feel like a kind of adventure if it weren't for all the disturbing events of the past weeks. Woofie, my protector, snored from George's chair.

The wind was picking up again and the cabin darkened from the thick front that was moving in. Round two was on its way. I wandered around the cabin, at a loss for what to do. I would have been willing to work on my Christmas card list, but that was in the computer. I could practice the cantata pieces but needed my electronic keyboard. Exercise? The fruitless shoveling had covered that. In fact, I really needed a shower. Of course, there was no water because of the electric pump. I rummaged around, looking for something to do and found a deck of cards. After losing a week's wages to myself playing solitaire, I stoked the fire and went back to the couch. A new layer of darkness crept into the cabin just as I settled down with a book that I had been reading.

"This is ridiculous. What in hell did people *do* before they had electricity?" I said. One of Woofie's ears twitched. "I think you've got the right idea Woofie. Sleep until it's over, but I had had way too much coffee. Hey, I know!"

I took my flickering flashlight up into the loft and explored the storage closets under the rafters. Eventually I found my backpack and after rummaging around, extracted the headlamp that I used for camping. When I twisted the light, it came on.

"Well, what do you know! The batteries are still good."

I took the headlamp back to the couch and settled down with my book. I had no idea why I thought it would be a good idea to read a horror story entitled: *Watched*. It was about a woman, Lilly, all alone in the woods during a snowstorm. Lilly, unlike me, was prepared for her life of solitude. She didn't use electricity and got her water from a creek and her food from the woods. She preferred her solitary lifestyle and had a loaded shotgun on hand for anyone who threatened it. But she was being watched by something that outmatched the shotgun—a creature, large and hideous. Perhaps a space alien, perhaps a freak of nature. It watched, it waited.

Nothing cluttering up Lilly's life. Her companions, a hybrid wolf she called Pariah and her twelve-gauge shotgun, never left her side. Lilly used both to hunt. She killed only for food, not sport. Now *she* was the hunted. Not an original plot, but neither was a love story or a good whodunit. The "Thing" watched her. The author shifted from Lilly's point-of-view to that of the creature—its base feelings primal and lustful. Was it going to rape her or eat her—or both? Clearly, the wolf and shotgun would be no match for the Frankensteinian creature that lurked outside Lilly's cabin. The wind blew, pummeling the windows with snow. Soon Lilly smelled its vile odor, felt its breath on her face, froze with terror as it came down on her...

As I read on through the harrowing rape scene, I chuckled. What a stupid book. In spite of the caffeine, my eyes drooped. I laid down the book, took off my headlamp and stretched out on the couch. Forced relaxation—not a bad thing. Except I was worried about George. That was the problem with becoming attached: grief and worry. I should have been more fiercely independent, like Lilly. Although I wouldn't fancy getting ravished by a Bigfoot mutant creature. Now *there* would be a pregnancy for the tabloids.

⚡ 12 ⚡

Woofie whined to go out.

"Just a minute, fella," I said as I fumbled for the headlamp. Woofie fussed and scratched at the door off the kitchen. Near darkness slowed my progress and the dog whirled and leapt with urgency. Forget the leash; Woofie was ready to explode. I flung open the door and he hurled himself into the darkness.

"Woofie! Come back," I shouted. I rushed back inside, grabbed my boots and coat, and stumbled out into the blizzard. I called at the top of my lungs, but my words were tossed back at me like paper confetti. He was lost, vanished in the storm. God, how what would I tell Bertie? I had to find him, but I needed light. Then I remembered the gas lantern that I used for camping—somewhere in the garage. I jammed on my headlamp. The thin pool of light barely cutting the darkness as I groped my way into the garage. Sometimes being a neat freak had its advantages, and I was able to find the lantern and some matches on the tidy shelves that lined the garage wall. It ran on white gas. I tried to remember the last time I'd used it—two, maybe three years ago? I shook it gently and it felt like there was some fuel in the reservoir. I pumped up the pressure, turned the knob and struck a match to the mantle. It lit with a whoosh and the garage filled with wonderful, beautiful light.

The force of the wind and blinding snow slammed me as I floundered into the yard. I yelled for Woofie, over and over, desperately trying to find tracks or any sign of him in the drifting snow. When I entered the woods that surrounded my cabin, the wind eased a bit and the snow wasn't as deep. I spotted some tracks, except they weren't Woofie's and they weren't mine. In fact, they didn't belong to any human or animal that I could imagine. I had spent a good deal of time hiking and camping in the woods and had become quite skillful at identifying animal tracks and signs. These were enormous and rectangular with a rough, fuzzy outline. They were too big even for a bear. Besides, bears were likely hunkered down in their dens. Howling penetrated the roar of the wind.

"Woofie!" I hollered, stumbling deeper into the woods. The shelter of the trees helped, but the fury that lashed the limbs made hearing difficult. "Woofie—come!" I raised the lantern, straining to see into the swirl of white. No use. My stomach knotted as I thought about the dog lost in the woods. How long before he would succumb to the cold? Then howling again—eerie, warbling.

Wolves.

My scalp prickled. I tried to convince myself that I was perfectly safe, living among the wolves. They were much maligned and mis-understood. Contrary to local legend, the Department of Natural Resources had no confirmed reports of wolf attacks on humans—ever. Lots of stories about them circling camps, stalking hunters, and such. Simple curiosity, wolf aficionados explained. Wolves are highly intelligent, but very shy. They avoid humans. For decades—centuries—humans have persecuted and exterminated wolves, thus their wariness of humans. Yes. Perfectly safe I told myself, but what about Woofie?

Highly territorial, wolves were known to injure and kill hunting dogs and even occasionally drag off the family cockapoo tied to the porch. Woofie was in serious danger. Why in hell hadn't I taken a minute to get the leash? So what if he had piddled on the floor? Big deal. Now I had to think about a big, sweet lummox of a dog either freezing to death or being ravaged by wolves.

And then there were the giant footprints leading in what seemed a random pattern through the trees then back to a more open spot where the stride appeared to lengthen, as if it running in a convoluted path before disappearing into the drifts.

The howling grew closer: deep and primal. Maybe not wolves. The prickle again and a feeling—like Lilly, being *watched*, by the creature that waited until she let down her guard, left her shotgun in the cabin. Pariah ran off, tail between legs. Some protector. Lilly hadn't put up much of a fight. I had been disappointed in Lilly. Until then, she had been a kind of role-model to me.

I hated to abandon Woofie and leave him out with whatever belonged to the giant footprints. I had laughed at the dubious reports of the Yooper Bigfoot. Most sightings made by drunken hunters or crazies that also claimed being victims of abductions by aliens who looked like Elvis. My feet were getting numb and the lantern had grown dim. Time to retreat. Wait until daylight, I told myself when the storm would be over, dissipating with the demons of an overactive imagination. Woofie had lots of fur—he was a walking, drooling carpet. Probably be just fine, I told myself as I stumbled back toward the cabin.

After stoking the fire and refilling the lantern, I sat on the couch huddled under a blanket. I hadn't eaten or slept much for what seemed eons. I could feel my eyelids droop and my head nod. Perhaps I would awake to normalcy. George's disappearance, the storm, Woofie lost—all a bad dream.

Howling at the door. My head jerked to attention. Scratching. Woofie—or something else? A tingling, paralyzing sensation crawled over me. I needed a weapon. I was not that paper tigress, Lilly, who stupidly forgot her shotgun. Clutching the poker from the fireplace tools and the lantern, I went to investigate the odd sounds at the door. "Woofie—is that you boy?" The scratching continued. I carefully unlocked the deadbolt and turned the knob. The door slapped open with enough force to knock the poker from my hand and send it clattering to the floor.

"Woofie! Thank God." I set the lantern down and threw my arms around him. Snow that had balled on his fur looked like dozens of string bolas undulating in the breeze. Something odd—barely visible—hung from his jaws.

"Whatcha got there fella?" I asked, giving the thing a pull. He growled without menace, as if wanting to play tug-of-war. Had the dog captured some unfortunate creature and brought it home for me to cook up? Whatever it was, he held on with steely determination.

"Treat!" I announced. Instantly Woofie let go of the "thing" and began to dance around the kitchen, flinging melting snow everywhere. Good to my word, I fished a dog biscuit out of the box, which he took from me with remarkable gentleness. Probably something Bertie insisted upon to avoid amputation of her children's fingers.

I was relieved to find that the treasure Woofie brought home did not appear to be a small mammal. I inspected the ragged, hairy thing. It did look like it had been torn *off* an animal—but what? Definitely not from a deer. Deep brown, nearly black and coarse. Maybe a bear—but I couldn't imagine a dog tearing a chuck of fur off a bear and living to tell about it. A carcass perhaps? It didn't seem to be off anything living—no blood oozing or offensive smell. It appeared to have been tanned, like for a coat.

"Where'd you get this Woofie?" He lifted his head and tilted it slightly, then began to leap around the kitchen again. Eventually he calmed and went to his empty food dish and looked at me. After crunching his way through a mound of kibble, Woofie retired to George's chair for a nap—the secret adventure in the blizzard safely locked in his doggie brain. Occasionally he whined and jerked while he slept.

* * *

Under the glow of my fading headlamp, I squinted at the test stick that had been sitting on the sink ledge since the power went out. I had hoped that after it dried out, it would come back with a verdict. Unfortunately, the mystery would continue as it had neither a plus nor minus but rather had turned an ambiguous shade of yellow. I sighed, wrapped it in toilet paper, and tossed it in the trash.

Then everything happened at once: The lights came on, the phone rang, someone pounded at the door, and Woofie commenced barking. I stumbled out of the bathroom and got to the phone after the robotic voice of the answering machine instructed the caller to leave a message.

"Janese dear, it's Mother. I hope you're all right. James and I have been watching the weather channel. *Please* call me."

More urgent pounding on the garage door accompanied by a voice, which was drowned out by Woofie's frantic barking.

"If you don't call me back, dear, James and I will jump in the car and head—"

I snatched the phone off the cradle and headed toward the door, dodging Woofie who threatened to entangle my legs. "Mother! I was in the bathroom. Sorry, I—"

"Oh, Janese, thank God you're alright! Is that a dog barking?"

"Dog, yes—a barking dog." I squinted through the peephole. Bertie! I jerked the door open and waved her in. Woofie leapt frantically around his mistress, overcome with joy.

"I've been doggie sitting."

"But Janese, you know I'm allergic."

"Well, perhaps you will need to stay at the resort until I'm done taking care of the pooch."

"How long will the creature be staying with you—and what is that noise?"

Bertie and Woofie were enjoying a reunion. Woofie had found his squeaky toy and was giving it a workout.

"What noise?" I said. I loved to mess with Mother. "I don't hear any noise."

"First the barking, now it sounds like something squealing—like when a belt goes out in the car."

"I don't know what you're talking about, Mother. Are you *in* the car now?"

Bertie tossed the dog toy across the room and Woofie lumbered after it.

"Of course I'm not in the car—whatever gave you that idea?" Mother asked.

"You said the belt in your car was slipping, so I assumed—"

"I *said* something on the phone line sounded like a squeal—there it goes again!"

Woofie passed close to me, gleefully squeaking his rubber bone.

"Funny," I said. "I don't hear it. Probably the storm affecting the phone lines. Although the wind has died down now and I think the snow's stopped."

By this time Bertie had caught on to my game and she was covering her mouth, trying not to laugh.

"Who's there?" Mother asked.

"Where?"

"*There!* You said someone was at the door."

"Oh, that was George. He had his arms full of firewood and needed me to let him in." I had always been able to lie easily to Mother on the phone. Face to face was another thing. "Is the fan belt still squealing?" I asked. "I don't think you should drive until you have it looked at."

"I suppose you're right," she said. "But I'm not driving, I—"

"What color is it now?" I asked.

"Color? You mean the car?"

"No—I thought we were talking about the resort—the redecorating. Goodness, Mother, are you okay?" I had to cover the mouthpiece of the phone so that I could release the pent-up laughter. Woofie came over with his rubber bone. I let him squeak it into the phone.

"There it goes again!" Mother shrieked.

"What—the car?" I said.

"No, the noise. Melon."

"Melon?" I said. "Do you mean the car is a *lemon?*"

"The resort, Janese," Mother said. "I wish you'd pay attention. We are going with Mellow Melon—like cantaloupe. It's quite nice. The blue was depressing."

Mother had turned the tables. Just like a wrestling match, she had quickly flipped her opponent—me—and was going for the shoulder pin.

"Well, gotta go," I said. "Time to brush the dog. Be sure to get the car fixed."

I hung up before Mother could respond. Bertie and I looked at each other and burst out laughing. After the hysterics faded a bit, I got up and made some coffee. I felt the hysteria taking a bad turn. Perhaps Bertie came to fetch Woofie, but she might also have some news about George.

"Thank God the power is finally back on," I said, handing her a cup.

"Amen to that," she said. Bertie was still in uniform, *sans* gun belt. She always locked it up at the station. Too many kids running in and out of her house, she said.

I looked at her—waiting.

"I don't know if I have good or bad news," she said.

I braced myself.

"They found his truck."

"At the art studio?" I asked.

"Well, no. A couple of the troops located it on Triple A Road—you know that goes to Big Bay, way out in the boonies, stuck in a snowdrift. Looks like there was actually some mud under the snow, which is what bogged it down. Anyway, some liquored-up snow-mobilers were out screwing around in the storm and thought it strange to find the truck abandoned out there a ways from any camps or houses. Nobody in the truck, and the engine hadn't completely cooled. They found a few drifted-over footprints heading off into the snow. In spite of their state of inebriation, they had the wherewithal to contact the authorities." She ran her finger around the rim of the coffee cup. "They ran the plate and the truck is George's."

I sat a moment, trying to digest the information.

"Another—well, strange thing," Bertie said.

It got stranger?

"There were clothes in the car—men's. A pair of lined jeans, a flannel shirt, undershirt, socks, coat, knit hat, gloves, and boots. Did George keep extra clothing in the truck?"

"Ah, no—I don't think so," I said. "What did the coat look like?"

Bertie thought for a moment. "Kinda gray. A little tattered."

"George's coat is gray and getting worn out. I told him he needs a new one..."

We sat silently for a moment, struggling to figure out why George's clothes—if they were his—were in the truck. Was George running around in his boxers? It made no sense that George would have been out in the backcountry during a blizzard. Even though the truck had four-wheel drive, it had its limitations. What did it have to do with a magazine interview by a woman who didn't exist? Bertie shifted in her seat. Woofie jumped into George's chair and settled down.

"They searched the area, spreading out in a widening spiral; even used the K-9 unit, but never found anyone or anything. We let the dog sniff George's clothes, but it never found a trail."

"What do you think?" I asked.

Bertie shrugged. "I don't know what to think. We already have a BOLO—be on the lookout— for George and for the Parks woman."

"The Parks woman? You mean Derry? I don't get the connection," I said.

"Well, she's a bit of a mystery too—having James Rush meet at Bucky's place, then James getting shut in the meat locker. And of course, Clarence Watkins's going to his reward. All a very strange coincidence. We sure would like to talk to her. We think maybe, just maybe, she and this Desiree Proof woman that George was meeting are one and the same. We know Pruce, or whatever her name is, lied about working at *The Potter's Wheel.*"

"But I don't see what it has to do with George or what he was doing on Triple A Road."

"We were wondering that ourselves," Bertie said. "I could see maybe him getting lost somehow on Triple A Road, but I have no idea why he would, um, take his clothes off. I thought maybe he had extra stuff in his truck. You know, how we keep warm things in our cars, just in case. Maybe he was trying to take a shortcut home."

Except Triple A Road did not head home. Even in the summer it was a nefarious road. In the winter it was mainly traveled by snow-mobiles. In a blizzard, it would be suicide. Panic then a niggling feeling began to meddle with my brain. Had George met some babe and they went out into the sticks for a little nookie? That would explain the removal of his clothes. Maybe an angry husband found them and George didn't have time to get dressed. The scenario was preposterous.

Bertie noticed the mystery fur that Woofie had brought home. When she asked about it, I told her about Woofie's great adventure— and fessed up about not using a leash. Bertie's husband was an avid hunter and she always helped with the butchering. She agreed that the patch of fur wasn't fresh and looked like it had been processed, like for a garment. We couldn't imagine where Woofie had gotten it.

We both stared into our coffee cups for a moment. Bertie looked beyond tired. I took a slurp of coffee. George on Triple A Road. It was nothing more than a goat path. George had no reason to be on Triple A Road.

"But wait, there's more," she said with thick sarcasm. "The assholes arrested Bucky this morning for the murder of Clarence 'Weasel' Watkins."

"No way!" I said.

"Way."

"But I thought it was accidental."

"Yeah. Well they got a search warrant for Bucky's trailer and found something rather incriminating, such as a knife with a broken blade, which –surprise, surprise—matches the blade recovered from the lock in the cooler," she said.

"Bucky may not be a genius, but I don't think he would be stupid enough to leave something that incriminating lying around," I said.

"Right, well it was in the kids' room—hidden under the mattress of one of the bunk beds."

"Yeah, but why not just throw it in the lake or something?"

"Because all of the lakes are frozen?" she said.

I got up and refilled our coffee cups.

George on Triple A Road. Bucky a murderer—over a stupid igloo contest? Now I had something else to feel guilty about. If George had lined up a romantic rendezvous with one of his artsie fartsie groupies, why not just meet at a sleazy motel like a normal lying, cheating, two-timing man?

"And one more thing—not totally unrelated," Bertie said quickly, likely picking up on my murderous expression.

I looked at her over the rim of my cup.

"Remember when you were attacked in your office—with the wastebasket?" she asked.

"Remember! I still have a bruise."

"Well, you might also remember that we took some hair that was caught in the wheel of your office chair; hair from the person who assaulted you."

"Uh huh," I said, still thinking about George. If he was having a nookie-fest in his truck, why would he leave his clothes and wander off?

"Well, the hair was fake," Bertie said.

"Huh?"

"You know, synthetic. Like from a wig. Fake, fake fake. No DNA there," Bertie said.

Another dead end, probably, I thought. I just couldn't decide if I was mad at George for cheating on me or worried because he might be in trouble. Serve him right. Men were pigs.

I took a swallow of cold, bitter coffee. The cheap stuff was no bargain. When would I learn?

⚡ 13 ⚡

Bertie left and Woofie stayed. Even though he and I had gotten off to a shaky start, he was starting to grow on me. Bertie probably figured I needed the company, if not the protection. I knew what she was thinking; I was thinking the same thing. George was a two-timing jerk, off with some floozy bitch. Strangely, I found little comfort in imagining him plunging buck naked into the blizzard. He would be dead from exposure by now. Perhaps *she* came to his rescue, wrapping him up in her mink coat or something. Bertie had told me that the police had George's truck towed to the impound lot. If George went back for his truck, it would be gone, along with his clothes. Surprise! You're fucked! Bad choice of words.

I plodded up the stairs to the loft and approached the closet where George had temporarily stored his potter's wheel and other accoutrements when Mother had arrived. I had arson on my mind. Open burning was legal in the winter so long as there was snow on the ground. I wondered how I would start it and how well it would burn. Woofie had joined me in the loft. He sat at my feet while I yanked at the closet door. It seemed jammed, but eventually gave way with a loud squawk. I stood, staring at the empty closet for a moment or two, allowing this new damning evidence to sink in. Woofie whined a little and went into the empty closet to sniff around. He lifted his leg and peed.

* * *

First, I took a long, scalding shower. It would take some time to put the cabin back in order. Besides the trail of firewood debris and doggie footprints, there was the mess in the kitchen. I had thrown and broken a few things. I quit when I realized I was traumatizing Woofie. George had planned it all along. When had he snuck his things out of the cabin? I was gone a lot, *working*. It would be easy enough.

After my shower, I jerked open the bedroom closet doors. As far as I could tell, his meager wardrobe was still there. Same with his dresser drawers: a jumble of boxers, tees, and socks. He could replace all that stuff. Same with toiletry items. His toothbrush sat in the holder, a blob of petrified toothpaste running down the handle. His cologne sat in its usual spot, top off. I dumped it and tossed the empty bottle into the trash, along with the sullied toothbrush. Was it so hard just to rinse it a little after using it? Was it asking so much just to make that teeny little commitment? He couldn't even commit to his toothbrush. Used it and left it a mess.

While I rummaged around for something to wear, I spotted the latest pregnancy test kit in my sweater drawer. Of course, it was just a useless box and instructions because the pee stick had been contaminated before it could give its verdict. I wondered if other women had this much trouble taking this simple privacy-of-your-own-home test. If so, I surely should consider buying stock in the company. Mother always said things like that—she wished she had stock in this or that. Actually, she probably did. Mother. She would smirk and say what bums men were, yet she always seemed to be in the market. I wondered how long before James would fall out of favor and end up on her compost heap.

I didn't want to think about EPTs or that whole mess. Clearly, if I were pregnant, I would be a single parent. I'd never see a nickel of support from George. The man couldn't even take care of a dirty toothbrush. Besides, I felt too empty to be pregnant. There was nothing there, inside. Just a bunch of laboring organs, pumping, pulsating, processing, inflating, deflating, filling, emptying. All working from instructions from some corner of the brain that somehow—really it was a wonder—orchestrated the whole thing, usually without a hitch. It was all impulsive, reflexive, and completely taken for granted.

* * *

I got my life back in order. Well, that wasn't entirely correct. I cleaned and straightened out the cabin. The plows cleared the snow on my street and eventually the wrecker arrived and gave the Subaru a jump. Woofie and I took a ride into town, searching for life. Things were getting back to normal, though huge piles of snow loomed along the streets, blocking visibility and burying mailboxes. An end loader worked on Main Street, its bucket consuming large bites of snow and depositing them into a dump truck. At least there would be plenty of snow for the igloo contest. I sighed. That damn igloo contest. If I could just get *that* out of my life. A person was dead, another in jail, and George had run off with another woman. The latter incident may not have been directly attributed to the igloo contest, but it just put the icing on the cake. Or maybe Mother was the icing. My cake was loaded with icing.

After consuming an enormous western omelet at The Copper Kettle, I headed into my office at the 4Cs. After the trashcan attack, I decided Woofie should stay with me whenever possible. Classes at the university had been cancelled for the day, and faculty and staff were not required to go in, but I needed the diversion. My office felt unfamiliar and remote, as if occupied by some spectral force. Same desk, same chair, and same damn blinking red light on my phone indicating I had messages.

Woofie spent several minutes sniffing the premises and seemed especially interested in the leg of my office chair.

"Don't even think about it, buster," I said.

He jumped up on my sagging guest chair, made a couple of circles and plunked down. He seemed to be staring at me through the veil of hair, though one could not be certain.

I put my phone on speaker and started cueing up the messages. All were old and pre-dated the snowstorm.

Message number one: no message.

Message number two: "Hey Janese, this is Walt." Walt was on the Igloo Committee. "When you get in, we need to talk about this igloo contest. I guess a big snowstorm is coming, so maybe no school, but we still need to talk. Things are getting a little out of hand. The president called me at home, for God's sake. Said we need to do something about the image. What the hell? Call me."

He left a cell phone number. Since the message was several days old, I figured Walt had things smoothed over. After all, it was *his* job as community relations director to make things good. That's why he got the big bucks.

Message number three was recorded at 6:32 p.m. on the day that George was supposed to meet the woman from the magazine—the day he disappeared.

There was a bit of dead air, then: "By the time you hear this message, I expect you'll wonder where George is." The connection was terrible, such as from a cell phone. Soft laughter—female? "I imagine James will be back to get that fancy car out of your garage. Soon, I hope, I do miss him."

Female, definitely a woman. Husky, maybe trying to disguise her voice. The caller log said *unavailable*.

A prickly chill washed over my scalp. I swear my hair levitated. I looked over at Woofie, whose head had popped up. He emitted a low growl, jumped off the hair and pressed up against my legs.

110

Who was protecting whom?

George missing and she knew why. If she were The Other Woman, why would she bother to call and flaunt it? And how did James fit in? She knew his car was in my garage, and she knew where I lived. No big deal, really. Everyone knew where I lived. Had this person been watching me? *Watched.* There had been menace and mockery in the woman's voice. I picked up the phone and called Bertie but got her voice mail. I decided not to leave a message just yet.

The studio. Maybe there would be a clue in the studio. I looked at Woofie. "I'm Sherlock Holmes. You wanna be my Watson and we can go look for clues?"

Woofie's tail thumped enthusiastically. A fine pair of sleuths.

* * *

The Community Center was deserted and locked up. I used my master key and Woofie and I entered the darkened gallery. He went to an abstract sculpture displayed in the atrium and sniffed the base. The sculpture had been a student's final exam project and because it weighed about 200 pounds, the student decided to put it on extended loan to the Community Center. I always thought it looked like a giant alabaster phallic symbol. It was entitled "cigar." The end did look a little like an ash ready to fall. The thing bugged me.

Woofie and I moved through the gallery and upstairs to the studios. Again, the master key gained me entrance, this time into the pottery studio. I flicked on the lights and waited for the clues to present themselves. Clue one: the phone had a red message light. Clue two: though potter's wheels pretty much all looked alike to me, there was no mistaking George's—the name LeFleur emblazoned on it—sitting in the corner, along with his stool, and canvas bags of mysterious materials that I assumed were essential in the creation of his pottery. Talk about a V8 moment. I could have slapped my forehead with the enlightenment or, in a more Holmes-like manner shouted *aha*! I looked at Woofie.

"Elementary, my dear Watson."

I had always wanted to say that. Woofie was unimpressed. He went to George's wheel, sniffed it, and growled. They say dogs were good judges of character, but this was only an object of George's, not the man himself. Probably Woofie didn't like the slimy, earthy smell.

To say one's heart leaps is not only a cliché, but also anatomically unlikely. Assuredly, however, my heart pulsed in my ears—thudding so hard it drowned out the clicking of Woofie's toenails on the wooden floor. An epiphany blurred my vision and made me light-headed. Okay, *fool*, so George had moved his stuff here, which was logical. Even though he had access to a classroom wheel, he likely preferred his own. I had helped him store it in the loft closet and it I had jumped feet first to a scandalous conclusion when I discovered the empty closet. Of course I should have realized that he would eventually move it to the studio, especially with Mother's vague estimated time of departure. And, of course, he didn't discuss it with me, but that was vintage George. My heart settled back to a normal rhythm. George was gone, but he hadn't *left*.

Back to clue one: George's voice mail messages. It was no problem breaking the code into his mailbox, since George always used the numerical password of 911. I hit the jackpot on the first message.

Hey, Mr. LeFleur. Desiree here from The Potter's Wheel. I made it into town, but I'm stuck here in some parking lot at the college, um lot number three. Could you and I meet—

The message ended, probably because George had dashed to the phone and managed to pick up. There were advantages to old phones like the one in the studio—you could still pick up when someone was leaving a message. The next three messages were from me, the pitch becoming shriller with the growing urgency of each call.

Lot C. That was the commuter lot, which was stuck way out at the edge of campus. It was remote and not visible from the main road. What the hell would she have been doing there? I called Bertie again on her cell.

"Yeah?" Sleepy-sounding and hostile.

"Bertie, we need to go to Lot C!"

"Who th' hell is this? Janese?"

"Yeah, the woman, she left a nasty message on my machine about George being missing and about James's car. It's in my garage, you know. Then on George's machine there's a message to meet in Lot C—it's a commuter lot on—"

"Where are you, Janese? Have you been drinking?"

I calmed myself and reiterated the phone messages and the location of Lot C, this time with a bit more coherence.

* * *

Snow removal machinery growled and grumbled around Lot C, systematically removing the snow and piling it in dump trucks, which would empty their loads into the Portage Canal. It would take Bertie at least twenty minutes to throw on some clothes and get there. I felt the thrumming again in my ears. There it was. I was sure of it. *Her* car—the only one in the lot, buried under a thick mantle of snow. I would have bet my meager 4Cs paycheck that it was hers—that Desiree someone—whatever her real name was. I debated whether or not to start knocking the snow off the car but decided I might be damaging a crime scene. I turned to Woofie who was watching a big yellow front loader eat its way through a snowbank.

"So, my dear Watson, where do you suppose the suspect is?"

Woofie, apparently, had no clue. And the larger more disturbing question: where was George? Surely, he wasn't running around without clothes. Holed up somewhere, waiting for help? Waiting for me? Hoping that I would ride in my aging Subaru, like a fractured fairy tale, and rescue him.

Bertie drove up and jumped out of her car. She had her two boys with her along with several extra kids. Woofie went berserk, whirling around like a dervish. I heard a cracking noise as Wolfie tried to crawl up on the dashboard to see out of the windshield. After I managed to get the door open to release the crazed dog, I noticed that the air vent on the dashboard had been broken out and lay in pieces on the floor. Once released, Woofie plunged into the cluster of children who shrieked with glee. They rolled around in the snow while the dog lathered them with slobber.

"My neighbor was watching Jeffie and Robby while I slept," Bertie said. "I figured she needed a break from hers *and* mine, so I went and collected them and loaded them up. God, I hate snow days. Anyway, I figured you'd bring Woofie and they could entertain each other."

"I guess I should give him back—Woofie," I said.

"Nah, you can keep him on loan for a while longer. The boys think it's great he's protecting their Auntie Janese. They have written a short, illustrated novel entitled *Woofie the Wonder Dog*."

"Well, I must admit we make a good crime-solving team."

"Sure," Bertie said. "So, how come you didn't start cleaning off the car? I need to see the plate and run it," Bertie asked.

"I didn't want to tamper with the evidence," I said.

"Right. Start cleaning," she said.

The vehicle emerged as a white Ford sedan. The plate came back as a rental from a place called Econo Cars located in Duluth, Minnesota. After the police dispatch called the rental place, they found it was past due for return and presumed abandoned or stolen. The credit card used by the woman who rented it went through at first then turned out to be lost or stolen. Its legitimate owner was an elderly woman named Mazie Wilson who resided in the Elder Years Nursing Home of Duluth.

The kids were yelling at each other playing a game, which involved pelting one another with snowballs and trying to overrun each other's forts. Woofie barked joyously, lumbering from one encampment to the other.

"Woofie wants to show no allegiance to either side, so he's working to encourage both. Hey! Take it easy on Robby! Hey Jeffie—help him up," Bertie shouted.

The child, Robby, had fallen. He writhed about, trapped in the bulky confines of his snowsuit. Woofie nosed Robby who wrapped his mittens around handfuls of dog hair and pulled himself up without human help.

"Yea!" shouted another boy. "The warrior is alive and ready for battle! Come Sir Robby, return to the castle and we shall plan our revenge!"

"Where do they get this stuff?" Bertie asked, shaking her head.

I smiled. Their imaginations that's where. These were amazing kids—collaborating on a novel, creating a reenactment from days of yore. I thought about the zombie-like youth wandering around the 4Cs campus, texting one another but never talking, music blaring in their ear buds. A spectacular sunset or soaring eagle would go unnoticed. Hell, a nuclear holocaust would go unnoticed. Bertie was adamant that her kids would not become tech addicts. Good luck, I thought.

Bertie checked out the inside of the sedan. No body parts, blood stains, mysterious hanks of hair, or loaded weapons were found. Bertie found a recent gas receipt from a BP. The identification number on it would enable them to track down which one. She also found petrified French fries, an empty cigarette package, a gum wrapper, and a dried-up ballpoint pen among the lint, grime, and crusty road salt ground into the floor mats.

"I think I'll have asshole Detective Burns come out from the crime lab and dust the thing. Typically, rentals have a zillion prints in them, but you never know," Bertie said.

Bertie stood up and arched her back, working out the kinks. "Hey, Trout, you realize I just got to sleep when you called?"

"Sorry," but I thought it was important.

She nodded.

"So, what are you thinking?" I asked.

"I'm thinking I smell something really fishy," she said. "We got two cars and no people. George is out there somewhere, *au naturel,* and this woman who doesn't really work for that potting magazine—"

"Pottery—potting would be gardening," I said.

"Whatever, I'm tired, okay? Anyway, she's missing, too. I want to listen to that phone call you got at work—I'm assuming from her—same person."

"Derry Parks," I said matter-of-factly.

"The one who skipped out on you in choir?" Bertie said.

"Yes, it's her—well I think. Okay, maybe not for everything. At least I don't think she was the one who attacked me, and I just don't know about Weasel Watkins, but she has something to do with George and James."

Bertie watched the kids demolish their snow forts. Woofie was watching too, or maybe he was sleeping.

"All right, Janese, we'll get the Parks waaa!" Bertie blurted as a snowball hit her in the back of the head.

"Robby did it!" shouted one of the boys.

"I'll get you all," Bertie replied, bending to scoop up a fist of snow. She paused and peered at something in the snow. "Well, hello," she said.

"Hello?" I said.

"Janese, take a step toward me."

"Okay, but—"

"In the fresh snow—where I can see the print," Bertie said.

I made a few prints in a fresh patch of snow.

"Janese—the print—it's like the one at the office when you were attacked. Did you wear these boots then? Did we think your prints belonged to the person who jumped you?"

I looked down at me feet. I was wearing the boots I'd bought at the Lutheran Church rummage sale. I explained to Bertie, who was now on her hands and knees looking at the impressions I had made, how I had come to own the boots *after* the attack in my office.

"Yup—lookie here. The chunk is missing from part of the tread," she said, ignoring a direct hit in the behind from a snowball.

"It could be a coincidence," I said, giving the evil eye to the older boy, who was looking far too innocent.

Bertie stood up. "Well sweetie, I'd bet my first born—WHO BETTER NOT THROW ANOTHER SNOWBALL IF HE KNOWS WHAT'S GOOD FOR HIM—that you picked up your assailant's boots at that church sale. Now we just have to find out who donated them, and we can put the thumbscrews to the bitch."

We stared at my feet as if the boots could tell their secret.

"And we'll get the Parks woman."

The choir warmed up before church on Sunday. Hannu was not pleased to find that James was still on hiatus. I assured Hannu that James would be back for the cantata. In fact, I had just spoken to Mother the night before, and she told me that the last color scheme painted at the resort would just have to do, as guests were arriving for the Christmas season. Mother felt she could leave things in the capable hands of her new manager for a few days so she could deliver James back to Moose Willow, TV 13, and the choir. They would arrive sometime next week. This gave me only a few days to come up with an explanation for George's disappearance. I would consider the truth—if I knew what it was.

I had warned Mother that a hairy dog was in residence. "We'll see," she had responded. That was her way of saying she may send the dog packing. I could feel a bit of adrenaline building in anticipation of a conflict. Woofie gave me something nobody else had—unconditional, slobbering love and devotion. I was grateful that Bertie and the boys had extended Woofie's loan to me and at the end of our rendezvous at the college parking lot, the pooch hopped happily into my car. Bertie had snapped up my rummage sale boots to take into the crime lab. Fortunately, I had a pair of backup sneakers in my car.

Bertie said the waffle tread of my boots was a match with the prints left by my attacker at the college. There was a piece of the sole missing from one of the boots and that cinched it. Nobody at the Lutheran Church remembered who donated the boots. According to the organizers, hundreds of items appeared in bags and boxes for weeks before the sale. No records were kept of donations and rarely did anyone request a receipt since non-cash donations were no longer worth fooling with at tax time. But why would anyone attack me? If it was the Parks woman, I had no idea what her problem was, unless it had to do with George. Or James. And then there was the meat locker debacle.

The whereabouts of Derry Parks a/k/a Desiree Pruce eluded Bertie. Parks obviously did not show up for choir practice and while this may have annoyed Hannu, it instilled an almost cheerfulness in Eleanor Heimlich. If Parks had any notion of reclaiming lead soprano, she would be eaten alive by Eleanor and neither Bertie nor I would have the opportunity to brace her for information on George's whereabouts. Why hadn't he tried to contact me? Didn't he wonder if I was pregnant? It had been her, I was sure, leaving the cryptic messages. She was screwing with me. Why?

These distractions cycled through my mind throughout the church service, obliterating the announcements, Gospel lesson, Epistle lesson, and sermon. I sang the choir anthem on autopilot. As I munched a cookie during the fellowship time afterward, our accompanist, Azinnia Wattles, plunked down next to me.

"Is your cookie burned?" she whispered.

"Huh?"

"My cookie is positively black on the bottom," Azinnia said, showing me.

"Um, mine's fine," I said, inspecting the bottom. "Maybe you should go get another one."

She put her cookie aside. "No, that would be rude. I'm just surprised that Agnes would serve burned cookies. I think she's upset ever since she had that—that thing in her yard."

"Thing? What thing?" I said, taking the bait. Azinnia didn't care about her burnt cookie. She had a story to tell.

"Oh! You haven't heard? I think you should know, since you live out there in her neck of the woods. Why in the good Lord's name she didn't move into town after Earl died, I have no idea, but there she is all by herself out in the boonies. Then this thing comes and pounds on her patio door or a window—I'm not sure—during that blizzard. I swear she turned gray overnight."

I chewed thoughtfully on my cookie. "During the blizzard?"

"Right, some *creature*," she said. "She called the police and they came and looked around. It had been blowing and drifting so much that there weren't any footprints or anything. And, of course, since Earl died, Agnes has been known to take a little sherry now and then. I ask you, who can blame her?"

"Not me," I said. No stones would be cast by me.

"So, they kind of patted her on the arm and told her she should get one of those neck pendant alert things to call for help. Now I tell you, what good is that? They're for when you fall and can't get up. Why, Agnes does that zombie class—"

"Zumba. I think it's a dance class called Zumba," I said.

"Zimba, Zumba, whatever. Anyway, she falls, she can get up. I don't care for the police thinking our Aggie is some dotty old woman."

"I agree. She's probably sharper than most of the college kids I run into."

I tuned out Azinnia, who prattled on about the injustices of growing old. I looked toward the refreshment table at Agnes, who was pouring coffee. A creature, knocking on her patio door or maybe a window, on the night of the blizzard? I thought about Woofie's great adventure into the snowstorm and the swatch of mysterious hair he came back with. I did see weird footprints. Maybe I should have called the police. Then there was the nonsense in the news about the two guys spotting something at their deer camp. Of course, that had probably been a bear. And Agnes did like her sherry. Still...

"If you'll excuse me, Azinnia, I'd like to chat with Agnes," I said.

"Oh, of course, dear. Maybe you could tell Aggie to call you or that fellow of yours—what's his name? Anyway, I think she saw something. She's a sharp cookie—even if she burns them."

The humor was not lost on me. I was pretty sure it was a smart cookie not a sharp cookie, though that made about as much sense. I worked my way into the unfamiliar territory of the church kitchen where Agnes was washing dishes.

"Need a hand?" I asked.

Agnes looked up, startled. She seemed to be trying to place me.

"Janese," I said. "We're actually fairly close neighbors."

"Of course, Janese. It's just that, well..."

"I know, I don't spend much time—well any time—helping in the kitchen," I said. I had once gone in there, but one of the church ladies had scolded me for putting a cup back in the cupboard with the handle facing to the left instead of the right—or maybe the other way around. She had explained that if the handles we lined up the same way, you could fit more cups in the cupboard. Even though half the cupboards were empty, this was apparently important. Though I have been accused of being OC, I never worried about coffee cup handles.

I picked up a dish towel and began drying silverware.

"Well, it's nice to have the help," Agnes said. "Thank you. I know some of the women can be fussy. I'm not one of them. Life's too short."

"Glad to hear it," I said, as I tossed silverware into the drawer. It was supposed to be neatly nested. Someone would need therapy after seeing the Janese Trout method of silverware storage.

119

"So, Agnes—"

"Please, call me Aggie. I *hate* Agnes," she said.

"Right, Aggie, I understand that you had a visitor on the night of the blizzard. I want you to know that I believe you," I said.

Aggie stopped washing. Her shoulders slumped. "Really? Why?"

"Because, Aggie, I think that thing was around my place, too."

Aggie stopped, looked around, and turned to me. "Janese, dear, why don't you come to my place for a cup of tea later today? I sure would enjoy that."

"It's a date," I said. I thought about Woofie. He had been left unsupervised while I was at church, and I didn't want to cause a doggie meltdown with more abandonment. "Oh, a favor?"

"Yes?"

"Could I bring my dog? I must warn you, he's very hairy."

Aggie's face lit up. "I love dogs, hair and all! Please bring him."

* * *

Mother was predictably unpredictable. She had told me she would arrive "sometime next week," which apparently meant Sunday afternoon. Technically Sunday is the first day of the week. According to the Bible, after God created heaven and earth, flora and fauna, pests and pestilence, He got the day off: Sunday. This makes Sunday seem like the end, but it is actually the beginning. Therefore, in spite of us saying "have a good weekend," as we leave our offices at 5:00 p.m. on Friday, we are really saying have a good weekend AND week beginning. This is just one of those biblical enigmas to deal with, unless you are Jewish or a Seventh Day Adventist, who get their worshiping done on Saturday.

Anyway, Mother, who was no slave to these concerns, decided to "surprise" me. Her car was in the driveway as I arrived home from church, which did not please me. However, James' car was no longer sequestered in my garage, which did please me.

"Mother! What are you doing here?"

"Hello to you too, dear."

She was sitting on the sofa, sipping tea. She let out a dainty sneeze.

"I put that beast in the bedroom," she said. "I mean, Janese, how could you?"

Frantic scratching and howling came from the vicinity of the bedroom door.

"I'm taking care of him for Bertie," I said.

"Well, it must go."

I didn't answer, hoping for the ultimatum "or I go," but it wasn't forthcoming.

A large cardboard box sat next to the sofa. The box had a picture of a white, gaudy Christmas tree on the label.

"Where is George?" Mother asked.

Whining and scratching. I would have to refinish the whole door by the time Woofie was sprung from prison.

"Where's James?" I countered. "And what's in the box and why is it in my living room?"

"I am not allowed to disclose James' whereabouts," Mother said. She gave a haughty sniff. "Let us just say that he is safe and will be returning to work tomorrow. The box, which I managed to drag in without any help, obviously contains a Christmas tree."

"I always get a live tree," I said. "I cut one down in the woods and it's really fresh that way."

Mother huffed. "Now Janice, you know I'm allergic. If you must get a live tree, you'll have to put it on the porch. This designer tree will be perfect over there next to the fireplace." She gave another dainty sneeze. "Where did you say George was?"

Mother won all her battles by being persistent to the point where merchants gave her free stuff, just to get her out of the store. Her auto mechanic wrote off any repair costs for her car rather than argue with her about how the funny noise started after the last oil change. In restaurants, Mother would return her food so many times that her dining companions, if she could find anybody to actually go with her, would be done eating and home watching television before she received a satisfactory meal. On the other hand, while Mother expected nothing less than perfection from her employees at her resort, she also compensated them well and gave them regular bonuses and recognition for their sterling performance. I, as her only child, defective at birth, and further subjected to impossible scrutiny throughout life, received no bonuses, metaphorical or otherwise, and rarely won a volleying match with Mother.

I had worked up what I believed to be a fairly viable story to explain George's absence. It would do no good to tell her that he was either a cheating bastard or that I had simply misplaced him. I didn't want to think about the unthinkable. Any of these scenarios would only reinforce her conviction that men were rarely worth the trouble. I had a feeling James had fallen a bit out of favor with Maddie the manslayer. She gave me a look.

"Well, where is he?" she demanded.

"Um, George went to an artist's conference in Duluth, and then he's doing some kind of a workshop for a while." Damn. Too fast and too pat.

Mother gave me an odd look, snorted and asked: "Do you know who *she* is, Janese?"

"I don't know what you mean," I lied.

Mother snorted again. Woofie howled. I got up and opened the bedroom door. He bounded across the living room, screeching to a halt at Mother's feet. She held her teacup in the air to avoid spillage.

"C'mon boy, let's go out!" I said.

Woofie lumbered over to the door. I slipped on my boots and snapped on his leash. This would give me time to gather my wits. Mostly it gave me time to experience hypothermia while Woofie searched for the perfect spot. He burrowed his snout into deer footprints, snuffling each one individually. Next he inspected a bright yellow spot, which apparently held little interest. After thorough inspection of a fresh pile of deer feces, Woofie lifted his leg then humped over producing a kind of two-in-one voiding exercise. I shivered, holding morosely to the end of the leash. I still had no idea what to tell Mother. Then I remembered I was supposed to go visit Aggie to discuss the *creature*. Perfect!

≈ 15 ≈

While Woofie prowled and I shivered, I mulled over the growing pile of questions that surrounded me. First, of course, where was George? And now James was supposedly ensconced somewhere "safe." I wondered if he returned to his luxury cabin in the woods, or perhaps was holed up in a hotel suite somewhere. I didn't think he was back at Mother's resort. Clearly an iceberg had sprouted between James and Mother.

Woofie, true to his name, began making soft woofing noises. The fringe of hair covering his face puffed out with each *ooof*. In spite of his veil of hair, he was looking up a tree, ooofing. A red squirrel scolded from a branch above the dog, its tail twitching with each reprimand.

And, of course, there were other looming personal questions about the likelihood of pregnancy and the situation had that started it all: Weasel Watkins and the meat locker death. I didn't think for a minute that Bucky Tanner intentionally caused his demise. Somehow, except for the question of potential motherhood, many of the pieces seemed to tie into Derry Parks, but I was too muddled to unknot the mess.

I headed back into the house and saw Mother's flame-red hair moving about in the loft.

I released Woofie and he bounded up to join Mother, who sneezed dramatically.

I trudged up after the dog. Mother's suitcase lay open on the futon, neatly folded clothing arranged in various piles next to it.

"What's going on?" I asked.

"I would think that would be obvious," she said, making a show of stifling a sneeze.

Woofie sat next to Mother and leaned against her.

"Honestly, why are they always attracted to people who don't want them around?" Mother said. I think her statement was a double entendre.

Woofie began licking Mother's shoes.

"He's trying to win you over, I guess," I said.

"Well, typical male," she said.

Ooof

"Anyway, you just got here. And besides Woofie—who is only here temporarily—what's the rush?" I said.

"Don't mention that *name* around me, Janese."

"Huh? Oh, James Rush?" I said.

"You see, I had to bring James back and I thought I'd stay a bit since the new manager seems to have things well in hand. But maybe I should just head back to the inn. Though I dread the drive." She stopped packing a moment, looking down at her hands. A tear slid down her face and she quickly wiped it away.

"Mother?"

"Oh Janese, I made such a fool of myself. Why do I always do that with men?"

"You're asking me? Mother, what happened?"

"I caught him putting the moves on one of the housekeepers at the resort. She is just a college kid trying to make some extra money. He is slime! I can't let these things go on under my nose! It's indecent. I won't have it. We came back here and James picked up his car and I don't care where he is, but I hope he's cold and miserable and freezes his balls off."

I was shocked. I'd never heard Mother say anything so crude. There was a reason why James had been married many times. While I was relieved that Mother was shed of him, I was thoroughly pissed at the philanderer.

Mother took a deep breath and said, "Darling, I should be asking you about things." She gave me a steady look. "I, er, saw the *box* you had hidden in the hamper. Are you preggies?"

"Am I wha...oh, well I don't think, um." Leave it to Mother to quickly turn the tables. I looked down at my stomach, as if it would provide an answer. Of course, all it told me was that the burnt cookie from after church had worn off and I was starved.

"Let me know if you want to talk," Mother said as she studied the piles of clothes arranged around her suitcase. She picked up a blouse and scrutinized it. "Do you think this is outdated?"

Then I remembered. Church. Aggie. Tea.

"Shit!"

Mother started, dropping a blouse on the floor, which Woofie immediately picked up and then ran off.

"My blouse!"

"Woofie, give it back," I shouted, chasing after him with Mother on my heels. I caught him at the bottom of the stairs. He turned to face me, tail thumping wildly against a nearby end table.

"Give me the blouse, Woofie. Good boy, give Auntie Janese the blouse."

Woofie emitted a playful growl and rotated his tail like a helicopter blade.

"DROP IT!" Mother commanded.

Woofie spat out the blouse and tucked his tail between his legs. He let out a small whimper. I remembered that voice—it was not to be trifled with. When Mother reached the bottom of the stairs, Woofie slunk over to her to offer penance. She picked up the blouse and sneezed.

"This will never do. It will have to go to Goodwill. There's a tooth mark, a *hole*. Goodwill won't even want it." She sighed and tossed it back at Woofie, who snatched it up and bounded with glee around the living room.

Mother and I looked at each other, both with questions, both with secrets. Typically, *she* would have her way with me—extracting secrets like festering slivers needing to come out. Best tactic was to change course. I figured by now Aggie was waiting for me.

"Mother, would you like to go have tea with me at a friend's house?"

Mother gave me a strange look. "Tea? You?"

"Sure, a church lady friend, and I'm late."

Mother arched an eyebrow. "Really? A church lady?"

"Sure, um, you remember Agnes whatsername? She recently lost her husband and, ah—"

"Why Janese, I'm proud of you. For once you're thinking of someone besides yourself."

Of course, that wasn't true. Aggie and I were going to discuss our similar sightings of the alleged Yooper Bigfoot. Mother would declare it to be poppycock—or would she? I had a sudden lapse of good judgment, I blurted out: "Mother, I think you should stay. I NEED you."

She had her back to me, heading up the stairs. She paused, turned, and gave me the strangest look. "Why, of course you do, dear. I'm here for you as long as you need me."

Oh Lord, what had I done?

125

Oooff oooff. Woofie shot past Mother, up the stairs, with the now severely shredded blouse dangling from beneath his mop face.

Mother sneezed.

* * *

"Why, I was getting worried, Janese! Maddie, how good to see you again!" Aggie said, standing at her front door to let us in. She held a bulky cardigan sweater around her. Mother, Woofie, *sans* blouse, and I entered a pleasantly warm sitting room. A cheery fire crackled in the fireplace. A silver tea service sat elegantly on a polished coffee table in the middle of the room. Delicate teacups with dainty floral patterns were arranged around the tea service. Soft, comfy chairs and a couch surrounded the table. Every piece of furniture was covered with multiple doilies: white, yellow, pink, blue, rainbow.

"Aggie, I hope it's okay that I brought my mother—you two know each other, of course. Mother is visiting me."

"Why of course. How are you Maddie? I was hoping you would be in church today so we could chat. Now we can chat over some tea and I've also got a few cookies left from today's fellowship. I'm afraid they are a bit scorched. I think my oven is on the fritz."

"Why this is just lovely," Mother said. "I've thought about having a proper tea at The Straights—my resort—but wonder if it would be appreciated. Thank you, Aggie, for having us. Woofie, NO!"

Woofie was poised to snatch a cookie off the coffee table. He backed off quickly, sat and portrayed the epitome of obedience. If for no other reason, I should keep Mother around to control the beast!

After we had all settled into pillowy cushions, teacups balanced on our knees, an awkward silence moved in. I was debating on how to bring up Aggie's creature sighting, without drawing scorn from Mother. As it turns out, Mother broke the ice.

"Aggie dear, do you crochet these doilies?" she said. "They are positively stunning." Mother picked one up off the arm of her chair and studied it. "My, the intricate work in these is astounding. You should consider selling on eBay."

"E what? Oh, I know what you're talking about. My nephew sold some of my departed Earl's things that way. Fetched a nice price too! I was able to pay off the roof loan and some other debts. They're not crocheted—it's called tatting. I just make them for my own use, and gifts, craft shows, and of course the church bazaar. I don't just make doilies you know. I also make ornaments, baby bonnets, and other things. I tatted this collar on my sweater, for example."

126

Mother and I simultaneously looked at Aggie's sweater collar. Sure enough, it was edged with lace.

"Very nice," Mother said. "I'm afraid neither Janese nor I have much skill in the domestic crafts."

"And it is becoming a lost art, I'm afraid. Tatting, crocheting, knitting, even sewing. Young ladies no longer consider it worth their time. Much too busy doing the face-looking, staring at their little computer screens. And don't even get me going on the tattoos and piercings. Work of the devil, you ask me."

Aggie sighed and took a sip of tea. We all took a sip of tea.

"Facebook, not facelook," Mother said. "It's all the rage. That and texting. Why, I've seen teenagers sitting at the table in the resort restaurant texting each other, playing games, and taking pictures of their food. They ignore everyone. They never even look at the beautiful view outdoors."

Everyone sighed and took another sip of tea. I reached for a cookie. I still hadn't had a proper lunch. It crunched loudly, crumbs scattering. Woofie sprang to life and quickly vacuumed up the mess. It was time to move from tatting and tattoos to other more important things. I cleared my throat.

"Um, so Aggie. We were having a little chat in church and you were telling me about an odd, well, visitor the other night—the night of the blizzard?"

Aggie refilled our cups. She took a dainty sip, peering at us over the rim of her cup. Mother cocked her head at me, then Aggie. Woofie continued to patrol the floor.

"Janese," Mother said, "did you and George have a prowler while James and I were gone?"

"Yes, Mother. I didn't want to alarm you, but during a blizzard something was prowling outside the cabin and when I let Woofie out—"

"You let the dog out in a blizzard?" Mother interrupted.

"Well, he had to go then he just took off. Anyway, he eventually came back with—"

"You mean he ran away. Oh Janese, I don't care for dogs, but that seems terribly irresponsible of you."

"Yes, well, whatever, that's not the point. It was an accident and all turned out fine. Anyway—"

"Maddie dear, it visited me too," Aggie interrupted. Bless her.

"Janese and I decided we needed to, well, compare notes and figure out what came around that night of the blizzard. People think I'm a dotty old woman, but when I saw that, that—thing, I called the cops. They patted me on the head and asked if I forgot to take my medication or had been hitting the sherry. The nerve! I saw it clear as I'm seeing you two. Anyway, the curtains on the patio door don't shut all the way. I heard knocking coming from the door. When I looked over there, I saw its face in the gap of the curtains, pressed against the glass and it began *pounding* on the door, as if it wanted to get in. I swear on a stack of Bibles. And when I heard that Janese saw it too!"

"Well, I never saw it—"

Mother's head swiveled from Aggie to me. "Saw *what*?"

"Why, the Yooper Bigfoot, of course," Aggie said, picking up a cookie.

Mother nearly spat out her tea but managed to swallow. She choked a little, coughing. I reached over and patted her on the back.

"As I was saying, I didn't see it but Woofie came back with a patch of some kind of mysterious animal fur in his jaw," I said. "Bertie looked at it and—"

"Bertie?" Mother interrupted. "Your old school chum—Alberta, or Bertha or—"

"Roberta," I corrected.

Aggie said, "Why she's our feisty little gal State Trooper is what she is. When I was lunch lady at the school I got to know her. She was a pip, let me tell you. That little miss didn't take any grief. Smart as a whip too! Straight As."

I said, "*Anyway*, Bertie determined it was tanned fur—not fresh off an animal. More like maybe from a coat or fur hat or something."

Aggie frowned and looked into her teacup. "Then I guess it wasn't a chunk off any Bigfoot, if it was tanned."

I said, "But I saw footprints, Aggie. Big ones, and shaped like, I don't know maybe an oversized bear or something. But bears should be hibernating by now, or at least not out in a snowstorm. Besides the footprints were rectangle, not oblong. And unfortunately they got covered up by the snow very quickly."

Mother sat with her mouth hanging open, teacup poised mid-air.

"And here's another interesting fact," Aggie said. "When I went out to Earl's workshop the next day—well it was his workshop, God rest his soul, but now I store some fruits and vegetables there. Anyway, I went out to get some rutabagas and something seemed, well, out of place. I'm positive that some of the apples were gone, and I could swear I smelled something very musty."

128

"They say the Yooper Bigfoot has a musky odor," I offered.

"Yes, well, musty is close to musky," Agnes continued. "But here's what is really odd. It was warm in there. Much warmer than it should have been. My Earl had an electric heater installed and I think it had been running. I do sometimes turn it on very low to keep things from freezing, but didn't remember turning it on so I checked, in case I may have done it subconsciously. But it was clearly turned completely off, so why was it warm?"

"Are their neighbor children who could be trespassing?" Mother asked.

"Well, I suppose. I don't keep it locked, but I guess I should. It's just an old shed. I'm not even sure it has a lock."

"Would a Bigfoot be smart enough to turn on a heater?" I said.

"Well, it might," Agnes said. "They are a humanoid and more intelligent that people may think. I've been reading up. Anyway, I tell you, *something* was out there. There have been rumors for years about a Yooper Bigfoot. Lots of sightings. Maybe there's a whole batch of them, like an extended family. I'm telling you both that I'm getting an alarm system installed this month. I have a little insurance money left from Earl's policy and I'm going to put it to good use." She took a chomp off her cookie. Woofie rushed over to clean up. "And I have a shotgun and I'm not afraid to use it. That's how I ran the thing off the night of the blizzard!"

"You shot at it?" I said.

"You betcha I did. Don't know if I hit the thing, but it took off. I really don't want to hurt anything, but I learned from my Earl how to defend myself. A widow woman can't be too careful; I keep the thing loaded."

Aggie nodded toward the front door where a previously unnoticed shotgun sat in the umbrella stand. We all looked at it. Mother hadn't blinked for several minutes. Her temporary paralysis faded and she slowly looked at me. "So where was George—that night—the night of the creature? I called you. You said he was there."

Busted.

"Well, see, here's the thing about George," I began.

"Men!" Mother spouted. "He left because you're preggies, didn't he?"

This time Aggie choked on her tea and dropped her cookie.

Woofie cleaned up.

≈ 16 ≈

Our drive home from Aggie's was painfully silent, except for the snuffled breathing of Woofie from the back seat. While Mother sneezed periodically, she put on a stoic front, not complaining about dog dander or other irritants. Problem was, Mother had hit a nerve about the potential of my being pregnant and the timing of George's disappearance. Still, he had to come back to the studio at some point, didn't he? He would not leave his pottery wheel and other things behind. And what if he were hurt or lost somewhere? Perhaps he had amnesia and was wandering around, lost and frightened. Or frozen, more likely.

Who was I kidding? In spite of popping up regularly in soap operas, amnesia was pretty rare. Still, if George and the Parks woman had run off, what did they run off in? Clearly the abandoned rental vehicle in Lot C was hers and George's truck, also abandoned, was now impounded at the police department pending an investigation into any foul play. Maybe she had several vehicles, which she rented with stolen credit cards. It was so easy for crooks to get hold of people's credit and debit card info; even have new plastic made. It had happened to me; a disaster that took weeks to straighten out. Good thing I had $100 cash in my underwear drawer.

So, Mother, the snoop, had found the pregnancy test. I knew she was *dying* to know the results. For that matter, so was I. It did give me a bit of pleasure to let her stew. I wouldn't tell her that like so many things in my life, I screwed up the test—well tests—and still had no idea as to my maternal status. I didn't *feel* pregnant. Okay, maybe a little queasy. And tired. And cranky. But with everything going on, who wouldn't be?

Woofie broke the silence with a noisy fart then he let out a little yip of surprise—or maybe an apology.

"Well, I never—" Mother said, vigorously waving her hand. I hit all four window buttons and let the frigid air waft through the car. We suddenly burst out laughing as snow swirled through the open windows. Woofie, impervious to the cold, stuck his head out his window, his mop of hair streaming in the breeze. Leave it to an 80-pound walking carpet to lighten the mood. I was still thoroughly pissed

130

at Mother for bringing up the pregnancy question in front of Aggie. The speculation of my "condition" had just started to fade from when I'd fainted in church and now it was infused with new life that would set the village rumor mill into full grinding mode. We pulled into the driveway and flung open the doors to clear out the lingering odor. I still couldn't pull into the garage since Mother delegated it for her la-de-da BMW.

We piled out of my car, with Woofie making a pit stop on a snowbank already pocked with yellow pee marks. Once in the house, ever hopeful, I checked the answering machine. Nada.

"I'm exhausted," Mother said. "Perhaps you can make dinner, Janese, while I lie down." She started up the stairs with Woofie on her heels.

"Go on, now, shooo!" Mother said then she sneezed. "Honestly, how long will this beast be staying here?" Woofie, undeterred, lumbered up the stairs ahead of her.

"Oh, just a few more days," I said, stifling a snicker. "I'm thinking about getting a dog of my own, though, once Bertie takes Woofie home."

"Oh for heaven's sake!" Mother said. "Now see here, Wolf or whatever your name is, get off the bed this instant."

"I think a big dog is the way to go," I continued. "While the terriers are cute and all, you can't beat the protection of, say, one of those Mastiff dogs, or maybe a Rottweiler. Or even a mix of the two!"

"I said DOWN!"

I heard a loud thud and then I believe Mother muttered something like "that's a good boy." Rare praise indeed. Clearly, Woofie was smitten with Mother and how could she not be flattered by a dog that worshiped her?

I opened the fridge to review dinner options. I was delighted to discover that there was some white zinfandel left in the wine box. I grabbed a glass and pulled the little spigot, watching the pretty pink liquid dribble in.

Just as I was poised to take a nice, healthy swig Mother yelled from afar, "Now Janese no alcohol if you're—you know. Of course, that is if you are, or think you are. Just thought I should mention."

Very clever, Mother. How did she know I was getting wine? Had she installed hidden cameras throughout the house? I took rebellious small sip and sighed. There was no getting it back in the box, so I dumped it. I could never live with the guilt if I had a child with an extra thumbnail or missing an earlobe because I drank too much wine.

Back to the fridge inventory. There was still lasagna, somewhat worse for wear but surely edible. I added some fresh shredded cheese on top, turned on the oven, and stuck it in. The crisper drawer revealed a semi-brown head of lettuce, a slimy cucumber, and some carrots. I threw the cucumber away and trimmed the brown off the lettuce, then broke it up into chunks and threw into a plastic bowl. Next I chopped some carrots and added them. It was a pathetic salad. After rummaging around in my "baking" cupboard, I found some sunflower seeds and raisins, which I added. Now it was looking a little more appealing. I stuck the salad back in the fridge and gave a yearning look at the box of wine. Salad dressing choices were limited to ranch. Mother would want something like raspberry vinaigrette or balsamic with toasted pine nuts or some damn concoction. Too bad. The final part of the meal would be garlic toast made with two heels of bread, smeared with butter, and sprinkled with garlic salt. I would stick it under the broiler at the last minute and try not to burn it.

After setting the table I turned on some music and, stupidly, checked the answering machine again. I picked up the phone and listened to the dial tone. I got my cell out and turned it on. One bar. Low Battery. No messages. I left it on, just in case, and plugged it in. Next I wandered outside, hugging my sweater around me. My Subaru sat stoically in the driveway. A light snow had begun to fall. No traffic on the street, no snow machines whining in the distance, no bird tweets or squirrel chattering; they were all tucked away for the night.

Back inside, the lasagna was beginning to fill the cabin with a nice garlicky aroma. I checked and it still wasn't bubbly. The kitchen activity was enough to draw Woofie away from Mother and he shambled into the kitchen. I assumed he was looking at me with soulful eyes, though it was hard to see much beneath the tangle of fringe. I gave him a bowl of dog kibbles, fresh water, and added a couple of chunks of cheese to the kibble, which he seemed to appreciate. After his doggie repast, I put on my coat and boots, snapped on his leash, and took him out for a walk around the cabin. Nightfall was closing in quickly and one by one, objects were smudged out by darkness. Woofie took his time, seemingly unconcerned about the cold, dark woods and the yip of coyotes giving chase to some hapless creature in the distance. Myself, I wished I had brought a flashlight. And maybe a gun.

The snap of a twig. Woofie gave a low, menacing growl. More snaps and cracks: closer. I stopped, frozen. Woofie tugged on the leash, pulling toward the darkness of the woods.

I thought I heard a muffled human-like voice, yelling something. Do Bigfoots have human-sounding voices? Now it crashed through the woods, moving fast. I heard more yipping. Coyotes nearer. Woofie exploded into full canine hysteria, howling and pulling against the leash so hard that he jerked me face down into a snowdrift. He dragged me for a while, until the leash slipped out of my hands, and he shot away into the woods.

"Woofie! Come back!" I screamed. "WOOFIE!" I clambered to my feet and continued to shout for him at the top of my lungs. Ferocious canine noises filled the air, primal and savage. Then a scream that turned my blood to ice. Whatever was being chased continued to crash through the darkness. I could hear but could see nothing. Blessedly, the driveway lights came on. Mother charged outside in her bathrobe and boots, brandishing the fireplace poker. Just then, something large, hairy, and creature-like burst into a pool of light in the driveway coming straight for me, with Woofie on its tail. Mother stepped forward, swung the poker and made a direct hit to the creature's head. It staggered and uttered a very humanoid F-bomb then crumpled to the ground. Woofie leapt through the air and landed on the beast, which emitted a soft whooshing noise, like air escaping a seat cushion.

Woofie was having a go at the creature's fur, tearing out chunks and flinging them around. Mother still clutched the poker, poised and ready to strike again. The yips of the coyotes faded off into the distance. With his prey subdued, Woofie's enthusiasm began to wane. I was still rasping for breath when the creature made another noise. More of a moan. A trickle of blood began to pool around its head.

"I—I think I might have killed it," Mother said. "I've never killed anything. Well, okay maybe those ants. You know, they get in everything. And I did have to use mouse poison once. I hated doing it though. But other than that, and eating meat, I don't kill things. I'm not a killer. Can you go to prison for killing a creature? It as self-defense, right? It was after you, Janese, my baby!"

She lowered the poker and sniffed loudly.

"It's okay, Mother. It's moving. It's still alive." Mother raised the poker as I took a cautious step closer. With what could only be described as incredible courage, I bent over to take a closer look. It moaned as I gently turned its face to the light.

"Ohmygod!" I said. "Call 911!"

* * *

The great thing about living in a small town is that when sitting in the emergency room at Moose Willow Memorial Hospital, you see familiar faces, which was mildly reassuring. I knew the EMTs who arrived with the ambulance. I went to high school with one of the ER nurses and the only other occupant in the waiting room, besides my group, was Frannie Loop, a woman from my church whom I also went to school with. She was Frannie Hulkinen then. We called her The Hulk. She could throw a mean softball. She wasn't fat, just bulky. Even the cliquey mean girls showed her respect. Frannie's son was having his arm X-rayed for a facture, which he sustained while monkeying around with a piece of cardboard and a snowbank.

It was a little like a mini reunion, though the atmosphere was subdued.

While the legend of a Yooper Bigfoot was at least partially dispelled—drunken hunting camp stories notwithstanding—why George was running around the woods wearing a bearskin rug with only boxer shorts underneath and had various animal skins taped to his feet with duct tape remained a mystery. The two EMTs, Buzzy and Bonnie Winfield, were a husband/wife team that owned and operated Superior Ambulance. When they examined George at the scene, they said he was alive though unconscious and his pupils were dilated. I knew, from watching doctor drama shows on television, that this was not a good sign. He was breathing just fine, though. And his heartrate came down after a bit. I had watched in horror as they strapped him to a board and stabilized his neck in case Mother snapped a vertebra or two along with cracking his skull. While the bleeding had slowed, drops of bright red blood smattered the white snow. Woofie, with pieces of fur still hanging from his mouth, had whined softly as if sensing that he had misjudged the situation.

I rode in the ambulance to the hospital. Mother followed in her car after racing back into the cabin to turn off the oven and throw on some clothes. Woofie, not to be left behind, was allowed to ride with Mother. Likely she would have to have the BMW professionally detailed or perhaps just sell it. After they had whisked George into an examining room, we were all directed into the ER waiting room.

Bertie arrived a few minutes later. Even though she wasn't on duty, she came as soon as I called. She spotted Woofie in Mother's BMW and got ahold of a neighbor to pick him up and take him to her house to be reunited with her husband and boys.

The officious Detective Burns arrived next. When he got my name, he suggested that I was the same Trout whom he had met at Bucky's infamous meat locker with Trooper Vaara when the deceased Watkins fellow was found. I allowed that I was, indeed, the same Trout. He refrained from making a crack about my name and asking if I liked to fish. Eventually, he asked me to replay the evening's events. I could tell by the contorted expression on his face that this was not the assignment that detectives dreamed about. The mystery of the creature that was bludgeoned by the fireplace poker by Mother in the dark in the driveway in the boonies on a Sunday night all seemed like a deranged version of the game "Clue" that I loved playing as a child. This was not so delightful.

Burns eventually completed taking my statement then turned to Mother, who was vacantly staring at a muted television screen.

"Now, ah, Mrs. Trout," Burns began.

"Caldwell," Mother corrected. "I remarried after Janese's father passed."

"My condolences," Burns said. "Okay, Mrs. Caldwell, can you please tell me the events of the evening?"

"Actually, you can call me Maddie. It's simpler," Mother said.

"Very well, Maddie, could—"

"I was protecting my baby, clear and simple. I heard a horrible noise—noises—and rushed downstairs. I had been napping in the loft. I thought someone was being murdered! Anyway, I called out for Janese. When I realized that she wasn't in the cabin, nor was that dog she's keeping, I assumed that something horrible was going on outside. Something to do with the dog or God-knows-what. I grabbed the first thing I could find, which was the fireplace poker, and after turning on the outside lights, I rushed outside to find Janese. Some horrible, hairy thing came bursting out of the woods and attacked Janese, so I wacked it. Of course, when we realized it was George, we immediately called the authorities. Again, I was protecting my daughter—or thought I was—from a vicious attack."

I think Detective Burns was contemplating if a law had been broken, but it all was a bit muddy. There was an assault, but this was not at all like the usual barroom brawl or family fight that he was used to where one or more of the parties were drunk and/or high on meth and the assault weapon was either a broken beer bottle or a truck.

Really, the whole thing was just a huge misunderstanding that involved a guy who had disappeared in a snowstorm and reappeared wearing a bearskin rug and not much else. Burns probably pegged George as a nutcase who went off his meds. When the wingnut (George) allegedly attacked his girlfriend (me), her old lady (Mother) walloped the guy with the first thing she could get her hands on (fireplace poker). Meanwhile, Bertie's big, harry dog was for some reason staying with the Trout woman and apparently was after the guy in the bear rug. Burns asked Bertie if Woofie had had his rabies shot and had he ever attacked anyone before. They might have to seize the animal; a prospect that got Bertie's hackles up, to say the least.

"Hey, Burns, all dogs are protective," Bertie said. "I lent him to Janese for protection because she was attacked at the school and you, *Detective*, have not done a damn thing to get to the bottom of that, now have you?"

"Take it easy, Vaara," Burns said, holding his hands up defensively, "just need to know if rabies adds to the LeFleur guy's list of troubles."

"I assure you, Burns, that my dog has had all of his vaccinations. I think maybe the blow to Mr. LeFleur's head is our main concern right now."

The two glared at each other. Burns, in an obvious attempt to change the subject said, "That taxidermist, Bucky Watz-his-name, got himself lawyered up and pled not guilty to neg hom charge with the guy that died in his meat locker."

Bertie started to open her mouth to say something when a doctor appeared, a woman doctor, unfamiliar. We all leapt to our feet.

"Any of you related to Mr. LeFleur?" she asked.

"I'm his fiancé," I said. Mother raised an eyebrow and gave me a curious look.

"There's nobody else," I added. "Just me." *And baby makes three,* said a voice in my head.

The doctor nodded. She looked tired. And young. And foreign, though her English was flawless. Her nametag said Dr. Shira. *Is that Jewish?* asked The Voice. *Jewish people are very smart and make excellent doctors. And lawyers. Am I being racist?*

"Okay, look, your fiancé is stable right now."

We all let out a collective sigh of relief. Well, thank God, The Voice said. Perhaps you will remember to REALLY thank God?

I have ordered an MRI for his head trauma. At the very least Mr. LeFleur has a serious concussion."

Mother let out a whimper.

"While he was dehydrated and suffering from hypothermia, the main concern is TBI—traumatic brain injury. We'll check for a facture and possible closed-head injury. I'm concerned about a diffuse axonal injury—it's a closed head injury. We definitely will watch for edema—swelling."

"Diffuse what?" I asked.

"Diffuse axonal injury. It's an injury to the brain—it can be very serious, but he could also simply have a concussion. We'll know more after we get more imaging. The next twelve hours or so will tell us more. We will be putting Mr. LeFleur in critical care. I am consulting with a neurologist, and depending what the MRI shows long with some other tests, we may need to transfer your fiancé to U.P. Regional or another facility that has a neurosurgeon on staff. It's possible that we may need to medically induce a coma to allow his brain to rest and heal. Like I said, we'll know more after some tests."

Coma! shrieked The Voice. *As in brain dead?*

We all stood in stunned silence. Even Burns looked properly subdued.

"Can I see him?" I asked. "Can I talk to him?"

"Not right now, I'm afraid," Dr. Shira said. "He has not shown any signs of regaining consciousness. We are watching for that. His body is protecting him right now."

Mother let out a louder whimper. "I'm so sorry, Janese. I—I thought—"

"It's okay Mom," I said, hugging her. "He's gonna be okay."

"It's going to be a while before anyone can see Mr. LeFleur," Dr. Shira said. "If you leave contact information with the nurse, we'll call if there's any change. Otherwise I suggest you get some rest and call in the morning. We'll have more information then."

We all nodded numbly.

Dr. Shira started to leave, stopped in her tracks and turned back to face us. "Do you have any idea why he was wearing a bearskin rug?"

We all shook our heads.

"Well, just curious. I will say that the bear's head apparently was covering your fiancé's head, and that likely saved his life by considerably softening the blow. A bit of good luck that he wasn't just wearing an ordinary hat."

Lucky? asked The Voice.

"Well, goodnight," the doctor said.

≈ 17 ≈

"Diffuse axonal injury occurs in about half of all severe head traumas. When acceleration or deceleration causes the brain to move within the skull, axons, the parts of the nerve cells that allow neurons to send messages between them, are disrupted."

I was in my office at the college, hunched over my computer. I had Googled *diffuse axonal injury* and was reading an excerpt to Bertie who was sitting in one of my guest chairs. She had brought along Woofie who was in my other guest chair and seemed uninterested in learning about traumatic brain injury.

"So what do they do to fix it?" Bertie asked.

I scanned down the article to *Treatment.* "It says that the most important thing is to reduce swelling inside the brain, which can cause additional damage. In most cases, they use medications, like steroids. If that doesn't work, they might medically induce a coma."

"Well, that scares the shit out of ya," Bertie said as she absently reached over and scratched Woofie around his ears.

I took a ragged breath. "I stopped by this morning. They said he was getting more imaging. The nurse said that Dr. Shira wasn't available and she—the nurse—could only say that he was still listed as critical. The good news was that a neurologist from U.P. Regional in Marquette was having a clinic at the hospital so he was going to review the MRI and all and examine George. But the nurse wouldn't tell me anything about George. Not even if he was conscious. I don't think he is or I'm sure someone would have called. I—I have my cell on. Someone is supposed to call." I took out my phone and looked at the little message icon. Nothing.

"Well, he's alive and they haven't transferred him to U.P. Regional or anything, so that's good, isn't it?" Bertie said.

"I guess. I think they might, though. I think if that neurologist doctor hadn't been there today, they would have."

Bertie stood up and stretched. "Well, I gotta go home and get some shuteye. I have the midnight shift. But I'm leaving my phone on. Call me if you hear anything. I'm sure you will, and I'm sure it will be encouraging. They're just taking precautions."

"Yea, okay," I said, my shoulders slumping. I would not have Bertie to lean on the rest of the day. Mother was a wreck. Her solution to handling the ordeal was to take a pill, lie down, and wait for things to get better. My therapy had been to go to work and wait for a phone call. Instead of actually working, I had spent my time surfing the internet for brain trauma information, which only served to frighten me with one ominous prognosis after another.

Bertie snapped a leash on Woofie and they headed out. She stopped at the door and turned back in. "Oh, and don't worry about watching Woofie while the hubby and I go to Hawaii. We decided to go in March, when the boys are on school spring break so that Mom doesn't have to tote them back and forth to school. She said something about taking them to Mall of America in Minneapolis. God love her. I'd rather poke my eyes out. Anyway, it's a ways off and maybe we can get him used to a kennel."

"Oh, well, I'm sure I'll be available to take Woofie by then," I said, staring at my computer screen. Terrifying words jumped out at me.

Diffuse axonal injury is one of the leading causes of death in people with traumatic brain injury.

Bertie opened her mouth as if to say something else, then closed it. I knew what she was wondering about. In all the chaos, I had forgotten about getting another pregnancy test. Maybe, when George was feeling better and things had settled, I'd just go to the damn doctor. I wondered if Dr. Shira was taking new patients.

"Later," said Bertie as she slipped out. Noise from the hallway briefly filtered in, then was again muffled as she gently closed the door.

Reluctantly, I closed an article from some neurologist at John Hopkins and opened my work e-mail. Several new messages popped up, demanding my attention. At least six were asking for an update on George. Because of privacy issues, our HR department wasn't allowed to mention a sick or injured employee. However, nothing stopped people from using Facebook.

Out of curiosity, I opened an e-mail from good ol' Brenda Koski— the one who kept squirming out of committee obligations for the igloo contest because she was too busy getting cozy with President Neil.

> Hey, Jan

"My name's Janese, you dumb cluck," I muttered.

> I saw on FB that George got attacked by a bear?

"Attacked by a bear? What the hell?"

Frannie Loop said she and you were in the ER together. I guess her kid broke his arm or something. Did the bear get in your house or what? OMG!

I deleted Brenda's e-mail and all the others that apparently had Facebooked with Frannie Loop and got a cockamamie story about a bear attack. Honestly, when people weren't posting photos of their food or grandchildren or Caribbean cruise on Facebook, they were perpetuating stories that strayed so far from the truth, they needed their own zip code. However, I wasn't about to dispel the bear-attack myth. It would get around quickly enough that Mother had clobbered my boyfriend with a fireplace poker; a story that was certain to take on a life of its own.

Next I scanned through the glut of e-mails concerning the igloo contest. A committee member, Frank "kiss up" Haataja wondered if Bucky—if he was in jail—would be able to get released to participate. If so, it was likely that President Neil would not be happy. Frank said it would taint the whole contest.

"Oh, stuff it Haataja," I said as I punched the delete key. I closed out my screen just as my cell phone began to chirp. Scrambling, I picked it up and managed to answer rather than accidentally disconnect, which is often the case.

"Hello?"

"Janice Trout?"

"It's Janese, but yes, this is she."

"I'm calling about your fiancé, Mr. George LeFleur?"

"Yes—how—"

"I'm Dr. Benjamin Bloom, doing a neurology clinic here at Moose Willow Memorial. We are still running some tests on Mr. LeFleur, and we are concerned that he still hasn't regained consciousness, but I believe that we are dealing with a concussion. A fairly severe one, but the prognosis is good. While he had a skull laceration that required a few stitches, there is no sign of a fracture."

A million pounds of lead weights slipped from my shoulders and I floated skyward. A buzzing filled my head, then I had a sensation of riding an elevator plunging out of control. Somewhere in the distance, a muffled voice said *hello, hello, Miss Trout?*

"Yea—yes, I'm here, um Dr. Bloom. Sorry, I'm just so relieved. Dr. Shira mentioned something about another thing." I quickly looked at my scribbled notepad. "Diffuse axonal injury, and it sounded so horrible."

"Well, I don't believe we are dealing with that. However, I would like Mr. LeFleur to come around soon, and I think he will. He's showing some preliminary signs of regaining consciousness. Once he wakes up, we can do a few tests and determine his cognitive ability and any other possible issues that may have been caused by the, er, accident and what, if any, rehabilitation is indicated."

I realized that I had been holding my breath while the doctor spoke. My heartbeat was thudding in my ears. I must have gasped when I started breathing, which startled the doctor.

"Miss Trout?" he said.

"I'm fine, I—when can I see him—George. When can I see George? I can be there in fifteen minutes."

"We will be moving him from critical care to a step-down unit. I would like you to try to talk to him—a familiar voice. Perhaps he will respond. I have some appointments and such, but I would like you to come around three this afternoon. He'll be settled and I'll hopefully be done with my appointments."

"Right! Three. I'll be there," I said. My breathing had slowed, my heartbeat no longer pounded in my ears. Things were coming back into focus.

We hung up and I sat very still. I looked at the clock. It was only 10:00 a.m. *It's going to be all right.* The Voice that had been speaking to me lately had resurrected itself in my psyche. My stomach growled. I hadn't eaten since having the burnt cookies and tea at Aggie's. The lasagna never made it to the table. For all I knew, it was still in the oven. Thank God Mother had thought to turn it off. The multiple cups of coffee I had guzzled were burning a hole in my stomach lining. *It's going to be all right,* repeated The Voice. *Eat!*

I picked up my purse, put my phone inside, and headed into the hallway.

"There she is!" shouted a woman in the hallway. "It's George's girlfriend. Hey, HEY!"

I stopped and turned to face a knot of several female coeds who raced toward me and soon had me surrounded. I felt like Custer making his last stand.

"How is he? You know, George?" demanded a tall, striking African American woman. She had long braids cascading everywhere. I wondered how many hours it took to do all that braiding. There were even little beads incorporated into the braids. I shifted my focus to her face; her eyes glistened with tears. "We heard he was in a terrible accident. That a bear attacked him and clawed his face off. Ohmygod! Tell me it isn't true. He was soooo, um so…"

"Beautiful. He IS, like, so bohemian. We are all so worried," sniveled a plump girl with rainbow-colored hair, a nose ring, and multiple ear piercings. I remembered her from somewhere on campus. While the hair was unforgettable, her name eluded me, as did the names of all the others. They were George's groupies. All artsy-fartsy females. Their circle tightened around me. I held up my hands like a cop directing traffic. "Whoa! Take it easy ladies!"

"We want to see him, or send flowers or balloons or something," said rainbow hair.

"Of course," I said. "First off, George did not have his face ripped off by a bear." I heard a collective sigh of relief from the girls. "He had an accident and bumped his head. And I'm sure George would appreciate all of your concern, but right now they are keeping him quiet. You'll have to wait on the balloon bouquet."

The girls let out a unified *awwww*.

"Maybe you could make him something, you know, something artistic. I promise I'll take it to him when he's better. Just have security open up my office for you and put it on my desk."

"Awesome," said one of the girls. "Who's going to take over teaching his classes?" asked another.

"I don't know. You'll have to ask the dean. I'm sure they will find someone to cover for him."

"But our final projects are due next week," whined rainbow hair. "I don't want anyone but George grading my work!"

They all nodded soberly.

"Well, I'm sure he feels the same way. I bet he'll be able to review all of your work when he's back on his feet," I said, edging my way toward a small opening in their human corral. They all grew silent and opened up a space for me to pass.

"Tell him we LOVE him, okay?" sniveled rainbow hair.

I hurried to the parking lot. It had snowed a couple of inches and I would have to clean off my car, or at least the windshield. I had heard that a warming trend was on the way, which meant we would be getting a lot of slush. Winter in the Michigan's Upper Peninsula always gave one or two false starts before settling in with a vengeance and maintaining a steely grip until April. We still had tons of snow left from the blizzard. If we got a few more inches here and there, we would be good for the igloo contest, even if we had to truck some extra snow in for folks to use. I stood in the lot, staring at my car, which was sandwiched in tightly between two other cars. I and glanced at my watch. A whole half hour had passed since I talked to Dr. Bloom. Only four and a half hours until I could see George. I envisioned holding his hand, speaking to him. His eyes would flutter open. He would see me and smile. I would smile back and—

A car horn blasted, causing me to jump.

"Hey lady, do you mind?" yelled a guy out his car window. "You're blocking that spot and I gotta go see my advisor."

I could see he was a student and that meant he wasn't even supposed to park in the faculty/staff lot. I let it go and moved out of his way. He waved and I waved back.

I squeezed into my Subaru and started it up then turned on the deicers to melt off the windshield. What day was it? *Get a grip,* said The Voice. Monday. The "accident" had happened Sunday night—just the night before. It seemed ages ago. The students would be out for semester break soon and while I wasn't faculty, I did get a few extra days off between semesters. That was good timing, what with George's situation, and *oh crap,* said The Voice. Choir practice popped into my head. That would be Wednesday. I might have to drop out. That would please Eleanor Heimlich no end. With that thought, I was determined to stay in. The Christmas Cantata—what, three weeks away—or less.

Suddenly I was starved beyond belief. I knew there wasn't much at the cabin. The front and rear window deicers had done their work so I set out on a mission for food at my favorite restaurant: McDonalds. The drive-through window quickly filled my order for three breakfast sandwiches, two hash browns, a large orange juice, a large coffee with extra cream, and a salad for Mother. She was proud of the fact that a fast-food sandwich had never passed her lips. I would take my greasy repast home for consumption, make a couple of phone calls, freshen up, and wait out the clock for my trip to the hospital. It was about 20 minutes from the cabin. I would factor in extra time in case I got behind a snowplow or an old man making his weekly journey into town in his rusty truck, which typically traveled significantly below the speed limit. So, I'd leave at 2:15, and barring a freak snowstorm or a meteor falling from the sky onto the road and blocking traffic, I would arrive at the hospital with time to spare.

* * *

Mother was puttering around the cabin when I entered.

143

"What is that dreadful smell?" she asked.

"Comfort food," I said. "I got you a salad and balsamic dressing."

"Oh, that's lovely. I could eat something." She paused. "Well?"

"Well, what?" I said. I wanted to make sure it wasn't my maternal state she was asking about.

"George? The man I assaulted last night. Your supposed fiancé. How is he, for heaven's sake? I've been on pins and needles for hours. I didn't want to call you at work."

"I didn't want to call you because I thought you were sleeping," I said. "Anyway, he is being moved from critical care to a step-down thing, which is good. I talked to the neurologist and he said it's likely a concussion, but no facture."

"Well, thank God," Mother said. She moved over to the bags of food sitting on the table.

"I'm going to the hospital at three to meet with the doctor and I get to see George," I said and I pulled food out of bags.

Mother eyed her salad, then looked at the sausage, egg, and cheese biscuit sandwich I was wolfing down. I could feel my arteries clogging. It was worth every molecule of plaque buildup.

Mother began toying with her salad, then looked at the two remaining breakfast sandwiches on the table. I stuffed a hash brown into my mouth and washed it down with a generous swig of O.J.

"Want one?" I asked.

"Don't talk with your mouth full, dear," she said.

I shrugged my shoulders.

"Well, perhaps just a taste," she said, tentatively reaching for a sandwich and removing its paper wrapper.

I took the lid off my coffee and blew on it. It was loaded with half and half. I took a careful sip. Perfect. McDonalds made excellent coffee and had real half and half, not that powdered stuff.

Mother took a bite of her sandwich. She did not spit it out. I tried not to smile. I was corrupting her. I thought of the alien Bork's line from Star Trek: *Resistance is futile.* I managed to suppress a snicker. The salad ended up in the fridge for a more desperate time.

⇗ 18 ⇖

Moose Willow Hospital is considered a gem by rural standards. It offers basic and even specialized care, which means that often patients don't need to go long distances for some of their medical needs. I drove around the hospital parking lot several times looking for a space. In the winter, when the lines are covered with snow, parking becomes dysfunctional as people must guess where to park. Inevitably, people guess poorly, and parking seems willy-nilly, even encroaching sidewalks and fire lanes. I finally found a space some distance from the entrance, locked up the Subaru, and trudged through the slush toward to hospital.

The hospital board found the word "hospital" outdated or too generic, thus the facility had a Vegas-style poison green and Day-Glo orange marquee proclaiming the facility to be MWMHCS, which formed no kind of pronounceable acronym. The full name was spelled out below: Moose Willow Memorial Health Care System. Most people just called it Moose Willow Hospital, Moose Willow Memorial, or simply "the hospital." The phrase "health care system" sounded like the building's boiler room and lacked the warm fuzzy image that folks hoped for when entrusting their lives to the machinations of a medical facility.

An attractive woman sitting at the front desk at the hospital entrance whose nametag proclaimed her to be "Anna, Information Services," directed me to the step-down care wing where I would need to check in with the nurse at that desk. I did as instructed and the desk nurse asked me to have a seat. She said Dr. Bloom was running late and I needed to wait for him before I went to see Mr. LeFleur. I was of course early, so that made my anticipated wait even longer. The small waiting area was devoid of any other "waitees" and featured several semi-comfortable chairs and a television tuned into a daytime talk show. The show involved a bunch of women sitting around a table blabbing about various hot-button topics, which seemed to arouse the hyped-up audience into frenzied cheers and boos. An assortment of magazines was strewn about the waiting area. None of them were particularly interesting to the average anxious waiting-room occupant:

Diabetes Today, WEB MD, Parenting, Healthy Living, and a stray issue of *Golf Digest.*

I looked at the cover of *Parenting*. It featured an attractive young mother and her adorable toddler. Below the photo was the storyline: "Are the Twos So Terrible?" I decided to forego *Parenting* and flipped through a dog-eared issue of *Healthy Living*. For some reason, I was always drawn to the recipes in magazines, which was ridiculous since I was not even a passable cook. Yet I found myself reading about Panko-crusted salmon, spinach salad with water chestnuts, sun-dried tomatoes, and citrus zest. My morning repast of two egg/cheese/sausage breakfast sandwiches, hash browns, juice, and jumbo coffee with extra cream grumbled away in my stomach, as if to scold me for my poor dietary choices. I was reading an ad about kelp and blueberry extract when I sensed someone coming down the hall.

As was the habit of those trapped in worrisome medical situations, I glanced up, hopeful for news, preferably good. A man wearing a crisp white lab coat approached. Clearly his name tag should have said "Dr. Dreamboat," because he was exceedingly good-looking, especially when he smiled and approached me. To say he was tall, dark, and handsome was an egregious understatement. But that is what he was: about six feet tall, trim, and ruggedly handsome in an all-male outdoorsy way. His black-with-just-a-touch-of-gray hair had been styled to look untidy and a shadow of a beard sprouted from a nicely chiseled chin. The "unshaven" look was all the rage. I suspected that looking fashionable was the motivation behind the scruffy masculinity rather than a lack of combs and razors in the house.

"Miss Trout?" he said.

"Yes, I'm Janese Trout," I said, leaping up causing the *Healthy Living* magazine to flutter to the floor.

"I'm Dr. Bloom," he said. "Sorry I'm a little late."

"Yes, sure, no problem. How is he—George?"

"I am very pleased. That's part of the reason I'm late. I wanted to check on him before I took you in to see him. While I was there, he regained consciousness."

"Oh, thank God!" I said.

"So, are you ready to go say hi?" he said.

I nodded and we headed down the hall. Dr. Bloom emitted an ever-so-faint whiff of musky cologne. It was not at all unpleasant.

"He's a little disoriented. Keep in mind he's on some pain meds, so that alone makes him groggy. He understands that he's in a hospital, though he is having trouble sorting out too many details of why he is here."

"Oh," I said.

"Again, this is not unusual with brain trauma. I'm hopeful you can, well, jar some of his memory, Janese." He flashed me a 100-watt smile of encouragement.

We arrived at George's room. Two nurses were in attendance. One, a male, was holding a Styrofoam cup with a straw up to George. The other, female, was fussing about with a multifarious-looking contraption on wheels. They both glanced at us when we entered. The female nurse gave Dr. Bloom a dazzling smile. George was less than dazzling and resembled a delegate from the living dead. It was obvious that someone had shaved his head, which was encircled with several yards of snowy-white gauze. Assorted tubes sprouted from him, including one sneaking from beneath the covers into a bag attached to the bed frame. It contained a liquid that looked suspiciously like pee.

"Now George, since you're drinking on your own, we can get this IV out of you," chirped the female nurse. "As soon as the doctor okays it, we'll pull that catheter too."

George muttered something to the nurse who was blocking his view of Dr. Bloom and me. He grasped the cup the male nurse had given him and took a few greedy sips. I made a noise as if clearing my throat and George glanced up. A smile twitched at the corner of his mouth.

"Hey, Trout," he said. His voice sounded thick.

"Hey yourself," I said, cautiously approaching his bed. The nurses stepped aside, letting me along with Dr. Bloom move up to the bed railing. George's appearance did not improve upon closer inspection. His beard had escaped the razor but was matted and mashed against one side of his chin. He sported two black eyes and looked withered in his hospital gown. Still, my heart thudded in my ears. Right away he recognized me! I hadn't realized until then that I was terrified that he would not know who I was.

"How are you?" I said, trying my best to control the sob stuck in my throat.

"Could be better," he said. I reached out and took his hand. It was cold but reassuring when he returned my grasp.

"We don't want to ask you too many questions right now, George," Dr. Bloom said. "But maybe Janese can ask a couple of things to get the ol' gray matter working."

Dr. Bloom looked at me and favored me with another smile.

"Okay, well, you sure had us worried," I said grinning idiotically. George looked at me expectantly.

"We are all wondering, sweetie, what happened to you. Where were you these past few days?" I said.

George gazed at me, flummoxed. "Here?"

"Okay, well then, do you remember, um why you were wearing that bearskin rug when you ran into the driveway?" I said.

"Because it was cold?" George responded with a hopeful tone.

"I see," I said. "And where were your clothes?"

George thought for a moment, scowled then brightened. "Gone. She took them. I had no choice but to wear the rug."

Dr. Bloom looked at me and I think he arched an eyebrow. Mother could arch an eyebrow. It meant *oh, really?*

"She?" I said. "Was it Derry Parks?"

"Who?" George said and yawned. "So tired."

"George, who was the woman who took your clothes?" I said.

"I think it was your mother. She took them to wash them. Where is she? Does she have my clothes?"

"Forget the clothes!" I snapped. *Patience!* warned The Voice. I took a deep breath and forced myself to be calm. "No, sweetie, I mean the woman who took your clothes to steal them."

"Someone stole my clothes?" George said, blinking. "You mean there is someone in the hospital stealing people's stuff?" He looked around at all of us and settled his gaze on the male nurse.

I looked at Dr. Bloom and shrugged. I knew what he was thinking. It was what everyone had thought all along. George had hooked up with another woman and now maybe he was being more evasive than suffering memory loss. But I didn't think George was lying and I knew him better than anybody else in the room. Clearly his brain just wasn't connecting the dots. He needed to try harder.

"Who. Was. She?" I repeated through clenched teeth. *Easy,* scolded The Voice.

But George's lids had slid shut. Dr. Bloom touched me on the shoulder.

"It's okay. He's sleeping now. I believe his memory will return. Sometimes it comes in bits and pieces. We just need to be patient. You can sit with him for a few moments, but just let him rest. You mentioned a woman taking his, um, clothes and all? Is it important?"

"I—I don't know. Kind of. His clothes were found in his truck, which was abandoned on Triple A Road during the after-Thanksgiving

148

blizzard. We have no idea why." I didn't add the information that the woman known as Derry Parks was missing and that someone attacked me with a trash can and that Weasel Watkins had died in a wild game meat locker. No need to sound like I was the one with an addled brain.

"I'll be heading back to Marquette tonight," Dr. Bloom said. "The staff here knows how to reach me at U.P. Regional—that's where my physician's group is based. I'll be back for another clinic here toward the end of the week and will check on your fiancé's progress. Meanwhile, he'll be in good hands. I believe Dr. Shira is rotating off ER duty and will be serving as a hospitalist the rest of the week."

"Hospitalist?" I said.

"Yes—a doctor solely assigned to the patients who are admitted."

With that Dr. Bloom took my hand and squeezed it then flashed another smile. I figured his teeth must be veneered. No toothpaste could get them that white.

* * *

Eventually, I located my car by repeatedly hitting the unlock button until I saw the Subaru's lights flash. I had been wandering around the lot, off by several rows when it occurred to me that there was no shame in using technology to assist directionally-challenged people such as myself. A warming trend had started, though it wasn't particularly pleasant. The day had become dark, gloomy, and damp. Piles of snow were revealing their dirty underbellies. And, of course, with the igloo contest just around the corner, we needed snow for the statues. We would definitely have to truck some in for the event if the meltdown continued. A west wind added to the misery. I often wondered why people, including myself, chose to live in such an unpleasant climate. Then there would be a beautiful winter's day, with an azure sky and the sun sparkling off the snow like diamonds, and all was forgiven.

It was too late to head back to the college, so I decided to go home and maybe give Bertie a call later before she left for her night shift. To me, one thing was certain: a woman—and we knew it was Derry Parks—had taken George's clothes. We figured the Parks woman had lured George to Lot C at the college for a rendezvous. George had told me it was to do with a magazine piece about his work. I believed him. Or at least I believed that Derry Parks brought him out under false pretenses. Of course, people would think that the two were meeting up to engage in non-literary activities. They would say that she got pissed off about something and took off with his truck and clothes. But the truck was found stuck and abandoned on Triple A Road. What happened to Parks? Did she have a snowmobile stashed in a bear den somewhere? And there was the gap of time between George's disappearance and reappearance. He obviously found shelter, water, and food—presumably in Aggie's storage shed—or he wouldn't be alive in a hospital recovering from an unfortunate assault from Mother.

The illicit sex-in-a-truck theory just didn't hold up. There were any number of places to shack up if you drove up the highway a bit. One was even called the No-Tell Hotel, with hourly rates and parking behind the building away from prying eyes. George's truck had no back seat and there was a console dividing the front. Even the most agile of teenagers would find having nookie a logistical nightmare in George's truck. Why mess around in a truck during a snowstorm on an abandoned road? George had the answer if we could just get it to surface.

Meanwhile, where was Derry Parks? I was getting nowhere finding answers.

I decided to stop at the grocery store to get some provisions before heading home. I contemplated picking up another pregnancy test at the drug store, but of course doing so in our tiny town would supercharge the rumor mill. Again, I wondered if Dr. Shira was taking new patients. The question of possible impending motherhood would have to remain a mystery a while longer.

At the IGA, I briefly toyed with the idea of making the Panko-crusted salmon I had read about in *Healthy Living*. I quickly discarded that idea when I saw the deli clerk taking some nice, juicy chickens off the rotisserie. I also got a tub of mashed potatoes and gravy and a container of broccoli salad, which may have been healthy if they hadn't added cheese, bacon, and a mayo dressing. In a righteous moment, I refrained from taking a fresh cherry pie from the bakery.

When I arrived home, I was pleased to see that Keskimaki had plowed the slushy mess out of the driveway and shoveled the walk. Inside Mother had morphed into a Whirling Dervish and cleaned the whole place, done laundry, and started a cozy fire in the fireplace. Perhaps she was doing penance for assaulting George. Or maybe she just couldn't stand my housekeeping habits, which had been lax as of late. Either way, it worked for me.

"I smell something good!" Mother said. "How's George?" she added.

"The doctor is pleased," I said. "George has come to and is talking. They're unhooking him from tubes and stuff. He still seems kind of out of it, though."

"Oh, praise God. Well, I'm sure he'll be his old self in no time. Will he come home soon?"

"Not sure," I said. I didn't tell Mother that while George was starting to come around, I couldn't help but feel that part of the original package was missing. I couldn't really put my finger on it. It wasn't just his confusion about what happened; something else just didn't seem right. It was as if his essence had changed.

Mother carried some plates and silverware to the table. She got a glass of water for herself and insisted that I have a large tumbler of milk. I knew what she was up to, force-feeding me calcium. Just in case. I wasn't crazy about milk, and she knew it. I only kept it around for un-condensing tomato soup or to add to my coffee. As a child, Mother had forced me to drink skim milk, which had a bluish tint to it. She said I didn't need the fat of whole milk and that young ladies needed to watch their waistlines.

While we ate, I brought Mother up to speed about George—that his bearskin ensemble was still a mystery. That he'd smiled at me, knew my name, and squeezed my hand. I mentioned that Dr. Bloom would be back at the end of the week. I may have slipped and called him Dr. Dreamboat. Mother gave me an inquisitive look.

"He's straight out of a soap opera," I said of Dr. Bloom. "He's so good looking that he doesn't seem real," I added. "Of course, not my type—a little old for me and all. And my heart belongs to George." The fiancé ruse was beginning to grow on me. Depending on how George's memory came back, perhaps our relationship would progress to the next stage. Especially if I was—

"I can't believe I ate half a chicken. I don't know what's gotten into me lately," Mother said, jolting me out of my reverie. "Now I'll clean up," she added.

Indeed, what *had* gotten into her? I took her up on the offer and went into the bedroom to give Bertie a call. Her youngest, Robby, answered—well breathed heavily at first, then said hello. When I identified myself, he was all excited to tell his Aunt Janese about teaching Woofie to beg for food and also shake hands. I infused the appropriate enthusiasm into my voice and decided that perhaps having a kid around might be kind of a nice thing. Robby was a gem in spite of his reputation for mischief.

"MOMMMMMEEEEE!" he screamed a mere inch from the receiver. "Auntie Janese thinks Woofie's the smartest dog in the whole world. She said so and she wants to talk to you." I heard some juggling of the receiver. "I love you Auntie Janese. Here's Mommy. Bye."

"Bye, sweetie," I said, slightly choked up.

"Hey, kiddo," Bertie said. "How's our George doing?"

I gave her an update.

"Well, Derry Parks is still MIA. And Bucky Tanner may be released as we speak. I'll tell you all about it later. Right now, Robby is teaching Woofie to beg using the leftover meatloaf I was going to heat up for dinner. Hey! Robert Michael—no! Oh crap. Woofie barfed. Gotta go."

Robert Michael was Robby's formal name that Bertie used when he was in deep doodoo. The mention of Bucky Tanner reminded me of the igloo contest. Entries closed that upcoming Friday and construction could start the day after Christmas, which was not far off. Even less far off was the Christmas cantata. When I checked my personal email, I had found a terse message from Hannu to choir members notifying us of a longer rehearsal on Wednesday. We were to start at 6:00 p.m. and go as long as necessary. He strongly encouraged us to practice on our own and listen to the CDs he had provided for each of the four-part harmonies. I had the soprano version, which I had been listening to in my car. Of course, the choir signing on the CD was Mormon Tabernacle quality accompanied by a symphony orchestra. It was intimidating. Besides, whether or not I even went to practice depended on how George was doing. My mind shifted on to Bucky Tanner. I had thought his arrest was premature, if not unfounded. Still, Weasel Watkins' demise was suspicious. I hoped Bertie could fill in some blanks when we talked again—hopefully soon.

I thought again of Robby, how something melted when he said he loved me. So uncomplicated, so pure. It made me smile.

≈ 19 ≈

Several things happened on Friday. Most of them were good, or at least not tragic, except maybe for Eleanor Heimlich.

First, classes at the Copper Country Community College were officially over for the semester, though there were still a few stray students racing around in various stages of meltdown desperate to get late assignments turned in. Several knocked on my door hoping I would know how to track down their teachers. The scenario was always the same. They had missed the drop-dead deadline and I was a convenient person to yell at because *professor so-and-so was NEVER in his/her office!* I would suggest a text or e-mail or prayer, if they were hoping for a miracle, which is what they needed at 4:59 p.m. on the Friday of the last day of the semester. Faculty were as scarce as buttercups in a blizzard.

Also, the deadline for the Habitat for Critters Igloo Contest had finally arrived. No more entries were allowed and construction could begin at 12:01 a.m. on December 26th. Snow would be trucked in ahead, as needed. Contestants were allowed to work around the clock until 11:59 p.m. on New Year's Eve. They could bring in lighting, water, food, non-alcoholic beverages, even a three-piece jazz combo, if they so desired. There was no limit or restrictions on who helped whom. Of course, anyone caught sabotaging another's creation or trash talking to the point of vulgarity was immediately disqualified. Contest stewards would patrol the igloo construction sites to keep an eye on things. Fortunately, I was an organizer, not an enforcer.

We had a total of fourteen entries—a new record—none of which strongly suggested anything lewd, lascivious, or otherwise inappropriate. While the wholesomeness of it may have dulled the excitement, it also made my life a lot easier. There was a last-minute entry entitled "Yooper Bigfoot's Lair." The accompanying sketch appeared to be a crude arrangement of branches and boughs and such into a kind of lean-to shelter. Missing was the requisite snow and/or ice. However, there was also a fire pit. Apparently, the Yooper Bigfoot had learned how to spark a fire and roast its prey. Area folklore yarned tales of "nests" that were claimed to be made up by Bigfoots. Skeptics said what it amounted to were hunting blinds, constructed by modern homo sapiens for the purpose of camouflage, which were eventually abandoned and had deteriorated over time.

The most intriguing entry was the plan for a snow and ice version of a Habitrail, which in normal scale was made of plastic and designed to entertain hamsters and their owners who have nothing better to do than watch them explore the labyrinth of tunnels. Of course, hamsters were domestic animals and Habitrails were found at Wal Mart, not in nature. But, nonetheless, a human-sized version was ambitious and clever rather than totally unimaginative like Bucky Tanner's beaver lodge.

Bucky Tanner would be able to participate in the contest without fear of tainting it—as if he ever cared—because all criminal charges against him had been dropped. Bertie said this was due to a new development, which she promised to tell me about. She also mentioned that some interesting information had come from a toxicology report that finally came back on Weasel Watkins. Technically, Bertie could not chat about the evidence associated with Watkins' death, but sometimes things had a way of slipping out.

The by-far best news of the day was that George was doing much better. He remembered me and that we were a couple. He didn't dispute the fiancé label nor feel me out for any potential paternity issues. Not sure if this was because of memory problems or denial issues. He remembered Mother, his pottery, the college where we both worked, he knew the make, year, model, and color of his truck. He wondered when he could get it back. He had no idea what day it was, but then he rarely did before the accident. He also could not bring up much detail about his romp in the woods during the snowstorm. His memory of the event was blotted out except a recollection of being chased through the woods by something that frightened him and then, wham, he woke up in the hospital. We were told that this was not unusual for a head injury. The good news was that George's headaches and vertigo had eased up and that he was getting antsy to "get the hell out of the hospital."

Mother insisted on coming with me when I visited George that morning. I suspected she was looking for atonement. I was hoping he would be discharged some time that day and be home for the weekend. I was encouraged because the incredible Dr. Bloom was doing a clinic at Moose Willow Hospital and had mentioned checking on George who had been moved into a regular hospital room. When Mother and I entered, we found George sitting up in a chair eating breakfast and watching television. It was tuned into a cooking show. George shoved a piece of toast into his mouth and chewed vigorously, all the while staring at the television and apparently unaware of Mother and me. I had always said that nothing ruined George's appetite. The room could be on fire, and he would still finish his meal. He had no tubes coming from any part of his body and he appeared to have showered. The large gauze that had previously covered most of his shaved head had been replaced with a smaller bandage. The black eyes were turning a lovely shade of yellow, giving him a jaundiced look. Nonetheless, vestiges of the old George were emerging along with some peach fuzz on his cue ball pate.

He looked up and smiled. "Scrambled eggs," he said. "And bacon. At least I think it's bacon. It could be a piece of shoe leather or maybe a petrified dinosaur turd. I'd kill for some real food. I bet these eggs are powdered. I mean is it so hard to crack a couple of eggs?" He nodded at the television. "These two teams are competing in a cooking contest. It's a hoot. They have to do something spectacular with only twelve ingredients, which they did not get to choose, and they must somehow use everything. They're bitching at each other and ranting and raving and not making much progress. And, of course, there's a time limit. Hell, I could do what they're doing with a lot less hoopla."

I took a seat next to George. He set down his fork, muted the television and took my hand. We kissed and George pulled me to him. Unfortunately, the arms of the chairs made things difficult. Mother cleared her throat and wandered around the room as if she were in an art gallery studying an interesting exhibit.

We took the hint and George said, "Did you bring me some clothes? I'm getting released when Dr. Broom gets here."

"Bloom, sweetie. It's Dr. Bloom," I said. "And yes, I brought some clothes, just in case."

"Dr. Bloom?" Mother said as she studied a dispenser of barf bags. "Is that your Dreamboat?"

I gave her a withering look, which she ignored and moved on to a laminated poster illustrating proper hand washing. It all went past George who dropped my hand and picked up the bacon on his plate and began to gnaw on it. "Like beef jerky," he said. "Only tougher."

Speaking of Dr. Bloom, I could feel the electrical surge before he came into the room; an aura that, much to my chagrin, made me tingle. Mother felt it too, I could tell. We both turned just in time to be imbued by one of his zillion-dollar smiles. At that moment, a cute nurse found it necessary to hustle in and make sure George was managing his breakfast and to see if he needed anything. Of course, I knew that wasn't Nurse Cutie Pie's real interest; that it was the dashing Dr. Bloom who had motivated her visit. But she didn't have a chance. While she had precious dimples and perky breasts, Mother oozed something that snagged a man like a fish on a treble-barbed hook. Dr. Bloom was caught the moment he and Mother made eye contact.

"Oh, hello," Dr. Bloom said. "Are you Janese's sister?"

Mother tittered a bit and confessed she was my mother and future mother-in-law of the patient.

"Just call me Maddie," she said, conspicuously holding out her left hand.

"Bernard," he replied, taking her hand and holding it for a couple of extra beats. He was obviously checking out the ring situation. Nothing, of course, on Mother's left ring finger. Nothing on his either, for that matter.

I did a mental eye roll. George took a sip of coffee and peered over the rim at Mother and Dr. Bloom. There could have been a code blue in progress and I doubt that Dr. Bloom or Mother would have noticed. Nurse Cutie Pie made a petulant little noise as she snatched George's food tray and bustled out the door. George watched her leave.

"Well, I guess I was done. Just as well. Those were the worst scrambled eggs that I ever had. Cold. Rubbery. Bland. I'm sure the health insurance companies encourage crappy food so that patients will beg to be released."

Dr. Bloom chuckled. "A sure sign that the patient is ready to go home; he complains about the hospital food."

Not that there was anything much to get excited about at home, food-wise at least. I made a mental note to make yet another quick trip to the store.

"How are you feeling today?" Dr. Bloom asked.

George shrugged. "Ready to blow this place. Not that you guys haven't been great and all, but I'd like to get outta here."

Dr. Bloom did a cursory examination of George. He checked his eyes, heart, and lungs. He held up fingers to be counted, had George touch his nose, walk around, squeeze the doc's hand, and pull his fingers. He looked at George's ankles, peered under the bandage on his head, and asked about his voiding experiences. The doctor asked what day it was, when he, George, was born, who was the president of the United States, and where he was when the twin towers were hit on the

9-11 attack. While George got 100% of the mundane questions, he flunked memory of the time frame relating to his foray in the woods wearing a bearskin rug.

"George, I'm sure you will do much better at home, so we'll get the discharge paperwork going," Dr. Bloom said. He turned to Mother and me. "Ladies, you need to keep him engaged. Listen to music, have him do crossword puzzles, play games, cook, do a craft project, drive around, and find familiar landmarks and visit special places. George, you need to not sleep too much. It's what you'll feel like doing but try to stay stimulated."

George gave me a mischievous look and I felt my face flush. "Stimulated, huh?" he said. "I might need some help with that. One must always obey doctor's orders."

I heard Mother once again titter. I'm sure Dr. Bloom caught the innuendo, but other than a slight twitch at the corner of his mouth, showed no reaction. At least he didn't gyrate his pelvis to accentuate the point.

Dr. Bloom said, "I'll have the nurse get those discharge papers ready. She'll set up a follow-up appointment with you, George, when I'm here for next week's clinic." Dr. Bloom gave Mother a wink. "I'll be in town for a couple of days, so I don't have to make the drive back and forth."

Mother said: "Well, perhaps you could come over one evening for dinner?"

Dr. Bloom said: "I'd like that." He took a card out of his pocket. "This has my cell number, along with my office and so on. Just let me know when and where."

I wasn't sure who was reeling in whom but stood amazed at my mother's ability to attract men.

* * *

A less affable event of that Friday had been a passing encounter with the prickly Eleanor Heimlich. As I scurried out of the hospital to pull the car up for George and Mother, I noticed Eleanor sitting in the doctor's office waiting area. While I tried to duck past, she glanced up just as I hurried by then she began to cough—a very nasty sounding cough at that. While I don't believe in death by mental telepathy, I was quite certain that Eleanor Heimlich would be thrilled to dance on my grave. Somehow, she blamed me for her being excused from choir practice. We had all shown up as commanded at 6:00 p.m. on Wednesday night. I had merely asked Eleanor if she felt all right. I had not been trying to get her expelled from the choir. It's just that I noticed that she looked a little flushed. When she tried to sing, her voice was raspy and she sneezed so violently that the offering plates sitting on the alter rattled. Hannu sent her away, lest she infect the whole choir and jeopardize the cantata. Eleanor needed to have a speedy recovery. I was not inclined to take over the solo she was singing in the cantata. I wasn't solo material and with everything that had been happening, the Christmas cantata hadn't been foremost in my mind. With Hannu, there was never any discussion. He told me to start practicing. He reminded me of the cantata CD (somewhere in the Subaru) and told me to start memorizing.

The main problem, though, was that Eleanor's contempt for me would only get worse. She was seeing a doctor—maybe that would speed up the recovery. Besides how was it my fault if she had some contagious bug or the plague or whatever? I swear I could feel the hate rays bore into my back when I slipped through the door leading to the hospital parking lot. I would not have been surprised if the glass door had shattered from the negative vibes. Somehow, Eleanor blamed me for all her misfortunes, including getting sick. She was sure I snuck germs in from the college for some deranged biological warfare so that I could gain status in the choir. I tried to assure her that I practiced stringent personal hygiene, but she always treated me as if I had come straight from a leper colony. It was ironic that she had the crud and I walked around with nary a sniffle, in spite of seriously neglecting things like good nutrition, exercise, sleep, and the pursuit of happiness.

* * *

George insisted we stop for provisions at the grocery store before taking him home. He had scratched out a shopping list on the back of his discharge papers. This was not like George at all. I almost took him back to the hospital and demanded they exchange him for the *real* George. The man I knew never made lists, and even if he did, they would not be for things like coriander, tilapia (whatever that was), boneless chicken breasts, wild rice, fresh spinach, baby redskin potatoes, blueberries, romaine, cage-free eggs, whole grain bakery bread (fresh!), and so on. Those were just a few of the items. I tore the list in half and Mother and I split up. I had no idea what tilapia was and wondered if George meant tapioca, and if so, was it the boxed pudding mix we all grew up on or the unadulterated stuff on top shelf. Fortunately, I ran across a kid stocking shelves. He told me tilapia was a fish (nothing to do with tapioca), but when I checked out the fish area in the meat case, they only had lake trout and salmon. It was purely dumb luck that I finally spotted the elusive tilapia in the frozen seafood section of the store, intermingling with other frozen aquatic species. After about a half hour, Mother and I rendezvoused at the check-out and laid out our goods.

Mother said, "I didn't know George cooked. Why, he's never even buttered a piece of bread that I've noticed."

I said: "This is what happens when you confine a man to a hospital room with nothing but soap operas, daytime talk shows, and the cooking network."

I about choked when the cashier announced the cost of our small collection of oddball groceries.

There were to be no culinary specialties emerging from the Trout kitchen that evening. We all had cereal and toast with peanut butter and jelly then watched the news and turned in early. In keeping with doctor's orders, George and I engaged in some long-overdue "stimulation" that night. I was pleased to find that things hadn't changed all that much after all, bald head notwithstanding.

* * *

The next day was Saturday, a day off for both Bertie and me. We decided to meet around 1:00 at Tillie's Bakery in town to have a chat. Tillie had seen a ripe opportunity to improve her bottom line by setting up a few tables and chairs and making assorted carafes of specialty coffee to go with her tasty treats. She had recently added things like cappuccino and decadent muffins to the menu.

Bertie's boys had a Judo class at the township hall, which would keep them occupied for an hour or so. Woofie was at the Pampered Pooch Pet Parlor, which also did doggie day care and boarding. According to Bertie, Woofie was fine with the grooming, but freaked if they tried to cage him. Since he was otherwise an easy-going boy, the groomers let Woofie hang with them before and after his sprucing up. He was a perfect gentleman so long as there was no chain link between him and the outside world. Bertie said she always tipped heavily.

"Here's the deal," Bertie said. "Those two boys of Bucky's are in a lot of trouble with their ol' dad." Bertie took a sip of her mocha cappuccino with double chocolate and extra whipped cream. I had the same.

"Cheyenne is the oldest," Bertie continued. "He's getting the most blame since he's almost twelve and should know better. The younger one, Dakota, is only seven and technically can't understand the legal ramifications of his actions."

"Don't tell me that the Tanner boys are responsible for their dad getting arrested," I said.

"Well, yes they kind of are," Bertie said, licking whipped cream off her upper lip. "Of course, they were just being boys, screwing around."

"So, are you going to tell me or what?" I said.

"Yea, of course. It's going to be in the newspaper anyway—public knowledge. See once the boys knew their dad was in deep doodoo, they thought they better come clean. The boys were not allowed to go into Bucky's game processing building—what with all those saws and dangerous stuff—unless accompanied by one of their parents. According to Cheyenne, they had heard their dad talking about a kind of beetle that eats the flesh off an animal skull. They thought maybe Bucky had acquired a batch of those disgusting bugs to clean up deer skulls before boiling them for his clientele."

"Major yuck," I said, setting down my cappuccino.

"All part of nature," Bertie said. "Anyhow, the youngest, Dakota, said he wanted to maybe work the beetles into a science project and win a trophy and show up some other kid in his class who was mean to him. Jeffie has told me about the bully. There's one in every batch. Anyway, our future mastermind criminals, Cheyenne and Dakota, snuck out of their room to check out their dad's meat locker. They were skulking in the shadows when they noticed two cars parked behind the place. In that a two track comes up the back way through the woods to the building, it's a favorite spot for kids and even adults to come for a little nookie and maybe a beer or two. Bucky said he's always cleaning up used condoms and empties along with an occasional hypodermic needle. The vegetation is so grown up around the place that it's hard to spot trespassers. Anyway, the Tanner boys had heard their dad complain more than once about the damn kids that carried on back there, so they figured that's what was going on. They didn't want to let on to their parents that they had spotted some activity—since they were supposed to be doing homework—so they shrugged it off. They waited, still determined to find carnivorous bugs. Eventually one of the cars left and they think there was just one person in it but didn't know if it was a man or woman and it was too dark to tell much about the car.

"The boys weren't sure what to do at that point because there was still a car left there, and they didn't see or hear anybody moving around. They were thinking about abandoning their search for flesh-eating beetles when the meat locker door opened and a man came out. It took some doing according to the boys since there was a board or wooden pallet wedged up against the door. The man looked around and hurried to the remaining car behind the barn and took off. The boys said they didn't get a good look, but he was an old guy who had light-colored hair. Of course to a kid, anyone over 20 is old. Anyway, it wasn't some teenager and according to the boys, they guy seemed kind of ticked off, saying the F-word and all and he walked like he was in a big hurry. When the guy left, he spun his tires, too, the boys said."

"I think we know who that was: James Rush," I said.

"More'n likely," Bertie said. "Looking for the Parks woman who was—for reasons not yet known—luring James out to the Tanner place to screw with him—figuratively, that is."

"Right," I said. "According to James, she said she had an explosive story that would gain him fame and fortune in the world of reporting. He fancies himself as a world-class investigative reporter, along with being irresistible to women." I thought about how he had treated Mother and felt my metaphorical hackles stand up.

Bertie and I both took a major swig of our cappuccinos.

Bertie said: "Rush is a has-been piece of fluff, you ask me. And probably looking for a little moonlight delight." She glanced at her watch and sighed. "I still got a few minutes before they release my boys back into an unsuspecting world."

"So, the Tanner boys hightailed it back in and kept mum?" I said.

"Oh no," Bertie said. She looked wistfully at the assorted fresh pastries in the glass case at the front of the shop. "I'm gonna get a blueberry muffin. You want one?"

"Sure," I said. "Even after seeing a stranger come from their dad's meat locker, they didn't go in and fess up?"

Bertie held up a finger to pause the conversation. When she returned with the muffins, she carefully peeled off the paper wrapper and took a bite. "They say these things are just as bad as donuts How can that be? It's got blueberries for God's sake."

I began working on my muffin. It was enormous—an entire meal—and sensational. Tillie had outdone herself.

"Anyway, the little dickens continued their quest to discover flesh-eating beetles. Dakota said that he wanted to go back because he was scared, but Cheyenne called him a sissy pants or some other name and double dog dared him to go into the locker. I can tell you from having two boys of my own that a double dog dare is extremely compelling."

I nodded and smiled. 'Only a triple dog dare trumps it—and that's reserved for things like bungee jumping and eating worms."

We had both finished our muffins and our cappuccinos. Bertie glanced at her watch again.

"Crap, gotta go in a minute. Anyway, the two youngsters did go in the locker and look around for a bucket of beetles snacking on a skull. They of course knew their way around since they'd go in with their dad sometimes and hang out. I think they were just as glad that there weren't any flesh-eating beetles to be found and were in agreement they should sneak back into the trailer before they were missed. The locker door had shut, probably automatically, when they went in. When they went to leave, it wouldn't open. Cheyenne accused Dakota of bawling like a girl and so on. Dakota said that it was all Cheyenne's fault that the knife blade snapped off and got stuck in the handle. Apparently, it was Dakota's knife—a prized possession—that Cheyenne tried to jimmy the door with."

"Aha!" I said. I had always wanted to say aha, though now it just sounded silly.

"Eventually they did get the door to open and went back to the house."

"All that excitement and the boys *still* didn't tell their folks?"

"Nope. Hid the remains of the broken knife under the bunk bed mattress."

"They thought they were home free," I said.

"Until they found out that *later that night* Weasel Watkins got trapped in there and died and of course Bucky got arrested by that numskull Burns after they found the broken knife under the bunk mattress. At first the boys said they didn't know how it got there. Then they wallowed in guilt for a while, caved and decided that the jig was up and they better come clean."

"How do we know they weren't coached on the story, to cover for Bucky?" I said.

"Got a professional in to talk to the boys," Bertie said. "Felt they were being truthful. Usually when a child has been coached on what to say, he falls apart pretty quickly. We teach them not to lie, after all. Besides, there is another piece to the puzzle. Hey, I gotta get my rug rats!"

We both got up and put on our jackets.

"Another piece of the puzzle?" I said.

"Yup. Can't say a lot right now, but let's just say that alcohol wasn't the only substance coursing through Weasel's veins."

≠ 20 ≠

Our choir pianist, Azinnia Wattles, was passing around a get-well card for choir members to sign. We were having an extra practice on Sunday after church. Cantata Sunday was rapidly approaching. Hannu was known to spring extra practices on the choir and heaven help anyone who didn't show up. The card being circulated was intended for Eleanor Heimlich who was stricken with laryngitis. According to Azinnia, Eleanor was under doctor's orders to restrict talking and no singing for at least two weeks. The consequence was obvious: plan B would be implemented, and I was on the hook.

We all signed the card with the usual get-well-soon platitudes and an occasional smiley face, which was open to interpretation. Azinnia collected the signed card back from the choir and said, "I took Eleanor some chicken soup to, you know, help her feel better. Poor Eleanor is writing things out on a pad of paper. She's beside herself. She'll have to miss the cantata."

There was a murmur amongst the choir and I could feel people looking at me.

"My opinion?" Azinnia continued, "Eleanor just practiced too much and blew out her vocal cords. I know she had a cold or something too, but the virus went straight to her throat." She gave Hannu a contemptuous look. "I think she was under a lot of pressure."

Hannu shrugged. "It's too bad, but maybe she just talks too much." He looked at Azinnia; the message was clear. So much for sympathy.

"Maybe Janese put a curse on her," suggested the ever-pompous James Rush from the back row. A couple of people chuckled. I gave James a poisonous look. I'd have loved to put a curse on him, the pervert. Mother had fallen for his cow patty rhetoric, but not me. I knew it was unchristian-like, but I wished James had stayed trapped in Bucky's meat locker long enough to freeze off a certain piece of his anatomy, thus doing the female population of Moose Willow a great service. The thought made me smile. *Careful!* warned The Voice. *You are in church for God's sake.*

My thoughts shifted from James the eunuch to the more troubling issue of me being Eleanor's understudy, as such. We had a total of five—now four—sopranos in the choir. Yet Hannu targeted me. I was a fraud. I could only hit an E flat on a good day, and there weren't all that many good days. The part in question wasn't considered a high soprano solo, but it wasn't a piece of cake, either. I could feel panic growing.

"Um, perhaps we should forget the solo?" I suggested.

Hannu ignored me.

"Well not forget it but, you know, the whole section could do the part where Mary sings to God," I continued. "Or perhaps one of the others?" I looked at my sister sopranos, all of whom quickly shifted their eyes down and intently studied their music.

The solo part in question was when God shows favor upon Mary and she realizes what it all means and sings to God that her soul has been glorified and she's on board with the deal. You know, the immaculate conception. In other words, Mary gets a holy bun in the oven. The irony was not lost on me.

"No, you are best for the part," Hannu said. As usual, his tone suggested that there would be no discussion.

I wasn't "best" because I was *best*. I knew what he was saying. The Virgin Mary was really just a girl maybe about fifteen. While my teenage years were in the distant past, I was still considerably younger than the three remaining sopranos: Loreen, Rose, and Carolyn, all of whom were a tad long in the tooth for the part. Of course, Derry Parks would have been perfect. That is if she had been authentic and not up to something besides singing His praises. And, of course, she was now a "person of interest" regarding assorted nefarious activities. Her underlying motive still remained a mystery. I did think, however, that if George's brain ever got back up to speed, he would have some answers to the Derry Parks mystery. If the authorities ever tracked her down, she would have some explaining to do.

"Okay, lets run through *My Soul Glorifies the Lord,*" Hannu barked. "Janese, you come in at the solo on measure 42."

I wasn't half bad. Get thee behind me, Eleanor!

* * *

The cooking smells were amazing. It wasn't Mother toiling over Sunday dinner because she was in St. Ignace checking on things at the resort. The weather forecast had looked good for driving, so she left Saturday for a quick trip with the promise that she'd be back in time for Dr. Bloom/ Dreamboat to come to dinner that week. She also said that she thought George and I needed some time alone to "sort things out."

"Oh good, you're home," George said. "Dinner will be ready in a few minutes. I hope you're hungry. I made pot roast."

I stepped into the kitchen. Shock and awe. George was wearing an apron, albeit a "man" apron, with a picture of barbeque tools emblazoned on the front. I had no idea where it had come from. George had gotten the okay to drive when discharged from the hospital and had borrowed my car on Saturday to apparently stock up on an assortment of culinary doodads and thingamajigs, along with more groceries. The pantry and fridge were overflowing. George's truck was still under lock and key at the impound lot. Bertie had promised to find out what the delay was in getting it released. I didn't appreciate having to readjust the seat, mirrors, and radio station after George drove the Subaru. Plus, God forbid he would put some gas in it.

The delicious aroma made my low gas warning light seem trivial. I wondered if it had little potatoes and carrots basting in the juices. And maybe gravy? The kitchen was a disaster. There was not one inch of the countertop that did not have a dish, cutting board, knife, spoon, bowl, or food debris on it. A salad had been prepared and placed on the dining table, along with a cruet of apparently homemade dressing. There was a basket of bread, a spread that I was later to learn was garlic butter (to die for), along with a jar of spicy brown mustard that was new to the household. The table was set rather elegantly. There was even a tablecloth. My wineglass was conspicuously absent.

George sidled over, pulled me to him and we kissed. "Hmmmm, you smell good," he said.

Something had definitely changed with George—and not just his temporary baldness. Since when did he notice how I smelled? Probably like gas, since I had to fill up on the way home from church. However, while I felt some concern about the new George, I also enjoyed being, well, noticed. I snuggled up against him. "You smell good too, in a savory, meaty kind of way."

George gently broke the embrace. "Better not get involved in anything," he said. "Food should be ready." He hustled over to the oven and pulled the door open. He grabbed a potholder and lifted the lid off a small roasting pan, then stuck something—a meat thermometer, which I didn't know I had—into the roast. Lifting the lid had released even more wonderful aromas. I was beginning to salivate.

"Medium rare—perfect," he said. "I need room to carve!"

The food was excellent. There were indeed little roasted potatoes, carrots, and pearl onions along with meat so tender you could cut it with a butter knife, all of which I drenched in gravy. There was also a fruit cobbler with real whipped cream for dessert.

Engorged, I pushed myself away from the table, set down my fork, and looked at George. "So, what's going on?" I said.

"What do you mean?" he said, licking the last vestiges of whipped cream off his fork.

"You know—the cooking. Since when did you become a domestic god?"

He looked thoughtful for a minute then shook his head. "Don't know."

"Not that I'm complaining, mind you, but you've—well, changed since the accident. I'm kind of worried."

George began to clear the table, then stopped halfway into the kitchen, still holding an armload of dirty dishes. "I'm beginning to remember," he said.

I rose to help clean up, which would be a monumental chore. "Remember?" I said.

"The woods. And a cabin. And a woman," he said.

I took the plates from him and set them on the counter. "Go on," I said.

"Snippets of things are coming back," he said. He went into the living room and sat on the couch. "I remember being afraid. And cold."

I joined George on the couch. "The woman—who was the woman? Was she the one who asked you to meet her at the college parking lot during the blizzard?" I surmised it was Derry Parks, but I was careful not to say so.

He shrugged his shoulders. "Just a woman. She said I had to be punished. She was wearing a facemask, you know, like when it's really cold and you are out shoveling or snowmobiling. I didn't see her face at least at first."

"Punished? For what?" I said.

"Don't know."

"Did you ever see her face—maybe later? Did she seem young, old, fat, thin?"

George shook his head. "Youngish, I think. Not fat. I can't remember her face. But she had a gun. Now I remember. She had a gun. Everything went blank until we got the cabin."

"A gun! Did she hold you at gunpoint?" I said.

"I think so—I—I don't remember exactly," he said.

"Where was the cabin you just mentioned?" I said.

George looked at me. "I don't know. We were just—there." He rose from the couch and went back into the kitchen and began to clang around. I followed him.

"You said everything went blank?"

"I think I passed out or she gave me something to knock me out."

"Gave you something? Like an injection or something in a drink. Did you drink anything?" I said.

George shook his head. "I don't think so. I just don't remember how we got there."

"Got where?"

"The cabin. I think I came to for a minute at some cabin, then went out again."

"Can you describe it—the cabin?" I said.

He shook his head again. "Everything was out of focus. I remember it smelled musty, unused. It's foggy, like a bad LSD trip from the 60s."

I looked at George. "LSD from the 60s? Where did that come from?"

"I don't know," he said. "I remember people talking about the 60s and the drugs and free love and everything. You know, it was part of our country's history, the whole counter-culture thing and I guess a bad LSD trip was nothing to take lightly. I heard it makes a user feel disconnected from reality as if floating and spinning in another universe. That's how I felt."

I rinsed off a few plates and handed them to George who, with great precision, loaded them into the dishwasher. "And now it's meth and fentanyl," I said. "Anyway, the cabin. What—besides being musty?"

"Next thing I remember was running through the woods and then I woke up for a minute in the hospital. There were all kinds people hovering over me, talking as if I weren't there. I knew I was safe, but my head hurt like a bitch and I thought I might be dying—you know, the way everyone was rushing around. I don't think I opened my eyes. It hurt too much. They must have given me something because I went out again. God! I wish I could remember!"

"You will," I said. George was looking anxious so I changed the subject while we finished cleaning up the kitchen. "Say, I'm singing a solo in the cantata. Eleanor Heimlich has laryngitis."

George barked out a laugh. "Now *her* I do remember. How could I forget that big poofy hair!"

"Right," I said. "She hates me and, by association, you. I'm not sure why."

We left the kitchen and went to the living room and George got a fire started in the fireplace. I turned on the television and began channel surfing. We were all cozy and warm when George turned to me and said, "I've been so out of it but I haven't forgotten, you know, I'm just wondering what's going on."

I muted the television and looked at him. "Sorry, I don't follow."

"You know—I wonder if you know for sure if you're—"

The phone rang. By the caller ID, I saw that it was Bertie so I quickly picked up.

"Hey, Bertie, what's up?" I said.

"Janese, we found Derry Parks," she said.

I grabbed the remote and muted the TV. George looked at me.

"God, really? Where is she—have you detained her?" I said. I looked back at George and mouthed the words *they found Parks.*

He mouthed back: *who?*

"Well, we haven't exactly detained her," Bertie said. "More like claimed her."

"Huh?"

"She's dead, Janese. Some guys on ATVs found her body earlier today. She was in a partially melted snowdrift, close to the ATV trail. One of the guys had his dog and it went nuts. They found her body and went to an area with cell service and called 911. It went to our post dispatcher. We retrieved the remains—I'm afraid a few critters found her first. Still, she's intact enough for a viable autopsy. They'll do it first thing tomorrow."

"Wow, dead? How—what happened?" I said.

"Don't know for sure," Bertie said. "Dumbass Burns got the call but I did talk to the ME and initial examination reveals nothing obvious so far as physical violence, you know like a gunshot or knife wounds. Again, some animals—um, anyway it could be exposure. Question being asked is how the hell did she get out there in the damn snowbank? It's like someone dropped her off, then left her to freeze to death? Anyway, they'll do a full workup."

I looked at George who had gotten up and was stoking the fire. "What do you mean, dropped her off?"

"Well, there was no vehicle around. Truth is, she was only about a mile from where we found George's truck. Anyway—she had to get out there somehow, and it was probably in the truck. George remember anything new?"

"A little—it's coming in bits and pieces. He mentioned a woman wearing a facemask. That she had a gun and maybe she somehow drugged him." I looked up at George, who seemed to be ignoring the conversation. He headed for the garage, carrying the firewood tote.

"Drugged him?" Bertie said.

"Well, he thinks something happened to incapacitate him," I said.

"Wait! A gun? This woman had a gun?" Bertie said.

"George's memory is fragmented. But he has a fuzzy recollection of her having a gun," I said.

"Did he say what kind of gun—like a handgun or a rifle, an assault rifle or what?" Bertie said.

"I just kind of assume a handgun of some type," I said.

I heard Bertie sigh into the phone. "I'll check, but I'm pretty sure there was no gun found with the body. And I'll check on the facemask, too. I don't know what she was wearing, clothing-wise, but I did hear that she was wearing a locket with a photo in it—probably her fella. Maybe it will be helpful."

The line was silent for a few beats. I could hear some yelling in the background and a dog—no doubt Woofie—barking excitedly.

"Um, Janese, it would be great if George could give us his side of the story—YOU GUYS, I'M ON THE PHONE. Sorry about that. Anyway, I'm pretty sure Burns will want to talk to him about his relationship with Parks a/k/a whomever she may be. And they'll be going over the truck again—see if Parks left behind any fibers or, ah, DNA."

I felt my heart skip a beat and watched George come back from the garage with his firewood. He dumped the load into a log holder I kept by the fireplace. Next, he opened the screen, picked up the poker and began jabbing at the logs, sending sparks up the chimney.

"They think George had something to do with Park's death?" I whispered.

"Nobody's saying that, Janese. But right now her death is suspicious. STOP IT RIGHT NOW!"

"What?" I said.

"Sorry, the boys are on a tear. I made fudge and popcorn and they're all sugared up tonight. And I have to go into work in a few hours. Look, I gotta go, but I wanted to give you a heads up. I'll keep you posted."

170

"Yeah, okay," I said, looking up at George. He stood a few feet from the fire, staring, apparently mesmerized.

"Hey, don't worry. We'll figure it out. I'm sure there's a logical explanation—we just need to find it out," she said. "Let me know if George remembers anything more that might help. And if he thinks he was drugged, maybe he could ask the doctor if there's any way to tell after this amount of time."

"Okay, thanks," I said and hung up.

George turned around and faced me. "There was a fire but it went out," he said.

"No sweetie, the fire is burning fine," I said.

"No. You don't understand. *The cabin* where she took me. There was a fire."

I nodded. "Like a fireplace or a wood stove?"

He shrugged.

"But it went out?" I said.

"Yes."

"Then what?"

"It got cold."

I gave him an encouraging look to continue. He rubbed his hand over his head stubble.

"I might need a warmer hat," he said. "Having no hair is weird."

"No worries. It will grow back," I said, waiting for him to get back on track.

George sat on the couch next to me. "Maybe you can get me one of those Stormy Cromer hats for Christmas. It's coming soon, right?" he said.

George was not getting back on track.

"Christmas? Very soon," I said.

"Good. I'd like a hat," he said, his eyes beginning to droop.

The television was still on and still muted. A car zoomed silently across the screen with several police cars on its tail. Eventually, the car being chased got boxed in by the law. Bertie would have laughed at the number of police cars that magically materialized out of nowhere. She often said that sometimes her backup was a half hour away—maybe more if the roads were bad.

George let out a snort; his head was resting on my shoulder. He jerked a little, then relaxed. I wondered if he were reliving something—if only I could tap into his secrets.

Speaking of secrets—I looked down at my abdomen. It seemed the only thing dwelling there was a lot of food being digested. I was pretty sure George was getting ready to ask for a maternity update when the phone rang. I had gotten a business card for Dr. Shira's office and vowed to call the next day to make an appointment. I looked at George. I needed to know. *We* needed to know.

≈ 21 ≈

Turns out you can't just cold call a doctor's office and simply make an appointment. Silly me. I had procrastinated most of the week as I wrapped up things at the 4Cs. My three-week vacation/holiday time off officially started at noon on Friday. Of course, I didn't actually break away until into the early afternoon and the moment I arrived home, George grabbed my car keys and flew out the door to make his appointment with Dr. Bloom, and apparently also to buy food for dinner. George's truck was still being held hostage.

Before there were any more distractions—I expected Mother any minute—I pulled out Dr. Shira's card and called her office only to be batted around like a wayward shuttlecock. First, I got a recording that said everyone was busy and if I had a medical emergency to hang up and dial 911. I, of course, opted to hold and was therefore subjected to a looping recording touting the state-of-the-art wonders of the hospital and its excellent care, skilled doctors, and caring staff. On the third rerun, a woman came on the line and asked me to hold. This time I listened to silence.

I glanced at my watch wondering what was keeping Mother who had gone to her resort to insert herself into the Christmas preparations. She was due back to my humble abode any moment to oversee, among other things, a nice dinner for Dr. Bloom.

When the receptionist came back on the line and asked how she could help me, I politely introduced myself and requested an appointment with Dr. Shira. No, I was not a current patient. No, it wasn't an emergency, per se, but I may be pregnant. I thought maybe that would light a fire. I was told that while Dr. Shira was taking on new patients, she only had office appointments two days a week, and was booking into mid-January. Furthermore, you didn't just go in to see her and find out if you were pregnant. No, no, no. The receptionist suggested that I utilize an early pregnancy test, since it would be weeks before I could see her. Also, Dr. Shira was an internist, and of course would happily monitor my lady parts, but if I were pregnant, she would likely refer me to an OB/GYN. I told her that I had one of those, but, frankly, things never clicked between us. I was looking for a change.

My conversation with Dr. Shira's office did end with an appointment—for a full physical. If I wanted to be her patient, I had to submit to an overall inspection including the sacrifice of bodily fluids along with providing a complete medical history, medical releases, insurance information, and so on. I could expect a weighty packet of pre-appointment paperwork in the mail in a few days. I was sternly advised that when I did arrive for my appointment in mid-January, that I should be there early to complete more paperwork. If I was late, I would be thrown into the recycle bin. Not exactly her words, but I got the message: tardiness would not be tolerated. *Yeah, get there early and wait an hour for the doctor, who is running late,* said The Voice in a rare bout of sarcasm.

I hung up just as Mother burst into the cabin, breathless and, uh oh, dragging a jumbo suitcase on wheels.

"Janese! Darling!" she said, hurrying over to me and giving me an airy kiss.

"Mother, I said. How was your drive?" I looked at my watch. "I expected you earlier."

"Well, I *thought* I would be here earlier because Dr. Bloom is coming for dinner you know and, well"— she looked around the cabin— "I thought there may be some, ah, preparation, shopping, tidying up and such needing to be done. Anyway, would you believe a stupid logging truck turned over on Highway 28 and spilled logs all over the road—including the shoulders? It took *forever* to clean up and there was really no way around. And, of course, no damn cell service. Then when there was, I didn't want to try to fiddle with my phone while driving. Anyway, thank God nobody was hurt. I'm just beside myself." She let out an exasperated puff of air and pushed a wayward lock of recently dyed red hair off her forehead.

"George and I have things under control." I said. "He, um, cleaned the cabin *again* this morning and is running to the store for stuff for dinner after his appointment, you know, with your Dr. Dreamboat."

"He's not *my* Dr. Dreamboat. I just thought it would be appropriate to offer him a home-cooked meal. I hope you aren't planning that lasagna again."

"I have no idea what George is planning," I muttered.

"George?" Mother said.

"Yes, he's taken to cooking. Big time."

"Really? I thought maybe it was just a temporary—outlet," she said.

174

"Go figure," I said.

Mother and I chatted a few minutes about the resort. The motel was completely booked over the holidays and her new concierge was a dream. Willa was her name and *she* was formerly a *he*. Mother said that Willa exuded assurance and self-confidence, which worked perfectly in her position. She was a fount of information about the local history, cuisine, and general points of interest. It was a little hard not to notice the prominent Adam's apple, but otherwise, Willa was all woman with impeccable taste, hair to die for, and a flair for applying makeup. She could even wear stiletto heels and fake fingernails like a pro.

I glanced down at my ratty-looking tennis shoes and nearly jumped out of them when George slammed into the cabin.

"A little help!" he said.

I hurried over and helped carry in a half dozen grocery bags.

"Hello, dear," Mother said. "How's your head?"

"Hello, Maddie," George said. "Still attached to my neck."

I peered into a grocery sack. "So, what's for din din?"

"Well, I had to figure out something quick. I had wanted to do marinated pork tenderloin medallions, but there is no time to marinade and besides, thank God I found out, Dr. Bloom really doesn't eat pork. I mean, duh, he's Jewish. Anyway, I wanted to do swordfish, but they only had frozen and there is no time to thaw—"

"Sooooo?" I said, peering in another grocery sack. George shoved me aside and began frantically pulling things out and tossing them on the kitchen counter. Mother stood by with her mouth agape.

"Ditto with any fish—all frozen," George said. "So, then I decided I better keep it simple—where the hell did I put the Parmesan cheese? I hope that stupid bag boy didn't forget—oh, here it is. Thank God," he said slamming the canister on the counter.

"I think we've gone way beyond simple," I said. "How much did all of this stuff cost anyway?"

"Yes, simple. Basil chicken breasts and rice pilaf. How much simpler can it get than that?"

Mother and I looked at each other. "I'm going to go unpack," she said.

"And tabbouleh," George said.

"Tab what ah?" I said.

"Tabbouleh. It's a salad with bulgur wheat. I opted out of the flowering kale."

"Good," I said. "I can live without kale."

"And a crusty bread," he said holding up the loaf. "And dessert—sorry, I had to buy a cheesecake from Tillie's Bakery. No time to whip anything up. I got some good cheddar cheese and crackers. Do we have wine?"

I nodded.

"Beer?"

"Uh huh."

"I know there's scotch. I think we're good," he said, sighing. "I wish I had more time to do this right."

"You're doing just fine," I said. "Whoever you are."

George ignored my comment and began organizing things. "Here—chop!" he said, handing me a bunch of green leafy stuff.

I got the cutting board and a knife and obediently began chopping.

"Smaller," he said. "Also, there's fresh parsley and mint. Chop chop!"

I gave George a sideways glance and began chopping. "Soooo, what did the doctor say?"

"Hmmm," he said, as he began messing with a large package of boneless, skinless chicken breasts.

"You know—Dr. Bloom—the brain doctor!"

"I'm doing great," George said. "He is pleased I'm starting to remember. Mainly, though he had a lot of questions about Maddie."

"Oh?"

"Yup. He's smitten. Anyway, he suggested I try to find things to help trigger my memory."

"Uh huh—such as?"

"Well, we got to talking about the bearskin rug I was wearing when they, ah, brought me in and I wondered what happened to it. Maybe the hospital threw it away."

"Nope. It's in a big white plastic bag marked 'Personal Belongings' and stashed in the back of the closet. I figure we'll give it away or something."

"Well, it's something that might help me remember. Damn it! Did I forget—nope. When you're done with the greens, get those tomatoes and take out the seeds and chop them up, okay?"

"Take out the seeds? How the hell? Oh never mind," I said. I grabbed a tomato and tried to cut it in half. The knife was a little dull and I had to apply a lot of pressure. Once the blade pierced the skin, tomato guts burst out all over the counter.

"Oh, give me that," George said grabbing the knife.

"Hey! Watch it buster," I said.

George ran the blade through a knife sharpener, which I didn't know I had, washed it, and gave it back to me. "Try again. Oh, and I asked about being able to check for any traces of drugs, you know like the gal cop mentioned—what's her name—your friend the state trooper?"

"Her name's Bertie Vaara," I said.

"Anyway, they of course pumped me full of shit while in the hospital, so it may not be a viable option. Apparently, they can check for traces of stuff in the hair follicles," George rubbed his hand over his stubbly head. "But they need to know what we're looking for *and* they need a court order. I mean, somebody's gotta pay and I'm pretty sure my insurance through the college won't."

"So, they can't tell if you were drugged?"

"Probably not," George said. "How are those tomatoes coming?"

I resumed chopping. "So, the bearskin—how would that trigger things?" I said.

"I dunno," he said. "Maybe the smell."

"I'll get it," I said, dropping the knife into the sink. I retreated from the kitchen, away from the lunatic who had taken up residence in the body of my boyfriend and so-called fiancé. I went into the bedroom and as I was rooting around in the closet, there was a knock at the door.

"Mother! Please get the door," I yelled as I crawled out of the closet dragging the plastic bag containing the bearskin rug. I heard Mother's heels click down the stairs from the loft and across the living room floor, followed by the sound of an opening door.

"You!" she said.

"Maddie," said an all-too-familiar male voice.

"James. What are you doing here?" Mother said.

"Could you just let me explain?" James said. "It was all really just a *big* misunderstanding. May I come in?"

"No. Don't let him in!" I shouted from the bedroom door, plastic bag in tow.

"Hello Janese," James said. I ignored him and continued to wrestle with the bag.

"Hey, Jimbo," George said from the kitchen. "Come to bring me get-well wishes?"

"Don't call me that," James said.

"Okay—then Rushinski."

"Come in, James," Mother said.

"No," I said.

"Don't call me Rushinski. I had my name legally changed, Georgie Boy."

"Don't call me that!" George said, brandishing a large kitchen knife.

"Everyone calm down," Mother said. "James, come in and sit down."

I continued to drag the plastic bag behind me. Not sure why.

"Got a body in there, Janese?" James said.

"Maybe," I said pulling open the drawstrings. The ungainly, furry mess spilled out onto the living room floor.

Mother sneezed dramatically. "Honestly, Janese, did you have to bring that out now?"

"What the?" James said.

"It's a trigger," I said.

"Like hell," James said. "My cabin was burglarized, and you, my dear Janese, are in possession of stolen property."

There was a knock at the door.

"Stolen?" I said, stomping over to open it.

Detective Burns stood at the threshold and unnecessarily flashed his badge. We all knew who he was.

"Looking for George LeFleur," he said.

"Oh, crap," I said.

"Forget him," James said. "Arrest her," he said pointing at me. "She's got my bearskin rug."

"Waaaa?" I said.

There was another knock at the door.

"Double crap," I said, yanking open the door. Dr. Dreamboat stood at the threshold, bedazzling smile on his face, bouquet of flowers and bottle of wine in hand.

"Good evening," he said. "I hope I'm not late. I had to park on the road."

* * *

While the bulgur boiled for the tabbouleh, we all crammed into my living room like a collection of suspects from a cheesy British whodunit. Mother introduced everyone. She put Dr. Bloom's floral arrangement in a vase while he uncorked the wine. The fire in the fireplace was stoked and crackled merrily. The cheese and crackers appeared. Beverages were served, some alcoholic, some not.

"I didn't realize you were having a mystery dinner party, Maddie," Dr. Bloom said, sipping his wine. "What's my role?"

"Unfortunately, this is not a game," Mother said. "Excellent wine, Ben."

"I'm glad you like it," Dr. Bloom said.

James glared at Dr. Bloom. "Why's he here?"

"We invited him," I said pointedly.

"So, ah, Miss Trout," Detective Burns said, "this fur thing is what Mr. LeFleur was wearing when he, um, ran out of the woods onto your property?"

"The very same," I said.

"George stole it!" James said.

"James dear," Mother said, "shut up."

"Nobody stole it," I said. "Don't you see? George was in James' cabin—that woman must have taken him there. Somehow, he ended up, um, wearing that thing. I still say she drugged him."

"Is that how you remember it, Mr. LeFleur?" Burns said.

"I don't remember," George said.

"That's convenient, isn't it?" James said. "Maybe it was the *other* way around."

"Shut up, James," Mother said. Dr. Bloom gave James a steely look.

Burns cleared his throat in an attempt to regain control. "It seems likely that you and this woman—the dead woman Derry Parks—went out to Mr. Rush's cabin. Perhaps for some privacy?"

"He did no such thing!" I shouted. "He got a call from someone—I know it was Parks—posing as a magazine reporter and lured George to the college parking lot. Then, well, I'm not sure..."

James snorted and took a drink from his glass of scotch.

George looked at me and his eyes brightened. "*The Potter's Wheel!* I remember the call."

"Go on," Dr. Bloom said. "Do you remember what you did after the call?"

"Excuse me Doctor," Burns said, "but I'm asking the questions. I'd appreciate it if everyone would quit interrupting me."

"I understand," Dr. Bloom said, taking a sip of wine. "However, I am Mr. LeFleur's doctor and frankly I'm not sure he's well enough to be interrogated."

"I'm not interrogating him. I just have a couple of questions and didn't expect to walk into this hornet's nest," Burns said.

"If I may speak?" James said, "It was my property that was broken into. Stolen property is right there in front of us." He pointed at the bearskin rug. "I suggest that George did the luring—to *my* cabin. He knew about it because I told him—in fact everyone in this room except the doc knew about it."

"Yeah, but you never gave us directions, James," I said. "And why was George running around in the woods wearing an animal skin?"

"I can think of an obvious scenario," James said.

"Does your so-called scenario include the lovely Derry Parks knowing about your cabin *because you showed her?*" I said. "How about that scenario?"

"Don't be absurd," James said.

"Well, I did see you two at the Bayview playing footsie. And, of course, you had your little rendezvous at Bucky's meat locker. Maybe you two got *busy* at the Rushinski family hunting spa?"

Burns held up his hand as if stopping traffic. "Trooper Vaara did mention that she thought it was you, Mr. Rush, at Tanner's meat locker that night that Weasel Watkins died. She said that the Tanner boys described someone that roughly matched your description. You were next on my list to talk to about that night."

James slammed down his empty scotch glass. "I was investigating a news story and—"

"Exactly what was the story?" Burns said.

"The *implication* was that that Indian—"

"Bucky Tanner?" Burns said.

"Yea—Bucky was doing *something* that would make a breaking news story. Anyway, I was, well, duped by the Parks woman. She tried to kill me and shut me in the cooler when I went in there to investigate."

"You do realize that you and the woman were trespassing?" Burns said.

James squirmed a bit. "People come and go from that property all the time. If you cops were doing your job, you'd be dealing with all the illicit activities that go behind that place."

"You entered the meat locker," Burns said.

"True. I feared that Miss Parks may have been in peril and felt it my duty to investigate."

Mother, George, and I all snorted simultaneously.

James gave us all an icy look. "As they say, no good deed goes unpunished and she obviously shut me in the damn locker and tried to kill me."

"But all you needed to do was open the door and leave," Burns said.

"Ah, yes but she tried to prop a board or actually a pallet against the outside handle to block the door. It didn't hold and I managed to escape." James looked around the room. "I did go to my family camp to hide out for a bit, then when the weather started deteriorating, I left and came here to get some help because I was concerned about being ambushed at my home. Maddie, George, and Janese will certainly vouch for my condition when I arrived."

We all nodded reluctantly.

"But you never made an official complaint against the Parks woman?" Burns said.

"Well—I admit I was a bit embarrassed. And in all truthfulness, I never actually saw her. For all I know, it could have been those kids playing games with the wooden thing wedging the door shut. Maybe Miss Parks got spooked and aborted the rendezvous. Anyway, I was pretty shook up."

"The Tanner boys did mention someone leaving before James," I said. "But they couldn't give a description. "

Burns let out a sigh. I suspected he regretted his unannounced visit to my place.

"Besides," James said. "The real issue is that dead man, Watkins. There was no dead guy in that locker when *I* got trapped in there. I'm lucky to be out with my life, not that anybody cares. Once and for all I had nothing to do with that old fart croaking."

Burns said, "I'm not saying you did but perhaps you can help us with some of the details of that night. Could you stop by the police station in the morning? I'd like to ask you a few questions. Strictly voluntary, of course."

The room fell silent except for the crackling from the fireplace. A loud pop made us all jump.

"I'm on the air in the morning, I couldn't possibly—" James began.

"Tomorrow's Saturday," I said. "I didn't think you worked weekends."

James gave me a poisonous look. "Well, I—"

"I'd appreciate it if you'd drop by," Burns said.

"I'll be calling my lawyer," James said.

"Of course that's up to you," Burns said. "This will be informal—just a little fact finding."

James picked up his glass and rattled the ice, trying to produce some liquid, then set the glass back down. "What about the break-in at my cabin? We have evidence right in this room."

"I really came here tonight to talk to Mr. LeFleur," Burns said. "Not discuss the alleged break-in at your cabin."

"Alleged!" James said. "I've heard enough. Maddie, perhaps we can speak another time."

Mother was deadly silent at the suggestion.

"I'll just be taking back my property," James said, heading toward the bearskin rug. "This is a family heirloom."

"Actually," Burns said, "it may be evidence and I will be the one taking it tonight. Of course you'll get it back—eventually."

"See that I do," James said. He grabbed his coat and slammed the door when he left.

"If you'll allow me," Dr. Bloom said, "I would like to ask George if he remembers this cabin and how he got the fur. This could be very important to his recovery."

"I understand, doc," Burns said. "But first I would like to go back to something Miss Trout said a while back about the possibility of Mr. LeFleur being drugged."

"Right," I said. "Bertie and I were talking and—"

"Drugged?" Dr. Bloom said. "George, is this true—do you remember?"

"I don't," George said. "I just blacked out and we thought, you know."

"Well, maybe you blacked out because you were tased," Burns said. We all said *huh* in unison.

"We didn't see it when we first found Miss Park's body," Burnes said. "The crime lab went back for another look-see and found a Taser near the deceased's body, along with what appeared to be a knitted face mask, such as for a really cold day."

"Taser?" Mother said.

"A stun gun," Burns said. "They're used to subdue perps without using lethal force. The one we found had both cartridges used."

"But how in the world do you get a Taser?" Mother said.

"You can order them online," Burns said.

At last a couple of pieces had fallen into place. Of course, there were still gaping holes.

George walked over to the bearskin and picked it up. "When I woke up, she was gone."

Dr. Bloom walked over to George. "Go on," he said. "What else?"

"So was my truck and my clothes, except my skivvies."

"The Parks woman. You can identify her?" Dr. Bloom said.

George shook his head. "Left me to die—to freeze in the cabin. My hands were taped—duct tape I think."

A timer went off in the kitchen.

"Bulgur's done," George said.

Bertie picked me up Monday morning for our pre-Christmas procrastinator's power shopping spree. I hadn't bought a thing for anyone. If it weren't for Mother, I wouldn't even have a Christmas tree—albeit white and glittery. I had plans to convince George to accompany me in the woods to cut down a real tree, which according to Mother would be relegated to the porch.

Bertie said she started her shopping early, but still had plenty of panic shopping to do, as her family was enormous, extended, and competitive in the gift-giving area. While small families may be anticlimactic, we aren't forced to buy tacky gifts for cousins, uncles, or assorted stepfamily members. I only had Mother (impossible), George (formerly easy, now difficult), and Bertie's two boys, Jeffie and Robby (easy peasy—Bertie would help) to buy for. I also planned on getting something nice for Woofie, such as a squeaky toy that would drive everyone batty. Bertie and I, of course, needed to buy for each other as well, but that would be a separate shopping trip. Bertie and I always got together some time after Christmas to eat at a fancy restaurant, drink mimosas, and exchange gag gifts. The previous Christmas I had gifted her with an enormous bottle of cheap lavender toilet water. She took it very literally and used it to freshen the toilet water in the boys' bathroom. She had gotten me a book entitled: *Worm Farming for Dummies*. This year I needed to find something exceedingly insulting such as purple polyester pants with an elastic waistband, or maybe some pads for bladder leakage. But first things first; the serious shopping needed immediate attention.

We made the long drive to the shopping mall in Marquette and started our traditional girls' outing with a stop at a coffee shop for a latte and scones. My favorite scone was cream cheese and Bertie's was chocolate chip. Once we had consumed a thousand or so calories each, we headed to Mother's favorite store, Over 40 Faves. This store did not cater to girls with pierced tongues, tattooed butt cheeks, and bouncing boobies. Yet, there was nothing frumpy about the styles. Nothing cheap, either. I found a jazzy bolero jacket with accompanying blouse and skirt that positively screamed *rich and classy*. The sales associate, ever the professional, easily convinced me to include complementing earrings and necklace to complete the ensemble. I used my already overworked charge card to close the deal. The salesclerk tucked a discrete sales slip (sans amount) in the box, which she gift-wrapped for "free." In spite of the outfit being perfect, there was a fifty-fifty chance that Mother would return it on the principle that I was incapable of displaying any sense of style or good taste. Apparently, I took after my father. Since he had no influence on me growing up due to his untimely demise, Mother surmised my deficits were genetic.

Next Bertie and I went to the Dollar Store where she checked several nieces and nephews off her list with glittery disposable items that would be gleefully destroyed within minutes after opening. Next, we ventured to an amazing toy store that totally intimidated me. I got Bertie's youngest, Robby, something called a Tot Town Activity Set. The theme of Tot Town was first responder oriented, with a police car, fire engine, and ambulance along with various Tots as police officers, fire persons (yes there was a girl fire Tot), a diverse set of ambulance drivers: one African American (female) and one Hispanic (male). The victims, too, were an assortment of people of all ages, ethnic groups, and even a gender-neutral person, which was not difficult to pull off in that the Tots had not yet reached puberty. There was an American flag flying over the combo police/fire/ambulance/ hospital. Bertie's oldest, Jeffie, got a more run-of-the mill action hero thing encased in a plastic castle/cave of some sort. Jeffie's idea of social justice was simple: death to the enemy and his caped hero (male and very manly) was just the guy to do it. With political correctness oozing from every cellophane wrapping, I was glad to escape the toy store without violating some social ethic.

Bertie and I headed for the car to make a package drop then began thinking about lunch. We decided on an upscale repast at a place called the Lands End Inn. It was an historic hotel and restaurant, with a lunch menu that went way beyond the burger. In keeping with our surroundings, we both ordered a salmon salad, bread toasted with olive oil and garlic, and wine for Bertie with a Virgin Mary for me. (Oh, the irony!) For dessert, we indulged in raspberry cheesecake. The very good-looking waiter drizzled dark chocolate on our desserts while we watched. He knew we would tip him extravagantly.

Bertie smacked her lips with her first bite of dessert. I held my first bite on my tongue, relishing the creamy richness. Tillie's Bakery had good cheesecake, but the Lands End had *outstanding* cheesecake. Having a hot waiter instead of Tillie's surly attitude helped too.

"So, how's George?" Bertie said, pouring herself some wine. I hadn't really counted but was thinking she was over the two-glass limit.

"Good, but weird," I said. "He doesn't seem to care anymore about his sculpture. All he does is fuss around the cabin and try new recipes. He has become obsessed with cooking and has even talked about going to chef school. I wish he would start seeing his therapist again. Now he's bonded with Dr. Bloom."

"Does seem a little weird—the cooking bug," Bertie said, taking a generous slug of wine. "This is ever since the bonk on the head, right?"

"Uh huh," I said, licking the last morsel of cheesecake off my fork. "Thing is, he was an okay sculptor and all, and a good teacher. The kids like him—correction: the girls *love* him. But he is positively passionate about cooking. Every day there is some new gadget in the kitchen and something unrecognizable in the fridge. Dinner is never plain ol' grilled cheese. Oh no, it has to have three kinds of gourmet cheese, special bread, and alfalfa sprouts on it. Yuck—I mean to the sprouts. Of course, Mother loves it. Says I could take a lesson."

"What does this Doctor Boom say?" Bertie said, frowning at her empty glass.

"Bloom. It's Dr. Bloom a/k/a Dr. Dreamboat. I don't know, but he seems very interested in George—kind of like a human guinea pig. Both George and I are going to meet with him next time he has a clinic here."

"Dr. Dreamboat?" Bertie said, scowling at me. Her gaze was a bit unfocused.

Just then our waiter floated up to our table, holding a padded leatherette binder, which obviously contained our bill.

"Could I get you ladies anything else?"

"We are all set, thank you—Michael," I said, reaching for the bill. Bertie and I weren't so gauche as to ask for separate checks. However, we were both cheap and neither of us offered to pick up the tab. Fortunately, we didn't quibble about minor differences and split things down the middle. Even cut in half, after adding a substantial gratuity, the bill would exceed my normal lunch expenses for a week at the 4Cs, where the cafeteria served up good, cheap food in substantial portions.

Michael floated away to allow us time to pool our cash—no plastic—and set the leatherette binder at the edge of the table. Once that was done, he swooped back, gave us a 25% gratuity smile, and again wished us an excellent afternoon, then left, leaving behind an ever-so-faint wisp of manly cologne.

We lingered a while, reluctant to face the mall mob again. Bertie gave me a wicked grin. She definitely had had more than the two-glass limit of wine.

"Sooo," she said. "I've been dying to talk about this Weasel Watkins thing." Except she had trouble enunciating and Watkins came out more like Whatkinsh. I was glad that I had command of the driving and had only consumed the Virgin Mary. Also, I doubted Bertie had gotten much sleep lately.

"Right," I said. "You mean with James Rush and the Parks woman and all?" I said.

"Well, there is that little tryst, but, you see, that while Mr. Whatkinsh had an impressive blood alcohol level—almost 2.0, it was the drugs that did him in."

"Drugs?" I said.

"Shhhhh," Bertie said, holding her finger up to her lips. "Don't tell anyone. Ish a secret."

She began to giggle and I nodded, hoping for more.

"Benza-something in the toxicology report. Wait, let me think. Benzodia—shit! Anyway, mix it with the booze and it's bye bye for ol' wazhisname. 'course he still basically died from exposure, but it was the alcohol and benza-stuff that made him black out first. Least that's what the report says."

Bertie burped a little then got the hiccups. She looked at me. "They think his ol' lady knocked him off."

"Aileen!"

"Shhhhh," Bertie said, looking around the room. "Yea. Her. It was her benza-whatever. A whole crap load of it in his system. Anyway, she had a 'scription for it, so ya put two and two together and you get a dead hubby."

"What the hell?" I said. "Aileen? The pillar of the church and epitome of righteousness. No way."

"Way," Bertie said, then added, "I don't feel so good." She suppressed another burp and suddenly looked very pale.

"We better get you home," I said.

Bertie jumped up and raced to the ladies' room. I suspected the expensive lunch was about to be lost.

* * *

"Phenox," Mother said. "Spelled with a P-H, not an F. Millions of those little happy pills are prescribed every year for anxiety, depression and so on. It's the designer drug. Used to be Proaloz but now it's Phenox. I'm sure it's gone generic by now."

"And how do you know so much about this, er, happy pill?" I said.

"Well, darling, I've had some ups and downs in my life. I don't leave home without them."

"Oh," I said, as I Googled Phanex. A bunch of hits came up asking if I meant PHENOX. Yes! Sometimes I loved computers, when I didn't hate them. They could read your mind. *Phenox (alprazolam-generic) a Benzodiazepine.*

"I'm going into town to get some wrapping paper. The stuff you have here looks like it's been around for a decade," Mother said as she scooped up her keys and coat.

I nodded. I felt a little smug knowing I had my own shopping underway *and* had my gift for Mother professionally wrapped. Then I frowned. But what about George? Should I get him a gift certificate to Chef Pierre's Culinary School or something? Send him to New York, never to see him again? George was always an enigma. The moment I had arrived home, he snatched the keys to my Subaru (his truck was *still* being held at the impound lot) and said he needed to go to the 4Cs to do some "business." When I asked if he was going to go tie up some loose ends from the semester he just shrugged and muttered "something like that."

I exited out of my phone and went to my computer so I'd have a bigger screen. Again, good ol' Google: *Benzodiazepine: side effects, risks.* Several pages of information were available, so I randomly selected one. It became clear that mixing a Benzodiazepine—or Benzo—with alcohol was playing Russian roulette, because they were both central nervous system depressants. I skimmed more info about metabolizing and the increased risk of overdose, suppressed breathing, reduction of cognition and physical reaction, brain and organ damage, and possible death. An example was given of a woman who had mixed the two, blacked out in her vehicle, and froze to death. This sounded all too familiar. Janese Trout: super sleuth.

Bertie made it sound as if Aileen Watkins was favored for being the culprit. I picked up the phone to call Bertie, hoping she was sober and awake. When I had delivered her home and poured her into bed, her hubby and the boys were gone doing some shopping of their own. I suspected that her drunken indulgence would come to an abrupt end anyway when they returned, so I keyed in her number. Just before voicemail would have kicked in, a groggy voice came on the line.

"'lo?"

I was feeling mischievous and tried to disguise my voice. "Hey Vaara You gotta come into work right away. A semi has spilled its load on 28 and dumped a bunch of live turkeys all over the highway." I stifled a snicker. "They're making a break for it. You gotta round them up!"

"Bite me," she said and hung up.

I pushed redial and it went to voicemail.

And again. Voicemail.

As I was ruminating about trying one more time and really pissing Bertie off, I heard someone drive up. I figured it was George, but then there was a soft knock on the door. When I swung it open, I was shocked to see Aileen Watkins.

"Aileen. What are you doing here?" I said. It occurred to me that I was home alone with a potential murderer glaring at me from my doorway.

"You mean instead of in jail," she said, pushing past me.

"Won't you come in," I murmured, looking around for the phone that I had not put back in its cradle. My cell was even further out of reach, plus it didn't usually work at the cabin, unless I went outside, stood on a stump, and faced Mecca.

"Are we alone?" Aileen said, inspecting the living room. She slipped out of her coat and let it drop to the floor. I half expected a gun or bludgeoning weapon of some sort to be tucked into her waistband. But then she killed with prescription medicines, didn't she? Besides, this woman before me didn't look like she could swat a fly. She seemed to have collapsed into herself. Her hair, normally tightly curled, appeared to have exploded out of her head and dwarfed her sallow face. The outfit she had selected for the day neither looked fresh nor matched. I was fairly certain the natty sweater she wore was both inside out and backwards, unless the latest fashion was to display clothing tags under one's chin. She had on one black and one brown shoe.

"Um, I expect George back any minute," I said, inching my way toward the door.

Aileen dropped wearily onto the couch. Unfortunately, I had left the phone sitting on the couch cushion, and I watched helplessly as it slid down the crack next to her. So much for dialing 911.

189

"They think I killed my Clarence." She let out a sob. "It's all because of that infernal igloo contest." She gave me a piercing look.

"Aileen, I—"

"I tried to tell them—they had me in for questioning, did you know that? It was humiliating. I admit that from time to time, I did sneak a few of my pills into Clarence's hot chocolate. It was to help him. I wasn't trying to kill him for God's sake! He wouldn't get professional help even though he had that post-traumatic stress disorder—you know from when he was overseas in the service. He told me he had stopped drinking, so I thought it was okay. He was so wound up about that infernal igloo contest; it was like he was back in Viet Nam somehow, on a mission. So, like any good wife, I tried to help. And he liked his cocoa for lunch. So every day I put a couple pills in his cocoa and it always worked. Like I said, it was to help him, you know. I find the pills very calming. That contest! It was like the most important thing in the world to him. I just don't understand it." She gave me a withering look. "It's because of the contest that he went to Bucky's meat locker."

After going to the bar, I thought.

"I was only trying to ca-calm him down, but I don't think they ba-ba-ba-leeve me!" she wailed.

I stood paralyzed, trying to decide if I should go pat her on the shoulder, or make a break for it.

"My la-lawyer says they might charge me. Oh, good Lord, what is happening?" she said. "I might take a lie detector test. I never was good at tests. I always get all flustered and discombobulated. I'll probably flunk, just like I did algebra." She sniffed loudly and wiped her nose on her sleeve.

Humanitarian that I am, I shoved a box of tissues toward her.

"I'll go to prison and become someone's sex slave! I've heard horrible stories." She gazed over at me. "I have prayed." She sniffed again and snatched a tissue from the box and noisily blew her nose. "I prayed for him—my Clarence, and the Lord gave me guidance."

"To, um, sneak pills into his cocoa?" I said.

Aileen sighed. "Yes. I pray and He answers."

I didn't know what to say. Was the woman implying that a voice in her head was telling her what to do? What was that? Schizophrenia?

Aileen fixed a steady gaze on me. I was no expert, but I was pretty sure that she had medicated herself beyond the recommended dosage that day. I didn't like the look in her eye. Not one bit. Her lips had

190

formed a very tight line, and I noted that the tissue she had been holding was reduced to balls of lint.

I cleared my throat. "Ah, Aileen. Why don't you let me call someone to take you home for a rest?" I thought about her tight knit group of church ladies. "Perhaps a couple of your friends from the church?"

"Humph," Aileen said. "They have abandoned me like rats on a sinking ship. Sisters in Christ, indeed! Harlots! All of them."

"Well, perhaps I could, um call you a cab," I said. Inching closer to the door.

She looked at me as if I had suggested she fly to the moon.

"There is a cab service in town now, you know. I think it's called Tribal Taxi. I've heard that they give good service. So why don't I just..."

Aileen sat, as if in a trance. For a moment I thought she might have slipped into a coma. Then she leapt up and scared the bejesus out of me.

"I must wash myself in blood!" she shrieked. "Then I will be clean and they will exonerate me."

Aileen moved toward me with surprising speed, fists clenched, eyes fiery. In my haste to make it to the door, I backed into an end table and lost my balance along with an ugly lamp that Mother gave me. We both crashed to the floor, with Aileen closing in. Stunned and possibly suffering a mild concussion, I lay there a moment like a wounded animal, hoping to blend with the underbrush. Aileen grabbed a shard of glass from the broken lamp and knelt on my chest. She had begun to babble about Jesus and blood and slashed at me with the shard. I managed to deflect her moves with my one functioning arm, but she had amazing strength and stamina. Just as she managed to make a slender slice across my neck, someone knocked on the door.

I heard someone scream for help.

I think it was me.

≈ 23 ≈

Fortunately, Detective Burns determined that a scream from within a domicile created exigent circumstances justifying a forced entry through the front door. This meant that he kicked it in, splintering the frame around the doorknob mechanism. That was all very dramatic, but too bad he didn't just try the knob, which was unlocked. In any event, I was not sorry to see him come storming in and yell: "Freeze! Police!" Again, unnecessary, at least for me and I was pretty much rendered immobile by Aileen whose boney knees had me pinned on the floor and her weapon of choice, a shard of pottery, kept my rapt attention. Unfortunately, the bop on my head made everything a bit out of focus and it all happened so fast.

Detective Burns, to his credit, quickly assessed the situation and grabbed my knobby-kneed assailant and tore her off me. I think he yelled in a very authoritative voice: "DROP THE WEAPON!" In that she was brandishing pottery rather than a gun, this may have been confusing to her, especially since she was likely not of sound mind. Nonetheless, she dropped the pottery shard and Burns neatly pulled handcuffs from their case on his belt and secured them around Aileen's wrists. He pushed her to the floor, then knelt next to me and said something like. "Hey, Miss Trout, are you injur—Ow!"

I should mention that I was not yet fully with it when the next few activities occurred. It seems that Detective Burns had knelt on a secondary pottery shard, and his reflexes kicked in causing him to lose his balance and fall on me. I was not in a ladylike posture and he was smack on top of me in the "missionary position" the moment Mother burst through the door, which of course had a forced-entry appearance.

"Get off her you fiend!" she screamed and raced over to Burns and began pummeling him with her purse, which I can guarantee weighed at least fifteen pounds.

"Mother! No!" I managed to squeak. "It's okay."

Mother stopped mid pummel.

Burns managed to roll off me and tried to help me up. Meanwhile, Aileen, who apparently needed child-sized cuffs, had slipped her shackles and was crawling toward the door when George walked in.

"Hey, Trout, is this some kind of yoga class?" Good ol' George. Always clueless.

Burns managed to detain Aileen before she made her escape and then tried to use his cell to call for backup and the paramedics. I pointed out to him that his cell wouldn't work and dug the cordless landline out of the crack of the couch for him to use. In no time at all, we could hear the wail of sirens.

* * *

Next thing I knew, I was whisked off to the hospital emergency room for assessment. You know the redundant saying: it was like déjà vu all over again. I had the strangest feeling this had happened before. And it had, sort of. First, the ER physician attended me, then the sparkling Dr. Bloom, who just happened to be doing a clinic that day, checked out the blow to my head. Both said that I would be just fine, and while the slash across my neck was disturbing, it didn't require stitches. For this I was grateful, as I did not want to wear turtlenecks for the rest of my life. Dr. Bloom said I may have received a mild concussion. He held up fingers for me to count. Asked me silly questions and looked into my pupils then abandoned me when Mother entered the room. While the two distracted one another, a nurse came in and had George sign discharge papers with instructions for my feeding and care. I was told that I was free to leave. After a surreptitious glance at Dr. Dreamboat, the nurse left the room.

As if that weren't enough to happen in one day.

It seems Detective Burns' visit to my cabin—albeit very good timing—had nothing to do with the seriously unglued Aileen Watkins, who had been whisked off by a female police officer perhaps to a cozy room with auto-locking door at the hospital for psychiatric assessment. I didn't plan to sign a complaint against her, so in all likelihood she would be evaluated and released the same day. Hopefully with some stipulation to undergo therapy.

Burn's unannounced visit actually had been an effort to talk to George about Derry Park's death. It also seemed that George did not go to the 4Cs to catch up on paperwork, but rather—and without any discussion whatsoever with me—to shift his career from clay to cuisine. He had resigned as an art teacher at the college and gave the dean a proposal for starting a culinary program, which he, George-who-had-learned-all-there-is-to-know-from-the-network-cooking-channel, could chair. Other than the fact that he totally lacked the proper credentials and that Upper Michigan's idea of haute cuisine was a Friday night fish fry, I'm sure they were ready to jump, feet first, into George's venture. You betcha.

I learned this little nugget of career-shifting news from George on our trip directly from the hospital to State Police headquarters, where his presence was requested by Detective Burns. Since I couldn't be left alone I was allowed to tag along. Mother was otherwise occupied. Supposedly she and Dr. Bloom would be going to my cabin to temporarily secure the splintered door then go out get a bite. A bite of what, I wasn't sure, nor did I want to know.

One fortunate thing did happen. Bertie showed up, wearing civilian clothes, and while she didn't save the day, she certainly improved it. Instead of holding George in the dank confines of an interrogation room, we were allowed to hang out in the visitor waiting area, which featured harvest gold plastic molded chairs and a table that held a dusty fake plant and few pamphlets about victims' rights.

Apparently, George was not a flight risk. And, for that matter, we still were in the dark as to why he would take flight. Eventually, Detective Burns and Bertie came over to where we were waiting and invited us to go to the currently unoccupied detective briefing room— or roomette, as it was not much bigger than a broom closet. Burns tried to pace, but the space was too small and he seemed momentarily at odds. Eventually, he leaned against the wall and took what I surmised to be a menacing pose: arms crossed and a well-practiced stern expression. Bertie sat down across from George and me. She took a long swig from a travel mug she had brought with her and released a yawn that left a lingering odor of cabernet and mouthwash.

"So, Mr. LeFleur, does the name Hal Aho ring a bell?" Burns asked, looking at his fingernails with extreme interest.

"Huh?" George said.

"Oh, can it Burns," Bertie said. "Okay, first off, this is just a fact finding not the inquisition. You are not under arrest, George, though we think you can fill in some of the blanks about this Derry Parks."

"A/k/a Diedre Parkila," Burns said smugly.

"Huh?" George repeated.

"That's her real name," Burns said. "We were able to get some prints out of the truck and ran them. Ms. Parks/Parkila has a bit of a record, it seems. But we'll get into that later. As you know, George, Hal Aho's the victim of that accidental death at Plante Forest Products where you worked as a lumberjack."

194

"Well, I was actually a loader and driver. I didn't fell the trees. That's done by the sawyers, like Aho. Jimbo was a scaler."

"Whatever," Burns said. "A man died."

"It was an accident," George said.

My eyes cut to George. Aha! The accident. I knew, of course, that George had worked for Plante. But how did Parks a/k/a Parkila fit in? There were definitely some blanks here. George looked at me then looked away.

Burns snorted. "Accidental, with negligence."

George shrugged and shook his head.

"You, Rushinski, and Hal Aho were boozing it up. Not very smart around that heavy logging equipment, is it?" Burns quipped.

I was not following any of this. Again, I looked at George.

"We had knocked off for the day, Hal, Jimbo—James, and me," George said. "Just having a few brewskies before heading home."

"But you weren't done for the day, where you?" Burns said.

"Our supervisor was an asshole," George said. "He told us to finish loading the pup trailer, even though it was getting dark, and I guess I should have turned on the loading lights, though that probably wouldn't have made any difference." George looked at me. "I was going to tell you about it—someday. My therapist said I would know when the time was right."

"But you haven't told me jack shit and haven't been going to your therapist," I said. "Just that Dr. Dreamboat—er Bloom." My head had begun to throb. I knew George's therapy had originally been court-ordered to assess his alleged "drinking problem." Even when the sentence was up, George had continued to see him or her—he never told me which. That is until all the craziness. Now George seemed content to talk to Dr. Bloom who was helping him retrieve his lost memory.

Bertie sighed. "Detective Burns, perhaps we should try to get to the point of this interview."

Burns, who continued to lean against the wall, shifted his weight from one foot to the other. He acted as if he needed to use the restroom. "Tell us again, Mr. LeFleur, how you met this Parkila woman."

"Who?" George said.

Bertie took a swallow from her mug. "Detective Burns is talking about the woman who said she was Derry Parks and also Desiree Pruce. Like we said, her real name is Diedre Parkila. Here's the deal, she was—shall we say—connected to Hal Aho."

"Connected?" George said.

"Right," Burns said. "Apparently intimately and, *shall we say*, in a business deal."

"Intimately?" George said. "But Aho was married. I sure remember his wife, Ruth the Ruthless. After the accident, she wanted to have James and me strung up by our you-know-whats for the birds to peck at. And our supervisor too. That was until she got a nice settlement from Plante."

"But Parks, or Parkila, got left out in the cold," Bertie said. "Because girlfriends of married men tend not to get a cut of a wrongful death settlement."

"What about James?" I said. "Did he get charged with anything or have court-ordered therapy?"

"Hell no," George said. "I took the main hit for the whole thing. I was running the scissor lift and loading the trailer. Jimbo was being his usual lazy self and doing nothing. I didn't know that all the uprights weren't in place. Like I said, it was getting dark and we were supposed to be done for the day. Anyway, once there was too much weight, the logs spilled and—"

"Crushed Aho." Burns completed the story.

"They dropped the negligent homicide charges," George said. "But I lost my job. Jimbo quit and went into his newscasting gig. There was plenty of blame to pass around. Hal should not have been standing where he was, I should have had on the loading lights, Jimbo should have checked the trailer, the supervisor should never have ordered us to load. Like I said, lots of blame all around."

I had been swiveling my head from one person to another so much listening to the story, I felt dizzy. "But Derry. Who?"

"Yea," said George. "I still don't know why you're asking me about that woman—Parks, Parkila, whatever. I swear I never saw her before all this shit came down."

"It's unlikely either you or James would have seen her when you worked for Plante," Bertie said. "After all, she was having an affair with a married man so was keeping a low profile."

"Well, I saw her," I said. "*Mystery woman* appeared out of nowhere when she came to our church and usurped Eleanor as lead soprano. Oh, and James didn't waste any time making his move. I saw them playing footsie at the Bayview Tavern."

"Probably she was trying to set him up for some kind of retaliation," Bertie said. "I think it backfired there at Bucky's meat locker."

"Retaliation for *what!*" George said.

"For crushing her dreams," Bertie said wistfully.

"Yea," Burns said. "Aho's untimely accident *and* Parkila's prison sentence most definitely derailed their cozy plans."

Bertie smiled slightly. "And made a bitter woman out of her."

"But I still don't see—" I began.

"Parkila was the director of a non-profit called The Plante Foundation," Burns said. "Supposedly connected to Plante Forest Products—the outfit Mr. LeFleur, Mr. Rushinski, and Mr. Aho worked for."

"Supposedly?" I said.

"Yup," Bertie said, draining her coffee cup. "Supposedly. It was a front. It's complicated, but Ms. Parkila set up a 501(c)3, which signifies the status as a non-profit. The clever gal even got a little office and began soliciting donations and grant funds for such things as outdoor programs for kids, outings for seniors, college service projects planting trees and diversity gardens—the list goes on. Plante Forest Products was sucked in."

Burns had taken off his rumpled sport coat and draped it on a file cabinet. He pulled out a chair and turned it around so he could straddle it and lean his elbows on the back, perhaps to look more formidable. "Nobody seemed to question who had actually authorized Parkila to set up the non-profit," he said. "She just appeared one day and said she was hired to get the things going. Thing is, she was so drop-dead gorgeous, she could manipulate people without them realizing it. At least men." Burns gave a meaningful look at George. "A lot of donors, when seeing the Plante Forest Products name attached, believed it to be a great organization to support. Parkila did organize a few activities, took lots of photos and such to make it look bona fide. What tripped her up was greed—it's always greed."

"Of course, she knew the ruse would eventually collapse," Bertie said. "But not before she had scammed close to a million bucks. We're pretty sure she was getting ready to disappear, with her honey bunny Hal. Our gal Parkila embezzled funds from the bogus foundation, fixing the books to look like legit expenditures. These payments ended up in accounts set up in multiple banks throughout Upper Michigan and parts of Wisconsin under all sorts of aliases. Both she and Aho had acquired false IDs to satisfy banking personnel. Still, it wasn't a very sophisticated scam, and they left a heck of a paper trail all over the place."

"She knew her house of cards was about to collapse," Burns said, "and had started to withdraw funds in her accounts when Aho went to the big logging company in the sky."

"Hey, a little respect," George said. "I worked with him."

Burns shrugged.

Bertie stood and stretched. "Parkila should have cut her losses and split. But again, greed. She wanted Aho's share too and was trying to finagle something as a beneficiary. All the accounts had been opened as individual not joint, probably to avoid being easily connected to each other. It was actually the Feds who nabbed her for some kind of banking fraud. Then, of course, the IRS, us staties, and God Himself came down on the bitch. She pled to embezzlement charges. Usually ten years, but she only got eighteen months and made a partial restitution. Got out last fall."

Burns looked at George. "You never heard about the arrest, the scandal? Splashed all over the newspapers. Nothing?"

George ran his hand over his stubbly pate and shook his head. The hair was taking its time growing back. "I didn't work for Plante anymore, remember?" he said. "Hal's accident was the main thing going on. The inquiry and all."

I was trying to remember what I'd heard about the whole thing. Maybe a story on channel 13? "I don't remember seeing anything about it," I said. "Or about the accident. Was it in *The Northern Sentry*?"

"Parkila's bogus non-profit was set up in Wisconsin," Bertie said "so that's where the proceedings took place and most of the media coverage, since it's the Plante Corporate Headquarters. It wasn't that big of a story around here. The accident and Aho's death might have been downplayed. Plante maybe pulled a few strings. Bad publicity and all."

George quit rubbing his head and continued to avoid eye contact with me. "So," he said, "the Parkila woman blamed Rush and me of screwing up her plans?"

"And sought her revenge," Bertie said. "She had lots of time in prison to plot."

Detective Burns looked at George. "Sure would be nice if you could remember some things to help us out." Burns had used air quotes when he said "remember."

George commenced rubbing his forehead, as if hoping to coax his memory into action.

"But that woman obviously kidnapped George and wanted to kill him," I said. "And she's dead. So—?"

"Exactly," Detective Burns said. "Dead."

"But I didn't kill her!" George said.

"But you don't remember," Burns said, "so how do you know?"

"It would have been self-defense, even if he had!" I said. My ears had begun to burn.

"I remember the cabin. It was cold," George said. "It smelled musty, like it had been empty for a long time. Someone's camp."

"James Rush's camp," Bertie said. "Maybe Rush had taken Aho there as a hunting buddy, showed him where a key was hidden. Then perhaps Aho took the Parkila woman there for a secret little love nest."

"And then Parkila, knowing how to get in, suggested you, Mr. LeFleur, and she could go there for a little privacy?" Burns said.

"Bullshit. She took my clothes. I was running around in a bearskin rug. The bitch left me there."

"Did she?" Burns said.

"What are you saying?" George said, standing up.

"I'm saying that maybe you went there willingly?" Burns said.

"Hey, wait a minute," I said. "He might meet someone to do a story about pottery, but he didn't go to some damn camp to screw around."

"After all, there are more convenient places if someone's looking for a rendezvous," Bertie said. "Such as the No-Tell outside of town."

"The woman was pure evil!" I said, my voice rising an octave. "She tried to trap James in Bucky's meat locker. She was wacko!"

Bertie gave Burns an icy look. "The report concluded that George was kidnapped. And they speculate that Parkila also attempted to murder George by leaving him to die of exposure. It does not speculate nor mention a tryst gone awry. There was a weapon, after all."

"Well, a weapon of sorts," Burns said.

"A damn Taser gun," Bertie said. "There's no way to get a confession from a dead woman, so we'll just have to follow the facts."

Burns gave a little snort.

"I got those calls, too, don't forget," I said. "Bertie listened to them. They're in the report. The call had to be her—teasing, probably enjoying the game. George was lured out by this woman in a damn snowstorm by promising to give him a big story in some potter's magazine that she lied about working for. And with James and Bucky's cooler, she lured *him* out there, offering a big news-breaking story, and probably oozed sexual innuendo all over the place. We know that James was hovering around the woman the minute she walked into Moose Willow Methodist Church." I turned to George, who had rubbed his forehead so hard that it was red. "You got a phone call at the studio, right? It was on the machine—I listened to it until it cut off!"

"I—I don't remember," George said.

"Hmm, convenient," Burns said.

"Hey!" I said.

"Fuck this," George said. "I'm leaving. When can I have my truck back?"

"We're releasing it," Bertie said. "Paperwork and keys are at the impound office. I'll take you."

"Can we go?" I snapped at Burns.

"Of course," he said, winking at me. "I'll be in touch."

George and I followed Bertie to the impound lot to retrieve George's truck. We all stood shivering out in the parking lot while George went over his truck with the impound officer, checking for any missing items or damage. Bertie and I watched out of earshot.

"Burns is an ass," Bertie said out of the side of her mouth. "This case, as far as I'm concerned, is closed. But I'm not the investigating la-de-da detective. Still, I think it's a done deal as far as the department is concerned. And, hey, a little bit of info that you *did not* hear from me."

"What?" I said.

"Burns has the hots for you, Janese. Hey, he knows that George is off the hook as far as any investigation, but that doesn't mean that he—Burns—can't make trouble for you and George. That way he can make a move on you."

"What!" I shrieked. George and the officer turned to look at me.

"Nothing," I said. "Hurry up. It's freezing out here."

"Of course, Burns doesn't know you're pregnant—right?" She gave me a hard look.

"I still don't know and George seems to have completely forgotten that there is a possibility."

"How convenient," Bertie said.

"I have a doctor's appointment in a few weeks, Okay? Those stupid home tests didn't work out. Anyway, when I know you'll know. And eventually everyone else, including George. Who, by the way barely has time for me, let alone some fling with a wingnut floozie ex-con."

"I agree. It's obvious to even a moron that Parkila abducted George, using her stun gun. After meeting in the college parking lot, I suggest that she pulled the gun and ordered him to move into the passenger seat. After he complied, she zapped him. Those things work at a close range of a few feet and emit an electric current that renders the victim immobile. Parkila climbed behind the wheel and drove to the Rush camp to carry out the next stage of her plan. The Taser we recovered, like most, has cartridges for two shots, which provides two opportunities to zap someone. George likely regained consciousness enough for her to lead him inside Rush's cabin, then she zapped him again. I don't doubt that he doesn't remember! He was out of it. Being tased is no picnic."

I nodded, shivering, and shifting from one foot to the other. I needed to pee pretty soon. "She took his clothes and left him to freeze to death, the bitch."

"Then Parkila took off in George's truck," Bertie said. "Probably going to take it back to the lot where she left her rental, exchange vehicles and be on her merry way."

"But she got stuck," I said. "On Triple A Road."

"Yup. Never underestimate the deadliness of a winter storm in Upper Michigan," Bertie said. "It's death waiting for the stupid and unprepared. Good ol' Mother Nature rendered a bit of Northwoods justice."

"She tried to walk," I said, "got lost in the blizzard, and died. God forgive me, serves her right."

"Took the Taser gun with her, which was a key piece of evidence," Bertie said. "I'll admit it was very good—maybe divine intervention— that we eventually found it with all the snow. And speaking of God, He must have been looking out for George, that's for sure. Pretty resourceful of him to use that bearskin rug. What an ordeal getting back to your place. Then your mother creams him."

"She thought she was protecting me," I said.

"Of course," Bertie said.

No question that George's saga would probably take a lot of therapy to work through. I looked over and saw him looking our way.

"Hey Trout, you need to hop in. We can get your car later."

"Right," I said. "I'm not supposed to drive today."

"I'll drive the Subaru for you," Bertie said, "and have a cruiser pick me up at your place."

"Appreciate it," I said.

Bertie Vaara: best friend ever.

⚡ 24 ⚡

The Saturday before cantata Sunday was a dress rehearsal, though no special dress was required. Most of us wore jeans and sweatshirts. I opted for a turtleneck, since my neck still bore traces of Aileen Watkin's handiwork before she was carted off for psychiatric evaluation. I reflected back on the attack in my office (still an unsolved crime) and wondered about Aileen as a suspect. She obviously hated my guts. *And* she was surprisingly strong for her size.

We knew that the boots I got at the Lutheran rummage sale had previously belonged to the culprit, and Aileen *was* an active member of that church. But she was probably not over five feet tall, and I couldn't imagine that my size eight bargain boots from the church sale would fit such a petite woman. Likely she shopped for her clothes and shoes in the children's department. Also, the hair caught in my office chair wheel was synthetic. I was pretty sure that Aileen's tightly permed steel-gray hair was not a wig.

I was right on time for our Saturday cantata rehearsal, which was the final chance to pull it all together. Hannu looked like hell—maybe a bit of liquid courage for breakfast, or maybe lack of sleep, or maybe he was bi-polar. Who knows? Personally, in light of all the recent drama in my life, obsessing over perfect pitch and dynamics seemed a bit trivial. However, to Hannu, it was anything but trivial. While he risked sucking the fun out of it by setting the bar too high, it was a vote of confidence that, somehow, we could and *would* pull it all together. But not so's you'd notice by the practice we stumbled through. As for me, having one's throat nearly sliced open seemed to have affected my ability to hit anything above a high C.

"Gargle with salt water!" Hannu said.

"Honey," said Azinnia Wattles from the piano. "A spoonful of honey morning, noon, and night makes you sweet and puts you right."

I doubted anything as simple as honey could make me sweet *or* put me right. Besides, I never cared for honey. I mean, it's bee regurgitation.

Keeping true to "The Show Must Go On" mantra, we forged through our final practice of *Come, Oh Light of the World!* It's all there: World in darkness and despair. Then the immaculate conception (where I sing my solo telling God I'm good with His plan), the anticipation of the arrival of the Christ child, His actual arrival in a lowly cattle stall, visits by shepherds and magi (where James has his solo), and a grand finale involving loud proclamations of jubilation shouted from metaphorical mountaintops. In the unlikely event that someone had never heard about the birth of the Christ child, the cantata was interspersed with narration telling the story. The thing would last about 35 minutes, give or take.

"Go home. Drink water. Don't talk and don't watch any sports and yell at the TV," Hannu said. "Be here at 9:30 tomorrow to warm up. And pray."

I was surprised by two things when I walked out of the church. The first was the weather. We were experiencing an unseasonable warming trend. While I usually welcomed a rare balmy winter day, the above-freezing temps did not bode well for the igloo contest. Christmas was only a few days away, and on December 26th, construction of Habitats for Critters would begin. But not if we had nothing but slush to work with. I made a mental note to look at the week-long forecast. Someone in the choir had mentioned rain. That would be disastrous.

The second surprise was that somebody had written something in the road grime that encrusted my Subaru. *SATAN!* was clearly etched across the driver's door. There was also a crude image of a snake, coiled and ready for action with a long, forked tongue and aggressive fangs. Yikes! Probably a prank. Damn kids. Outside of a church, too.

I ran the Satan-mobile through the car wash and eliminated any reference of the devil or his minion, the serpent. When I arrived home, I was pleased to find room in the garage for the Subaru. When I walked into the cabin, George was busy preparing something exciting for lunch while Mother fussed around the hideous white, glittery Christmas tree, arranging packages.

"Janese, darling, you're home! How was practice? I hope it's okay that I invited Ben—you know, Dr. Bloom, to church tomorrow for the cantata and, of course, dinner afterward. What about this weather? It's melting like crazy. Why, a bunch of snow slid off the roof and nearly scared me to death. Doesn't lunch smell marvelous?"

"Mother!" I shouted before she passed out. "Have you been drinking a lot of caffeine or something?"

"Oh, perhaps. It's just that I do love Christmas, and I need to leave Monday morning to head back to the inn, and I so hope we can exchange gifts ahead of time, because of course I won't be here on

Christmas day. I've gotten a little something for Ben, so he won't feel left out. He's one of the few men I know who still wears cufflinks, so I got him a pair. That is if you feel it's appropriate, I mean dinner, not the cufflinks. But then, I've already invited him. I do hope it's okay."

"Well, sure," I said. "We can do it tomorrow after church." I would need to finish wrapping my gifts. Thank God for online shopping. I was able to find several websites for chef-quality kitchen products for George—a set of sauté pans, a mysterious steamer gadget, spatulas and spoons, and a hand-crafted cutting board. Additionally, I ordered a crisp white chef's jacket and goofy hat called a *toque blanche*. Kind of a joke, the hat, but if he was serious about starting a culinary school at the college, he needed to look the part. I also had gotten him a lined flannel shirt and firewood carrier with wheels. I hoped Mother would like the classy outfit I bought her when shopping with Bertie. While online, I'd also ordered her favorite perfume along with some leather driving gloves. I wondered if George had given any thought whatsoever about what to give me. A ring might be nice. Did he even remember that I may be pregnant?

"Ben will be going with me to St. Iggy for Christmas. Isn't that wonderful?"

"Sure," I said without much enthusiasm. St. Iggy was a nickname for St. Ignace where Mother's inn was located. I just hoped her romance with Dr. Bloom would go better than when she and James made the trip.

"Lunch!" George shouted from the kitchen.

We all enjoyed homemade soup—he called it a bisque—and garlic toast. For dessert, we had creamy peppermint ice cream. It was delish.

"You know, George dear, I think you've found your calling," Mother said. "It's too bad you and Janese don't live closer to the inn. I'd hire you as a chef in a heartbeat."

Just shoot me, I thought.

George grinned. "I've never felt so—free."

"Free?" I said. "Don't you miss making your pottery? And what about your students?"

George pondered this for a moment. "The students come and go. As for my pottery, I really don't miss it at all. That part of me seems to have disappeared. The cooking, it's like—I don't know, it's like I've opened a part of myself that was waiting to get out."

My spoon, holding the last of my ice cream, paused mid-air, and I suspect my jaw dropped to my navel. George sounded, well, not like

George at all. He was so…philosophical, and he hated all that touchy-feely stuff. At least the *old* George had.

"Oh George, I think you should share these thoughts with Dr. Bloom," Mother said. "He says you have repressed so many things for so long. Anyway, all this stuff aside, what shall we have for our early Christmas dinner tomorrow?"

While Mother and George went over menu ideas, I cleared the table and began cleaning up the kitchen, which had undergone George's signature disaster. How could making soup dirty so many dishes? A low rumble from the steel roof of the cabin rattled the windows as another slab of melting snow and ice slid off. Speaking of disasters. The warming trend, which, according to the Channel 13 weather report was to continue for the foreseeable future, cast an ominous future on the igloo contest.

* * *

It was finally cantata Sunday and the warm weather brought people out of the woodwork. While I waited with my choir-mates in the fellowship hall, a couple of church ladies directed their hubbies to haul out some folding chairs, which would be set up in various nooks and crannies of the sanctuary to handle the overflow.

The choir members had cleaned up pretty good, including me. I was wearing my one and only long black skirt (no pantyhose), a white blouse bejeweled with some sparkly beads, and my Lutheran Church rummage sale boots. My hair had pretty much flopped, but what's new? My only jewelry was a pair of diamond earrings and a simple necklace with a gold cross that Mother passed on to me from her mother. It had been in the family for generations, I am told. While not particularly valuable, I cherished it. I had never met any of my grandparents before they died and somehow that tiny gold cross provided a bit of family history to cling to.

Hannu had instructed us to either talk in low tones or, better yet, save our voices and not talk at all. While he pretended to be talking to the whole group, he was eyeing James, who was regaling everyone with his booming broadcaster voice. James spotted me and bustled over.

"Janese!" he bellowed, making me jump. "Hello fellow soloist," he chortled. "Too bad you're having some issues with those pesky high notes. I'm tip top today. I think having this whole conundrum with the Parks/Parkila woman coming to fruition is lifting a burden from my shoulders."

"Sure," I said, not in the mood to chitchat about George's role in that goat rodeo.

"I see that Maddie is out there. She's looking positively radiant," James continued.

"Uh huh."

"Perhaps we could all go out for a bite afterwards," James said. "The four of us," he added.

I smiled. James had apparently not noticed that Mother had the incomparable Dr. Bloom escorting her today.

"I'll catch her after the program," he said, looking across the fellowship hall, and apparently noticing someone more interesting than I. "Gotta go! Break a leg."

"Yea," I muttered. "You too." James was acting like he was in a Broadway hit instead of a small-town church cantata.

Hannu gathered us around an electronic keyboard for a quick warm up. There was still a question as to whether or not I would be able to pull off the F sharp in my solo. Over the years, however, I had become a master at choosing an alternate note when necessary, and usually could do it without anyone but Hannu noticing. The prospect of trying to hit that high note had kept me awake a good deal of the night, along with other major concerns such as the prospect of the igloo contest melting into a puddle, George's career shift, Mother's blooming relationship with Dr. Bloom, and last but not least, the fact that I was very late for my time of the month.

I peeked through the glass of the fellowship hall door out into the narthex, which is a kind of reception/lobby area where congregants first enter the church. The stream of people had thinned to a few scurrying latecomers, and the greeters had left their post and slipped into the sanctuary. This meant that the service had begun and after some announcements and a few prayers, it would be showtime.

"Line up," Hannu instructed.

The insides of my boots had heated up pretty good and my feet were getting soggy. I wondered if my church rummage sale bargain boots were constructed of man-made materials (plastic) rather than leather. And of course they were lined, which didn't help. No wonder someone gave them away. In any event, I was feeling a bit clammy all over. We filed through the narthex and entered the sanctuary two by two, which reminded me either of the beasts boarding Noah's ark or lambs being led to slaughter. While we processed, we bellowed out the beloved anthem "Oh Come, All Ye Faithful" along with everyone in the packed, overheated church. Someone had actually cracked the emergency exit doors to allow a bit of fresh air in. At last check, temps had risen to the 40s and the sun was making an unlikely appearance. It felt more like Easter than Christmas.

We were positioned on the risers and belted out the last few measures of the song, OH COME LET US AHHHH DOOORRR HII IIMM, CHRIIIIII IIIIIST THE LORD!

The congregation/guests sat with a muffled thud. A narrator began telling the story from a microphone on the podium, Azinnia softly (for her) played the opening measures of the first song, then as the narrator finished, the piano volume grew, and we were off and running, practically exploding in our petition for the coming of Christ.

Three songs into the cantata came my solo. I had it memorized and there was no need to stare at my music. My eyes shifted from Hannu, to a brief scan of the audience. There was Mother, smiling warmly at me and snuggled up to her Dr. Bloom, who, though Jewish, seemed very comfortable in his Christian surroundings. He was also smiling, though it may have been because of whatever promise was in the air with Mother rather than the birth of our Savior. Then there was George, looking awkward but nicely spruced up. He grinned and gave me a thumbs up. Next to him was my bestie, Bertie. I knew she was supposed to be sleeping and looked tired. She'd probably hustle home right after the cantata. When our eyes locked, she put her fingers in her ears and stuck her tongue out at me. That made me smile as I shifted my focus back to Hannu—only a few measures left to the piano prelude before I started my solo. Then I saw her: the ever-evil Eleanor Heimlich sitting a few rows back from Mother and company. Her smug glare oozed malice and I felt as if I had been zapped by the Parks/Parkila woman's taser gun.

One measure. I dragged my eyes back to Hannu, who had a somewhat concerned expression. He pointed a finger at me. My mouth opened and, praise God, singing came out. The right words, the right notes, which had been tattooed in my brain over the past few days. No cracking voice, no flat notes. Then came the F sharp. I went for it and based on the fact that Hannu was smiling and not grimacing, I figured it was fairly much in tune. Then the rest of the choir came in, my solo was over, and Eleanor Heimlich's black spell had fizzled. I half expected her to melt into a puddle like the wicked witch in the *Wizard of Oz*.

More songs of the Good News, James' flawless solo as a wise man, a melodious command to go tell it on the mountain and it was over. All the practice, all the stress behind us. All I could think of was getting home and getting out of my good clothes and into my sweats. First, however, we all went to the fellowship hall for coffee and cookies in a kind of afterglow gathering.

"Good job, darling," Mother said as she gave me a hug. "Ben is having a theological discussion with Pastor Sam. I wanted to rush right in and congratulate everyone for the most wonderful program, well, in quite some time."

I knew the implication was that we didn't compare to the good ol' days when she was the darling of the choir. I would never fill her shoes. God knew I didn't want to even try. I looked around and spotted George studying the cookie selection on the refreshment table when James sauntered over to him.

"Hey Georgie boy," James bleated. "How's the ol' cranium doing?"

Before George could respond, James homed in on Mother. "Maddie!"

As if on cue, Dr. Bloom appeared and smiled at me. "I really enjoyed this," he said. "You Christians know how to do it right." He turned to Mother and beamed with obvious affection then looked at James.

"Ben, James, you remember each other, of course," Mother said.

The two men plastered on smiles and shook hands, muttering the appropriate cordialities. George shuffled over, munching on a cookie.

"Soooo," I said.

"Yea, Trout, you were awesome. The whole thing was terrific. I kind of had goosebumps. Hey, who made the chocolate chip cookies? I want the recipe. I'm trying to figure out if there's a touch of mint or maybe some rum in them."

Good ol' George.

"Well, nice to see you again, Ben," James said. "Okay if I call you Ben?"

"Sure, *Jim*," Dr. Bloom said. "I'll make a point to watch you on the news."

James looked a little stiff as he backed away from our group. He had his ever-present smile arranged on his face, which was beginning to sag a little, wasn't it? And the one eye seemed a little droopy. I had never noticed that before.

"Okay my loves," Mother said. "Let's go have Christmas!"

"Cornish hens," George said. "And rice pilaf, winter salad, and baked Alaska. Oh, and braided Swedish cheddar bread."

"What? No figgy pudding?" I said.

"Maybe next time," George said, flinging his arm around my shoulder.

"And presents," Mother said, smiling up at Dr. Bloom.

It was hard not to feel warm and fuzzy.

☞ 25 ☜

We had taken several vehicles to church. Mother and Benjamin traveled in his tricked-out Jeep, George drove his truck, and I in my trusty Subaru. Saturated with marginal coffee and too many sweets, we went our separate ways when leaving the church. I minced my way around several puddles of snow melt heading for my car parked down the street. No question about it, the igloo contest was in peril of melting into oblivion. I would need to get ahold of the committee and discuss. While I was wool gathering, my feet sank into a slushy mess piled along the curb.

"Guess it doesn't matter if I get my feet wet," I muttered to myself, "since the boots are obviously plastic."

I thought it a little strange that the driver's door of my car was ajar. Must not have shut it properly, I thought. Sometimes the seatbelt didn't retract all the way and jammed the door. And I might not have locked it. After all, it was Sunday. Usually the crime rate in Moose Willow was nonexistent on Sunday mornings since all the lowlifes were still sleeping off their Saturday night sins.

I whipped open the door and tossed my purse across to the passenger seat. Then I saw it. A huge, ugly snake making itself at home on the driver's seat. I let out a yelp, stumbled backwards, and stepped squarely into a deep, watery pothole. In spite of waving my arms frantically for balance, I fell over backward, hitting the pavement hard, leaving me winded and gasping for air. Fortunately, Pastor Sam was just locking up the church and heard what probably sounded like someone in her death throes and rushed over.

There are few things that truly frighten me. I am not afraid of the dark, or surly teens, or maybe getting a tattoo. But snakes, even though they are relatively harmless in Upper Michigan, scare the bejesus out of me. I believe it goes back to having an unfortunate garter snake dropped down my shirt in kindergarten by a delinquent sixth-grade boy who enjoyed terrorizing little girls. I understand he's in prison now, but that's beside the point. Because of my playground trauma, I remain scarred for life and become paralyzed with fear when I see a snake that may be doing nothing more than sunning itself on a rock.

Thus, the humiliating tumble into the dirty, slushy snow held not a candle to the unbridled terror I felt seeing a *snake* snoozing on the front seat of my car. Now I would have to sell the car or maybe have it crushed and melted down.

After helping me up, Pastor Sam ineffectively tried to dry me off with his handkerchief while I made incoherent noises and pointed at my car.

"Janese," the pastor said soothingly, "are you hurt? Should I call someone?"

All I could do was make a hissing noise and point.

"What is it?" he said.

"sssss—snn—snnnnaaah!"

"Something in the car?"

I nodded.

Pastor Sam pulled open the door. He let out a little gasp, then smiled. "Rubber," he said.

"Huh?"

"It's a rubber snake, like you'd get in tourist places. You know, along with the miniature spoons, shot glasses, and little bags of polished stones."

He grabbed it and held it out for me to see. It *was* very lifelike as it gyrated in the pastor's grasp and I nearly fell over backward again.

"Kids!" Pastor Sam said. "If families would come to church, our youth wouldn't be idling around on Sunday morning with nothing to do but cause mischief."

"Uh huh," I said, still feeling a big shaken and very silly. I was beginning to sense a theme when combining this incident with the previous day's serpent artwork on the car door. Was this some kind of gothic ritual or initiation for teens?

"So, shall I dispose of it, or do you want to keep it as a souvenir?" he asked, giving it a little shake, which again activated its writhing movement.

"Huh? No!" I said. "I mean, no thanks." I looked down at my soggy long, black skirt. "I feel like an idiot."

"Not at all," he said. "For me, it's ticks. They give me the willies. And, of course, non-believers. They just break my heart. We all have our phobias and fears and things that keep us awake at night. But remember, our Lord and Savior is always there to lend a hand. All you have to do is reach out and take it." With that, he reached out and gave my shoulder a squeeze.

Clergy didn't dare hug anyone for fear of accusations of inappropriate behavior. I really needed a hug, too. I nodded, feeling strangely like crying. I hoped it wasn't hormones, but simply the events of the past few days coming to roost. Now wasn't a time to collapse into his arms and pour out my soul. Maybe later. I mustered up a brave smile and thanked the pastor, then climbed into the faux reptile-mobile and headed home.

"Janese, darling, what happened to you?" Mother shrieked as I squished into the cabin. She and her Dr. Bloom were sipping cocktails. A fire snapped and popped in the fireplace.

"Oh, nothing," I lied. "I turned my ankle in a pothole and fell into a puddle."

"Are you okay?" asked Dr. Bloom, standing and looking at me earnestly. "Should we have that ankle looked at?"

"I'm fine, really. Just feeling kind of klutzy," I said, again suppressing a strong urge to burst into tears. "But thanks. Where's George?"

"He said he was getting out of his dressy duds," Mother said. "Then he's putting the game birds in the oven and we'll open our gifts while things cook."

"Guess I'll get out of my dressy duds, too," I muttered, heading for the bedroom.

When I walked in on George, the first thing I noticed was that he was only wearing his boxer shorts—the ones with little hearts on them. This made my heart speed up a few beats. The second thing I noticed was that he was fumbling around with some Christmas wrapping paper and a box. A small one. Be still my heart!

"Hey, Trout, don't you knock!" he said.

"It's my house. Remember? Whatcha doin?"

"None of your business," he muttered, as he tried to maneuver a ribbon around the box. During the struggle, the wrapping paper began to unfold and threatened to fall off.

"Want me to tie that ribbon for you?" I asked.

George turned to look at me. "Hey, quit looking, you—what the hell happened to you?"

"I fell in a puddle. There was a snake," I added, my lip beginning to quiver.

"In the puddle? A snake?" he said.

"No, in my car. It was fake, but still..." I sighed, trying to regain my composure. It was stupid to be so upset. I started to snivel, and I felt my eyes well up. "Rubber! Pastor Sam had to take it out of the car. I felt like a damn helpless female." Suddenly, I burst into uncontrolled sobbing, obviously startling George, who gave up on the ribbon and rushed over to me, enclosing me in a nice warm hug.

"Hey there, what's going on?" he said.

"I—I don't know," I said, somewhat distracted by things pressing against me. "It's just, you know, so much uncertainty," I blubbered.

"I haven't forgotten, you know," he said.

"Haven't forgotten?"

"I mean, I *did* forget, but it came back. In church. When you sang your solo. Poof, it triggered a memory that you might, I mean we might be, you know."

"Pregnant?

"Yea. That. Still don't know, right?"

"Right. I have an appointment pretty soon."

"Okay, good. Now, you're like hugging a sponge," he said. "Go change."

* * *

The phone rang just as I went into the living room to join the others.

"Oh, heavens," Mother said. "I hope it's not the inn."

I answered it and it was not the inn. Rather it was none other than the president of the 4Cs, Patrick Neil.

"Janice," he said, mispronouncing my name, "the snow is melting."

"Yes, I noticed. I was, um, going to contact the committee tomorrow and discuss what to do." I wanted to add that this was Sunday and I had plans to eat a nice family dinner (albeit a somewhat dysfunctional family) and then open presents. I was dying to know what was in the awkwardly-wrapped little giftbox, which was now prominently displayed under the tree and obviously intended for me. But my curiosity would have to wait since I needed my job, and Prez Neil apparently felt that my job included all days and hours of my life.

"You know it's only five days until Christmas," he said unnecessarily.

"I do," I replied.

"I talked to Bill who was going to haul snow in for the igloo contest. It's a no go," he said.

Bill was the head of maintenance. I had learned over the years that there was no arguing with Bill, not that I would have wanted to. I could barely contain my glee with this latest news. One less glitch in my life. I had grown to really despise the igloo contest, which had started out as wholesome and fun but had morphed into a mean-spirited hate fest.

But, of course, I didn't relay my true feelings. "I'm terribly sorry this has happened," I said. "It's devastating. Such good publicity for the college. So much work and planning. I feel terrible."

"Not your fault, Janice. But here's the deal. You need to come up with a plan B. Should have had one all along."

I suppressed a seething resentment of having my name mis-pronounced *and* being expected to come up with a so-called Plan B. I had suggested this all along at meetings and was basically brushed aside and accused of being a Debbie Downer when I emphasized that weather could be an issue. However, unknown to others and even myself, I had been thinking of what to do if we had to cancel the igloo contest. Besides jump for joy, that is.

"How about we just have the dinner buffet as planned, and maybe have a drawing to give out the prizes?" I suggested.

"Maybe," he said.

"We could have a dance!" I said, warming to my own idea. "Perhaps we can find some dance instructors to lead traditional dances, like the polka, swing, waltz—you name it. Not sure about a band at the last minute on New Year's Eve, though."

"I know a band!" he said. "My brother, Ed, and his buddies. I think they call themselves the Moody Booties—something like that. They have an accordion, fiddle, guitar, keyboard, bass, kantele, drums—the whole enchilada. Got their own sound system, too. They fill up a panel van with all their equipment. And Ed owes me. *Big time.* I know they are available because they were supposed to do a gig at the Holiday Inn but got cancelled and replaced by one of those deejay outfits. More appeal to the millennials, I guess. Far as I'm concerned, all they do is play loud, recorded music. Anyway, they cancelled out Ed and his Booties, or whatever."

"Well, then, we just need to get the word out," I said.

"Absolutely! I'm counting on you for that. I know you have all the connections—emails, phone numbers, social media. Text me when you've got it done, Janice."

And with this final command, he hung up.

"It's JanESE," I muttered.

"Who was that, dear?" Mother said.

"President Neil," I said. "We're cancelling the igloo contest, and going to a hastily arranged Plan B. I'll need to get the word out after we're done here."

"Oh, my," Mother said.

I smiled. No judging. No bitter rivalry, except maybe on the dance floor. No underhanded sabotage. No trash talk. I only wished the igloo contest had never existed to begin with. Maybe, just maybe Weasel Watkins would still be alive, living a semi-content life with his wife, Aileen. And Bucky went through the arrest, bonding out, probably had some stiff lawyer fees, and the public humiliation. Well, maybe not too much, as Bucky never really much cared what people thought. But his boys probably endured a lot of teasing and bullying at school *and* likely were permanently grounded for messing around where they didn't belong and hiding the evidence of their misdeeds.

All because of a stupid contest that was supposed to be unifying.

* * *

It was not a ring. But it was jewelry, sort of. A gift card to H & H Jewelers, located downtown. At first, I was crushed at getting a gift card. Not exactly personal. Then George whispered in my ear that we could pick out something *special* together. Was I wrong to think a diamond ring? The gift card would not cover much more than a quarter of a karat but still...

After a delicious meal, served by Chef George donning his crisp new chef's attire, Benjamin left for home and Mother scurried upstairs to pack for their trip to The Straights Inn. The holiday activities at the inn would soon be in full swing and would stretch through New Year's Day. Then the clientele would swiftly convert to winter enthusiasts, such as snowmobilers, skiers, and ice fishermen. Somehow, Mother managed to shift the atmosphere of her establishment from elegant and formal to rustic and moderately campy with menu changes, decorations, and the attire worn by her employees. During the Christmas season, employees were expected to wear black pants or skirts and crisp white shirts or blouses accented with little black bow ties. Once the snowmobilers and fishermen entered the doors, they were greeted by employees wearing jeans, flannel shirts, mukluks, and jaunty toques. Christmas wreaths were replaced by multiple species of mounted fish and an abundance of antlers. (Mother loathed animal-head trophies.) The restaurant switched its Friday night special from salmon almandine to an all-you-can-eat fish fry.

While George was cleaning up the kitchen mess from our festive repast, I went to the computer and sent out a group e-mail to the committee with a copy to President Neil, Lempi Hempanin who was my contact in the college catering service, and Bill in maintenance who would have to see to making a dance floor work.

> *Dear Igloo Committee,*
>
> *Unfortunately, due to the warm weather, the igloo contest has been cancelled. The buffet will go on as planned. Prizes will be distributed as door prizes. We will have dancing to a band arranged by President Neil. I will be attempting to get some dance instructors to help make things work.*
>
> *We appreciate all the hard work and planning that has taken place, but I'm sure that we can still have a successful alcohol-free New Year's Eve sponsored by the Copper Country Community College that will be a night for the community to remember.*
>
> *Emergency meeting TBA. Suggestions welcome!*
>
> *Janese Trout, Committee Chair*

I clicked "send" and sighed with great satisfaction. Now, the hard part. Getting ahold of all the contest entries and pretending that I felt just *awful* about cancelling. I had a bit part in a high school drama during which I feigned burning love for the leading man, whom I loathed in real life. I was so convincing that he asked if, after the cast party, I wanted to, like, sneak out to his car and have something stronger than Hawaiian Punch and, you know, make out. I told him, like, I'd rather eat glass.

I had e-mails for most entries and sent out my sad regrets of having to cancel the igloo contest. It all ended with a positive spin on Plan B.

Relief washed over me as I mentally checked the various stress-inducers off my list. First, of course, was getting George back. Although a somewhat transformed George, he was beginning to grow on me. The Christmas Cantata was in the rearview mirror. The Igloo Contest had simply melted away. Mother and her latest beau were departing in the morning, which left George and me to sort things out and maybe visit the jewelry store to pick out something very special.

≈ 26 ≈

Serving green bean casserole was not what I had envisioned. Not at all. I had thought George and I would have a nice, lazy Christmas. I planned on wearing the spiffy new outfit Mother had given me, which was comfortable yet stylish—at least according to her. George could build a fire, we'd decorate the little tree we had cut down and set up on the porch, watch a couple of sappy movies, and maybe mess around. All made possible because Mother, with Dr. Bloom in tow, was at her inn in St. Iggy. And while the warm weather had pretty much eliminated an enchanting Currier and Ives landscape, I had hoped to spend a quiet day connecting with the new, possibly improved, George.

Instead, I was at the Lutheran Church helping serve Christmas dinner to the less fortunate and lonely. I was rubbing elbows with Pastor Greg, the Lutheran minister, who was in charge of mashed potatoes, stuffing, and gravy. Another server handled the sweet potatoes and cranberries. Several helpers replenished food, cut up pie, and took meals to those who were unable to go through the buffet line. George, *who had no idea how much trouble he was in*, served the turkey and ham. I was given the vegetable assignment because I was the rookie.

My hands sweated inside the disposable gloves. How did surgeons stand to wear the things? Also, I was wearing a fetching hairnet and apron that had started out crisp and white and somehow had gotten smeared with turkey gravy that had been dribbled on the serving table. I was given strict instructions to measure the precise amount of green bean casserole for each guest by using what looked like an undersized ice cream scoop. Food was kept warm with little canisters of Sterno fuel that blazed under a row of chafing dishes. I was feeling a bit queasy with the heat and obnoxious smell of green bean casserole. Eventually, I came to the bottom of my chafing dish and foolishly thought I was off duty when someone snatched it up and hustled it to the dishwashing area. I snapped off the miserable gloves to let the heat escape from my hands.

"Hot stuff! Comin' through," bellowed a large, imposing woman who bumped me aside with her hip and plopped a fresh batch of the offensive casserole into place over the Sterno. "Get some new gloves, honey. We've only just begun. Senior center just dropped off a busload, and those folks can eat!"

I may have looked ready to weep.

"Maybe Janese can help carry plates," Pastor Greg said, wiping sweat off his brow with his apron. "Many of the elders need to be served. Maybe you should get a clean apron," he said to me. "You don't need gloves. And it's nice to sit and chat with the folks."

I glanced over at the person, my George, who got me into the mess. He had sprung it on me Christmas Eve Day after our shopping trip to H & H Jewelers where we went to look at diamonds. No, not diamond rings, but necklaces, which was not quite what I had hoped for but way better than, say, a new pair of mukluks. After the salesclerk had placed the sparkling diamond necklace in a velveteen box and gift bag emblazoned with the store name, George and I had lunch at The Copper Kettle.

"You like that necklace?" George had asked.

"I love it," I gushed.

"Good. I mean you don't wear a lot of jewelry, not like your mother, and I didn't want to pick out something you hated."

"If it's from you, I would never hate it," I said. Somewhat of a stretch of the truth, but it seemed the appropriate response in a rare tender moment. I was thinking the moment might lead to a serious discussion about the future Mr. and Mrs. LeFleur. No more fishy jokes about my last name.

And then the moment ended.

"So," George said, "how would you like to help out the less fortunate at Christmas dinner?"

Not one bit would I like it. Were we going to invite some meth addicts to dinner? I admit that my service to the less fortunate was scant. But Christmas dinner? I had envisioned brunch, binge watching, and bonking.

"It's kind of funny how this all happened," George said with a forced chuckle.

"I'm listening," I said, without a chuckle.

"Well, I never mentioned it after the cantata, but the pastor—Pastor Greg—from the Lutheran church was there."

"Right, I saw him. He usually comes to the cantata because the Lutheran service is over by the time ours starts. He's friendly with our pastor."

"So, anyway, he and I got to talking and I find out he does this Christmas dinner for the community."

"Uh huh."

"And that the fellow who was supposed to oversee cooking the meat—guess it's turkey and ham—was headed to Mayo Clinic with his wife, who also helps with the meal. Pastor Greg said that he was not at liberty to discuss the health crisis that the family was facing, but that it was very serious and they needed our prayers. Guess he assumed since I was in a church that I, you know, would fit in."

Uh oh. George was having a come-to-Jesus moment.

"So, I guess I kind of volunteered to help out and figured you would want to do what you could too, so I said we'd be there." He gave my shoulder a congenial squeeze.

"Uh huh."

"So, are we good?"

I sighed and fingered my new diamond necklace. The setting was platinum and swirled gracefully into a heart encrusted with chip diamonds. In the center glittered a quarter karat diamond flanked by two deep-blue sapphires. It was quite lovely. Soooo much better than mukluks.

"Sure," I said. "We're good."

Which is how I found myself serving God's less fortunate.

I was excused from the steamy serving line as a horde of elders swarmed into the dining hall, some in wheelchairs and scooters, some with walkers and canes, and some via their own two feet. The small musical combo, which had been on break, returned to their instruments. They had been playing Christmas music earlier in the day, but they started their new set with a Beatles tune "When I'm Sixty-Four" from the sixties, except the band modified the lyrics to "when I'm a hundred and four," which was met with a thunderous response from the audience.

I had to admit that the senior infusion really livened the place up, and several of the children, who had been picking listlessly at their food, wondering why Santa missed their house, brightened considerably when the elders piled wrapped gifts on a table along the wall. As I began delivering plates of food to our new arrivals, I was told that each gift had either a red or green bow, so that—even in this PC era—boys and girls would be receiving gender-appropriate gifts. A white bow meant that it could go either way.

"I always hated dolls," confessed one woman. "I liked playing doctor. I finally married my gynecologist."

A man who shared her table cackled and raised his eyebrows. "I always used to poke the eyes out of my sister's dolls. 'course she thought it was 'cause the boogieman was out to get 'er."

I quickly moved away from the table before learning more about unspeakable doll abuse and the details of playing doctor.

"Yoohoo, Janese!" someone hollered from across the room. "Here!"

It was Aggie, my partner in bigfoot sightings. I waved and went to get some plated dinners for her table. She had only one dining companion, a rather dashing gentleman, who, with the aid of a snazzy cane, stood as I approached and asked me to join them for dinner, as if we were at the Ritz rather than a church fellowship hall. Since part of my job was to sit and chat, I got myself a plate of food and joined the two. When getting a slab of turkey from George, I asked if he could take a break to eat, but he declined, citing the need to carve another bird and pig.

"Oh Janese, that necklace is positively *beautiful*," Aggie said as I sat down. I had worn my Christmas present for all to see. Perhaps not appropriate among folks who had to come for a free Christmas dinner, but hey, I had my own deprivations in life to bear.

"Thank you, Aggie," I said.

She eyed me with a twinkle in her eye. "That from your fella?"

"Uh huh. I love your sweater, Aggie," I said, quickly changing the subject. Clearly her tatting skills had been applied to the cuffs, neck, and hem of the garment. Mother would have been proud that I had volleyed a compliment back to help create an amiable atmosphere, as she called it.

"Why thank you Janese. I thought this might be a bit too festive, but what the heck," she said, touching the bright red lace collar bedazzled with beads and sequins. "Anyway, Janese, this is Winston Beauford. He's of the Beaufords who make baby formula. You know, with the motto: 'Your baby is part of our family.' We met at the senior center."

"Pleased to meet you," I said. I had no idea who the baby formula Beaufords were, but it was likely a very lucrative enterprise.

"Charmed, my dear," he said, reaching to take my hand, which for a moment I thought he might kiss. As his sleeve slid back in the

221

gesture, I noted he was wearing a Rolex. And, also, that his ring finger bore no gold band or other adornment.

My, my. Aggie had hooked herself quite a fish.

We all tucked into our food for a few moments. The band played and sang "Feeling Groovy" then segued into "Santa Baby."

"So, Janese," Aggie said, her voice lowered in a conspiring whisper. "I have something to tell you. Winston knows." She looked at him and he nodded while focusing on buttering his roll.

"It came again," she said.

"It?"

"Yes," she said, as if that cleared things up. "Bigfoot," she added.

I paused my forkful of mashed potatoes halfway to my mouth. "Bigfoot?"

"Yes. Only not the same one."

"I see," I said. This was somewhat of a relief to hear, in that it was generally concluded that my mysterious George was the original Bigfoot, though faux in that he was simply a man wearing a bearskin rug. It had been George who had found warmth and food in Aggie's shed and eventually peeked into her patio door that cold winter's night, seeking help. What he had received was a close call with a twelve-gauge shotgun. I was uncertain if this was before or after George, when trying to find my cabin that stormy night, had been run off by Woofie, who adorned with balls of snow, resembled a hairy monster not of this world. Then, of course, when George finally did reach my cabin sometime later, he was greeted by Mother brandishing a fireplace poker. I was absolutely positive that it was a scenario that George did not care to repeat and under no circumstances would ever again peek into Aggie's house.

"I know the first one was George," Aggie said, as if reading my mind. "But this one was different. Much more ape-like. And white, like a polar bear."

"White?" I said.

"Probably a Yeti," Winston chimed in. "You know, the abominable snowman? Not surprised with the damn winters we have up here. The regular Bigfoots prefer the milder temps of the Pacific Northwest."

And we trusted this man to make food for babies?

"Yeti, schmeti," Aggie said. "Whatever, you call it, it was peeking in my kitchen window."

"Did you call the police?" I said.

222

"Humpf," she said. "And be called a dotty old woman again? Nope. I just got my shotgun out of the umbrella stand and shot off a load out the kitchen door. Next thing I knew, I saw its harry white butt hightailing it for the woods."

"I believe you Aggie," Winston said, dabbing the corner of his mouth with a napkin.

"Thank you, dear," she said. "I feel like I'm losing my mind."

"You know, Aggie," I said, "there may be a logical explanation, just like when George was running around the woods. One way or the other, I believe you too."

"I'm worried about my Aggie living out there alone," Winston said.

His Aggie?

"I have asked her to consider moving into the condo complex where I live. It's strictly for seniors and very nice."

"And expensive!" Aggie said. "I've lived in my house for fifty years. Earl, rest his soul, and I loved that house. We raised our children there. So many wonderful times and priceless memories." Aggie began to tear up.

"Maybe you could get a dog," I offered.

"I suppose," she said. "But what happens to the dog when I join my Earl in heaven? It would be irresponsible."

"An alarm system?" I said.

"Perhaps," she said, sniffing. "I did call a company and they gave me a quote. It was quite a bit more than I would like to spend."

"Now, now dear," Winston said. "No need to make any decisions now. Just think about it as a new beginning. There are so many wonderful people in the condo association. We do some pretty exciting stuff. Last year we went to Italy. Very reasonable, too, I might add."

"Italy?" Aggie said, perking up.

He nodded. "I think we're going to Hawaii next. We have a travel service that takes care of everything. Food, lodging, travel arrangements. I think there are hula lessons included too."

That made Aggie laugh. She had a keeper there.

The band finished a jazzy version of "White Christmas" that had attracted several couples to a small, improvised dance floor. The next song, "Here Comes Santa Claus!" was for the children. A few of the kids jumped up and started leaping around the room in a frenzy, shouting for Santa. Suddenly a storage room door burst open and out came the man himself wearing a well-stuffed Santa suit and sporting a brilliant white beard. He looked over his shoulder and shouted, "Take

223

care of the reindeer, will you? They're tired from delivering all those toys!"

Then he turned to the swirling clot of children and bellowed: "HO HO HO! Where are all the good little girls and boys?"

A couple of elders jumped up and yelled that they had been very, very good.

"HO HO HO! I mean the *little* boys and girls. I have my list that I've checked twice, and I know that there are only good boys and girls here today. HO HO HO!"

That voice was all too familiar.

George.

☙ 27 ☙

George and I staggered into the living room just in time to hear Mother leaving a terse message on my answering machine. All I caught was that she wanted George to call her immediately. George had shed the Santa suit at the church and brought it home to be washed. Not one but two children had thrown up on him. Probably from all of the excitement one mother had proclaimed. Yeah, that and the fact that her kid ate a whole pumpkin pie. While I had not been barfed on, no doubt I carried a lingering odor of the day's menu.

I hit the replay button on the answering machine.

"George, tell Janese to answer her cell once in a while. This is an emergency. Call me."

Unsure if I should be hearing alarm bells or just be annoyed, I looked at George and shrugged. The emergency could range from something trivial such as a shortage of party favors to a major catastrophe. Perhaps the inn burned down or maybe Dr. Bloom ran off with one of the waitresses. It was true that I had neglected to turn on my cell phone all day to check messages. Since there was no service in half of the county, I tended to forget.

After depositing our soiled clothing into the laundry hamper and slipping into comfy clothes, George and I looked at the answering machine, which had stopped blinking, but still held the mysterious message.

"You call her. She's your mother," George said as he shoved some Styrofoam containers into the fridge. We would be having leftovers for a few days as George had taken home generous amounts of turkey, ham, and a few sides. Unfortunately, there was no pie left over, unless you counted what had been upchucked on the Santa suit.

"She asked for you," I said.

"Because she was mad at you for not turning on your phone."

I sighed and picked up the landline phone and punched in Mother's number. She picked up on the first ring.

"Where have you been?" Mother shrieked. "I've been worried sick."

"Well, we—"

"Anyway, I have a situation here and I need George."

George but not me. For some odd reason I felt rebuffed.

"Well, is he there?" she added impatiently.

I grabbed George as he tried to scurry from the room and shoved the receiver at him. He gave me a poisonous look and snatched the phone.

"Hello, Maddie. What's up? Uh huh. Uh huh. Is he going to be okay? Wow, that's a bummer. Uh huh."

I poked at George's shoulder and mouthed *what?*

"How long? Well, I suppose. Un huh, he can order stuff, just not...I see. Really?"

I poked harder.

"Just a minute," George said and turned to me, "The chef got hurt. Something about a shelf falling on him."

"So, what's that got to do with you?"

George held up a finger, indicating for me to wait a minute, then he returned to his cryptic phone conversation. "Uh huh. Okay, yea sure. Tomorrow looks okay with the weather and all. I don't know if she can come, though. Work, you know. Uh huh. Sure. Okey dokes. Bye."

I didn't like the sound of this one-sided conversation. Not at all.

"Well?" I said. "What's she up to now?"

"Mario broke his hand. He can't cook. She wants me to step in."

"What! You?"

"Sure, why not? It'll be a hoot. Me: Chef George. Or maybe I'll be Jorge or Georgio, or something more apropos."

"You do know that you'll be working closely with Mother, who cannot be pleased. I bet that Mario intentionally had an *accident* in a suicide attempt."

"What can I say?" George said. "She's my future mother-in-law."

Whoa.

"Boy, I guess that kind of slipped out," George said, looking sheepish.

"You guess?" The proverbial bombshell just "slipped out" of the man harboring a million secrets? True, I had been inserting the term fiancé into an occasional conversation but George had never referred to me as anybody but "Trout." I wondered if there was substance to the slip.

"Anyway, I said I'd fill in—well I never really said it, I just agreed to her, er, request."

"Command," I corrected. "So, back to your slip of the tongue."

"Right, it was a command," he said, ignoring the second part of my comment. "But it's cool. I mean it'll be good experience. I'm not sure the college is going to go along with a degree in cuisine, at least not this year, and I may need to find another, er, outlet for now. I don't suppose you'd want to come too? You could be my assistant, like at the church Christmas dinner."

"First off, I wasn't your assistant. Partner, maybe. Second, I can't because I've got to somehow pull off this New Year's Eve thing, minus the igloo contest. I was hoping *you'd* be able to help *me*." I had decided to table the mother-in-law comment for the time being. But it was not going far.

"Well, no offense, Trout, and I did forget to mention this. Maddie said I'd be paid handsomely."

"That so?" I said. "Well, I have a way of showing my gratitude, too." Unfortunately, this line was delivered sounding more petulant than coquettish.

George gave me a peck on the cheek. "I'll just have to find some other way to, ah, earn your gratitude. But I think I should go first thing tomorrow and try to get up to speed. Mario can still direct the operation but can't physically cook. Once New Year's is over, I'll be back and we'll—talk."

"'bout what?"

"Stuff. Anyway, can you wash my Chef George duds? And maybe iron them, too? Do you have any spray starch?"

The look I gave him was the only starch in the house.

"Never mind, I'll do it," he said hurrying off toward the bedroom. He poked his head out of the door. "The washer's in the basement, right?"

I sighed and trudged toward the bedroom. The washer and dryer were in the utility room off the kitchen, behind the folding doors. Apparently, the domestic transition of George LeFleur needed more work.

* * *

I was several days into living solo at the cabin. George had arrived safely at Mother's inn and sounded beyond elated in his new role as assistant chef, for which he would be *handsomely* compensated. I was determined that Mother would not get her claws into him with some devious plan to use him as a lure to get me closer to her domain. She often mentioned job openings at various educational institutions within driving range of the inn. Or, of course, I could work at The Straights in middle management. I'd rather poke my eye out with a fork.

Meanwhile, I was alone with no distractions from planning the community New Year's Eve bash at the college. Well, there may have been one distraction, which constantly loomed. I thought about trying one more time for the pregnancy test, but when I slunk into the local drug store to make the purchase, I ran into three people who decided to chat me up, making it impossible to buy anything discreetly. I ended up picking up a new hairbrush and a pack of hair clips as cover. I had heard that EPTs could be ordered online, along with other embarrassing products, such as for bladder leakage, impotence, marital enhancement, yadda yadda yadda. Or I could just wait to see the doctor. I had Googled symptoms of early pregnancy, now that I could do so without someone creeping up on me and looking over my shoulder, but the results were inconclusive. Obviously, the most prominent sign was missing a cycle, or period, such as in my case. Other indicators included nausea (sometimes), tenderness in areas (not really), mood swings (yeah, okay), and a collection of other unseemly conditions such as swollen ankles, rashes, weight gain/loss, changes in hair integrity (whatever that meant), and so on. However, it also mentioned that one or all of these symptoms could be caused by other conditions, such as diabetes, kidney failure, heart failure, auto-immune disease, cancer, peri or full- blown menopause, stress, eating disorders, or perhaps some exotic disease from Africa.

I wondered about this peri-menopause thing. It said it can start as early as the mid-thirties, which I was rapidly approaching. That put a whole new spin on things.

Even though I seemed to be physically unraveling (my hair perhaps had lost its integrity), things were coming together well for the New Year's Eve bash. President Neil had texted and e-mailed repeatedly, announcing that the Moody Booties band would be delighted to play. I had made up entry slips for the giveaway of prizes that previously were to be awarded to igloo contest winners. The caterers were good to go and all of the entrants along with the general public had been notified about the change of plans.

While most who had entered the contest had expected a change of plans due to the warm weather, die-hard Bucky Tanner had a fit. That was until I mentioned that the grand prize was going to be given away in a drawing. I also mentioned the dancing, costumes, and free food, which lightened the mood a bit.

Since I was unable to line up any bona fide dance instructors I was hopeful that, indeed, everyone would find their dancing niche. We had been assured by the band that the Finns would have their moment with their Finnish tango, schottische, some ballroom steps, and the ever-popular polka. The young people would, of course, have the opportunity to engage in whatever dance steps or gyrations that were currently the rage for youth. And while all the shaking and quaking was going on, I would be the proverbial wall flower in that George was several hundred miles away, cooking for a bunch of inebriants at The Straights Inn. I had always wanted to dance with George—especially a waltz. Well, perhaps at a future wedding.

I shook myself out of my bizarre train of thought and went to look out the window at the patches of slushy snow scattered around my yard, seemingly being pushed aside by emerging dead winter grass. It wasn't at all pretty, but I knew that plenty of the white stuff would be returning.

When it was time to watch the channel 13 local news, I wished I could just have one tiny glass of wine. A cup of tea was not the same, but until I knew whether I was with child or facing some horrible disease, it would have to do.

I caught the last couple of minutes of *persona non grata*, James Rush, giving his closing news report. I will give him credit, he looked pretty good, glowing almost. I wondered if he had resurfaced his pearly whites and gotten a spray-on tan at the local salon. His silvery hair seemed even thicker than usual. Plugs? Maybe a good toupee?

"And now, we have a look at the weather for the New Year's holiday. Standing in for Gail Storm is reporter Ted WEEner with the latest forecast. Have a good night and stay safe!" Rush pointed his index finger at the camera and winked. I swear his eyes twinkled. How did he do that?

"Good morning America! Ted VEEner here with the latest on the weather, er I'm here for Gail Squall. I mean Stormy."

While the yokel on the screen's last name was intentionally mispronounced by James, it was the only thing Weiner got right in his weathercast. First off, his opening gaffe was a plagiarism from a prominent show of the past called *Good Morning America!* Secondly, it wasn't morning, but evening. Yes, he did correct Gail's last name, but still got it wrong. Word was Weiner was someone's nephew. The slaughter continued.

"What we all want to know is what the weather is gonna do for Christmas Eve."

"No, Ted, New Year's Eve," I muttered.

"Did I say Christmas? Hee hee. Hope Santy was good to all the naughty little boys and girls. Did he come down your chimney, or get stuck? Hee!"

For some reason, this felt tinged with sexual innuendo and made my skin crawl.

"Anyway, time fugits and it's almost the New Year. Wow! Out with the new and in with the old land sign. What? Oh, we have to break for a commercial, I guess. Anyway, snow is coming. I'll tell you—"

Then it cut to a commercial from a local furniture store that invited us in for their New Year's mattress sale! I wandered into the kitchen to look for something to eat. There was still some ham left from Christmas, and a little bit of sweet potatoes, both well beyond their prime. I tossed it in the trash and looked in the freezer for a pot pie. I had always loved chicken pot pies and got them often as a child because Mother worked a lot. She always fussed because I picked out the peas and carrots, which left only the chicken, gravy, and crust.

I stuck the pot pie in the microwave and went back to the living room to catch channel 13's most inept employee point at a weather map. Unfortunately, he was blocking a good deal of it, but the gist of the situation was that a moderate snowstorm was headed our way, just in time for the New Year's Eve holiday. I was surprised by the next segment, which featured none other than my bestie, Bertie Vaara, spit polished in her crisp uniform. She had on a touch of makeup, which suggested there was a woman in that mannish uniform, tasteful and no-nonsense. Her hair, streaked with gold highlights, was neatly pulled into a bun at the back of her head.

"We want everyone to have a safe and happy holiday. We would like to have zero arrests and no serious accidents this New Year's celebration time. Please everyone, have a wonderful time celebrating with your friends and family, but always have a designated driver, or just stay the night if you've had too much to drink. And remember, too much to drink is only a couple. We will be out in full force keeping things safe and sane out there. We have some snow coming, which will make things slick, so remember to drive safely and responsibly."

Next Weiner came back on.

"Thank you, Mrs. Policeman, er woman. Anyway, please do take her advice and keep it safe out there. I'll be back tomorrow morning—

right? Yes, tomorrow morning, which is I guess New Year's Eve day, for a weather update and to tell you about a costume contest going on at the college. It was supposed to be an igloo contest, but what with the melt and all—what? Oh, I guess Jim Rush is going to report. He's trying to get his story together, I guess. Anyway, this is Ted VEEn—"

Then, mercifully, they cut him off. I had to chuckle at Weiner's comment of James trying to get his story together. So true.

So, this story—I wondered if the pompous James Rush was planning on calling me. If so, I'd have to make it clear it wasn't a costume contest, just a party, with a drawing. The microwave beeped. Dinner was served.

I may have had a stress-induced headache, but then again, it may have been the unrelenting blare of the recorded music pounding in my head. The band had not yet started, and some God-awful recorded stuff boomed over the loudspeakers. Somehow, this wretched noise inspired partygoers to form a conga line and proceed to do laps around the gym floor. Leading the serpentine was Bucky Tanner wearing a crude-looking outfit of animal skins, including a pair of antlers lashed to his head. A flimsy cardboard and aluminum foil spear hung from a rope belt around his waist. I suspected that the skins were the spoils of his game processing industry and originally intended as igloo embellishment.

"He thinks he's Nimrod," said his wife. "I told him he just looks like a fool. He's going to gore someone with those antlers." Mrs. Tanner herself had pulled together a very respectable version of Mother Nature or maybe a wood nymph. She wore a flowing frock festooned with vines and leaves, and a wreath of flowers in her hair. She dressed her two boys, Dakota and Cheyenne, as Ninja warriors—likely repurposed costumes from Halloween.

Other participants wore a mishmash of attire ranging from heavenly angel to a hockey-masked chainsaw murderer. And none of them showed any signs of tiring, as the conga line made its thirty-first lap around the dance floor.

I had dressed up as a lumberjack—or jane—with a flannel shirt, jeans, boots, and a bombardier hat with flaps turned up. It wasn't going to win any prizes, but it was stuff I had around the cabin and I didn't have to fuss with my hair. For makeup I had smeared some soot from the fireplace on my face. At the opposite end of the spectrum was Brenda Koski, who appeared to be a graduate of the Coitus School of Prostitution. Only she could convert the sexless cap and gown into a costume that oozed sex and debauchery.

I jumped when President Neil came up behind me and shouted in my ear. "Way to pull it off, Janice," he bellowed.

"It's JanESE," I corrected.

"What?"

I shook my head and looked at the crowd on the dance floor. At last they appeared to be tiring. The thumping music came to an end and for a blessed moment the hall fell to relative peace and quiet, with only the chatter of the audience.

President Neil was dressed as a Viking, complete with horned helmet, cape, tights, and a plastic sword. I had heard that the horns on a Viking's helmet were just a Hollywood prop, but who was I to point that out to Erik the Prez?

"Nice crowd," said the Viking King.

"Yes, I think everyone is having fun."

"Yes indeed. Oh look, the band is getting ready to play. Time to cut the rug. I better go find The Wife."

"The wife?"

"Yup. She's dressed as a Grecian Goddess," he said scanning the room. Then he muttered something like, *not that she in any way resembles one.* "Well there's Brenda. My, she's looking festive."

"Uh, huh."

"Hmm. Talking to my wife. Gotta go!"

"Well, give them my best," I said as he scurried over to the Koski/Wife combo.

"Check-check-check-check-check," came over the loudspeakers. Deafening microphone feedback squealed, which triggered complaints from the audience. Some adjustments were made, then more check-check-checking, minus the squeal.

"Good evening everyone. I'm Ed. I'm the lead singer and bass guitar here for the Moody Booties. (polite clapping) Hey, the place looks great! I'm wondering who blew up all these balloons! I'd like to meet her! (laughter and whistling) Anyway, over there at the keyboard is Herb." Herb nodded and played a perky tune on the keyboard. "Sally Ann is our drummer." Ed gave a little wave and wink to Sally Ann, who did a drum roll and cymbal crash, which was followed by more polite clapping.

"Johnny is our lead guitar and also a singer, then we got this old dude on accordion. We call him Fruit Fly!" Fruit Fly ran his fingers deftly up and down the keys, which drew cheers and whistles from the crowd. Someone shouted, "You show 'em Fruit Fly!"

"And last, but *certainly* not least, is Heather Meadows on her fiddle. She fiddles *and* dances, folks." Heather Meadows took a bow, her long blond hair cascading down over her shoulders. She did a little energetic fiddling, which really got the crowd whistling and cheering—

that and the fact that she wore a miniscule glittery dress and spike heels, and was drop-dead gorgeous. I had a feeling that she could have been playing the spoons and still have great crowd appeal.

"We'll start out with a little dance music. How about a polka? Grab someone you care about and let's get rockin'!"

They weren't bad, albeit loud. The older members of the crowd knew how to polka. The college kids watched in horror, until one or two young couples ventured out and soon others joined in and seemed to have fun in spite of the hopelessly outdated music.

Ed was right, the place did look great. In addition to about a million balloons, the maintenance guys had hung a mirrored disco ball from the ceiling, which rotated and sparkled magically around the room. Streamers were festooned from one end to the other, and an enormous banner, stating the quintessential "Happy New Year!" was strung across the back of the stage. At midnight, the plan was to drop a bunch of confetti from the control booth where the house and stage lighting control panel was located. Of course, the band would play Auld Lang Syne and noisemakers would be handed out prior to the Big Moment to provide something to do for those who had no one to kiss, such as me. Along one wall was an impressive buffet and non-alcoholic beverage table, which was doing a brisk business after the marathon conga line gambol.

"Care to dance?" came a voice from behind me.

"Huh?" I said, turning around to look at one of the biggest, strangest women I'd ever seen.

"It's me, James."

"James?"

"Yup."

Oh crap. I had forgotten that Channel 13 would be coming to cover the dance. I had not noticed the cameraman and a few other Channel 13 crew had come in when I wasn't looking and were working the room for a story. It looked like President Neil and The Wife were doing some dancing for the camera. Brenda Koski was dancing with a zombie/mummy combo who was impossible to identify. She managed to bump the Prez's backside a couple of times on the crowded dance floor.

"So, James, is this the *real* you?" I said, looking him up and down. Was he actually primping in a compact mirror he had pulled from a little clutch purse?

"Well," he said, "I decided to lean toward political correctness and show, er, that Channel 13 supports the gay community, as well as transgender and tri-sexuals and all of that," he said, snapping the compact shut and sliding it into the purse. "Perhaps boost our ratings."

"But dressing up as a woman doesn't have anything to do with being gay or transgender. It means you're a cross-dresser," I said.

"Whatever," he said, looking around the room. He made a signal to the cameraman who had a portable unit perched on his shoulder.

"I'm really surprised you didn't come as some kind of macho man or superhero," I said, "rather than a knock-off of Monty Python in drag."

"Weather girl!" he said, flipping back a stiff lock of his platinum wig. He wore a very tight, red sequined dress, greatly enhanced at the bosom with foam. There had to be at least an inch of makeup troweled on his face and a thick coating of blood-red lipstick smeared on his lips. Vibrant aqua-blue eye shadow glittered beneath mascara-caked eyelashes. He wore long, dangly earrings, which tended to snag in the wig. The dress was sleeveless and of course short, and while there was an overabundance of leg and arm hair exposed, he didn't make an entirely bad-looking woman.

"You don't look like any weather girl I've ever seen."

He fanned himself with a clutch purse. "Oh, look who's talking. You're dressed as a man, and a slob at that. How uninspired can one be? You must have spent three minutes putting that together," he said jutting the little purse at me and giving his head a toss.

I looked down at my hastily put together lumberjack/jane costume. He had me there. I may have actually only spent two minutes putting together my ensemble.

"So, shall we dance?" I've got the cameraman ready to get a shot. And these shoes are *killing* me. How do you gals stand them?"

"All us *gals* don't own a pair and I'd rather dance with Freddy Krueger over there with his PlaySkool chainsaw than with a sexist cross-dresser."

"Well! I never!" James said, adjusting his foam bosom. "As if anyone else is asking. Where's ol' Georgie Boy?"

"I could dance with anyone here. I'm not afraid to ask. George is helping out Mother at the resort. Her chef got, um, injured."

"I see. And how is Madeline?"

"She's fine. And so is Benjamin. You know, the *doctor*. He's there with her."

"Well, how nice. I guess we've all moved on," James said. "Now, how about that dance? You're the only girl dressed up like a boy here and I need the photo op."

What the hell. I sighed and allowed myself to be led to the dance floor as my so-called weather girl partner tottered ahead on his/her high heels.

The band began playing a plucky little tune, which I was to learn was a schottische—a type of folk dance. I had to admit, The Viking King and his Grecian Goddess wife were doing a fine job of showing how it was done. Eventually, others joined in and everyone was prancing around the dance floor, pointing toes, twirling, and skipping.

"Let me lead," I said. "I'm the token male." We flailed our arms around a bit, trying to get the proper dancing posture for the schottische, which seemed to require performing side-by-side.

"No way," James snapped. "You are too small. I'm leading."

"Ouch!" I shrieked, breaking our tenuous grasp and hopping on one foot. "What the hell are you wearing? Spears on your feet?"

"They're spike heels and I'm not afraid to use them," he said.

James noticed that the cameraman was laughing and getting it all. Also, someone had shoved a microphone under my chin. A small group had formed a circle around us, laughing and pointing.

"Get over here," James said through clenched teeth. "Hey, that is NOT going on the air," she snarled at the cameraman.

By now the schottische had mercifully ended and the band struck up, of all things, the "Hokey Pokey." I couldn't believe that the young people in the audience had never done the Hokey Pokey. Wasn't that every child's first dance routine?

"Hey everyone, you know what it's all about, eh? Form a circle and let's do THE HOKEY POKEY," screamed all the members of the band in unison.

I had to admit, I was having a blast. And I didn't have to touch Girlie Girl Rush, who had kicked the ridiculous shoes under a table and whose mascara was running a bit. Also, his tarty dress had slipped down considerably, allowing a substantial amount of chest hair to pop out of its foam prison.

By the time we got to putting our heads in and our heads out, everyone had caught on to the nonsensical routine. Lastly, we put our whole-selves in and out and then shook all about, and that what it was enough Hokey Pokey to last for some time.

Then the band took a break and we all headed for the food and drinks. I stepped outside for a few minutes of air and noticed that wet, heavy snowflakes were coming down in earnest. They had predicted a moderate snowstorm, but we all knew that weather predictions were about as reliable as political polls. This had the feel of beyond moderate. I was glad things would be winding down soon and everyone could perhaps beat the weather. It was good to know that those leaving the party would be stone-cold sober. The concern would be those on the highways and byways who *weren't* sober.

After a few more sets by the band, they took a break and the drawings got underway. A rotating cage on wheels had been borrowed from the VFW where it was normally used for Bingo night. Instead of Bingo balls, door prize entry forms had been filled out by most everyone and tossed into the cage throughout the night. The unit was brought up on stage and several students took turns twirling it and pulling out entry slips then announcing names of the winners. A table next to the stage featured the various prizes, including tees, hats, and other token items along with more interesting prizes, such as a massage at the Magic Hands Spa and a weekend package at the Slippery Slope Ski Resort. Items were selected one by one on a first come, first served basis.

Except, of course the Grand Prize, which was on reserve. It was represented by a simple set of keys that belonged to a spanking new shiny red off-road vehicle. The ORV had been on display at the edge of campus for a few days, chained to a utility pole, where people driving by could see it. Someone had whipped up a sign: WIN ME! COME 2 THE NU YRS PARTI! I hoped the sign—an obvious victim of texting lingo—had not been created by an English major.

The night had slipped away and it was 15 minutes until confetti time. President Neil stepped up to the microphone and cleared his throat.

"And now, ladies and gents, the moment we've all been waiting for! It's time to find out who wins the new four-wheeler." President Neil had gotten the set of keys off the now-empty prize table and held them high in the air. "Of course it was to have gone to the first-place winner of the Habitat for Critters Igloo Contest, but, hey, some crazy weather put the kibosh on that!"

The audience clapped and whistled. There was a drum roll and a slight squeal from the mic as the prez snatched it out of its stand and joined Mrs. Neil, who was vigorously spinning the rotating cage. The basket slowed and stopped, Neil opened the little door, dramatically closed his eyes, reached in, and pulled out an entry.

"And the winner is..." (drum roll) BUCKY TANNER!

"HOT DAMN!" yelled Bucky from the dance floor.

"Come on up here, Bucky, and get the keys to your brand new, Suzuki Z2000, all-terrain vehicle!"

Everyone liked Bucky, who couldn't care less if anyone liked him or not. However, he grinned broadly as the audience cheered, whistled, and stomped their enthusiasm. Bucky straightened his antlers, strutted up, and took the keys from President Neil then held them above his head and gave them a jingle. He favored the audience a rare full-wattage smile, minus a few teeth. More than a few, actually.

"Hey, yous don't know how much this will help me, eh?" Bucky said. "Me and the missus and the boys will take real good care of 'er." The missus scurried up on the stage with their two boys and mobbed Bucky and President Neil, who seemed to recoil a bit. Perhaps everyone was a little ripe from all the dancing.

The rotating cage was removed from the stage and the musician at the keyboard ran a few scales to get everyone's attention. Ed gently wrenched the microphone out of President Neil's grasp, who got the hint and left the stage.

"Hey ladies and gents, look at the time," said Ed pointing to a clock above the buffet table. "Five minutes until midnight. Grab your gal and we're going to get in some dancing as this old year goes into the review mirror. I think you'll like this one!"

The band burst into "Rock Around the Clock," which while an oldie, was something all ages could shake, rattle, and roll to. And as the lyrics moved through the hours, the symbolic passing of time made it a perfect final tune for the departing year. Plus the beat just made you want to boogey.

That is, if you had someone with whom to boogey.

James had long since abandoned me as a dance partner and was shaking it up with Brenda Koski. I was surprised that their sequins didn't melt together with all the heat being generated from their bumps and grinds. I was the proverbial wallflower, having not attracted any dance partners besides James. I decided to make myself useful and mosey up to the control booth where the confetti would be dropped. I interrupted a bit of heavy breathing up there as the two college kids in charge of the confetti drop had taken advantage of the privacy.

"You might want to save it for later, guys. You've got less than two minutes before showtime. What's your names?"

"Oh, hey," said the guy, trying to straighten his costume, which was some sort of gnome or Robin Hood. Or maybe an elf, who knows. Anyway, he wore tights and it was good he didn't stand to shake my hand.

"I'm Maryellen. This is Jesse," said the girl, who appeared to be dressed as a girl from ye olden days—perhaps Maid Marian, which would make sense if Jesse were Robin Hood. "I know you. Janese, right? George LeFleur's girlfriend?"

"I guess that's me," I said.

"He's an awesome teacher. I'm going to switch to the culinary program if he teaches it."

"Good for you," I said.

TEN...NINE...EIGHT

"You guys ready?"

"Yup," said Jesse, now standing and holding a box of confetti out the booth window.

SEVEN... SIX... FIVE

Maryellen moved next to Jesse and took one side of the box.

FOUR...THREE...TWO...ONE

HAPPY NEW YEAR!!!

I was amazed at how much confetti the box held as I watched the cloud of paper flakes flutter down onto the cheering crowd.

Maryellen and Jesse had abandoned the box and were mashed together in a very passionate kiss. The band struck up "Auld Lang Syne," Ed began to sing and after everyone came up for post-kissing air, they joined in.

I'd never felt more alone.

≉ 29 ≉

All the cars looked alike because they were covered in at least four inches of snow. I was amazed at how quickly it had piled up. I finally found my Subaru and beeped it open. It gave a double beep, which I chalked up to hitting the unlock a second time. I found my snow brush and went to work while the car warmed up. I was pretty sure this was beyond what was considered a moderate snowstorm. Once inside the car I activated my phone and brought up the weather. The advisory had elevated to a storm warning, with snowfall at a rate of up to two inches an hour, combined with a nasty northeast wind, which could cause possible whiteout conditions. Good Lord. I could only imagine what all the poor cops who had to work were thinking. Drunks plus bad roads and poor visibility. I was glad that when the party had wound down the band leader warned everyone to drive carefully. I felt a tingle of angst thinking about my ten-mile drive home on the winding, hilly, Big Lake Road, which was notorious for accidents even in good weather.

Things went pretty well until I was past the streetlights. Once the brightness of town faded behind me, I entered the land of white doom. The huge flakes torpedoed my windshield with a vengeance, then darted off into the night. Mailboxes had disappeared and only the headlights of a rare oncoming vehicle or the weak glow from one of the few houses along the way broke the monotony of white. No plow had been down the street since the onslaught of the storm, and my Subaru waged a valiant battle through the deepening drifts.

An idiot light came on, indicating I was intermittently losing traction.

"Oh, like I hadn't noticed," I snarled. "I know I'm in deep doodoo."

My phone gave a little chirp, causing me to glance over to the passenger seat. I caught a movement out of the corner of my eye. I glanced back at the road. White. I was now down to about 15 miles per hour. At this rate it would be daylight before I reached the safety of my cabin. The movement, again. I flicked on the interior light and took a quick look but saw nothing. I flipped the light back off. Eyes back on the road—or what may have been the road. My defroster and wipers were not keeping up with the thick slush building up on the windshield. My phone pinged again. Probably a low battery warning. I reached down, fumbling, to try to swipe it off and save what little juice was left.

That's when I felt something odd. And it moved. I jerked my hand away and looked down. A pair of eyes shone back at me and I caught a glimpse of my passenger. A snake. Not a rubber snake, but a real, live snake riding shotgun. For some reason, I though speeding up would help, as if I could somehow outrun a menace that was riding merrily along next to me. It began moving again, this time toward my lap.

"Holy Mary Mother of God!" I shrieked and stupidly tried to stand up, which allowed the snake to glide silently behind me onto my seat. This action caused me to inadvertently floor the accelerator and jerk the wheel. I know there's no idiot light for how stupid that was, but there should be. I felt the rear end of the Subaru lose traction and tried to steer into swerve. I may not have done it correctly because I'm pretty sure the snake and I experienced a 180 circle before careening into a ditch, flipping, and hitting something with a compressive thump, which activated the airbag and locked the seatbelt. In spite of all these safety features, I hit my face on something and the last thing I remember was feeling the snake work his way up my jacket into the cozy warmth of my lumberjane flannel shirt.

* * *

I'll give credit to Subaru Motors on the tenaciousness of their seat belt design. Mine held me firmly upside-down. As I emerged from the fog of unconsciousness and pushed the deflated airbag off me, I noted my hair seemed to defy gravity by hanging toward the vehicle's ceiling. I took a mental inventory of myself. While I felt a bit tingly, I didn't have any excruciating pain though my nose felt weird and warmly liquid. Well, a bloody nose was no big deal. I tried to reach down to unhook the seatbelt. No luck. Even when right side up and in place, seatbelts were a pain in the ass, especially with thick winter clothes. Nonetheless, I couldn't hang upside-down forever and I was afraid that I would pass out. As I fumbled around, grunting with the effort I felt my old nemesis Mr. Snake exploring his options. Though it was difficult to tell, offhand it seemed he had survived our ordeal just fine. With the help of a brief adrenalin rush, I managed to hit the seatbelt latch just right and with an abrupt lurch, fell onto the ceiling. The snake, much better designed for tight, awkward spaces, deftly slid into our new position and continued its pursuit of a cozy warm spot, such as inside my coat.

Then I discovered three things. Two were good. I was able to reach the switch for the interior light and switched that on. Also, the console had popped open and my emergency flashlight lay near me along with tissues, a granola bar, a frozen bottle of water, and a Tic Tac container, which had popped open and spilled its contents. I flicked on the flashlight and was relieved to find that it still worked.

The last thing I discovered was bad. When I shone the light out the car windows, all that could be seen was white. I quickly concluded that I was in a roadway ditch buried in the snow, rubber-side up and shiny-side down, with the doors hopelessly impacted. For a moment I panicked, worried about carbon monoxide, then relaxed when I realized that the motor was silent. Praise God.

Clearly, I needed help. Phone. I played the flashlight beam around looking for my cell phone, hoping that if could just get my hands on it I could get help. It could have been wrapped up in the deflated airbag or perhaps wedged under the seat. In any event, it was nowhere to be found, not that it mattered since it was probably dead and there was small likelihood of any cell service in a ditch on a desolate stretch of Big Lake Road.

I squirmed around, trying to get into a tenable position and managed to grab onto a partial packet of tissues from the console to staunch the flow of blood trickling down my chin. The activity apparently disturbed Mr. Snake, who moved away from me and wrapped itself around the steering wheel. While I may have just been imagining it, I swear he was looking at me in a meaningful way. I was too large to be considered potential prey, so could only assume those beady eyes were somehow trying to communicate. Probably something like: *What th' hell?* in snake lingo.

"Hey, snake-guy," I said. "I guess we're all in this together."

The snake flicked his tongue out a few times then he slid off the steering wheel onto the ceiling next to me. He arranged himself into a tight coil, with his head sticking out. The eyes continued to stare. *Do something, human!* He was probably getting cold or maybe hungry. I figured the snake would eventually lapse into a dormant state until things improved. Lucky snake. Being human, I would simply freeze to death. Already I couldn't feel my toes. Also, it was getting stuffy in the car.

I squirmed around and managed to reach the door handle and felt around until I located the window control. When I pushed the little lever, nothing happened. I squirmed some more, positioning my feet against the window and tried to kick, but I couldn't get any leverage and the window remained mockingly intact.

"Any ideas?" I asked the snake. He lifted his head then slowly began to uncoil. I fixed the flashlight on him in case he decided to come my way, but instead he headed toward the dashboard and began exploring the passenger side vent—or the gaping hole that had held a vent louver before Bertie's dog, Woofie, had smashed it with his snout and broken it. I had removed it a while back with the plan to find a replacement on eBay or Amazon, eventually.

I watched the snake slowly disappear into the hole. Perhaps he wasn't so big after all. I wondered what was on the other side, maybe some lingering warmth in the engine. I also wondered if he could possibly work his way through the engine compartment and out the bottom of the car to freedom. In any event, he was gone, or at least out of sight.

"When you get out big fella, bring help!" I yelled. Then I began to giggle and hiccup. And my nose hurt like a sonofabitch, though the bleeding had seemed to slow. My hands were joining my feet in numbness and I was yawning incessantly. Not a good sign. I tried kicking the window again. No luck. I looked frantically around for something, anything, to try to bust my way out. I located a snowbrush wedged in the seat headrest and managed to grab it. I commenced beating on everything in sight until I became light-headed and exhausted. And my nose was really starting to throb along with my shoulder and maybe a couple of ribs. My ears joined the frostbite club. I tried to push down the panic. One of my many great fears—along with being trapped under the ice, speaking to large groups, getting scurvy from not eating my fruits and vegetables, and snakes—was being buried alive. Taphophobia was playing out at that very moment.

I resorted to useless yelling, then lost my voice at some point and was probably using up a limited oxygen supply. Damn, my nose hurt. Maybe it was frozen, but somehow it still hurt. How could that be?

Dear Lord, if you get me out of this, I promise to be a better person. I'll even be nice to James Rush, Brenda Koski, and even Eleanor Heimlich—though of course you know it's really Eleanor who has the problem. And also, I'll do whatever Mother asks. I will honor and obey. And if I'm having a baby, I promise not to be a terrible mother.

Yes, that's it. Even if I've sinned repeatedly dear Lord please think of this potential innocent child that maybe I am carrying and please spare it. And of course me too. In Jesus' name I pray. Amen.

* * *

Muffled thudding noises bounced around in my brain and a cold waft of air hit my face like a gift from heaven. What I saw when I thought I had opened my eyes was not St. Peter nor God or anything remotely heavenly, but rather a white, hairy, and startling apparition. I thought maybe it was Woofie in that all I could see was a mop of hair. Whatever it was, it had somehow gotten the driver's door partially open and allowed fresh air to circulate. But of course Woofie couldn't do that.

"Bertie?" I muttered. Maybe she and Woofie had come to rescue me. "Get me outta here Bertie!" I croaked.

But the hairy thing only grunted. It wasn't Woofie or anything canine, but it was too dark out to tell what I was looking at. I heard a siren in the distance. The hairy thing muttered something and then vanished.

The siren arrived and I heard some activity then a face—a human face—poked into the crack of the door.

"It's okay Miss, we'll get you out of here. Are you bleeding anywhere or feeling any pain?"

"Nosh," I responded. "Cold."

"Yes, okay, what's your name?"

"Jaheese. Trod."

"Hey Janese, it's me, Buzzy. Buzzy Winfield."

Another head appeared in the open door. A woman. "Hi Janese. You remember me, right? Bonnie Winfield?"

"Uh hud," I said. I was having trouble breathing and my mouth was so dry. "'hanks fah cuhmin."

I heard more sirens as apparently more first responders arrived.

It was Bertie who next stuck her head into the open door. "Hey girl. What the hell happened?"

"Snaa," I said.

"Did the witness stick around?" she said to the Winfields," We got a call from a passerby."

"Nope," said Bonnie. "In fact, we would never have even found the vehicle if that kind of weird thing hadn't been sticking up out of the snow. Like a big stick put for a marker, but it disappeared."

Doughnuts to dollars it was Mr. Snake they saw.

Another face appeared in the door crack. Based on his hat, I figured him to be a fireman.

"Okay, Miss now we're going to try to get you out through this door once we can get it cut off. Don't be frightened. The machine makes a racket."

Which it did. I wondered how Mr. Snake was feeling about the screaming noise as the driver's door was severed and torn off like the lid on a can of soup. After the pesky door was gone, it was just a matter of getting my semi-paralyzed body to unfold and slide onto a board they had positioned outside the door. Someone had put a bandage over my nose and once finally out and on the board, covered me and stuffed padding around my head.

Bertie helped the EMTs maneuver me onto the board and carry me through the deepening snow to the road. I was lifted onto a gurney and wheeled toward the ambulance. I giggled as I wondered if the gurney had sled runners. Bertie's radio squawked and she spoke into a microphone clipped to her shirt. All I heard was something about a possible ten-fifteen on Townline Road.

"Got another accident," Bertie said to the Buzzy and Bonnie team as they dropped down the gurney and prepared to lift me into the ambulance. I knew that ten-fifteen meant a personal injury.

"Okay," Buzzy said. "It's been one of those nights. I think the other team freed up shortly after we got this call. Man! Will this snow ever quit?"

Up I went into the back of the ambulance.

Bertie stuck her head in. "Do you want me to contact your mother?"

"Uh huh," I responded. "Ad duh resort. Shudda na drive." I was wondering if they had given me something because I was feeling very groggy and my tongue felt thick and dry. Someone slapped an oxygen mask over me making talking even harder.

"Okay, I'll tell them to hold off coming. You'll be fine. No worries. Gotta run!"

With that Bertie's face disappeared and I soon heard her cruiser siren kick into life as she blasted off.

"No need for a code run here," Buzzy said. "We'll just drive nice and sensibly and get you into the hospital for a going over. How's that nose?"

"Hurds," I said.

"Yeah, it took a beating. Warming up yet?"

"Uh hud," I muttered, feeling myself drift off. Then I thought about the snake left behind. Cold and frightened. My eyes popped open. "How's duh snah? He hokay?"

"Not sure what you mean, sweetie," Bonnie Winfred said. "Maybe you shouldn't try to talk right now with that mask on. You'll be just fine. I'm afraid you'll need a new car though, or at least a new door. A wrecker will pull it out and take it on in and you can call your insurance company. Everything will be fine. Now we're on our way. Hope you enjoy your ride," she said jokingly as she patted my shoulder.

Then I remembered the white hairy thing that had somehow got my car door open. Had I imagined that? Maybe my kicking had somehow pushed the door open and my rattled brain had played tricks on me. It muttered something kind of human sounding. Why did it leave?

"Harrr crechur," I said. "See 'em?"

"Sure, sure honey. Hey, her BP is dropping. She might be getting shocky. Maybe you better hit it," Bonnie said to Buzzy.

I felt things lurch into action and heard the siren come on. I wondered if I was dying. I hated the idea. I wanted to thank my white hairy savior. And poor Mr. Snake. How did he get in my car? The unlock beeped twice. Someone had been in my car while I was at the New Year's gig. I wanted to yell ah ha!

"Ish beed twash," I said.

"Okay, sure," Bonnie said. "That's the siren you hear, sweetie."

"No, unlock beep twas." I just couldn't get my mouth to work and the stupid plastic mask was making everything so dry and my nose felt so weird.

"BP looking okay now."

Good. I was going to live. Then the horror hit me. All those promises to God—Mother! What had I done? Suddenly I felt deep cramping in my gut. Lord, don't let me soil myself.

"Uh oh," Bonnie said. "Heart rate just accelerated and she's hyperventilating. Hey, just breathe nice and easy there, honey bun. Buzzy and Bonnie are here to take care of you."

Then she turned around and shouted at Buzzy, "Step on it!"

⩔ 30 ⩔

So, this was what it felt like to die. Weird smells, strange noises, and an ethereal sense of physical and spiritual disconnect. I wondered if I'd meet Mother's late husbands, one being my father.

First I heard her, then I saw her. Mother.

"Janese, darling, can you hear me?"

"Hey Trout."

George?

Someone said: "She's coming around."

And I did. No heavenly angels singing, no fluffy clouds, no face of God. On the contrary, my coming around revealed beeping noises, tubes, a wicked hospital bed, and the face of Mother—the person I had promised God that I'd be nice to if He got me out of the mess.

And the spectacular Dr. Bloom was also among those clustered around my hospital bed.

I tried to speak, but my mouth felt like a pair of woolen hunting socks. I never thought of spit as a wonderful thing but would have given a boatload of cash for a good mouthful of it.

"How are you feeling?" Dr. Bloom asked.

I telepathically told him that I felt like shit. I think he got the message.

"I believe we can give her some ice chips," Dr. Bloom said.

Someone magically produced a Styrofoam cup of ice chips. Mother held it for me and helped me get a few into the vast wasteland that once was my tongue. As I sucked away, I could tell my nose was heavily bandaged. At least there was no oxygen mask.

"Hansh," I managed.

"Do you remember what happened?" asked Dr. Bloom.

I bet he wondered what the odds were that both George and I would get amnesia almost at the same time. But I remembered perfectly what happened. Sort of.

"Snaaa—aach," I said. "Bweep twash, Schnoo stah," I added. There, that explained everything. Someone put a snake in my car. I had a bad case of distracted driving, the weather was bad, and I rolled into the ditch. It happens.

247

"You have a broken nose," Dr. Bloom said. "Not too bad. You had to go into surgery to get it realigned. Also, you have a mild concussion, so we are keeping an eye on that."

George squeezed my hand, the one without an IV. "You look like a boxer that went one round too many," he said. "Like I did after your Mother bludgeoned me!"

Good ol' George. Always making everyone feel better.

"I was protecting my baby!" Mother said.

I caught Dr. Bloom out of the corner of my eye as he slipped from the room. Coward.

"Anyway, darling," Mother said. "They say you can go home tomorrow. I'll stay and take care of you."

"I can take care of her," George said.

"Of course, dear. We'll both take care of her."

God have mercy.

"George has been a complete godsend at the resort," Mother said. "He is the best chef I have ever had!"

"Well, I have a good boss who gives me what I need," George said. I could hear him preening.

A Mother/George lovefest. This sounded dangerous.

* * *

"I'm telling you, something big, white, and hairy got my car door partway open, then the sirens started and it ran off," I said. My nose was killing me, so I popped one of the wonderful little white pills they had given me. I had been given a stern warning about the pills and all the harmful side-effects, such as a feeling of nirvana, which could lead to addiction and drug abuse, then undoubtedly a downward spiral into the gutter. Whatever.

Bertie had come to visit me and finish up her police report. I saw the corner of her mouth twitch. I remembered when we were kids it meant that she thought I was full of shit.

"Well," Bertie said, "we did get a 911 call of a rollover—that being yours—and never did figure out who called it in. Since there is no cell service out where you had your accident, we figured it was a passerby who didn't want to stop—maybe needed to drive to get cell service, or maybe too much celebrating—and went on to his or her destination and called it in. Probably a throw away phone because no caller ID was available according to the dispatcher."

"But the big hairy thing..."

"Well, I've been thinking about that," Bertie said with the twitch returning. "Maybe someone was at a costume party and stopped to help."

"But it took off!"

"Probably afraid of the cops because he was drunk or maybe just didn't want to get involved. It happens a lot."

"But he left when the sirens started."

"Sure," Bertie said. "He knew you'd be okay and he was outta there."

"In a white, hairy costume. He would have taken the head off, don't you think, when he looked at me? And he never really spoke but made humanoid mumbling noises. And strong! How did he get the car door open? I mean I was buried pretty good."

"I don't know. A lot of people carry a shovel in their trunk," Bertie said looking down at the notes she had been scribbling.

"Really?" I said. Now it was my turn to give a little smirk. "Did you happen to find evidence of that?"

"Well, no, but we weren't really looking. Of course Buzzy and Bonnie got there first because I was way the hell over on the other side of the county. They were concerned about you and didn't scout the area for clues. Their job was to render aid. And it was snowing so hard, any footprints were gone pretty quickly."

"Hmm," I said. "Too bad. If there had been giant animalistic footprints that would have been helpful."

"Are you saying that you think you were rescued by a bigfoot?" Bertie said. Now she had the smirk.

"Well, I will say that Aggie—at my church—saw something in her window. She pulled a shotgun on it and—"

"I don't even want to hear this," Bertie said. "I've heard about Agnes Whim and her itchy trigger finger. Now, about the snake—"

"Yeah," I said. "He rode along on the passenger seat next to me, then tried to get inside my coat, which freaked me out and I lost control. After the accident he left through a hole in my dash."

"A hole? In the dash?"

"Right, your pooch bashed the heat vent with his snout back when I doggie sat and I removed the broken piece to get a replacement."

"Oh, well sorry about that. I'll pay. So anyway, a snake was on the seat and you didn't notice right away?"

"I think it was on the floor to start with. And it was dark. Anyway, he moved up onto the seat then toward me while I was driving in that whiteout. As you can imagine, I got a bit distracted."

"Of course. Who wouldn't?"

"Someone put it in my car."

"Well, I'd say that's a safe assumption, since it's unlikely snakes are indigenous to Subarus, especially in the wintertime when they are generally buried in their winter getaway spots. And of course snakes come from tropical rain forests and live in aquariums with heat lamps, not dashboards."

"When I went to get in my car after the party, I hit the unlock and it beeped twice. I think that meant that the car was already unlocked."

"Okay, it was already open. Assuming you didn't leave it open, how did someone get in?"

"Dunno," I said. "Thinking back, it's happened a couple of times I've found my car unlocked. One time there was a rubber snake."

"A rubber snake," Bertie said.

"Uh huh," I said. "After the church cantata. You can ask Pastor Saaranen. He was there when I freaked out. Very embarrassing. A stupid rubber snake like you get at the dollar store. We figured kids. But how did they get in? I always lock the car. Sometimes the seatbelt gets caught though—doesn't retract, so maybe it was open when the rubber snake was put in. But this last time, I know it was locked. I left my purse in the car and just took my keys and phone to go to the New Years' party. I am positive I would have made sure it had locked."

"Okay," Bertie said. "Who has a key?"

"Well me, obviously. I keep a spare at home, and then just the car key in a magnetic box stuck to the fender. Hmm."

"The one in the magnetic box, have you checked that lately?"

"Not since I bought the car a couple of years ago. It was a little bonus thing from the salesman—the magnetic box to put a manual key in. In case you locked your keys in the car."

"Did you mention this to anyone?"

"I don't know, maybe. I think I did suggest it to James Rush at choir practice because he was late one night after locking his keys in the car. Apparently, you can do this by leaving the keys in the ignition then hitting the lock button on the armrest and shutting the door."

"Yes, it can happen. We get calls for help. Takes a special tool now that typically automotive places and locksmiths have. We used to carry Slim Jims for the old mechanical locks, but not too many of those around anymore. So, you say James and everyone else in your choir knew you had the little magnetic box?"

"I guess, if they were paying attention. I didn't make a general announcement of it or anything," I said.

"I see," Bertie said, staring out the cabin window.

"Why would anyone do something so bizarre?" I asked.

"You seem to attract bizarre behavior," Bertie said. "Um, how are you feeling, by the way—you know..."

"Oh, my nose hurts. I took a pill, which is taking its sweet time kicking in. I try to avoid mirrors because of the two shiners and bandages."

"Right, but I mean in all of this, I haven't forgotten your dilemma—you know, if you're pregnant. Did you ever have a chance to do the test?"

"Well, no, but now I don't need to. See, things, well, you know I started probably from the accident and hanging upside down and all. I was kind of a mess from head to toe. They fixed me up at the hospital, probably chalked up to the trauma triggering things. Anyway, I guess this means that I'm not pregnant. Or at least not anymore. Thanks for asking. Nobody else has. George keeps giving me these looks, but I think he's too chicken to—you know. It's hard for a guy."

I felt as if I'd swallowed another woolen sock. I didn't know how I felt about the whole thing. I had an appointment with Dr. Shira the next day to have it looked into. The office just happened to have a cancellation and squeezed me in. I felt relieved in a way, but empty. Mother hadn't brought it up at all, but just bustled around me like a wind-up toy. I was sure she knew.

"Are you okay?" Bertie asked.

"Sure, I guess," I said. Then I burst into tears.

Bertie came over and hugged me. "Hey, it's okay. Things happen for a reason. They really do. Nobody can say that you have a dull life! And if you want kids, you still have plenty of time. Or you can borrow mine!"

I blubbered some more and gulped a couple of times and tried to wipe the snot off my nose bandage. Then I had to giggle thinking about Bertie's two hooligans.

"Better?" Bertie said.

I nodded. I did believe in God's plan, but it would be nice if it came with a roadmap.

251

"Hey!" Bertie said, brightening. "I have something that might cheer you up."

"Yeah?"

"That second accident—you know when I had to leave you quickly after getting a call, well it seems someone else ended up having a bad night too."

"Uh huh? And this cheers me up?"

"Yup. It was Eleanor Heimlich. She ended up in the ditch, too, only right-side-up. But no mysterious hairy guy came and let her out. She had to crawl out of her sunroof—I didn't know they even had those anymore—and walk to a house in the snowstorm and they pulled a gun on her and made her wait on their porch while they called the police."

I tried to snort, but it didn't work so well with the nose issue. "She okay?" I asked, remembering my promise to God to be nice.

"She did have a sprained wrist and some bruises," Bertie said. "She was not too far from you in the ER when she was being checked out. Of course she was treated and released and you were whisked off to surgery."

"Guess it's good she's okay," I muttered. I was feeling a bit wiped out from my crying jag.

"Yes, she was lucky. Said she was coming home from helping a sick friend."

"Hmm," I said. I avoided making a snarky comment about *what friend.*

"So, hey, where's George and your mother?"

"Wend to da store, tank Gah." For some reason my tongue had stopped working and the perpetual plugged feeling in my nose intensified. Finally, the little white pill was doing its stuff.

"They seem to have gotten close," Bertie said, standing up and putting on her coat.

"Ihd in soh mush trhubble," I said, feeling groggy. The pain pill was definitely kicking in.

"Well, sweetie," Bertie said, "you are a trouble magnet. I mean, a snake in the vent?"

"Uh hud." I bolted up. "Duh snaa!"

"Well, he *or* she's a small python—a baby. The man towing your car found it coiled around your rearview mirror. Turns out he's an animal guy and he took the thing to some reptile/raptor refuge near Marquette. I love the people in this community!"

"Oh gud," I mumbled.

"Get some rest," Bertie said. "We'll do lunch soon. Hey, we gotta exchange gifts yet."

"Ud hud," I said as I drifted off. Maybe *Bigfoots and Snakes for Dummies!* I thought about visiting the snake at the refuge. After all, I was pretty sure it was the snake that helped the ambulance drivers find me buried in the snowdrift. A bigfoot and a snake to the rescue! Who woulda thunk?

⚶ 31 ⚶

My nose bandage was now reduced to just a single strip and my black eyes had turned yellowish-green. Even though I could easily have been cast in a horror movie, I was told the look was totally normal and that I was "one lucky gal!"

I had to admit to myself that George must really love me to be able to look at me without wincing. He even brought me roses, which I put in the middle of the dining room table. Mother had settled back in for a few days to determine if George was capable of being a caregiver. Being the lucky gal that I was, I really didn't need a lot of pampering, but decided not to look a gift horse in the mouth.

Mother and I were at the table feasting on quiche Lorraine, which George had made before he headed over to the college to talk to someone or other about his proposed culinary school.

"Well," Mother said, "George is a wizard in the kitchen. There's more than eggs in this quiche."

I nodded and took a bite, thinking about other things George could be a wizard at, though it had been a while.

Mother looked uneasy for a moment, a rarity. "Janese dear, are you doing okay?"

"Sure," I said, nibbling on a piece of toast. "I know I look like hell, but it hardly hurts and I can breathe a lot better now."

"Yes, of course," Mother said. "I mean, I did see the, er, *box* in the hamper."

I set the toast down. I had figured as much. The hamper was a stupid hiding place for a pregnancy test. "It's all good," I said. I knew I didn't sound very convincing. "I mean, I thought maybe—but it was a false alarm. I saw a wonderful new doctor—they squeezed me in—and she could tell there had been, well, nothing there. You know."

Mother nodded. "So, just running late?"

"I guess," I said. There was that woolen sock stuck in my throat again.

"Will you have things checked out more thoroughly? I mean as a teen you were always irregular."

"Yes, well, I guess I'm what you might call perimenopausal."

"What! At your age?"

"I'm told that it can happen in a woman's thirties."

"My baby," Mother said. "In her thirties."

"Yup. Tick toc," I said, reaching for piece of Danish from the plate that George had left for us.

Mother gave me a steady gaze then said in a rather severe tone: "I want grandchildren. Get on with it, Janese!"

"Huh," I said, crumbs falling from my mouth.

"Marry that man and get on with it," she snapped.

"Marry?"

"Well, yes darling, I'm old fashioned that way."

"But he hasn't asked," I said.

Mother's diabolical look was very unsettling.

"Now I know that look, Mother. Don't even think about it!"

"Hmm," she said, with a little smile. She reached for the Danish.

* * *

Even though the semester/Christmas/New Year's break wasn't officially over, employees trickled in and out of their offices at the 4-Cs to touch bases with one another. When I opened my e-mail at the office, I quickly wished I hadn't touched bases. There was an ominous message from hizzonor, President Neil.

> Janice,
>
> *I have some exciting news. Please set up an appointment to meet with me.*
>
> PN

"It's Janese," I snapped at the computer. I wondered if the man would ever get my name right. Using "exciting" as an adjective in academia was a coverup for something less than exciting and often downright dreadful.

"Your timing is perfect, Janese," Natalie, the president's admin assistant said when I called for an appointment. "Not only is President Neil in, so is Brenda Koski."

A warning bell clanged in my head. "Brenda's there?"

"Uh huh. Guess it involves all three of you," Natalie said. "My other line's chirping. Come right over and go on in he says. And good luck!"

Good luck? That never bodes well. The last time I had good luck was when I got not one but two special decoder rings in a box of Sugar

Bomb cereal when I was little. I lost one and broke the other. That was the extent of my good luck.

I saw Natalie pull out as I pulled into the parking lot of the administration building, which we underlings called The Head Shed. It housed President Neil's office, along with others that dwelled in the higher echelon of the 4-Cs.

"Janice!" the president bellowed as I timidly knocked on the frame of his doorway. "Come in, come in! Wow! What does the other guy look like?" he snorted.

I let the mispronunciation of my name pass. I had almost forgotten how hideous I looked, but sure appreciated the reminder.

"You know Brenda!"

"Of course," I said.

Brenda sat in the comfy guest chair in President Neil's office. Even though she balanced some papers on her lap, the unabridged exposure of her legs was the focal point of the room.

"Hi Brenda," I said, trying to instill perkiness in my tone. Unfortunately, the nose injury still inflicted a nasally, underwater effect when I talked.

"Hey, Jan. Sorry about your accident," Brenda said. She uncrossed and re-crossed her legs and began bouncing the top one. I wasn't the only person in the room who noticed this.

"Yeah, thanks," I muttered.

"So, Janet, have a seat," President Neil said. "I have some great news!"

Now I wasn't even Janice, but Janet. The only seat left to take was an orange plastic molded chair apparently reserved for the lower strata such as myself.

"Well, Bren and I have been talking and I think I've found a solution to a couple of problems."

Problems? That was right up there with good luck. I tried to look attentive, but imagined I just looked pathetic. And he called her Bren, not Brenda. How cozy.

"Bren here has been my right hand in external affairs—you know, keeping me out of trouble with the community," he said with a chuckle.

I had thought external affairs was building relations with the community, but apparently not in this case.

256

"And of course you, Janet, have been our campus coordinator, but you know it kind of reaches into the community too, like the ice contest—"

"Igloo," I corrected. Stupid of me. One never corrects one's boss.

"Right, and of course we know that went down the drain," he added.

"Yes, because of the weather," I said.

"Oh sure. Not your fault," he said.

"And the party was awesome!" Brenda chirped in.

"Right," Neil muttered "My wife's still going on about it."

"I loved the band!" Brenda said. "So—retro."

"ANYWAY," the president said, "I've made Bren here the V.P. of Community Connections."

"Community connections?" I repeated.

"Right," he said. "I thought that sounded so much better than external affairs. Anyway, she'll be your supervisor and so you no longer have to go through me—I know I'm tough sometimes to connect with, Janet—and I think things will run, er, much smoother."

"My supervisor?"

"Isn't it just positively awesome, Jan?" Brenda said. "We get along so great. I won't be, like, your boss at all, but we'll be a team! You are such a majorly great organizer, I'll just let you do your thing."

"My thing?"

"Sure, you know, all the super community activities and programs. And then the campus stuff, too, like graduation and that honorary buffet."

"Honors banquet," I corrected. I couldn't help myself.

"Uh huh. I'll just stay right out of your way and let you do stuff."

"I see. But you'll be my, um, supervisor?"

"Sure. We'll, like, have a meeting and you can tell me what we're doing and I'll tell Patrick what we're doing."

In other words, I do all the work and she gets the glory. How lucky is that?

"It will be win-win!" Brenda chirped.

"Sure," I said rather flatly. "Everyone's a winner."

"So, then," Neil said, "it's settled! Hey, you two gals should go do the cafeteria and have lunch on me. Bren, tell them to give you the president's privilege, since you're a V.P. now."

For some reason this made "Bren" giggle. Me, not so much.

257

⇜ **32** ⇝

Had anyone been home when I got there, they would have received the full brunt of my rage. No such luck. I could slam and rant all I wanted and other than perhaps a couple of freeloading mice, it would fall on deaf ears.

I had gotten a cryptic text from Mother on my way home from the college, stating, "going on a little biz." Whatever the hell that meant. As far as I knew, George was still at the 4-Cs plotting the rollout of his culinary school.

When George slammed the door, it sounded like a gunshot. Given my recent bizarre experiences, my heart didn't just skip a beat but went into full cardiac arrest. Fortunately, my brain managed to jump start it before I collapsed. I whirled around to confront George for his startling entrance but then saw his face contorted with fury and thought better.

"What a bunch of condescending assholes!" he said.

I waited.

"They said I didn't have the credentials for a culinary school and that perhaps I could teach a cooking class to old ladies at the senior center since young, ambitious students had brighter goals on the horizon. Yeah, right, like such useful things as how to cultivate marijuana or how to find white supremacy in your corn flakes. It's like crazy! Everyone has to eat and someone has to cook the food! Will they next deny *eating* and maybe call it a socially-motivated racist myth. I can't stand it. I hate that place!"

I nodded. I was not feeling the love myself.

"Would you believe that prick, Dean Mantis, said that I should stick to throwing pots because it attracted the girls, like athletics attract men. I mean first that's insulting, and second it's so sexist!"

It was true. George's blobby pottery class did have the women all googly-eyed. And it was the boys who played sports. The women had some teams too, because if they didn't there would be no state funding, but for the most part it was a man's world. That's why the men's basketball game was on Friday night and the women's at 7:00 a.m. on Sunday morning. And I would never tell George in a million years, but if he taught cooking to old ladies, they would fawn shamelessly over him. What it boiled down to was that George's ambitions were not being taken seriously. Welcome to my world!

"So, I quit!"

Whoa!

"I need some boxes and then I will go get my stuff this afternoon," he said, sounding a bit shaky. They said I had until tomorrow to clear out my stuff."

It was never good to act in anger and haste, but it did feel good for the moment. When I had learned that "Bren" Koski was my new boss, and it was obvious that I was to do all the work while she got all the glory so long as she and the prez were bonking, though it would have felt good to exhibit righteous indignation and quit, I decided to think things over and consider my rather limited options. It would be just a matter of time before Brenda Koski found herself abruptly demoted to the mail room, or worse, when the president's wife became suspicious of hubby's excessive out-of-town business travel. Perhaps she'd hire a detective to get some incriminating photos for the "divorce" file. President Neil's vision was blurred by the happy place below his belt. Things rarely ended well for married men with wandering willies.

The door burst open again and Mother swished in as if her royal court awaited her.

"Darlings!" she chirped. "So glad you're both here. I have *marvelous* news."

I didn't know how much more news, marvelous or otherwise, I could take.

"I need some boxes. We have boxes, Trout?" George muttered as he paced in a circle.

Mother ignored him and floated into the living room, tossed her coat and purse on the footstool, and let out a huge, dramatic sigh as she plunked into the armchair. "Will someone please get me a big glass of wine? Better yet, is there any bubbly? It's time to celebrate!"

This could mean any number of things ranging from a new nail salon to an announcement that she was running for public office. We waited.

"Well, is there?" she demanded.

"I don't think there is any champagne. I'll get you some wine," I said. I had become accustomed to passing up alcohol during the limbo/mommy issue, but since it was no longer necessary, I got two glasses. Wine consumption, which had slowed, was about to pick up again. Of course George steadfastly remained on the wagon.

"Ah, thank you darling! Is this the screw-off cap stuff, or did it have a real cork?" Mother asked.

"Comes in a box, actually," I said.

"Boxes? Where?" George said.

"George, dear, chill," Mother said, grimacing as she took a sip of wine. "Please, everyone sit down and let's chat. Oh, I'm *so* excited I could burst!"

George and I plunked down on the couch. He was starting to defuse a bit and I had to admit I could use something to get excited about. I suspected this was *not* a new nail salon or even a bid for village manager of Moose Willow.

George and I looked at Mother expectantly. It did no good when Her Highness wanted to prolong the suspense. There was no hurrying through the scene.

"So," Mother said. "As you know, I am greatly impressed with George's cooking ability. And those who know me," she added, "know that I don't easily dish out compliments."

"Got that right," I muttered.

"What was that Janese?" Mother said.

I didn't answer lest things drag out even longer.

"And, of course, Janese here is a *wonderful* organizer and really such a people person!"

"I am?"

"Of course, darling. Otherwise, why would you be running so many things at that college?"

Indeed, why? My career seemed to have melted into a giant puddle, literally and figuratively.

"You all know of the old Pine Lodge—a ways off the beaten path there in Trillium?"

I had heard of the lodge. It was a summer resort for a wealthy automaker who liked to retreat to Upper Michigan for hunting, fishing, and probably canoodling. As generations came and went, the old lodge eventually fell out of favor and sat vacant on a beautiful piece of property overlooking Lake Superior. The structure, though not used for years, had been minimally maintained and property taxes paid. There had been talk of it being donated to the township and converting it into a museum, but the idea never got off the ground. Especially since the taxes were indeed current.

"Well, my dear family, I have closed a deal on it and plan to convert it to a bona fide inn, with fine dining, luxurious and unique guest rooms, mystery dinners, perhaps boat cruises, a gift shop—so much potential for such a steal!"

The next sound was George's and my jaws hitting the ground.

"And you, George will be my chef and Janese, dear, will run the place. You will need to upgrade your wardrobe," she said, giving me a critical look. "We'll need to hire lots of good people—perhaps some students from the college can work in the summer."

"Um," I said. "I have a job."

"I don't," George said, a grin spreading over his face.

Mother looked at him for a moment with a glimpse of curiosity, then shrugged.

"Of course," she said, taking another sip of wine, "you'd both get full benefits, nice salaries, corporate perks—did I mention I've incorporated? Anyway, once we have things settled, you two will have full control. You won't have me hovering over you as Ben and I will be busy in St. Iggy with The Straights. He's been offered a wonderful position at the hospital there. It's just perfect, don't you think?"

"Have to admit there is something to this door closing and another opening," George said.

Oh brother, the George/Mother lovefest strikes again. I knew we were doomed.

"Oh," Mother said. "Also, Ben and I are getting married."

I jumped up, nearly spilling my wine. "Whaaa—you barely—"

"Janese, dear, more wine please," Mother interrupted.

I snatched her glass and stomped into the kitchen. George, on the other hand—the king of suck-up—went over and hugged Mother and gave her a kiss. Cripes, he hadn't kissed me since my nose had been smushed.

When we were all settled back, wine glasses refreshed, George looked like he was having a nirvana moment while I was feeling a bout of indigestion coming on. Still, Mother was a fact in my life, so why not just capitulate. I could feel a smug smile form on my face as I began to mentally draft my letter of resignation to President Neil. Wait! This was Mother. We were being lured into her lair. Mother: the one who had reminded me daily as a child of my shortcomings. What made me think that she had undergone a miraculous transformation? No, there was manipulation here. A catch. A condition. A trap.

"And my loves," Mother said, sounding a bit like The Queen, "there is one caveat."

Aha!

"I was thinking a double wedding," she said, avoiding eye contact.
"Really?" George said. "Who's the other lucky couple?"
Oh George.

* * *

"I was just kidding," George said.
"Hah!" I said.
We were left alone to "consider" Mother's proposition. It wasn't really optional. He knew it and I knew it, but we all pretended that we had a choice.

Not that I was totally opposed to the idea of marriage, it's just that I'd have preferred George to have come up with the idea minus the Mother Mandate. Clearly, visions of chefdom were dancing in his head. When mother wasn't manipulating, she was bribing. For example, I got the cabin due to her largesse, with the stipulation that she could pop into my life at her leisure, then, of course, leave whenever it suited her as well.

"Seriously," George said. "It was a joke. Of *course* I knew that we'd be, um, couple number two."

George was not saying the right things at all. The correct thing—the thing that would repair the damage—would be, oh, I don't know, something like: *Darling Janese. I love you and want to spend the rest of my life with you. Will you marry me?*

"I, uh, have been giving this some thought," he said.

"Uh, huh," I said. Good to know I was worthy of some dispassionate thought.

It had grown mighty chilly in the cabin. George got up and went into the bedroom and I could hear a drawer open and close. Perhaps he was getting out his chef's hat for starching. When George returned, *sans* chef hat, he carried something in his hand.

"I know that we might have picked something out together, but this—well, it's a family thing. I mean. Oh, Christ, Janese, will you marry me?" he blubbered, then belatedly dropped to one knee and flipped open a little box, which held a ring.

"It was my grandmother's engagement ring. It's an antique. She gave it to me and asked me to, well, keep it until the right one came along."

"Oh George!" I blurted and jumped to my feet. "That is so romantic."

"Well?" he said.

"Well what?" I said.

Now it was his turn to give a look.

"Yes!" I said. "Of course I'll marry you."

George slipped the ring on my finger. It was a little large, but we'd get it sized.

"Granny raised me, you know. Never knew my father and my mother, I guess, was pretty young when she had me. Anyway, I want to keep it going with you, Janese. You've put up with a lot from me, and I do really love you. I even love your slightly smushed nose."

"I love you too," I whispered, staring at the beautiful marquise cut diamond, which was surrounded by emeralds and more small diamonds. It was beyond exquisite.

George stood and grabbed me, then we had our first kiss as an engaged couple.

"Of course, Mother didn't know anything about this, right?" I said after we pulled apart.

"I might have mentioned it to her," he said. "You know, casually."

"Uh, huh. I've been had!" I said.

"Problem?" George said, sliding his hand under my sweater.

"Nothing that can't be fixed," I said.

"How so?" he asked.

As if he didn't know.

⚡ 33 ⚡

Bertie and I were in Tillie's Bakery stuffing our faces with Tillie's giant blueberry muffins and guzzling coffee. I had driven there in a rental car, which I would use until I got something to replace my wrecked Subaru—a situation that gave me great sadness.

"Guess what Mother wants sung by the church choir at our wedding—guess!" I said. "'What I Did for Love' from that musical—*A Chorus Line*," I continued without giving Bertie a chance to answer. "Can I borrow your gun to shoot myself?" I blathered, pointing an imaginary gun at my head and pulling the trigger.

"Well, at least she doesn't want 'Singular Sensation'," Bertie said. She glanced at her watch. "Still time before my, um, appointment."

"Then at the reception, she wants the dance band to play 'Only You' and 'Tomorrow' and 'We've Only Just Begun,' and only God knows what else. And since Ben is Jewish, Mother decided we should form a Horah and dance the Hava Nagila instead of a conga line."

"Sounds like a real musical mashup," Bertie said.

"Actually, I don't really care," I said, so long as we don't have that sappy wedding song 'There is Love' OR Eleanor Heimlich singing in the damn choir. Appointment for what?"

"Doctor appointment. Well, it's *very* unlikely that Eleanor will be making any kind of an appearance at your wedding," Bertie said, as she picked up muffin crumbs with her moistened thumb.

"Yea?" I said.

"She's, er, being evaluated. I can't really say too much about *where* this is taking place, but I can tell you why. Since you were her victim."

"Evaluated? For what?" I said. "Want another muffin?"

"Sure, why not. Maybe they won't weigh me at the doctor's office."
I looked at Bertie. "You okay?"

"Sure. Get me a chocolate chip this time," she said reaching for her purse.

"It's on me! After all, you are my matron of honor," I said. I came back with two fresh muffins. Bertie's chocolate chip and a cream cheese and cranberry for myself.

"So?" I said.

"So, what?" Bertie said.

"Eleanor? What's the deal?"

"Well, remember the night of your accident?" Bertie said. "I love chocolate chips. I think they should add some peanut butter icing to these things."

"Of course I remember the night of my accident," I said. "Peanut butter icing? You've got to be kidding."

"Anyway, as you know, there was a snake in your car, presumably put there by someone. I mean, pythons aren't exactly indigenous to the boreal forest."

I waited.

"So, as you probably also remember, Eleanor was also out and about in the blizzard and went into a ditch."

"Uh huh," I said. "Wonder what she was doing out in that weather. I mean, I can't believe she was out partying or visiting a friend."

"She was out because you were out," Bertie said.

"You mean, like stalking me?"

"Kind of. Well, anyway, they found an animal crate in Eleanor's vehicle when it was towed in. No biggie, right? Just an ordinary cat or small dog carrier."

"Didn't know the bitch had any pets."

"Oh, yes, but not the cuddly kind."

"You mean..."

"Uh huh. Eleanor is a snake lady. Of course, no law against that per se, so long as you have the right permits. But if you put a snake in someone's car and cause an accident, it's considered assault with intent to do great bodily harm. Eleanor did confess, but said she was only playing a joke. Like the rubber snake in your car at the church. Oh, and about the attack in your office with the wastebasket over your head. Guess what?"

"No!"

"Yup, she has a hairpiece and while fake hair can't be directly tied to an individual, like with DNA—"

"I knew all that hair couldn't be hers. I mean it's like two feet high!"

"And it was the same type of synthetic hair we got from your office chair and from her hairdo. Eleanor admitted she did it—and that the boots that you purchased from the Lutheran Bazaar where, indeed, donated by her. Thus, the distinct mark they made outside your office building ties up the package rather neatly. Of course, a half-wit lawyer could shoot a few holes in it, but we have a confession."

"Good. Save the taxpayers' money," I said. "But back to the snakes!"

"The Polar Bear Frozen Foods delivery guy about had a stroke when he saw all the dead rats—snake food—stashed in Eleanor's freezer. Apparently, he went to the wrong freezer to put her order away. See, Eleanor wasn't home at the time. I guess they are often given permission by the customers to enter the house and put the goods away, even when the owner is not there. Kind of like the old milkman days. Turns out that Eleanor didn't give permission, but the guy was new and just assumed he could knock and go in through the unlocked garage door toting a bunch of frozen lasagna and whatnot. Anyway, he reported all the dead rodents to the police. Again, nothing illegal, except of course he just said something about multiple frozen carcasses and forgot to mention that they were rodents. Anyway, naturally we jumped to life and our beloved Detective Burns got a warrant. I guess he about wet himself when he saw all the snakes writhing around in their aquariums stored in Eleanor's spare bedroom. Seems she didn't have a permit for all those exotic snakes, and they got confiscated and are currently housed at Reptile World in Marquette. The rest is history."

I sat there with my mouth hanging open, then said, "Why does she hate me?"

"I guess," Bertie said, "because you could hit the high note, and she couldn't."

"Seriously?"

"I've seen lesser reasons—such as the desire to win a stupid igloo contest."

"True," I said. "But Weasel Watkins wasn't really murdered."

"Nope, but had he not been so occupied with the contest he would be happily enjoying an adult beverage at the bar."

"Now I feel guilty."

"Don't—he was pretty screwed up from 'Nam and somehow transformed his experiences in the jungle to Bucky's meat locker. And it was his wife who drugged him, not you. I mean, what was she thinking?"

"True. How's Aileen doing?"

"Getting some help," Bertie said. "Maybe she and Eleanor can be in the same group session. That is if you wish to press charges against Eleanor and if you are good with her getting psychiatric treatment instead of the slammer, or maybe probation. Burns is going to be getting in touch."

I thought of George and how after the logging accident in which alcohol was a factor; he had been ordered to go to "get help."

"Do you think I should?" I said. "I mean, she's wacko, right. Needs help, like Aileen."

"I do. It's imperative that Eleanor be monitored. We're learning there's a history here, going back to other things, including the rather mysterious death of her husband. Though that never went anywhere and was chalked up to mishandling snakes."

"Snakes again! Seriously?"

"Uh, huh. So she needs to be reeled in. Now Aileen is another story. Since Burns witnessed her attacking you, doesn't matter that you didn't press charges. We're making sure she gets evaluated as well. She's a different case from Eleanor, who actually planned things and I believe was completely aware of what she was doing, albeit totally off the rails." Bertie glanced at her watch and sighed.

"So, everything okay with you? I said.

"Sure. When is the wedding?"

"Last Saturday in July," I said.

"Hmmm," Bertie said, polishing off her muffin. "So, tell me more."

"Oh," I said, "the music is just the tip of the proverbial iceberg. *Everyone* will be invited. We will not be able to get married in the Moose Willow Methodist Church, partly because there isn't room and partly because Ben is, as mentioned, Jewish. So, the ceremony, which will take place on the grounds of The Trillium Inn—formerly the Pine Lodge—weather permitting, will be multi-denominational, with both our pastor and a rabbi officiating. While my list of friends basically includes you and your fam, and maybe a couple of people from the college, Mother and George whipped up a guest list that rivals a presidential inauguration. Their reasoning is that this is a good marketing ploy, to get The Trillium Inn On The Map." I made air quotes.

"About my dress—" Bertie began.

"So, in order to make things 'Unforgettable,' which is the first dance song for the bride and groom, there will be an orchestra/band replete with vocalists along with a portable dance floor for cutting the metaphorical rug. And get this. George has asked James Rush to be his best man AND he—James—is going to sing something. Again, please, just lend me your gun!"

"I'm thinking my dress should be, well, flowing," Bertie said.

"Sure," I said. "Whatever you want. No matter what, you'll look great against Aggie Whim, whom Mother asked to be her matron of honor."

"Don't be so sure," Bertie mumbled.

I took a deep breath. "As they say in late-night infomercials, WAIT, THERE'S MORE! The reception will be inside and outside, and will include an open bar, buffet style food, a seven-tier wedding cake, the aforementioned live music, a wireless microphone for drunken speeches, a bouncy house and magic show for the kiddies, tiki lanterns, fairy lights, a portable fountain that spews boozy punch, and an ice sculpture depicting either a swan, a bigfoot, or a penis, depending on the perception of the observer. The sculptor, Raul somebody, is a casual acquaintance of George's. According to George, Raul's 'a free spirit' who usually carves gnarly logs with a chainsaw and makes woodsy things for the tourists, but has recently been tinkering with ice chainsaw carving."

"You've got to be kidding," Bertie said. "A chainsaw ice sculpture of a penis?"

"Well," I said, "Since he's not very experienced with doing ice, he really can't commit to what actually is going to emerge from the block of ice. And of course it will be summer, so the logistics will involve Bucky Tanner's freezer and an abundance of dry ice."

"Holy crap," Bertie said. "Things are circling back to Bucky's vault of death!"

"Creepy, isn't it?" I said.

"So, this inn your mother bought. Tell me about it," Bertie said.

"The Pine Lodge," I said. "It's in fairly good shape and will begin its transformation from rustic hunting lodge getaway to a la-de-da B&B experience. The new name will be The Trillium Inn and while not open to the public until after the wedding, the guest rooms will be available free of charge for out-of-town guests. Apparently, the entire staff from Mother's resort in St. Ignace will be coming to handle many of the thirty million details. The Straights will be temporarily closed and I'm not to worry about a thing, except of course everything. George's instructions are to rent a tux and to show up for the rehearsal as well as the wedding. Mother and I will see to things like themes, favors, colors, music, food, invitations—the list is endless."

"Maybe you could elope," Bertie said.

"What? And give up having Mother's claws in George and me for the rest of our lives? Don't be silly. George is so jazzed up about becoming head chef at The Trillium that he seems to be forgetting about the wedding. If we eloped, Mother would not only pull the proverbial rug out from under both of us, she'd likely disown me and walk out of my life."

"Hmmm," Bertie said. "How would that make you feel?"

"What are you, my shrink? Anyway, I will admit that in spite of her annoying, meddling ways, I guess I want Mother in my life—at least from a distance."

"So, sounds like a very unorthodox wedding. People will be talking about it for years," Bertie said. She glanced at her watch again and stood up.

"Oh," I said, "Get this. Mother's fiancé, Dr. Bloom, will be giving me away and George will be giving Mother away. I have no idea how that will work. And maybe your boys can be ring bearers. Wear cute little bow ties and suits."

"Why do you hate me?" Bertie demanded.

⸎ 34 ⸎

"I wonder how long the reception went on," I said.

"Depends on how long the booze held out," George said.

We were in the deluxe suite at our first destination of a whirlwind honeymoon tour of upscale inns and B&Bs. We had left the insanity of our wedding reception around 9:00 p.m. and drove off in Mother's Mercedes. (She insisted—so long as no tin cans or "just married" signs desecrated the vehicle.) In that George and I had been acting like an "old married couple" for some time (Mother's words) she suggested we combine business and pleasure, something she has always embraced. The idea was to check out the competition and stay at a half dozen places and take notes. Our first stop was at the Waterview Inn in Sault Ste. Marie.

The room was very posh with an enormous bed, in which George and I were ensconced. Also included was a two-person bubbly tub, wet bar, gas fireplace, enormous television, kitchenette, balcony overlooking the harbor, and a two-person shower. When we had arrived around midnight, a cheery fire blazed away in the fireplace—in spite of the air conditioning being on—and a bottle of expensive champagne was chilling in an ice bucket next to a bowl of plump strawberries. In addition, an enormous bouquet of roses filled the room with a heavenly aroma and each pillow had not just a mint, but a mini box of expensive chocolates. I believe that there may have been a complimentary breakfast that we missed due to oversleeping and other things. Mother had insisted on paying for the room, which had more amenities than the entire collection of the guestrooms at The Trillium Inn, and likely cost more than George's and my projected combined monthly salaries as The Trillium's head chef and lodging manager, respectively. After a late checkout—a very late checkout—we would catch the ferry to Mackinac Island and stay at another obscenely overpriced inn.

Mother and Benjamin stuck it out at the reception, where the festivities likely had raged on into the wee hours. Mother wanted to make certain the 100-year-old lodge/inn was still standing in the morning when things finally wound down.

"So, what do you think of this place, Trout?" George asked.

"That's Mrs. LeFleur to you." I gave his rib a poke.

"You'll always be Trout to me. And I do love the way your schnoz is a little off kilter since your snaky accident," he said, tweaking my nose.

My hand went up to my so-called schnoz, which I thought had gained character through its ordeal. "Don't change the subject," I snapped. "The only reason I married you was to get rid of my ridiculous last name," I said, noticing that his hand was doing some interesting things that had nothing to do with my nose. "Therefore, I want an annulment."

"Ummm hummmm," he said. "Too late."

"What a bummer for Bertie," I said.

"Hmmm?" he said.

"You know, she couldn't drink alcohol or eat the sushi. I'm such an idiot. She dropped like a million hints that she was pregnant way back when she was only a little ways along. I'm so dense. Said something about moving to an unlisted address if it's another boy." I sighed. "Mother thought it was great to have Bertie in all her pregnant glory waddling down the aisle. A good omen, she said. And those two boys! So dang cute. Do you think anyone noticed us at all?"

"Hmm?" said George. "Oh, I think they noticed you, Trout. You were drop-dead gorgeous."

"Except my own mother one-upped me," I said. I had opted for a simple dress, tea length, off-white, some bedazzled areas of pearls around the bodice. No puff and ruffle nonsense. No veil either, just a couple of flowers in my hair, and a simple bouquet of roses. Mother wore a slinky long dress, pale pink, which glittered like a disco ball. She also wore flowers in her hair—gardenias, I think and had a bouquet of silk trillium.

"Well, you both were the stars of the show, until that damn dog got loose."

"Woofie?" I said. "I Guess no leash can hold him. Mother was horrified that we had 'that beast' at the wedding. Apparently, Jeffie and Robby insisted and used it as a bargaining tool for the clip-on bowties they were resisting. Besides, Woofie was a good boy. There was a squirrel getting into the mixed nuts on the buffet table. He was doing his doggie duty, so to speak."

"Well, Woofie and I had an issue back in my Sasquatch days," George said. "Of course, it was your mother who wacked me on the head. And I've forgiven her. But knocking over the ice penis sculpture is totally on Woofie, not your mother."

271

"It wasn't a penis. It was a swan with a very long neck," I said.

"Whatever it was, it pointed right at Rush during his solo."

"That was okay, since I hated what he was singing," I said.

"And the way it melted right out of—well, it was pretty funny," George said.

I tried to suppress a giggle. "That moment will be forever burned in my brain. Right when he was segueing from the dreaded 'There is Love' into 'Unforgettable'."

"What a disaster," George muttered. "Sooooo glad at least a dozen people have it recorded. He raised up on one elbow and looked at me. Things did improve—later on," he added with a smirk.

"Indeed they did," I said. "Other than 'There is Love' being slaughtered by James and the ice thingy mishap, the music was perfect. I mean, where did mother get a frickin' orchestra?"

"Where does your mother get anything? George said. "Such as fresh oysters. My God, we're a million miles from the ocean. Anyway, I mean *later*."

"I'll admit the choir was at its best being accompanied by a real orchestra instead of Azinnia's assault on the keyboard," I said. "Bless her," I quickly added lest God strike me down for being catty. "I think that Finnish Tango number may have been the reason that Bertie went into labor. Or maybe it was the 'Hokey Pokey' when she put her whole self in. She seemed kind of ticked off that she had to leave to go the hospital. I'm waiting for a text to see what she had and all the other details."

"I turned your phone off, Trout. I mean, it is our honeymoon."

"Oh pooh. Just like any other night for an old married couple. You know, have wild sex a couple of times, get drunk on bubbly, mess around in a hot tub. Same ol', same ol'." I said.

"It was three times—sort of," George said with a touch of indignance.

"Of course, dear," I said.

"I do need to learn how to make those Oysters Rockefeller," George said. "I must have eaten a half dozen. Hey, you know what they say about oysters!"

"So, do you think we can make it?" I said.

"Wasn't that the third dance song?" George said looking around the luxurious room. "I think we have it *made*!"

I thought about Mother and the tightening gyre on the George/Janese duo. "More like we've been had," I said.

"I know I had my way," George muttered. "And I think I liked it. Wasn't that another song the band played?"

"No, you bozo! I mean with the inn and *Mother!*"

"We can work it out," George said.

"Will you stop with the stupid song lyrics?" I said.

"I will if you'll just stop talking and give me some lovin'."

"How many oysters did you have?"

"I believe I exceeded the recommended dosage," George said.

"Shall we call the doctor?" I said, turning to him.

"Is that a song?" He said.

"Yup, I got a bad case of lovin' you," I said.

"Back at ya, Trout. Now c'mere."

About the Author

Terri Martin and her husband moved to Upper Michigan nearly 22 years ago and have no desire to live anywhere else, in spite of the 250 inches of snowfall each winter. *Moose Willow Mystery: A Yooper Romance* is Terri's first full length adult novel, which is set firmly in Upper Michigan's culture. Terri is a regular contributor to *UP Magazine* (Porcupine Press) where she finds an outlet for her humorous writing. Many of her stories from *UP Magazine* have been anthologized in her two books: *Church Lady Chronicles: Devilish Encounters* (2020) and *High on the Vine* (2022).

Terri has a published two middle-grade children's novels: *A Family Trait* (Holiday House, 1999) and *The Home Wind* (2021), which received the 2022 U.P. Notable Book Award.

Terri has a master's degree in English and has taught college success courses, tutored English at the college level, and served as an aide for college composition classes.

Visit Terri's website at www.terrilynnmartin.com or e-mail her at gnarlywoodspub@gmail.com

CPSIA information can be obtained
at www.ICGtesting.com
Printed in the USA
JSHW050324180822
29383JS00001B/2